MURDER AND MYSTERY ON THE STREETS OF LONDON

SHORT STORIES OF CRIME AND MURDER FROM THE UNDERBELLY OF LONDON

British Library Cataloguing-in-Publication Data
A catalogue record for this book is available from
the British Library

CONTENTS

The Adventure of the Worst Man in London

SIR ARTHUR CONAN DOYLE

IT IS YEARS since the incidents of which I speak took place, and yet it is with diffidence that I allude to them. For a long time, even with the utmost discretion and reticence, it would have been impossible to make the facts public; but now the principal person concerned is beyond the reach of human law, and with due suppression the story may be told in such fashion as to injure no one. It records an absolutely unique experience in the career both of Mr Sherlock Holmes and of myself. The reader will excuse me if I conceal the date or any other fact by which he might trace the actual occurrence.

We had been out for one of our evening rambles, Holmes and I, and had returned about six o'clock on a cold, frosty winter's evening. As Holmes turned up the lamp the light fell upon a card on the table. He glanced at it, and then, with an ejaculation of disgust, threw it on the floor. I picked it up and read:

> CHARLES AUGUSTUS MILVERTON,
> APPLEDORE TOWERS,
> HAMPSTEAD.
>   *Agent.*

'Who is he?' I asked.

'The worst man in London,' Holmes answered, as he sat down and stretched his legs before the fire. 'Is anything on the back of the card?'

I turned it over.

'Will call at 6.30 – C.A.M.,' I read.

'Hum! He's about due. Do you feel a creeping, shrinking sensation, Watson, when you stand before the serpents in the Zoo and see the slithery, gliding, venomous creatures, with their deadly eyes and wicked, flattened faces? Well, that's how Milverton impresses me. I've had to do with fifty murderers in my career, but the worst of them never gave me the repulsion which I have for this fellow. And yet I can't get out of doing business with him – indeed, he is here at my invitation.'

'But who is he?'

'I'll tell you, Watson. He is the king of all the blackmailers. Heaven help the man, and still more the woman, whose secret and reputation come into the power of Milverton. With a smiling face and a heart of marble he will squeeze and squeeze until he has drained them dry. The fellow is a genius in his way, and would have made his mark in some more savoury trade. His method is as follows: He allows it to be known that he is prepared to pay very high sums for letters which compromise people of wealth or position. He receives these wares not only from treacherous valets or maids, but frequently from genteel ruffians who have gained the confidence and affection of trusting women. He deals with no niggard hand. I happen to know that he paid seven hundred pounds to a footman for a note two lines in length, and that the ruin of a noble family was the result. Everything which is in the market goes to Milverton, and there are hundreds in this great city who turn white at his name. No one knows where his grip may fall, for he is far too rich and far too cunning to work from hand to mouth. He will hold a card back for years in order to play it at the moment when the stake is best worth winning. I have said that he is the worst man in London, and I would ask you how could one compare the ruffian who in hot blood bludgeons his mate with this man, who methodically and at his leisure tortures the soul and wrings the nerves in order to add to his already swollen money-bags?'

I had seldom heard my friend speak with such intensity of feeling.

'But surely,' said I, 'the fellow must be within the grasp of the law ?'

'Technically, no doubt, but practically not. What would it profit a woman, for example, to get him a few months' imprisonment if her own ruin must immediately follow? His victims dare not hit back. If ever he blackmailed an innocent person, then, indeed, we should have him; but he is as cunning as the Evil One. No, no; we must find other ways to fight him.'

'And why is he here?'

'Because an illustrious client has placed her piteous case in my hands. It is the Lady Eva Brackwell, the most beautiful *débutante* of last season. She is to be married in a fortnight to the Earl of Dovercourt. This fiend has several imprudent letters – imprudent, Watson, nothing worse – which were written to an impecunious young squire in the country. They would suffice to break off the match. Milverton will send the letters to the earl unless a large sum of money is paid him. I have been commissioned to meet him, and – to make the best terms I can.'

At that instant there was a clatter and a rattle in the street below. Looking down I saw a stately carriage and pair, the brilliant lamps gleaming on the glossy haunches of the noble chestnuts. A footman opened the door, and a small, stout man in a shaggy astrakhan overcoat descended. A minute later he was in the room.

Charles Augustus Milverton was a man of fifty, with a large, intellectual head, a round, plump, hairless face, a perpetual frozen smile, and two keen grey eyes, which gleamed brightly from behind broad, golden-rimmed glasses. There was something of Mr Pickwick's benevolence in his appearance, marred only by the insincerity of the fixed smile and by the hard glitter of those restless and penetrating eyes. His voice was as smooth and suave as his countenance, as he advanced with a plump little hand extended, murmuring his regret for having missed us at his first visit.

Holmes disregarded the outstretched hand and looked at him with a face of granite. Milverton's smile broadened; he shrugged his shoulders, removed his overcoat, folded it with great deliberation over the back of a chair, and then took a seat.

'This gentleman,' said he, with a wave in my direction. 'Is it discreet? Is it right?'

'Dr Watson is my friend and partner.'

'Very good, Mr Holmes. It is only in your client's interests that I protested. The matter is so very delicate—'

'Dr Watson has already heard of it.'

'Then we can proceed to business. You say that you are acting for Lady Eva. Has she empowered you to accept my terms?'

'What are your terms?'

'Seven thousand pounds.'

'And the alternative?'

'My dear sir, it is painful to me to discuss it; but if the money is not paid on the fourteenth there certainly will be no marriage on the eighteenth.' His insufferable smile was more complacent than ever. Holmes thought for a little.

'You appear to me,' he said at last, 'to be taking matters too much for granted. I am, of course, familiar with the contents of these letters. My client will certainly do what I may advise. I shall counsel her to tell her future husband the whole story and to trust to his generosity.'

Milverton chuckled.

'You evidently do not know the earl,' said he.

From the baffled look upon Holmes' face I could clearly see that he did.

'What harm is there in the letters?' he asked.

'They are sprightly – very sprightly,' Milverton answered. 'The lady was a charming correspondent. But I can assure you that the Earl of Dovercourt would fail to appreciate them. However, since you think otherwise, we will let it rest at that. It is purely a matter of business. If you think that it is in the best interests of your client that these letters should be placed in the hands of the earl, then you would indeed be foolish to pay so large a sum of money to regain them.' He rose and seized his astrakhan coat.

Holmes was grey with anger and mortification.

'Wait a little,' he said. 'You go too fast. We would certainly make every effort to avoid scandal in so delicate a matter.'

Milverton relapsed into his chair.

'I was sure that you would see it in that light,' he purred.

'At the same time,' Holmes continued, 'Lady Eva is not a wealthy woman. I assure you that two thousand pounds would be a drain upon her resources, and that the sum you name is utterly beyond her power. I beg, therefore, that you will moderate your demands, and that you will return the letters at the price I indicate, which is, I assure you, the highest that you can get.'

Milverton's smile broadened and his eyes twinkled humorously.

'I am aware that what you say is true about the lady's resources,' said he. 'At the same time, you must admit that the occasion of a lady's marriage is a very suitable time for her friends and relatives to make some little effort upon her behalf. They may hesitate as to an acceptable wedding present. Let me assure them that this little bundle of letters would give more joy than all the candelabra and butter-dishes in London.'

'It is impossible,' said Holmes.

'Dear me, dear me, how unfortunate!' cried Milverton,

taking out a bulky pocket-book. 'I cannot help thinking that ladies are ill-advised in not making an effort. Look at this!' He held up a little note with a coat-of- arms upon the envelope. 'That belongs to – well, perhaps it is hardly fair to tell the name until tomorrow morning. But at that time it will be in the hands of the lady's husband. And all because she will not find a beggarly sum which she could get in an hour by turning her diamonds into paste. It *is* such a pity. Now, you remember the sudden end of the engagement between the Honourable Miss Miles and Colonel Dorking? Only two days before the wedding there was a paragraph in the *Morning Post* to say that it was all off. And why? It is almost incredible, but the absurd sum of twelve hundred pounds would have settled the whole question. Is it not pitiful? And there I find you, a man of sense, boggling about terms when your client's future and honour are at stake. You surprise me, Mr Holmes.'

'What I say is true,' Holmes answered. 'The money cannot be found. Surely it is better for you to take the substantial sum which I offer than to ruin this woman's career, which can profit you in no way ?'

'There you make a mistake, Mr Holmes. An exposure would profit me indirectly to a considerable extent. I have eight or ten similar cases maturing. If it was circulated among them that I had made a severe example of the Lady Eva I should find all of them much more open to reason. You see my point ?'

Holmes sprang from his chair.

'Get behind him, Watson. Don't let him out! Now, sir, let us see the contents of that notebook.'

Milverton had glided as quick as a rat to the side of the room, and stood with his back against the wall.

'Mr Holmes, Mr Holmes!' he said, turning the front of his coat and exhibiting the butt of a large revolver, which projected from the inside pocket. 'I have been expecting you to

7

do something original. This has been done so often, and what good has ever come from it ? I assure you that I am armed to the teeth, and I am perfectly prepared to use my weapon, knowing that the law will support me. Besides, your supposition that I would bring the letters here in a notebook is entirely mistaken. I would do nothing so foolish. And now, gentlemen, I have one or two little interviews this evening, and it is a long drive to Hampstead.' He stepped forward, took up his coat, laid his hand on his revolver, and turned to the door. I picked up a chair, but Holmes shook his head, and I laid it down again. With a bow, a smile, and a twinkle Milverton was out of the room, and a few moments after we heard the slam of the carriage door and the rattle of the wheels as he drove away. Holmes sat motionless by the fire, his hands buried deep in his trouser pockets, his chin sunk upon his breast, his eyes fixed upon the glowing embers. For half an hour he was silent and still. Then, with the gesture of a man who has taken his decision, he sprang to his feet and passed into his bedroom. A little later a rakish young workman with a goatee beard and a swagger lit his clay pipe at the lamp before descending into the street. 'I'll be back some time, Watson,' said he, and vanished into the night. I understood that he had opened his campaign against Charles Augustus Milverton; but I little dreamed the strange shape which that campaign was destined to take.

For some days Holmes came and went at all hours in this attire, but beyond a remark that his time was spent at Hampstead, and that it was not wasted, I knew nothing of what he was doing. At last, however, on a wild, tempestuous evening, when the wind screamed and rattled against the windows, he returned from his last expedition, and, having removed his disguise, he sat before the fire and laughed heartily in his silent, inward fashion.

'You would not call me a marrying man, Watson?'

'No, indeed!'

'You will be interested to hear that I am engaged.'

'My dear fellow! I congrat—'

'To Milverton's housemaid.'

'Good heavens, Holmes!'

'I wanted information, Watson.'

'Surely you have gone too far?'

'It was a most necessary step. I am a plumber with a rising business, Escott by name. I have walked out with her each evening, and I have talked with her. Good heavens, those talks! However, I have got all I wanted. I know Milverton's house as I know the palm of my hand.'

'But the girl, Holmes?'

He shrugged his shoulders.

'You can't help it, my dear Watson. You must play your cards as best you can when such a stake is on the table. However, I rejoice to say that I have a hated rival who will certainly cut me out the instant that my back is turned. What a splendid night it is!'

'You like this weather?'

'It suits my purpose. Watson, I mean to burgle Milverton's house tonight.'

I had a catching of the breath, and my skin went cold at the words, which were slowly uttered in a tone of concentrated resolution. As a flash of lightning in the night shows up in an instant every detail of a wide landscape, so at one glance I seemed to see every possible result of such an action – the detection, the capture, the honoured career ending in irreparable failure and disgrace, my friend himself lying at the mercy of the odious Milverton.

'For Heaven's sake, Holmes, think what you are doing!' I cried.

'My dear fellow, I have given it every consideration. I am never precipitate in my actions, nor would I adopt so energetic and indeed so dangerous a course if any other were possible. Let us look at the matter clearly and fairly. I suppose that you will admit that the action is morally justifiable, though technically criminal. To burgle his house is no more than to forcibly take his pocket-book – an action in which you were prepared to aid me.'

'I turned it over in my mind.

'Yes,' I said, 'it is morally justifiable so long as our object is to take no articles save those which are used for an illegal purpose.'

'Exactly. Since it is morally justifiable, I have only to consider the question of personal risk. Surely a gentleman should not lay much stress upon this when a lady is in most desperate need of his help?'

'You will be in such a false position.'

'Well, that is part of the risk. There is no other possible way of regaining these letters. The unfortunate lady has not the money, and there are none of her people in whom she could confide. Tomorrow is the last day of grace, and unless we can get the letters tonight this villain will be as good as his word, and will bring about her ruin. I must, therefore, abandon my client to her fate, or I must play this last card. Between ourselves, Watson, it's a sporting duel between this fellow Milverton and me. He had, as you saw, the best of the first exchanges; but my self-respect and my reputation are concerned to fight it to a finish.'

'Well, I don't like it; but I suppose it must be,' said I. 'When do we start?'

'You are not coming.'

'Then you are not going,' said I. 'I give you my word of honour – and I never broke it in my life – that I will take a cab straight to the police-station and give you away unless you let me share this adventure with you.'

'You can't help me.'

'How do you know that? You can't tell what may happen. Anyway, my resolution is taken. Other people besides you have self-respect and even reputations.'

Holmes had looked annoyed, but his brow cleared, and he clapped me on the shoulder.

'Well, well, my dear fellow, be it so. We have shared the same room for some years, and it would be amusing if we ended by sharing the same cell. You know, Watson, I don't mind confessing to you that I have always had an idea that I would have made a highly efficient criminal. This is the chance of my lifetime in that direction. See here!' He took a neat little leather case out of a drawer, and opening it he exhibited a number of shining instruments. 'This is a first-class, up-to-date burgling kit, with nickel-plated jemmy, diamond-tipped glass cutter, adaptable keys, and every modern improvement which the march of civilization demands. Here, too, is my dark lantern. Everything is in order. Have you a pair of silent shoes?'

'I have rubber-soled tennis shoes.'

'Excellent. And a mask?'

'I can make a couple out of black silk.'

'I can see that you have a strong natural turn for this sort of thing. Very good; do you make the masks. We shall have some cold supper before we start. It is now nine-thirty. At eleven we shall drive as far as Church Row. It is a quarter of an hour's walk from there to Appledore Towers. We shall be at work before midnight. Milverton is a heavy sleeper, and retires punctually at ten-thirty. With any luck we should be back here by two, with the Lady Eva's letters in my pocket.'

Holmes and I put on our dress-clothes, so that we might appear to be two theatre-goers homeward bound. In Oxford Street we picked up a hansom and drove to an address in Hampstead. Here we paid off our cab, and with our greatcoats buttoned up – for it was bitterly cold, and the wind seemed to blow through us – we walked along the edge of the Heath.

'It's a business that needs delicate treatment,' said Holmes. 'These documents are contained in a safe in the fellow's study, and the study is the ante-room of his bedchamber. On the other hand, like all these stout, little men who do themselves well, he is a plethoric sleeper. Agatha – that's my fiancée – says it is a joke in the servants' hall that it's impossible to wake the master. He has a secretary who is devoted to his interests, and never budges from the study all day. That's why we are going at night. Then he has a beast of a dog which roams the garden. I met Agatha late the last two evenings, and she locks the brute up so as to give me a clear run. This is the house, this big one in its own grounds. Through the gate – now to the right among the laurels. We might put on our masks here, I think. You see, there is not a glimmer of light in any of the windows, and everything is working splendidly.'

With our black silk face-coverings, which turned us into two of the most truculent figures in London, we stole up to the silent, gloomy house. A sort of tiled veranda extended along one side of it, lined by several windows and two doors.

'That's his bedroom,' Holmes whispered. 'This door opens straight into the study. It would suit us best, but it is bolted as well as locked, and we should make too much noise getting in. Come round here. There's a greenhouse which opens into the drawing-room.'

The place was locked, but Holmes removed a circle of glass and turned the key from the inside. An instant afterwards he had closed the door behind us, and we had become felons in the eyes of the law. The thick warm air of the conservatory and the rich, choking fragrance of exotic plants took us by the throat. He seized my hand in the darkness and led me swiftly past banks of shrubs which brushed against our faces. Holmes had remarkable powers, carefully cultivated, of seeing in the dark. Still holding my hand in one of his, he opened a door, and I was vaguely conscious that we had entered a large room in which a cigar had been smoked not long before. He felt his way among the furniture, opened another door, and closed it behind us. Putting out my hand I felt several coats hanging from the wall, and I understood that I was in a passage. We passed along it, and Holmes véry gently opened a door upon the right-hand side. Something rushed out at us, and my heart sprang into my mouth, but I could have laughed when I realized that it was the cat. A fire was burning in this new room, and again the air was heavy with tobacco smoke. Holmes entered on tiptoe, waited for me to follow, and then very gently closed the door. We were in Milverton's study, and a *portière* at the farther side showed the entrance to his bedroom.

It was a good fire, and the room was illuminated by it. Near the door I saw the gleam of an electric switch, but it was unnecessary, even if it had been safe, to turn it on. At one side of the fireplace was a heavy curtain, which covered the bay window we had seen from outside. On the other side was the door which communicated with the veranda. A desk stood in the centre, with a turning chair of shining red leather. Opposite was a large bookcase, with a marble bust of Athene on the top. In the corner between the bookcase and the wall there stood a tall green safe, the firelight flashing back from the polished brass knobs upon its face. Holmes stole across and looked at it. Then he crept to the door of the bedroom, and stood with slanting head listening intently. No sound came from within. Meanwhile it had struck me that it would be wise to secure our retreat through the outer door, so I examined it. To my amazement it was neither locked nor bolted! I touched Holmes on the arm, and he turned his masked face in that direction. I saw him start, and he was evidently as surprised as I.

'I don't like it,' he whispered, putting his lips to my very ear. 'I can't quite make it out. Anyhow, we have no time to lose.'

'Can I do anything?'

'Yes; stand by the door. If you hear anyone come, bolt it on the inside, and we can get away as we came. If they come the other way, we can get through the door if our job is done, or hide behind these window curtains if it is not. Do you understand?'

I nodded and stood by the door. My first feeling of fear had passed away, and I thrilled now with a keener zest than I had ever enjoyed when we were the defenders of the law instead of its defiers. The high object of our mission, the consciousness that it was unselfish and chivalrous, the villainous character of our opponent, all added to the sporting interest of the adventure. Far from feeling guilty, I rejoiced and exulted in our dangers. With a glow of admiration I watched Holmes unrolling his case of instruments and choosing his tool with the calm, scientific accuracy of a surgeon who performs a delicate operation. I knew that the opening of safes was a particular hobby with him, and I understood the joy which it gave him to be confronted with this green and gold monster, the dragon which held in its maw the reputations of many fair ladies. Turning up the cuffs of his dress-coat – he had placed his overcoat on a chair – Holmes laid out two drills, a jemmy, and several skeleton keys. I stood at the centre door with my eyes glancing at each of the others, ready for any emergency; though, indeed, my plans were somewhat vague as to what I should do if we were interrupted. For half an hour Holmes worked with concentrated energy, laying down one tool, picking up another, handling each with the strength and delicacy of the trained mechanic. Finally I heard a click, the broad green door swung open, and inside I had a glimpse of a number of paper packets, each tied, sealed, and inscribed. Holmes picked one out, but it was hard to read by the flickering fire,

and he drew out his little dark lantern, for it was too dangerous, with Milverton in the next room, to switch on the electric
light. Suddenly I saw him halt, listen intently, and then in an
instant he had swung the door of the safe to, picked up his
coat, stuffed his tools into the pockets, and darted behind the
window curtain, motioning me to do the same.

It was only when I had joined him there that I heard what
had alarmed his quicker senses. There was a noise somewhere
within the house. A door slammed in the distance. Then a
confused, dull murmur broke itself into the measured thud of
heavy footsteps rapidly approaching. They were in the passage
outside the room. They paused at the door. The door opened.
There was a sharp snick as the electric light was turned on.
The door closed once more, and the pungent reek of a strong
cigar was borne to our nostrils. Then the footsteps continued
backwards and forwards, backwards and forwards, within a
few yards of us. Finally, there was a creak from a chair, and the
footsteps ceased. Then a key clicked in a lock, and I heard the
rustle of papers. So far I had not dared to look out, but now I
gently parted the division of the curtains in front of me and
peeped through. From the pressure of Holmes' shoulder
against mine I knew that he was sharing my observations.
Right in front of us, and almost within our reach, was the
broad, rounded back of Milverton. It was evident that we had
entirely miscalculated his movements, that he had never been
to his bedroom, but that he had been sitting up in some
smoking- or billiard-room in the farther wing of the house,
the windows of which we had not seen. His broad, grizzled
head, with its shining patch of baldness, was in the immediate
foreground of our vision. He was leaning far back in the red
leather chair, his legs outstretched, a long black cigar projecting at an angle from his mouth. He wore a semi-military
smoking-jacket, claret-coloured, with a black velvet collar. In
his hand he held a long legal document, which he was reading

in an indolent fashion, blowing rings of tobacco smoke from his lip as he did so. There was no promise of a speedy departure in his composed bearing and his comfortable attitude.

I felt Holmes' hand steal into mine and give me a reassuring shake, as if to say that the situation was within his powers, and that he was easy in his mind. I was not sure whether he had seen what was only too obvious from my position – that the door of the safe was imperfectly closed, and that Milverton might at any moment observe it. In my own mind I had determined that if I were sure, from the rigidity of his gaze, that it had caught his eye, I would at once spring out, throw my greatcoat over his head, pinion him, and leave the rest to Holmes. But Milverton never looked up. He was languidly interested by the papers in his hand, and page after page was turned as he followed the argument of the lawyer. At least, I thought, when he has finished the document and the cigar he will go to his room; but before he had reached the end of either there came a remarkable development which turned our thoughts into quite another channel.

Several times I had observed that Milverton looked at his watch, and once he had risen and sat down again, with a gesture of impatience. The idea, however, that he might have an appointment at so strange an hour never occurred to me until a faint sound reached my ears from the veranda outside. Milverton dropped his papers and sat rigid in his chair. The sound was repeated, and then there came a gentle tap at the door. Milverton rose and opened it.

'Well,' said he curtly, 'you are nearly half an hour late.'

So this was the explanation of the unlocked door and of the nocturnal vigil of Milverton. There was the gentle rustle of a woman's dress. I had closed the slit between the curtains as Milverton's face turned in our direction, but now I ventured very carefully to open it once more. He had resumed his seat, the cigar still projecting at an insolent angle from the corner of his mouth. In front of him, in the full glare of the electric light, there stood a tall, slim, dark woman, a veil over her face, a mantle drawn round her chin. Her breath came quick and fast, and every inch of the lithe figure was quivering with strong emotion.

'Well,' said Milverton, 'you've made me lose a good night's rest, my dear. I hope you'll prove worth it. You couldn't come any other time – eh?'

The woman shook her head.

'Well, if you couldn't you couldn't. If the countess is a hard mistress you have your chance to get level with her now. Bless the girl, what are you shivering about? That's right! Pull yourself together! Now, let us get down to business.' He took a note from the drawer of his desk. 'You say that you have five letters which compromise the Countess d'Albert. You want to sell them. I want to buy them. So far so good. It only remains to fix a price. I should want to inspect the letters, of course. If they are really good specimens — Great heavens, is it you?'

The woman without a word had raised her veil and dropped the mantle from her chin. It was a dark, handsome, clear-cut face which confronted Milverton, a face with a curved nose, strong, dark eyebrows, shading hard, glittering eyes, and a straight, thin-lipped mouth set in a dangerous smile.

'It is I,' she said, 'the woman whose life you have ruined.'

Milverton laughed, but fear vibrated in his voice. 'You were so very obstinate,' said he. 'Why did you drive me to such extremities? I assure you I wouldn't hurt a fly of my own accord, but every man has his business, and what was I to do? I put the price well within your means. You would not pay.'

'So you sent the letters to my husband, and he – the noblest gentleman that ever lived, a man whose boots I was never worthy to lace – he broke his gallant heart and died. You remember that last night when I came through that door I begged and prayed you for mercy, and you laughed in my face as you are trying to laugh now, only your coward heart cannot keep your lips from twitching? Yes; you never thought to see me here again, but it was that night which taught me how I could meet you face to face, and alone. Well, Charles Milverton, what have you to say?'

'Don't imagine that you can bully me,' said he, rising to his feet. 'I have only to raise my voice, and I could call my servants and have you arrested. But I will make allowance for your natural anger. Leave the room at once as you came, and I will say no more.'

The woman stood with her hand buried in her bosom, and the same deadly smile on her thin lips.

'You will ruin no more lives as you ruined mine. You will wring no more hearts as you wrung mine. I will free the world of a poisonous thing. Take that, you hound, and that! – and that! – and that! – and that!'

She had drawn a little gleaming revolver, and emptied barrel after barrel into Milverton's body, the muzzle within two feet of his shirt-front. He shrank away, and then fell forward upon the table, coughing furiously and clawing among the papers. Then he staggered to his feet, received another shot, and rolled upon the floor. 'You've done me,' he cried, and lay still. The woman looked at him intently and ground her heel into his upturned face. She looked again, but there was no sound or movement. I heard a sharp rustle, the night air blew into the heated room, and the avenger was gone.

No interference upon our part could have saved the man from his fate; but as the woman poured bullet after bullet into Milverton's shrinking body, I was about to spring out, when I felt Holmes' cold, strong grasp upon my wrist. I understood the whole argument of that firm, restraining grip – that it was no affair of ours; that justice had overtaken a villain; that we had our own duties and our own objects which were not to be lost sight of. But hardly had the woman rushed from the room when Holmes, with swift, silent steps, was over at the other door. He turned the key in the lock. At the same instant we heard voices in the house and the sound of hurrying feet. The revolver shots had roused the household. With perfect coolness Holmes slipped across to the safe, filled his two arms with bundles of letters, and poured them all into the fire. Again and again he did it, until the safe was empty. Someone turned the handle and beat upon the outside of the door. Holmes looked swiftly round. The letter which had been the messenger of death for Milverton lay, all mottled with his blood, upon the table. Holmes tossed it in among the blazing papers. Then he drew the key from the outer door, passed through after me, and locked it on the outside. 'This way, Watson,' said he, 'we can scale the garden wall in this direction.'

I could not have believed that an alarm could have spread so swiftly. Looking back, the huge house was one blaze of light. The front door was open, and figures were rushing down the drive. The whole garden was alive with people, and one fellow raised a view-halloa as we emerged from the veranda and followed hard at our heels. Holmes seemed to know the ground perfectly, and he threaded his way swiftly among a plantation of small trees, I close at his heels, and our foremost pursuer panting behind us. It was a six-foot wall which barred our path, but he sprang to the top and over. As I did the same I felt the hand of the man behind me grab at my ankle; but I kicked myself free, and scrambled over a glass-strewn coping. I fell upon my face among some bushes; but Holmes had me on my feet in an instant, and together we dashed away across the huge expanse of Hampstead Heath. We had run two miles, I suppose, before Holmes at last halted and listened intently. All was absolute silence behind us. We had shaken off our pursuers, and were safe.

We had breakfasted and were smoking our morning pipe, on the day after the remarkable experience which I have recorded, when Mr Lestrade, of Scotland Yard, very solemn and impressive, was ushered into our modest sitting-room.

'Good morning, Mr Holmes,' said he, 'good morning. May I ask if you are very busy just now?'

'Not too busy to listen to you.'

'I thought that, perhaps, if you had nothing particular on hand, you might care to assist us in a most remarkable case which occurred only last night at Hampstead.'

'Dear me!' said Holmes. 'What was that?'

'A murder – a most dramatic and remarkable murder. I know how keen you are upon these things, and I would take it as a great favour if you would step down to Appledore Towers and give us the benefit of your advice. It is no ordinary crime. We have had our eyes upon this Mr Milverton for some time, and, between ourselves, he was a bit of a villain. He is known to have held papers which he used for blackmailing purposes. These papers have all been burned by the murderers. No article of value was taken, as it is probable that the criminals were men of good position, whose sole object was to prevent social exposure.'

'Criminals!' exclaimed Holmes. 'Plural!'

'Yes, there were two of them. They were, as nearly as possible, captured red-handed. We have their footmarks, we have their description; it's ten to one that we trace them. The first fellow was a bit too active, but the second was caught by the under-gardener, and only got away after a struggle. He was a middle-sized, strongly built man – square jaw, thick neck, moustache, a mask over his eyes.'

'That's rather vague,' said Sherlock Holmes. 'Why, it might be a description of Watson.'

'It's true,' said the Inspector, with much amusement. 'It might be a description of Watson.'

'Well, I am afraid I can't help you, Lestrade,' said Holmes. 'The fact is that I knew this fellow Milverton, that I considered him one of the most dangerous men in London, and that I think there are certain crimes which the law cannot touch, and which therefore, to some extent, justify private revenge. No, it's no use arguing. I have made up my mind. My sympathies are with the criminals rather than with the victim, and I will not handle this case.'

Holmes had not said one word to me about the tragedy which we had witnessed, but I observed all the morning that he was in the most thoughtful mood, and he gave me the impression, from his vacant eyes and his abstracted manner, of a man who is striving to recall something to his memory. We were in the middle of our lunch, when he suddenly sprang to his feet. 'By Jove, Watson! I've got it!' he cried. 'Take your hat! Come with me!' He hurried at his top speed down Baker Street and along Oxford Street, until we had almost reached Regent Circus. Here on the left hand there stands a shop window filled with photographs of the celebrities and beauties of the day. Holmes' eyes fixed themselves upon one of them, and following his gaze I saw the picture of a regal and stately lady in Court dress, with a high diamond tiara upon her noble head. I looked at that delicately curved nose, at the marked eyebrows, at the straight mouth, and the strong little chin beneath it. Then I caught my breath as I read the time-honoured title of the great nobleman and statesman whose wife she had been. My eyes met those of Holmes, and he put his finger to his lips as we turned away from the window.

THE TRIAL FOR MURDER

By Charles Dickens

I have always noticed a prevalent want of courage, even among persons of superior intelligence and culture, as to imparting their own psychological experiences when those have been of a strange sort. Almost all men are afraid that what they could relate in such wise would find no parallel or response in a listener's internal life, and might be suspected or laughed at. A truthful traveller, who should have seen some extraordinary creature in the likeness of a sea-serpent, would have no fear of mentioning it; but the same traveller, having had some singular presentiment, impulse, vagary of thought, vision (so-called), dream, or other remarkable mental impression, would hesitate considerably before he would own to it. To this reticence I attribute much of the obscurity in which such subjects are involved. We do not habitually communicate our experiences of these subjective things as we do our experiences of objective creation. The consequence is, that the general stock of experience in this regard appears exceptional, and really is so, in respect of being miserably imperfect.

In what I am going to relate, I have no intention of setting up, opposing, or supporting, any theory whatever. I know the history of the Bookseller of Berlin, I have studied the case of the wife of a late Astronomer Royal as related by Sir David Brewster, and I have followed the minutest details of a much more remarkable case of Spectral Illusion occurring within my private circle of friends. It may be necessary to state as to this last, that the sufferer (a lady) was in no degree, however distant, related to me. A mistaken assumption on that head might suggest an explanation of a part of my own case—but only a part —which would be wholly without foundation. It cannot be referred to my inheritance of any developed peculiarity, nor had I ever before any at all similar experience, nor have I ever had any at all similar experience since.

It does not signify how many years ago or how few, a certain murder was committed in England, which attracted great attention. We hear more than enough of murderers as they rise in succession to their atrocious eminence, and I would bury the memory of this particular brute, if I could, as his body was buried in Newgate Jail. I purposely abstain from giving any direct clue to the criminal's individuality.

When the murder was first discovered, no suspicion fell—or

I ought rather to say, for I cannot be too precise in my facts, it was nowhere publicly hinted that any suspicion fell—on the man who was afterwards brought to trial. As no reference was at that time made to him in the newspapers, it is obviously impossible that any description of him can at that time have been given in the newspapers. It is essential that this fact be remembered.

Unfolding at breakfast my morning paper, containing the account of that first discovery, I found it to be deeply interesting, and I read it with close attention. I read it twice, if not three times. The discovery had been made in a bedroom, and, when I laid down the paper, I was aware of a flash—rush— flow—I do not know what to call it—no word I can find is satisfactorily descriptive—in which I seemed to see that bedroom passing through my room, like a picture impossibly painted on a running river. Though almost instantaneous in its passing, it was perfectly clear; so clear that I distinctly, and with a sense of relief, observed the absence of the dead body from the bed.

It was in no romantic place that I had this curious sensation but in chambers in Piccadilly, very near to the corner of St. James's-street. It was entirely new to me. I was in my easy-chair at the moment, and the sensation was accompanied with a peculiar shiver which started the chair from its position. (But it is to be noted that the chair ran easily on castors.) I went to one of the windows (there are two in the room, and the room is on the second floor) to refresh my eyes with the moving objects down in Piccadilly. It was a bright autumn morning, and the street was sparkling and cheerful. The wind was high. As I looked out, it brought down from the Park a quantity of fallen leaves, which a gust took, and whirled into a spiral pillar. As the pillar fell and the leaves dispersed, I saw two men on the opposite side of the way, going from West to East. They were one behind the other. The foremost man often looked back over his shoulder. The second man followed him, at a distance of some thirty paces, with his right hand menacingly raised. First, the singularity and steadiness of this threatening gesture in so public a thoroughfare attracted my attention; and next, the more remarkable circumstance that nobody heeded it. Both men threaded their way among the other passengers with a smoothness hardly consistent even with the action of walking on a pavement; and no single creature, that I could see, gave them place, touched them, or looked after them. In passing before my windows, they both stared up at me. I saw their two faces very distinctly, and I knew that I could recognise them anywhere. Not that I had consciously noticed anything very remarkable in either face, except that the man who went first had an unusually lowering appearance, and that the face of the man who followed him was of the colour of impure wax.

I am a bachelor, and my valet and his wife constitute my whole establishment. My occupation is in a certain Branch Bank, and I wish that my duties as head of a Department were as light as they are popularly supposed to be. They kept me in town that autumn, when I stood in need of change. I was not ill, but I was not well. My reader is to make the most that can be reasonably made of my feeling jaded, having a depressing sense upon me of a monotonous life, and being 'slightly dyspeptic'. I am assured by my renowned doctor that my real state of health at that time justifies no stronger description, and I quote his own from his written answer to my request for it.

As the circumstances of the murder, gradually unravelling, took stronger and stronger possession of the public mind, I kept them away from mine by knowing as little about them as was possible in the midst of the universal excitement. But I knew that a verdict of Wilful Murder had been found against the suspected murderer, and that he had been committed to Newgate for trial. I also knew that his trial had been postponed over one Sessions of the Central Criminal Court, on the ground of general prejudice and want of time for the preparation of the defence. I may further have known, but I believe I did not, when, or about when, the Sessions to which his trial stood postponed would come on.

My sitting-room, bedroom, and dressing-room, are all on one floor. With the last there is no communication but through the bedroom. Time, there is a door in it, once communicating with the staircase; but a part of the fitting of my bath has been—and had then been for some years—fixed across it. At the same period, and as a part of the same arrangement, the door had been nailed up and canvased over.

I was standing in my bedroom late one night, giving some directions to my servant before he went to bed. My face was towards the only available door of communication with the dressing-room, and it was closed. My servant's back was towards that door. While I was speaking to him, I saw it open, and a man look in, who very earnestly and mysteriously beckoned to me. That man was the man who has gone second of the two along Piccadilly, and whose face was of the colour of impure wax.

The figure, having beckoned, drew back, and closed the door. With no longer pause than was made by my crossing the bedroom, I opened the dressing-room door, and looked in. I had a lighted candle ready in my hand. I felt no inward expectation of seeing the figure in the dressing-room, and I did not see it there.

Conscious that my servant stood amazed, I turned round to him, and said: 'Derrick, could you believe that in my cool senses I fancied I saw a——' As I there laid my hand upon his breast, with a sudden start he trembled violently, and said, 'O Lord, yes sir! A dead man beckoning!'

Now I do not believe that this John Derrick, my trusty and attached servant for more than twenty years, had any impression whatever of having seen any such figure until I touched him. The change in him was so startling, when I touched him, that I fully believed he derived his impression in some occult manner from me at that instant.

I bade John Derrick bring some brandy, and I gave him a dram, and was glad to take one myself. Of what had preceded that night's phenomenon, I told him not a single word. Reflecting on it, I was absolutely certain that I had never seen that face before, except on the one occasion in Piccadilly. Comparing its expression when beckoning at the door with its expression when it had stared up at me as I stood at my window, I came to the conclusion that on the first occasion it had sought to fasten itself upon my memory, and that on the second occasion it had made sure of being immediately remembered.

I was not very comfortable that night, though I felt a certainty, difficult to explain, that the figure would not return. At daylight I fell into a heavy sleep, from which I was awakened by John Derrick's coming to my bedside with a paper in his hand.

This paper, it appeared, had been the subject of an altercation at the door between its bearer and my servant. It was a summons to me to serve upon a Jury at the forthcoming Sessions of the Central Criminal Court at the Old Bailey. I had never before been summoned on such a Jury, as John Derrick well knew. He believed—I am not certain at this hour whether with reason or otherwise—that that class of Jurors were customarily chosen on a lower qualification than mine, and he had at first refused to accept the summons. The man who served it had taken the matter very coolly. He had said that my attendance or non-attendance was nothing to him; there the summons was; and I should deal with it at my own peril, and not at his.

For a day or two I was undecided whether to respond to this call, or take no notice of it. I was not conscious of the slightest mysterious bias, influence, or attraction, one way or other. Of that I am strictly sure as of every other statement that I make here. Ultimately I decided, as a break in the monotony of my life, that I would go.

The appointed morning was a raw morning in the month of November. There was a dense brown fog in Piccadilly, and it became positively black in the last degree oppressive East of Temple Bar. I found the passages and staircases of the Court-House flaringly lighted with gas, and the Court itself similarly illuminated. I *think* that, until I was conducted by officers into the Old Court and saw its crowded state, I did not know that the Murderer was to be tried that day. I *think* that, until I was so helped into the Old Court with considerable difficulty, I did not know into which of the two Courts sitting, my summons would take me. But this must not be received as a positive assertion, for I am not completely satisfied in my mind on either point.

I took my seat in the place appropriated to Jurors in waiting, and I looked about the Court as well as I could through the cloud of fog and breath that was heavy in it. I noticed the black vapour hanging like a murky curtain outside the great windows, and I noticed the stifled sound of wheels on the straw or tan that was littered in the street; also, the hum of the people gathered there, which a shrill whistle, or a louder song or hail than the rest, occasionally pierced. Soon afterwards the Judges, two in number, entered, and took their seats. The buzz in the Court was awfully hushed. The direction was given to put the Murderer to the bar. He appeared there. And in that same instant I recognised in him the first of the two men who had gone down Piccadilly.

If my name had been called then, I doubt if I could have answered to it audibly. But it was called about sixth or eighth in the panel, and I was by that time able to say, 'Here!' Now, observe. As I stepped into the box, the prisoner, who had been looking on attentively, but with no sign of concern, became violently agitated, and beckoned to his attorney. The prisoner's wish to challenge me was so manifest, that it occasioned a pause, during which the attorney, with his hand upon the dock, whispered with his client, and shook his head. I afterwards had it from that gentleman, that the prisoner's first affrighted words to him were, '*At all hazards, challenge that man!*' But that, as he would give no reason for it, and admitted that he had not even known my name until he heard it called and I appeared, it was not done.

Both on the ground already explained, that I wish to avoid reviving the unwholesome memory of that Murderer, and also because a detailed account of his long trial is by no means indispensable to my narrative, I shall confine myself closely to such incidents in the ten days and nights during which we, the Jury, were kept together, as directly bear on my own curious personal experience. It is in that, and not in the Murderer, that I seek to interest my reader. It is to that, and not to a page of the Newgate Calendar, that I beg attention.

I was chosen Foreman of the Jury. On the second morning of the trial, after evidence had been taken for two hours (I heard the church clocks strike), happening to cast my eyes over my brother jurymen, I found an inexplicable difficulty in counting them. I counted them several times, yet always with the same difficulty. In short, I made them one too many.

I touched the brother juryman whose place was next to me, and I whispered to him, 'Oblige me by counting us.' He looked surprised by the request, but turned his head and counted. 'Why,' says he, suddenly, 'we are thirt——; but no, it's not possible. No. We are twelve.'

According to my counting that day, we were always right in detail, but in the gross we were always one too many. There was no appearance—no figure—to account for it; but I had now an inward foreshadowing of the figure that was surely coming.

The Jury were housed at the London Tavern. We all slept in one large room on separate tables, and we were constantly in the charge and under the eye of the officer sworn to hold us in safe-keeping. I see no reason for suppressing the real name of that officer. He was intelligent, highly polite, and obliging, and (I was glad to hear) much respected in the City. He had an agreeable presence, good eyes, enviable black whiskers, and a fine sonorous voice. His name was Mr. Harker.

When we turned into our twelve beds at night, Mr. Harker's bed was drawn across the door. On the night of the second day, not being disposed to lie down, and seeing Mr. Harker sitting on his bed, I went and sat beside him, and offered him a pinch of snuff. As Mr. Harker's hand touched mine in taking it from my box, a peculiar shiver crossed him, and he said, 'Who is this?'

Following Mr. Harker's eyes, and looking along the room, I saw again the figure I expected—the second of the two men who had gone down Piccadilly. I rose, and advanced a few steps; then stopped, and looked round at Mr. Harker. He was quite unconcerned, laughed, and said in a pleasant way, 'I thought for a moment we had a thirteenth juryman, without a bed. But I see it is the moonlight.'

Making no revelation to Mr. Harker, but inviting him to take a walk with me to the end of the room, I watched what the figure did. It stood for a few moments by the bedside of each of my eleven brother jurymen, close to the pillow. It always went to the righthand side of the bed, and always passed out crossing the foot of the next bed. It seemed, from the action of the head, merely to look down pensively at each recumbent figure. It took no notice of me, or of my bed, which was that nearest to Mr. Harker's. It seemed to go out where the moonlight came in, through a high window, as by an aerial flight of stairs.

Next morning at breakfast, it appeared that everybody present had dreamed of the murdered man last night, except myself and Mr. Harker.

I now felt as convinced that the second man who had gone down Piccadilly was the murdered man (so to speak), as if it had been borne into my comprehension by his immediate testimony. But even this took place, and in a manner for which I was not at all prepared.

On the fifth day of the trial, when the case for the prosecution was drawing to a close, a miniature of the murdered man, missing from his bedroom upon the discovery of the deed, and afterwards found in a hiding-place where the Murderer had been seen digging, was put in evidence. Having been identified by the witness under examination, it was handed up to the Bench, and thence handed down to be inspected by the Jury. As an officer in a black gown was making his way with it across to me, the figure of the second man who had gone down Piccadilly impetuously started from the crowd, caught the miniature from the officer, and gave it to me with his own hands, at the same time saying, in a low and hollow tone— before I saw the miniature, which was in a locket—'I was younger then, and my face was not then drained of blood.' It also came between me and the brother juryman to whom I would have given the miniature, and between him and the brother juryman to whom he would have given it and so passed it on through the whole of our number, and back into my possession. Not one of them, however, detected this.

At table, and generally when we were shut up together in Mr. Harker's custody, we had from the first naturally discussed the day's proceedings a good deal. On that fifth day, the case for the prosecution being closed, and we having that side of the question in a completed shape before us, our discussion was more animated and serious. Among our number was a vestry-man—the densest idiot I have ever seen at large—who met the plainest evidence with the most preposterous objections, and who was sided with by two flabby parochial parasites; all the three impanelled from a district so delivered over to Fever that they ought to have been upon their own trial for five hundred Murders. When these mischievous blockheads were at their loudest, which was towards midnight, while some of us were already preparing for bed, I again saw the murdered man. He stood grimly behind them, beckoning to me. On my going towards them, and striking into the conversation, he immediately retired. This was the beginning of a separate series of appearances, confined to that long room in which *we* were confined. Whenever a knot of my brother juryman laid their heads together, I saw the head of the murdered man among theirs. Whenever their comparison of notes was going against him, he would solemnly and irresistibly beckon to me.

It will be borne in mind that down to the production of the miniature, on the fifth day of the trial, I had never seen the

Appearance in Court. Three changes occurred now that we entered on the case for the defence. Two of them I will mention together, first. The figure was not in Court continually, and it never there addressed itself to me, but always to the person who was speaking at the time. For instance: the throat of the murdered man had been cut straight across. In the opening speech for the defence, it was suggested that the deceased might have cut his own throat. At that very moment, the figure, with its throat in the dreadful condition referred to (this it had concealed before), stood at the speaker's elbow, motioning across and across its windpipe, now with the right hand, now with the left, vigorously suggesting to the speaker himself the impossibility of such a wound having been self-inflicted by either hand. For another instance: a witness to character, a woman, deposed to the prisoner's being the most amiable of mankind. The figure at that instant stood on the floor before her, looking her full in the face, and pointing out the prisoner's evil countenance with an extended arm and an outstretched finger.

The third change now to be added impressed me strongly as the most marked and striking of all. I do not theorise upon it; I accurately state it, and there leave it. Although the Appearance was not itself perceived by those whom it addressed, its coming close to such persons was invariably attended by some trepidation of disturbance on their part. It seemed to me as if it were prevented by laws to which I was not amenable, from fully revealing itself to others, and yet as if it could invisibly, dumbly, and darkly overshadow their minds. When the leading counsel for the defence suggested that hypothesis of suicide, and the figure stood at the learned gentleman's elbow, frightfully sawing at its severed throat, it is undeniable that the counsel faltered in his speech, lost for a few seconds the thread of his ingenious discourse, wiped his forehead with his handkerchief, and turned extremely pale. When the witness to character was confronted by the Appearance, her eyes most certainly did follow the direction of its pointed finger, and rest in great hesitation and trouble upon the prisoner's face. Two additional illustrations will suffice. On the eighth day of the trial, after the pause which was every day made early in the afternoon for a few minutes' rest and refreshment, I came back into Court with the rest of the Jury some little time before the return of the Judges. Standing up in the box and looking about me, I thought the figure was not there, until chancing to raise my eyes to the gallery, I saw it bending forward, and leaning over a very decent woman, as if to assure itself whether the Judges had resumed their seats or not. Immediately afterwards that woman screamed, fainted, and was carried out. So with the venerable, sagacious, and patient Judge who conducted the trial. When the case was over, and he settled himself and his papers to sum up, the murdered man, entering by the Judges' door, advanced to his Lordship's desk, and looked eagerly over his shoulder at the pages of his notes which he was turning. A change came over his Lordship's face; his hand stopped; the peculiar shiver, that I knew so well, passed over him; he faltered, 'Excuse me, gentlemen, for a few moments, I am somewhat oppressed by the vitiated air'; and did not recover until he had drunk a glass of water.

Through all the monotony of six of those interminable ten days—the same Judges and others on the bench, the same Murderer in the dock, the same lawyers at the table, the same tones of question and answer rising to the roof of the court, the same scratching of the Judge's pen, the same ushers going in and out, the same lights kindled at the same hour when there had been any natural light of day, the same foggy curtain outside the great windows when it was foggy, the same rain pattering and dripping when it was rainy, the same footmarks of turnkeys and prisoner day after day on the same sawdust, the same keys locking and unlocking the same heavy doors—through all the wearisome monotony which made me feel as if I had been Foreman of the Jury for a vast period of time, and Piccadilly had flourished coevally with Babylon, the murdered man never lost one trace of his distinctness in my eyes, nor was he at any moment less distinct than anybody else. I must not omit, as a matter of fact, that I never once saw the Appearance which I call by the name of the murdered man look at the Murderer. Again and again I wondered, 'Why does he not?' But he never did.

Nor did he look at me, after the production of the miniature, until the last closing minutes of the trial arrived. We retired to consider, at seven minutes before ten at night. The idiotic vestryman and his two parochial parasites gave us so much trouble that we twice returned into Court to beg to have certain extracts from the Judge's notes re-read. Nine of us had not the smallest doubt about those passages, neither, I believe, had anyone in the Court; the dunderheaded triumvirate, however, having no idea but obstruction, disputed them for that very reason. At length we prevailed, and finally the Jury returned into Court at ten minutes past twelve.

The murdered man at that time stood directly opposite the Jury-box, on the other side of the Court. As I took my place, his eyes rested on me with great attention; he seemed satisfied, and slowly shook a great grey veil, which he carried on his arm for the first time, over his head and whole form. As I gave in our verdict, 'Guilty', the veil collapsed, all was gone, and his place was empty.

The Murderer, being asked by the Judge, according to usage, whether he had anything to say before sentence of Death should be passed upon him, indistinctly muttered something which was described in the leading newspapers the following day as 'a few rambling, incoherent, and half-audible words, in which he was understood to complain that he had not had a fair trial, because the Foreman of the Jury was prepossessed against him'. The remarkable declaration that he really made was this: '*My Lord, I knew I was a doomed man, when the Foreman of my Jury came into the box. My Lord, I knew he would never let me off, because, before I was taken, he somehow got to my bedside in the night, woke me, and put a rope round my neck.*'

Trent and the Fool-proof Lift

E. C. BENTLEY

ONE OF THE commonest forms of fatal accident in the life of the town is falling down a lift shaft. Every coroner of large urban experience has dealt with cases by the score, whether due to short-sight, negligence, faulty construction, or defective safety mechanism. And there is another possibility.

One perfect day in June M. Armand Binet-Gailly, who held an important agency in the wine trade, left his office in Jermyn Street rather earlier than usual, and strolled homewards through the Parks to his bachelor flat at 42 Rigby Street. This was a tall old house, 'converted' from the errors of its pre-Victorian youth. There were five flats, and M. Binet-Gailly's was the second above the ground level. About 5.30 – so went his statement to the police – he entered by the front door which always stood open during the daytime, and went to the lift at the end of the hall. The lift was not at the ground floor, as he could see through the lattice gate, and he pressed the button which should bring it down. But nothing happened.

M. Binet-Gailly was very much annoyed. A portly man, he did not relish the prospect of climbing two flights of stairs on a warm day when he had paid for lift service. He aimlessly seized and shook the handle of the lattice gate. To his amazement, the gate slid aside as if the lift were in place. It should, of course, have been impossible to move it unless the lift were there. The whole system was out of order, he thought. He put his head into the shaft and looked upwards. There was the lift, so far as he could judge, at the top floor. Then, as he drew back his head, his eye was caught by something at the bottom of the shallow well in which the lift-shaft ended. There was a strong electric ceiling lamp always alight at this dark end of the hall, and it showed M. Binet-Gailly quite enough.

Like most of his countrymen, he had served in arms, and things of this kind did not upset him. Plump though he was, he began to clamber down into the well; then he bethought himself. Certainly there could be no life in that crumpled bundle of humanity. The thing to do was to leave it untouched until the arrival of the police. M. Binet-Gailly went to the door communicating with the basement and bellowed downstairs for Pimblett, the caretaker. 42 Rigby Street, though distant by little more than the breadth of Oxford Street from the elegance of Mayfair, did not rise to the luxury of a uniformed porter, and neither Pimblett nor his wife was usually to be seen after the morning job of cleaning the hall and staircase was done.

Pimblett, who also had served in arms, and had seen more dirty work than had M. Binet-Gailly, took in the situation at a glance. Wasting no words, he strode to the hall telephone and rang up the police station. Both men then mounted the stairs to find which gate it was through which the unknown – for the face of the corpse could not be seen – had plunged to his death. On the floor immediately above M. Binet-Gailly's they found the gate drawn back. On this floor was the flat occupied by Mr Anthony Villiers Maxwell – a young man of sporting tastes – and his valet. M. Binet-Gailly proposed ringing the bell of the flat to make inquiries, but Pimblett remarked that the police would prefer to have all that left to them.

An hour later M. Binet-Gailly, sipping a glass of Campari in his own rooms, discussed with his servant, by name Aristide, what he had just learnt of this mysterious affair. The dead man had turned out to be his own landlord, Mr Stephen Havelock Hermon, who had bought the house a few years before, and had installed his nephew, Anthony Maxwell, in the flat above-stairs on its falling vacant soon afterwards. There had been some slight lack of sympathy between M. Binet-Gailly and Mr Hermon, owing to the fact that Mr Hermon had among his eccentricities a passionate hatred of liquor in every form, and when he purchased the place had not concealed his chagrin on finding that one of the sitting tenants was engaged in the wine trade, which Mr Hermon preferred to call the drink-traffic.

No one in the building had seen Mr Hermon enter it that afternoon. No one had seen him at all before the finding of his body. No one had known of his intention to come to the house. Mr Clayton Haggett, the famous surgeon, who had the top flat, had not been at home; his housekeeper had heard no ring. Anthony Maxwell also had been out, and his valet had had the afternoon 'off'. Aristide could vouch for it, as he had already informed the police that no one had called at M. Binet-Gailly's. Mr Lucian Corderoy, the eminent dress designer, and his wife had both been at his shop in Malyon Street, and their 'daily' servant was never in the place after twelve noon. As for Sir George Stower, the Keeper of Phoenician Antiquities at the British Museum, he was enjoying a hard-earned holiday at Margate, and his flat on the ground floor had been shut up for some days past.

'But naturally,' remarked Aristide, fingering a swarthy chin, 'the old gentleman wished to call upon his nephew.'

'It is very probable,' M. Binet-Gailly agreed. 'He was devoted to that young animal, and they say he had no other relative living. The nephew will be his heir, no doubt, and he will make the money roll a little faster than the uncle ever did.'

'Ah! when one is young,' observed Aristide sentimentally.

'And when one is a waster by nature,' M. Binet-Gailly added. 'Well, Aristide, it is time for me to dress.'

Philip Trent, in his first outline of the case for the readers of the *Record*, had given these facts about the other tenants of the building. 'It is naturally assumed [he wrote] that Mr Hermon had called, as he often did, to see his nephew, to whom he is said to have been much attached. His ringing at the door had been resultless, and he had turned away to go down by the way he had come. He had opened the gate, believing the lift to be in position there – and stepped out into emptiness. He was known to be extremely short-sighted. His neck, so says the police surgeon, was broken, and there were other injuries that must have been immediately fatal. When his body was found he had been dead not more than an hour.

'This is very simple, but it leaves all the important questions unanswered.

'Why was not the lift where he expected it to be? He had only just left it; and according to the information gathered by the police there had been no one leaving or entering any of the flats since the early afternoon, when Mr Clayton Haggett and Mr Maxwell went out.

'Why was it at the top floor?

'How was it that he had been able to open the gate, which should have been locked automatically the moment the lift moved from that floor?

'Why was the gate on the ground floor unlocked? Why

indeed? Conceivably the mechanism of the upstairs gate had gone wrong, so that Mr Hermon could open it; but the gate at the bottom could not be opened by a dead man.

'Why were all the other gates in working order – the top gate, where the lift was, unlocked; the other two locked?

'On this very vital point I have had some conversation with the expert who was sent to investigate by the firm which built and installed the lift. The mechanism, he told me, was tested by the makers at monthly intervals, and had been in perfect order at the last examination, ten days before. The system was as nearly fool-proof as it could be. "But," he added, "it isn't tool-proof. Any engineer could see with half an eye that both those locks had been forced."

'Here are the elements of a very sinister mystery. Some one who was not Mr Hermon forced the ground-floor gate. Presumably he forced the other. The only persons known to have been in the house from three o'clock onwards were the caretaker in the basement, the French manservant in M. Binet-Gailly's flat, and the housekeeper in Mr Haggett's. Did some one enter the house before Mr Hermon; or did some one accompany him? To this point the inquiries of the police are being directed – so far, I believe, without result.

'If Mr Hermon was a victim of violence, it is hard to think that any feeling of ill-will could have been at work. It is true that he was a man of strong opinions, often violently expressed in public controversy – the hard knocks exchanged between him and his tenant, Mr Clayton Haggett, in their dispute over vivisection last year will be remembered. But he was always a fair and even a chivalrous fighter, on the friendliest footing with opponents to whom he was personally known. His nature was kindly and generous, his great wealth was largely devoted to works of benevolence; the hospital endowments made by him as memorials to his late wife are but a part of his service to humanity.'

Trent did not try to intrude on the sorrow of Anthony Maxwell, but he had from the young man's valet, Joseph Weaver, some material information. He learnt that the nephew felt his loss very deeply indeed; that he did not look like the same man. He had, Weaver said, a feeling heart. A little wild he might have been – young gentlemen would be young gentlemen – but he had what they call a nice nature. He owed everything to Mr Hermon, who had been a father to him after his parents died when he was a child. Naturally he was very much upset.

Trent reflected privately on the deceitfulness of appearances; for he knew Anthony Maxwell by sight, and would not have said that either his eye, his mouth, or his bearing proclaimed the niceness of his nature. Perhaps Weaver was being loyal to his employer. He did not look particularly loyal; but then he did not look anything to speak of. He had the expressionlessness of his calling. His quiet voice, neat clothes, and sleek black hair suggested nothing but discretion. Trent asked a question.

Mr Hermon, Weaver said, came up fairly often on business from his place in Surrey, and when he did so, always visited his nephew. Sometimes he came on purpose to see him. No; Mr Maxwell had not been expecting him on the day of the accident; he had given no notice that he was coming. If he had done so, Mr Maxwell would naturally have been at home. Weaver thought it unlikely that Mr Hermon had been intending to call on any of the other tenants. He did do so from time to time, to talk about some matters of repairs or other landlord's business; but that would always be by appointment, and not during the working day. All the tenants, Weaver pointed out, were busy men, with the exception of Mr Maxwell; they would seldom be at home until the evening.

Yes; Mr Hermon attended personally to the management of all his house property in the West End. There was a good deal of it, and it gave him occupation. No; he was not what they call a hard landlord; quite the contrary, Weaver would say. Mr Hermon liked to do things for people, being a very generous man, as Weaver had good reason to know.

'You mean that he was generous to you,' Trent suggested. 'A present for you when he called here – that sort of thing?'

'Mr Hermon always behaved like a gentleman,' Weaver said demurely. 'But I meant more than that, sir. You see, I was two years in his service before I came to Mr Maxwell; that is how I came to know so much about his habits, and to appreciate his kindness. Then when Mr Hermon went on a tour round the world, he suggested I should go to Mr Maxwell, who was not satisfied with the valet he had then; and I have remained in his service since then – about nine months ago it would be.'

When Trent went to talk it over with his friend Chief-Inspector Bligh, he found that officer cheerfully interested in what he described as a very nice case.

'There's nothing easy,' he said, 'about it so far. Of course, it's a murder – that's certain. You have heard what the lift company's man says. And, of course, it was meant to look as if it might be an accident.'

'Then how about the ground-floor gate being forced as well as the other? That doesn't look like an accident.'

'Well, what does it look like?' Mr Bligh wanted to know.

'It looks to me as it looks to you, I suppose. When the old man had been pushed into the lift-shaft, the murderer realized that something had gone wrong with his plan. Hermon had had something on him that might give the murderer away if it was found on the body. The only thing for him to do was to run downstairs, prise open the bottom gate, and take what he wanted off the body. If Pimblett or anybody appeared while he was doing so, he could say he had seen the old man open the gate and fall down the shaft, and had rushed down and forced the gate to see if he was still alive.'

The inspector nodded. 'Yes; that's the idea. And he did get what he wanted, presumably; and nobody did see him. Of course, it's the sort of place where nobody is about most of the time, and the man who did the job knew that.'

'Well, how about the people who live here? Are they all above suspicion?'

'There is no such thing,' Mr Bligh declared, 'as being above suspicion – not if I do the suspecting. And it just happens that most of them haven't an alibi. The Museum man has, of course; his flat was shut up, and is still. And the Corderoys were at their dress shop till after six. But the Frenchman was alone when he came in and reported having found the body; and his story of how he found it, and what time he entered the house, is quite unsupported. Maxwell says he lunched at his flat, went out immediately afterwards, and spent all the afternoon at Lord's watching Lancashire take a licking from Middlesex; then went to his club with some other bright boys, had drinks, and came home to dress for dinner. But Lord's is a place you can dodge out of and return to later, and it's no distance for a car to Rigby Street. Then there's Clayton Haggett, the surgeon. He had lunch in his flat too, after a morning at the hospital; went down to his car at two-thirty, had an operation at a nursing-home and another at a private house; finished by four-fifteen, had a cup of tea, and then spent two hours driving about down Richmond way – just to take the air, and nobody with him all that time, which is a pity.'

'He didn't like Hermon,' Trent remarked. 'He was very bitter in that tussle they had over vivisection.'

'Yes, and he's got a naughty temper when he's crossed. Loses his self-control. He had to resign from the Hunter Club for knocking a man down in the smoking-room. Nobody would have anything to do with him if he wasn't such a wizard with the knife.'

'And what about the servants in the building? Do they come into the picture at all?'

'All I can tell you is that none of their stories can be checked. Pimblett says he was in the basement all the afternoon until the Frenchman shouted for him; his wife was away calling on her sister in Highbury. The French manservant and Haggett's housekeeper say they never opened the doors of their flats until the police looked them up after the finding of the body. Maxwell's man says he had the afternoon off, went out after his master had gone, and sat through the cinema programme at the Byzantine, getting back a little before Anthony did. Well, what good's that? Like the other three, he can't prove anything at all about where he was for some hours before the police were called in.'

'Any of them ever been in trouble?'

'Nothing known against any of them. Ex-Sergeant Pimblett – excellent record. Mrs Hargreaves, the housekeeper – ditto. Weaver used to be employed at Harding's the big barber shop in Duke Street, where old Hermon used to go when he was in town. He always had Weaver to attend to him, and at last he took him on as his valet. Afterwards—'

'Yes, he told me; he was switched on to Anthony. Perfectly respectable. And the French domestic?'

'All I know about Aristide Recot is that he has a wooden face and side-whiskers, and doesn't mind being seen in an apron. What I'm told by his master is that he has been with him for some years, and given every satisfaction. But what's the use? We had to consider the servants, of course; but what motive could any of them have had? It's a different thing when you come to their employers. Haggett, for instance.'

Trent looked the inspector in the eyes. 'You were talking about motive,' he said gently. 'Is Haggett's resentment really the strongest you can think of? I don't like being teased.'

'All right; I was coming to it,' Mr Bligh responded with a faint grin. 'Yes, I suppose the expectation of coming into the greater part of a very large fortune might operate as a motive. That is what Maxwell will do, according to our information. Unless something happens to him. His uncle made him a very generous allowance, and he lived rent free, and Weaver's wages were paid by the old man. Maxwell ought to have been grateful, and perhaps he was; but there you are – he's a vicious young brute, and always in debt; and though Hermon wasn't strong, he might have lived to any old age. Now then! Will that do for you?'

'Something of the sort had crossed my mind,' Trent admitted. 'Certainly it will do – until something better comes along.'

Mr Bligh raised an impressive finger. 'And now,' he said, 'I'll tell you something that hadn't crossed your mind. It's information received. If it's right, the coroner will hear it at a later stage, but at present we would rather the murderer didn't know about it. You remember I mentioned that Clayton Haggett left his flat at two-thirty that afternoon. Well, he had more to tell us than that. He went down by the lift, he said. It's rather a slow-motion lift. As it passed down by the floor below – Anthony's floor – Haggett heard some words spoken. He could see as he passed that the door of the flat was just being opened from inside, and as it opened he heard a loud bullying voice call out, ' You do what I say, and look sharp about it. If you get on the wrong side of me, you know what to expect.' That is as near as Haggett can go to the actual words he heard – I asked him to be particular.'

Trent stared at the inspector with kindling eyes. 'You do like saving up the best bit to the last, don't you? And you had this – this! – simply handed to you. On a plate.'

'With parsley round it,' added Mr Bligh unashamed.

'I have heard you use that phrase before,' Trent said thoughtfully. 'It meant, I think, that you were rather mistrustful of good things that came so easily. But now, what about this remarkable addition to the record? Did Haggett recognize the voice? Did he see anybody?'

'No. Haggett says it might have been Maxwell he heard talking; but he only knows Maxwell by sight, has never spoken to him, and has no idea what his voice would sound like if it was raised. And, of course, it might have been anybody else in the world. Then I asked him what class of voice it was – like a curate's, or a dustman's, or what. All he could tell me was that it was not a coarse voice, and not a refined one; just middling. Very useful! But that isn't all. As the lift got to the bottom he heard a door above slam violently, which he assumed to be the one he had just seen being opened; and as he was getting into his car, Maxwell came out of the street door, with his hat on, looking furiously angry and very red in the face, and walked away rapidly.'

Trent considered this. 'So that is Haggett's information. And what does Maxwell say about it?'

'He hasn't been asked – yet. He is being given a little more time to make mistakes. But, of course, it may all be a lie. Yes, you may look surprised; but Haggett isn't out of it yet, as I told you. There's another piece of news I've got for you which certainly isn't a lie. When Jackson did the post mortem he found something that wants a lot of explaining.'

'What! Another thing you are keeping dark?'

'For the present. He noticed that the finger nails of the right hand looked as if they had been scratching hard at something, and there was a very faint odour that he couldn't place; so he took some scrapings from the nails to be analyzed. They found some tiny scraps of human skin; also traces of some things with hydrocarbo scientific names that don't seem to tell you much, and one thing that I have heard of quite often before.'

'Yes. What?'
'Chloroform.'

Thinking it over in his studio, Trent could make no more of this at first than Mr Bligh and he had made between them. If there had been a struggle, and if chloroform had been used, it did seem to point to the one resident in the house who might be presumed to know all about chloroform and what could be done with it. And Haggett was known to be violent tempered and a good hater, as well as a very able and successful professional man – not an unknown combination of qualities. But Trent found it hard to believe in such a character expressing its dislike in murder done by tricky and treacherous means. A quarrel; yes. An assault; possibly. An assault with a fatal result, legally a murder; such things did happen. But a planned and cold-blooded crime, with the murderer scheming to avoid detection by means of a trumped-up tale – Trent did not see it. In his experience, trained faculties, high responsibility, and professional distinction did not go with dirty actions and circumstantial lying.

But if Haggett's story of what he had heard and seen was true, how could it be fitted to the known facts? Maxwell's own statement about the time at which he had left the building agreed with Haggett's. Weaver's statement was that he had, as was natural, gone out a little later. Both of them had said nothing of this loud-voiced unknown who had used threatening language in Maxwell's flat. It might have been Maxwell himself. Could it have been Hermon? But Hermon had been fond, even foolishly fond, of his nephew. Unless – and here opened a new vista of ugliness – both Maxwell and his servant had been concealing the truth on that point, building up the fiction of a generous benefactor whom for worlds Maxwell would not have injured. There might be purpose enough in their doing so. The inspector had not thought of that; at least (Trent reflected with a wry smile) he had not mentioned it. Hermon's visit, by the way, had been a surprise visit according to Weaver.

Trent, at this point in his meditations, rose and began to pace the studio. Soon he went across to the model's dressing-room and examined his appearance in the mirror there. His hair had been cut fairly recently, but another trimming would not upset the balance of nature, he thought. Within the hour he was one of a dozen sheeted forms, sitting in a strange chair before a tall mirror, and had met the attendant's opening comment on the warmth of the day with the due rejoinder that it looked like rain later on.

Trent, like many other men, found his thoughts the clearer for being written down, and would often prepare for the drafting of a dispatch that could be published by a private memorandum, including all that could not. That evening he sat at his bureau, and did not rise until the account of what he had discovered, and the conclusions drawn, was complete in black and white.

'Starting with the belief that Haggett's story was true [he wrote], I had to make out who the person in Maxwell's flat was who gave some order, in offensive words, coupled with a vague threat; and who the person ordered about and threatened was. As Bligh said, it might have been any one who used those words; some one who had not as yet come into view in the case. But it was as well to consider first those who were known to have been in the place; and one of these was Hermon. But the accounts we had of Hermon made this seem unlikely; and they were not only the accounts given by Maxwell and his valet. Hermon's general reputation was that of a man who would be the last in the world to bully and threaten. As for the others who had been in the other flats, there was no visible shadow of a reason for suspecting any one of them.

'There remained Maxwell and his valet.

'Maxwell might be capable of bullying and threatening. He is not a nice young man. Could he have been the speaker, and either Hermon or Weaver the man spoken to?

'Well, is it likely? Maxwell is not a lunatic. No man in his senses would talk like that to his rich uncle whose fortune he expected to inherit; nor to his valet unless he was prepared for the man leaving him on the spot, and for being obliged to do his own valeting and cooking and housework until he could get another servant. Unless, of course, he had got either of them under his thumb in some way. Has Hermon, or Weaver, a guilty past, known to Maxwell?

'I had got as far as this when a new point occurred to me. Weaver, when I saw him, had told me that Maxwell had not been expecting his uncle's visit. As this looked very much like a plain lie, I thought some attention paid to Weaver might be worth the trouble; and so I went and had my hair cut at Harding's.

'The man who cut it was as ready for conversation as barbers usually are. I spoke of the fatal accident to Mr Hermon, and the barber, who may have been reading my own remarks on the subject, said that it was a funny sort of accident, giving his reasons for that view. Then I mentioned that I knew Mr Hermon's former valet had once had a job at Harding's. The man remembered both of them very well. He only wished he had the chance of bettering himself as Weaver had done. He had not known that Weaver had become Mr Maxwell's valet, but he had known that Weaver had done very well for himself. Besides that, Weaver had come into a bit of money of his own; he had mentioned it confidential. He was quite the gentleman now, especially in the last six months. He had taken to having his hair done at Harding's once a fortnight, probably just to show off a bit among his old pals. Gold wrist-watch, diamond tie-pin, quite the swell. Liked to do himself well, too, in his time off; and why not if you could run to it? Sometimes he would have my barber and other friends from Harding's to meet him after hours, and would stand drinks like a lord; and you could always see he had had a few beforehand.

'So far, my visit to Harding's had yielded more than I had any right to expect. But this was not all. My man came at length to that stage of the proceedings at which it is usual for the barber to hint delicately that the condition of one's scalp is not all that could be wished, and that this could be remedied by the use of some sort of hair-wash. With a flash of inspiration I asked what Weaver was in the habit of buying for himself. The best hair tonic there is, said my barber with enthusiasm; Harding's own preparation, Capillax – just the thing for me; and I would understand that Weaver knew, as a hairdresser, how excellent it was. I thought, when I was told the price of it, that Weaver also knew how impressively costly it was. I was shown a bottle of Capillax; a green fluted bottle, with NOT TO BE TAKEN stamped in the glass. Why, I asked my barber, should I be forbidden to take Capillax if I should choose to buy Capillax?

'He turned the bottle over, and showed me on the back a tiny pasted label. It read:

> This preparation, containing among other valuable ingredients a small amount of Chloroform, is, in accordance with the Pharmacy Act, hereby labelled
> POISON.

'I ordered a bottle, of course. I thought my barber had earned his commission on the sale. And I asked him if he could tell me why chloroform should be used in a tonic for the hair, because I had thought it was for putting people to sleep. He said yes, but that was only the vapour of chloroform; in solution it acted as a stimulant to the skin, and had cleansing properties.

'My reconstruction of this crime is that Weaver planned the murder of Hermon. He had found out something that Maxwell did not dare have known about himself; he put the screw on him and bled him for every shilling he could raise. A servant who knows too much about his employer is a figure common enough in the odorous annals of blackmail. Weaver had 'come into money' indeed! Probably he got rid of a lot of it by betting. Anyhow, the more he got, the more he wanted. He had tasted easy money; he could not do without it; and there was no more in sight. But he knew that Maxwell, when his uncle died, would be a rich man. Weaver thought it over; and he formed a plan, to be carried out the first time that opportunity offered.

'On the morning of Hermon's death Maxwell heard, by letter or telephone, that his uncle intended to call that afternoon. Weaver's tale, that the old man had given no notice of his coming, was hardly credible. It was the height of summer, and it was utterly unlikely that Maxwell would be staying indoors that afternoon unless he was expecting a visitor. Hermon would certainly have let him know he was coming. This was what Weaver had been waiting for. After lunch he told Maxwell to leave the flat, go somewhere where he could mix with friends, and stay away until dinner-time. I do not believe Maxwell knew what was intended, because Haggett's story makes it plain that he protested against this. He did not see why he should deliberately absent himself when his uncle had asked him to be at home; why should he affront the old man? Weaver then went to the door of the flat, and as he opened it he raised his voice in the bullying words that Haggett caught as the lift went down. Maxwell, in a furious temper, did as he was told.

'When Hermon arrived, coming up by the lift, Weaver

opened the door to him. He framed some lie to account for Maxwell's absence, and asked him to come in, perhaps for a rest and a cup of tea. Hermon did so; and while he was alone in the sitting-room, Weaver slipped out, took the lift to the floor above, and forced the lift gate on Maxwell's floor. When the old man went, Weaver saw him to the lift, opened the gate, and thrust him into the empty shaft. He knew better than most people how bad Hermon's sight was, and how little strength he had for a struggle. And here the plan went wrong. Hermon realized at the last instant that the lift was not there, and grabbed at Weaver as he felt the push given him. His right hand clutched Weaver's hair, tearing some of it out as he fell to his death, and lacerating the man's scalp.

'Weaver had seen instantly that if hair was found in the dead man's hand there would be an end of the theory that he had met with an accident. The police would be looking for a man with black hair and a scratched head; and they would not have far to look. There was only one thing for it. Weaver ran down to the ground floor, forced the gate there, stepped into the well, and carefully removed the hair he found in the dead man's grasp. There was nothing else he could do. He must simply stick to the story he had already made up, and trust to luck. After all, as far as he knew, there had been no witness whatever to anything that had passed.'

It was late by the time Trent had finished his memorandum. He read and re-read it, then slipped it into an envelope, addressed it to Mr Bligh at Scotland Yard, went out and registered it at the district post office.

Trent was at work in his studio next morning when the telephone bell called him.

Mr Bligh, not an effusive man by nature, said that Trent's report had reached him. 'There's no doubt but what you're right,' he went on. 'It's a pity, though, that we shall never hear what it was Weaver knew about Maxwell. It might very well have been a job for us.'

'Well, you called him a vicious young brute,' Trent said. 'With my morbid imagination and your fund of horrid experience, we ought to be able to guess a few of the things that it might have been. But why do you say you will never know? If you bring the murder home to Weaver, he will probably give Maxwell away, having no further use for his secret. It would be just like him.'

'Weaver won't do that.' There was a note of grimness in the inspector's voice. 'At eight fifteen last night Weaver was on his way down Coventry Street. He had been drinking, and couldn't walk straight. A dozen people saw him stumble off the kerb and into the road, right under a passing bus. He was killed instantly. His injuries—'

'Thanks, I don't want to hear about his injuries.' Trent wiped his brow. 'They were fatal – that's enough for me.'

'Yes, but there were some that weren't fatal. On the head, concealed by the hair, there were four deep scratches, not completely healed, and the signs of some hair having been torn out by the roots. I thought you'd like to know.'

The Mysterious Death on the Underground Railway

BARONESS EMMUSKA ORCZY

* * *

It was all very well for Mr Richard Frobisher (of the *London Mail*) to cut up rough about it. Polly did not altogether blame him.

She liked him all the better for that frank outburst of manlike ill-temper which, after all said and done, was only a very flattering form of masculine jealousy.

Moreover, Polly distinctly felt guilty about the whole thing. She had promised to meet Dickie – that is Mr Richard Frobisher – at two o'clock sharp outside the Palace Theatre, because she wanted to go to a Maud Allan matinée, and because he naturally wished to go with her.

But at two o'clock sharp she was still in Norfolk Street, Strand, inside an ABC shop, sipping cold coffee opposite a grotesque old man who was fiddling with a bit of string.

How could she be expected to remember Maud Allan or the Palace Theatre, or Dickie himself for a matter of that? The man in the corner had begun to talk of that mysterious

52

death on the Underground railway, and Polly had lost count of time, of place, and circumstance.

She had gone to lunch quite early, for she was looking forward to the matinée at the Palace. The old scarecrow was sitting in his accustomed place when she came into the ABC shop, but he had made no remark all the time that the young girl was munching her scone and butter. She was just busy thinking how rude he was not even to have said 'Good morning', when an abrupt remark from him caused her to look up.

'Will you be good enough,' he said suddenly, 'to give me a description of the man who sat next to you just now, while you were having your cup of coffee and scone.'

Involuntarily Polly turned her head towards the distant door, through which a man in a light overcoat was even now quickly passing. That man had certainly sat at the next table to hers, when she first sat down to her coffee and scone: he had finished his luncheon – whatever it was – a moment ago, had paid at the desk and gone out. The incident did not appear to Polly as being of the slightest consequence.

Therefore she did not reply to the rude old man, but shrugged her shoulders, and called to the waitress to bring her bill.

'Do you know if he was tall or short, dark or fair?' continued the man in the corner, seemingly not the least disconcerted by the young girl's indifference. 'Can you tell me at all what he was like?'

'Of course I can,' rejoined Polly impatiently, 'but I don't see that my description of one of the customers of an ABC shop can have the slightest importance.'

He was silent for a minute, while his nervous fingers fumbled about in his capacious pockets in search of the inevitable piece of string. When he had found this necessary 'adjunct to thought', he viewed the young girl again through his half-closed lids, and added maliciously:

'But supposing it were of paramount importance that you should give an accurate description of a man who sat next to you for half an hour today, how would you proceed?'

'I should say that he was of medium height—'

'Five foot eight, nine, or ten?' he interrupted quietly.

'How can one tell to an inch or two?' rejoined Polly crossly. 'He was between colours.'

'What's that?' he enquired blandly.

'Neither fair nor dark – his nose—'

'Well, what was his nose like? Will you sketch it?'

'I am not an artist. His nose was fairly straight – his eyes—'

'Were neither dark nor light – his hair had the same striking peculiarity – he was neither short nor tall – his nose was neither aquiline nor snub—' he recapitulated sarcastically.

'No,' she retorted; 'he was just ordinary-looking.'

'Would you know him again – say tomorrow, and among a number of other men who were "neither tall nor short, dark nor fair, aquiline nor snub-nosed", etc.?'

'I don't know – I might – he was certainly not striking enough to be specially remembered.'

'Exactly,' he said, while he leant forward excitedly, for all the world like a Jack-in-the-box let loose. 'Precisely; and you are a journalist – call yourself one, at least – and it should be part of your business to notice and describe people. I don't mean only the wonderful personage with the clear Saxon features, the fine blue eyes, the noble brow and classic face, but the ordinary person – the person who represents ninety out of every hundred of his own kind – the average Englishman, say, of the middle classes, who is neither very tall nor very short, who wears a moustache which is neither fair nor dark, but which masks his mouth, and a top hat which hides the shape of his head and brow, a man, in fact, who dresses like hundreds of his fellow-creatures, moves like them, speaks like them, has no peculiarity.

'Try to describe *him*, to recognise him, say a week hence, among his other eighty-nine doubles; worse still, to swear his life away, if he happened to be implicated in some crime, wherein *your* recognition of him would place the halter round his neck.

'Try that, I say, and having utterly failed you will more readily understand how one of the greatest scoundrels unhung is still at large, and why the mystery on the Underground railway was never cleared up.

'I think it was the only time in my life that I was seriously tempted to give the police the benefit of my own views upon the matter. You see, though I admire the brute for his cleverness, I did not see that his being unpunished could possibly benefit anyone.

'In these days of tubes and motor traction of all kinds, the old-fashioned "best, cheapest, and quickest route to City and West End" is often deserted, and the good old Metropolitan railway carriages cannot at any time be said to be overcrowded. Anyway, when that particular train steamed into Aldgate at about four p.m. on March eighteenth last, the first-class carriages were all but empty.

'The guard marched up and down the platform looking into all the carriages to see if anyone had left a halfpenny evening paper behind for him, and opening the door of one of the first-class compartments, he noticed a lady sitting in the further corner, with her head turned away towards the window, evidently oblivious of the fact that on this line Aldgate is the terminal station.

' "Where are you for, lady?" he said.

'The lady did not move, and the guard stepped into the carriage, thinking that perhaps the lady was asleep. He touched her arm lightly and looked into her face. In his own poetic language, he was "struck all of a 'eap". In the glassy eyes, the ashen colour of the cheeks, the rigidity of the head, there was the unmistakable look of death.

'Hastily the guard, having carefully locked the carriage door, summoned a couple of porters, and sent one of them off to the police station, and the other in search of the stationmaster.

'Fortunately at this time of day the up platform is not very crowded, all the traffic tending westward in the afternoon. It was only when an inspector and two police constables, accompanied by a detective in plain clothes and a medical officer, appeared upon the scene, and stood round a first-class railway compartment, that a few idlers realised that something unusual had occurred, and crowded round, eager and curious.

'Thus it was that the later editions of the evening papers, under the sensational heading, "Mysterious Suicide on the Underground Railway", had already an account of the extraordinary event. The medical officer had very soon come to the decision that the guard had not been mistaken, and that life was indeed extinct.

'The lady was young, and must have been very pretty before the look of fright and horror had so terribly distorted her features. She was very elegantly dressed, and the more frivolous papers were able to give their feminine readers a detailed account of the unfortunate woman's gown, her shoes, hat, and gloves.

'It appears that one of the latter, the one on the right hand, was partly off, leaving the thumb and wrist bare. That hand held a small satchel, which the police opened, with a view to the possible identification of the deceased, but which was found to contain only a little loose silver, some smelling-salts, and a small empty bottle, which was handed over to the medical officer for purposes of analysis.

'It was the presence of that small bottle which had caused the report to circulate freely that the mysterious case on the Underground railway was one of suicide. Certain it was that neither about the lady's person, nor in the appearance of the railway carriage, was there the slightest sign of struggle or even of resistance. Only the look in the poor woman's eyes spoke of sudden terror, of the rapid vision of an unexpected and violent death, which probably only lasted an infinitesimal fraction of a second, but which had left its indelible mark upon the face, otherwise so placid and so still.

'The body of the deceased was conveyed to the mortuary. So far, of course, not a soul had been able to identify her, or to throw the slightest light upon the mystery which hung around her death.

'Against that, quite a crowd of idlers – genuinely interested or not – obtained admission to view the body, on the pretext of having lost or mislaid a relative or a friend. At about eight-thirty p.m. a young man, very well dressed, drove up to the station in a hansom, and sent in his card to the superintendent. It was Mr Hazeldene, shipping agent, of 11, Crown Lane, EC, and No. 19, Addison Row, Kensington.

'The young man looked in a pitiable state of mental distress; his hand clutched nervously a copy of the *St James's Gazette* which contained the fatal news. He said very little to the superintendent except that a person who was very dear to him had not returned home that evening.

'He had not felt really anxious until half an hour ago, when suddenly he thought of looking at his paper. The description of the deceased lady, though vague, had terribly alarmed him. He had jumped into a hansom, and now begged permission to view the body, in order that his worst fears might be allayed.

'You know what followed, of course,' continued the man in the corner, 'the grief of the young man was truly pitiable. In the woman lying there in a public mortuary before him, Mr Hazeldene had recognised his wife.

'I am waxing melodramatic,' said the man in the corner,

who looked up at Polly with a mild and gentle smile, while his nervous fingers vainly endeavoured to add another knot on the scrappy bit of string with which he was continually playing, 'and I fear that the whole story savours of the penny novelette, but you must admit, and no doubt you remember, that it was an intensely pathetic and truly dramatic moment.

'The unfortunate young husband of the deceased lady was not much worried with questions that night. As a matter of fact, he was not in a fit condition to make any coherent statement. It was at the coroner's inquest on the following day that certain facts came to light, which for the time being seemed to clear up the mystery surrounding Mrs Hazeldene's death, only to plunge that same mystery, later on, into denser gloom than before.

'The first witness at the inquest was, of course, Mr Hazeldene himself. I think everyone's sympathy went out to the young man as he stood before the coroner and tried to throw what light he could upon the mystery. He was well dressed, as he had been the day before, but he looked terribly ill and worried, and no doubt the fact that he had not shaved gave his face a careworn and neglected air.

'It appears that he and the deceased had been married some six years or so, and that they had always been happy in their married life. They had no children. Mrs Hazeldene seemed to enjoy the best of health till lately, when she had had a slight attack of influenza, in which Dr Arthur Jones had attended her. The doctor was present at this moment, and would no doubt explain to the coroner and the jury whether he thought that Mrs Hazeldene had the slightest tendency to heart disease, which might have had a sudden and fatal ending.

'The coroner was, of course, very considerate to the bereaved husband. He tried by circumlocution to get at the point he wanted, namely, Mrs Hazeldene's mental condition lately. Mr Hazeldene seemed loath to talk about this.

No doubt he had been warned as to the existence of the small bottle found in his wife's satchel.

' "It certainly did seem to me at times," he at last reluctantly admitted, "that my wife did not seem quite herself. She used to be very gay and bright, and lately I often saw her in the evening sitting, as if brooding over some matters, which evidently she did not care to communicate to me."

'Still the coroner insisted, and suggested the small bottle.

' "I know, I know," replied the young man, with a short, heavy sigh. "You mean – the question of suicide – I cannot understand it at all – it seems so sudden and so terrible – she certainly had seemed listless and troubled lately – but only at times – and yesterday morning, when I went to business, she appeared quite herself again, and I suggested that we should go to the opera in the evening. She was delighted, I know, and told me she would do some shopping, and pay a few calls in the afternoon.

' "Do you know at all where she intended to go when she got into the Underground railway?"

' "Well, not with certainty. You see, she may have meant to get out at Baker Street, and go down to Bond Street to do her shopping. Then again, she sometimes goes to a shop in St Paul's Churchyard, in which case she would take a ticket to Aldersgate Street; but I cannot say."

' "Now, Mr Hazeldene," said the coroner at last very kindly, "will you try to tell me if there was anything in Mrs Hazeldene's life which you know of, and which might in some measure explain the cause of the distressed state of mind, which you yourself had noticed? Did there exist any financial difficulty which might have preyed upon Mrs Hazeldene's mind; was there any friend – to whose intercourse with Mrs Hazeldene – you – er – at any time took exception? In fact," added the coroner, as if thankful that he had got over an unpleasant moment, "can you give me the slightest indication which would tend to confirm the suspicion that the unfortunate lady, in a moment of mental anxiety or derangement, may have wished to take her own life?"

'There was silence in the court for a few moments. Mr Hazeldene seemed to everyone there present to be labouring under some terrible moral doubt. He looked very pale and wretched, and twice attempted to speak before he at last said in scarcely audible tones:

' "No; there were no financial difficulties of any sort. My wife had an independent fortune of her own – and she had no extravagant tastes—"

' "Nor any friend you at any time objected to?" insisted the coroner.

' "Nor any friend, I – at any time objected to," stammered the unfortunate young man, evidently speaking with an effort.

'I was present at the inquest,' resumed the man in the corner, after he had drunk a glass of milk and ordered another, 'and I can assure you that the most obtuse person there plainly realised that Mr Hazeldene was telling a lie. It was pretty plain to the meanest intelligence that the unfortunate lady had not fallen into a state of morbid dejection for nothing, and that perhaps there existed a third person who could throw more light on her strange and sudden death than the unhappy, bereaved young widower.

'That the death was more mysterious even than it had at first appeared became very soon apparent. You read the case at the time, no doubt, and must remember the excitement in the public mind caused by the evidence of the two doctors. Dr Arthur Jones, the lady's usual medical man, who had attended her in a last very slight illness, and who had seen her in a professional capacity fairly recently, declared most emphatically that Mrs Hazeldene suffered from no organic complaint which could possibly have been the cause of sudden death. Moreover, he had assisted Mr Andrew Thornton, the district medical officer, in making a post-mortem examination, and together they had come to the conclusion that death was due to the action of prussic acid, which had caused instantaneous failure of the heart, but how the drug had been administered neither he nor his colleague were at present able to state.

' "Do I understand, then, Dr Jones, that the deceased died, poisoned with prussic acid?"

' "Such is my opinion," replied the doctor.

' "Did the bottle found in her satchel contain prussic acid?"

' "It had contained some at one time, certainly."

' "In your opinion, then, the lady caused her own death by taking a dose of that drug?"

' "Pardon me, I never suggested such a thing; the lady died poisoned by the drug, but how the drug was administered we cannot say. By injection of some sort, certainly. The drug certainly was not swallowed; there was not a vestige of it in the stomach."

' "Yes," added the doctor in reply to another question from the coroner, "death had probably followed the injection in this case almost immediately; say within a couple of minutes, or perhaps three. It was quite possible that the body would not have more than one quick and sudden convulsion, perhaps not that; death in such cases is absolutely sudden and crushing."

'I don't think that at the time anyone in the room realised how important the doctor's statement was, a statement which, by the way, was confirmed in all its details by the district medical officer, who had conducted the post-mortem. Mrs Hazeldene had died suddenly from an injection of prussic acid, administered no one knew how or when. She had been travelling in a first-class railway carriage at a busy time of the day. That young and elegant woman must have had singular nerve and coolness to go through the process of a self-inflicted injection of a deadly poison in the presence of perhaps two or three other persons.

'Mind you, when I say that no one there realised the importance of the doctor's statement at that moment, I am wrong; there were three persons, who fully understood at once the gravity of the situation, and the astounding development which the case was beginning to assume.

'Of course, I should have put myself out of the question,' added the weird old man, with that inimitable self-conceit peculiar to himself. 'I guessed then and there in a moment where the police were going wrong, and where they would go on going wrong until the mysterious death on the Underground railway had sunk into oblivion, together with the other cases which they mismanage from time to time.

'I said there were three persons who understood the gravity of the two doctors' statements – the other two were, firstly, the detective who had originally examined the railway carriage, a young man of energy and plenty of misguided intelligence, the other was Mr Hazeldene.

'At this point the interesting element of the whole story was first introduced into the proceedings, and this was done through the humble channel of Emma Funnel, Mrs Hazeldene's maid, who, as far as was known then, was the last person who had seen the unfortunate lady alive and had spoken to her.

' "Mrs Hazeldene lunched at home," explained Emma, who was shy, and spoke almost in a whisper; "she seemed well and cheerful. She went out at about half-past three, and told me she was going to Spence's, in St Paul's Churchyard, to try on her new tailor-made gown. Mrs Hazeldene had meant to go there in the morning, but was prevented as Mr Errington called."

' "Mr Errington?" asked the coroner casually. "Who is Mr Errington?"

'But this Emma found difficult to explain. Mr Errington was – Mr Errington, that's all.

' "Mr Errington was a friend of the family. He lived in a flat in the Albert Mansions. He very often came to Addison Row, and generally stayed late."

'Pressed still further with questions, Emma at last stated that latterly Mrs Hazeldene had been to the theatre several times with Mr Errington, and that on those nights the master looked very gloomy, and was very cross.

'Recalled, the young widower was strangely reticent. He gave forth his answers very grudgingly, and the coroner was evidently absolutely satisfied with himself at the marvellous way in which, after a quarter of an hour of firm yet very kind questionings, he had elicited from the witness what information he wanted.

'Mr Errington was a friend of his wife. He was a gentleman of means, and seemed to have a great deal of time at his command. He himself did not particularly care about Mr Errington, but he certainly had never made any observations to his wife on the subject.

' "But who is Mr Errington?" repeated the coroner once more. "What does he do? What is his business or profession?"

' "He has no business or profession."

' "What is his occupation, then?"

' "He has no special occupation. He has ample private means. But he has a great and very absorbing hobby."

' "What is that?"

' "He spends all his time in chemical experiments, and is, I believe, as an amateur, a very distinguished toxicologist." '

'Did you ever see Mr Errington, the gentleman so closely connected with the mysterious death on the Underground railway?' asked the man in the corner as he placed one or two of his little snap-shot photos before Miss Polly Burton.

'There he is, to the very life. Fairly good-looking, a pleasant face enough, but ordinary, absolutely ordinary.

'It was this absence of any peculiarity which very nearly, but not quite, placed the halter round Mr Errington's neck.

'But I am going too fast, and you will lose the thread.

'The public, of course, never heard how it actually came about that Mr Errington, the wealthy bachelor of Albert Mansions, of the Grosvenor, and other young dandies' clubs, one fine day found himself before the magistrate at Bow Street, charged with being concerned in the death of Mary Beatrice Hazeldene, late of No. 19, Addison Row.

'I can assure you both press and public were literally flabbergasted. You see, Mr Errington was a well-known and very popular member of a certain smart section of London society. He was a constant visitor at the opera, the racecourse, the Park, and the Carlton, he had a great many friends, and there was consequently quite a large attendance at the police court that morning.

'What had transpired was this:

'After the very scrappy bits of evidence which came to light at the inquest, two gentlemen bethought themselves that perhaps they had some duty to perform towards the State and the public generally. Accordingly they had come forward, offering to throw what light they could upon the mysterious affair on the Underground railway.

'The police naturally felt that their information, such as it was, came rather late in the day, but as it proved of paramount importance, and the two gentlemen, moreover, were of undoubtedly good position in the world, they were thankful for what they could get, and acted accordingly; they accordingly brought Mr Errington up before the magistrate on a charge of murder.

'The accused looked pale and worried when I first caught sight of him in the court that day, which was not to be wondered at, considering the terrible position in which he found himself.

'He had been arrested at Marseilles, where he was preparing to start for Colombo. I don't think he realised how terrible his position really was until later in the proceedings, when all the evidence relating to the arrest had been heard, and Emma Funnel had repeated her statement as to Mr Errington's call at 19, Addison Row, in the morning, and Mrs Hazeldene starting off for St Paul's Churchyard at three-thirty in the afternoon.

'Mr Hazeldene had nothing to add to the statements he had made at the coroner's inquest. He had last seen his wife alive on the morning of the fatal day. She had seemed very well and cheerful.

'I think everyone present understood that he was trying to say as little as possible that could in any way couple his deceased wife's name with that of the accused.

'And yet, from the servant's evidence, it undoubtedly leaked out that Mrs Hazeldene, who was young, pretty, and evidently fond of admiration, had once or twice annoyed her husband by her somewhat open, yet perfectly innocent, flirtation with Mr Errington.

'I think everyone was most agreeably impressed by the widower's moderate and dignified attitude. You will see his photo there, among this bundle. That is just how he appeared in court. In deep black, of course, but without any sign of ostentation in his mourning. He had allowed his beard to grow lately, and wore it closely cut in a point.

'After his evidence, the sensation of the day occurred. A tall, dark-haired man, with the word "City" written metaphorically all over him, had kissed the book, and was waiting to tell the truth, and nothing but the truth.

'He gave his name as Andrew Campbell, head of the firm of Campbell & Co., brokers, of Throgmorton Street.

'In the afternoon of March eighteenth Mr Campbell, travelling on the Underground railway, had noticed a very pretty woman in the same carriage as himself. She had asked him if she was in the right train for Aldersgate. Mr

Campbell replied in the affirmative, and then buried himself in the Stock Exchange quotations of his evening paper.

'At Gower Street, a gentleman in a tweed suit and bowler hat got into the carriage, and took a seat opposite the lady. She seemed very much astonished at seeing him, but Mr Andrew Campbell did not recollect the exact words she said.

'The two talked to one another a good deal, and certainly the lady appeared animated and cheerful. Witness took no notice of them; he was very much engrossed in some calculations, and finally got out at Farringdon Street. He noticed that the man in the tweed suit also got out close behind him, having shaken hands with the lady, and said in a pleasant way: "Au revoir! Don't be late tonight." Mr Campbell did not hear the lady's reply, and soon lost sight of the man in the crowd.

'Everyone was on tenter-hooks, and eagerly waiting for the palpitating moment when witness would describe and identify the man who last had seen and spoken to the unfortunate woman, within five minutes probably of her strange and unaccountable death.

'Personally I knew what was coming before the Scots stockbroker spoke.

'I could have jotted down the graphic and lifelike description he would give of a probable murderer. It would have fitted equally well the man who sat and had luncheon at this table just now; it would certainly have described five out of every ten young Englishmen you know.

'The individual was of medium height, he wore a moustache which was not very fair nor yet very dark, his hair was between colours. He wore a bowler hat, and a tweed suit – and – and – that was all – Mr Campbell might perhaps know him again, but then again, he might not – he was not paying much attention – the gentleman was sitting on the same side of the carriage as himself – and he had his hat on all the time. He himself was busy with his newspaper – yes – he might know him again – but he really could not say.

'Mr Andrew Campbell's evidence was not worth very much, you will say. No, it was not in itself, and would not have justified any arrest were it not for the additional statements made by Mr James Verner, manager of Messrs Rodney & Co., colour printers.

'Mr Verner is a personal friend of Mr Andrew Campbell, and it appears that at Farringdon Street, where he was waiting for his train, he saw Mr Campbell get out of a first-class railway carriage. Mr Verner spoke to him for a second, and then, just as the train was moving off, he stepped into the same compartment which had just been vacated by the stockbroker and the man in the tweed suit. He vaguely recollects a lady sitting in the opposite corner to his own, with her face turned away from him, apparently asleep, but he paid no special attention to her. He was like nearly all businessmen when they are travelling – engrossed in his paper. Presently a special quotation interested him; he wished to make a note of it, took out a pencil from his waistcoat pocket, and seeing a clean piece of paste-board on the floor, he picked it up, and scribbled on it the memorandum, which he wished to keep. He then slipped the card into his pocket-book.

' "It was only two or three days later," added Mr Verner in the midst of breathless silence, "that I had occasion to refer to these same notes again.

' "In the meanwhile the papers had been full of the mysterious death on the Underground railway, and the names of those connected with it were pretty familiar to me. It was, therefore, with much astonishment that on looking at the paste-board which I had casually picked up in the railway carriage I saw the name on it, Frank Errington."

'There was no doubt that the sensation in court was

almost unprecedented. Never since the days of the Fenchurch Street mystery, and the trial of Smethurst, had I seen so much excitement. Mind you, I was not excited – I knew by now every detail of that crime as if I had committed it myself. In fact, I could not have done it better, although I have been a student of crime for many years now. Many people there – his friends, mostly – believed that Errington was doomed. I think he thought so, too, for I could see that his face was terribly white, and he now and then passed his tongue over his lips, as if they were parched.

'You see he was in the awful dilemma – a perfectly natural one, by the way – of being absolutely incapable of *proving* an alibi. The crime – if crime there was – had been committed three weeks ago. A man about town like Mr Frank Errington might remember that he spent certain hours of a special afternoon at his club, or in the Park, but it is very doubtful in nine cases out of ten if he can find a friend who could positively swear as to having seem him there. No! no! Mr Errington was in a tight corner, and he knew it. You see, there were – besides the evidence – two or three circumstances which did not improve matters for him. His hobby in the direction of toxicology, to begin with. The police had found in his room every description of poisonous susbtances, including prussic acid.

'Then, again, that journey to Marseilles, the start for Colombo, was, though perfectly innocent, a very unfortunate one. Mr Errington had gone on an aimless voyage, but the public thought that he had fled, terrified at his own crime. Sir Arthur Inglewood, however, here again displayed his marvellous skill on behalf of his client by the masterly way in which he literally turned all the witnesses for the Crown inside out.

'Having first got Mr Andrew Campbell to state positively that in the accused he certainly did *not* recognise the man in the tweed suit, the eminent lawyer, after twenty minutes' cross-examination, had so completely upset the stockbroker's equanimity that it is very likely he would not have recognised his own office-boy.

'But through all his flurry and all his annoyance Mr Andrew Campbell remained very sure of one thing; namely, that the lady was alive and cheerful, and talking pleasantly with the man in the tweed suit up to the moment when the latter, having shaken hands with her, left her with a pleasant "Au revoir! Don't be late tonight." He had heard neither scream nor struggle, and in his opinion, if the individual in the tweed suit had administered a dose of poison to his companion, it must have been with her own knowledge and free will; and the lady in the train most emphatically neither looked nor spoke like a woman prepared for a sudden and violent death.

'Mr James Verner, against that, swore equally positively that he had stood in full view of the carriage door from the moment that Mr Campbell got out until he himself stepped into the compartment, that there was no one else in that carriage between Farringdon Street and Aldgate, and that the lady, to the best of his belief, had made no movement during the whole of that journey.

'No; Frank Errington was *not* committed for trial on the capital charge,' said the man in the corner with one of his sardonic smiles, 'thanks to the cleverness of Sir Arthur Inglewood, his lawyer. He absolutely denied his identity with the man in the tweed suit, and swore he had not seen Mrs Hazeldene since eleven o'clock in the morning of that fatal day. There was no *proof* that he had; moreover, according to Mr Campbell's opinion, the man in the tweed suit was in all probability not the murderer. Common sense would not admit that a woman could have a deadly poison injected into her without her knowledge, while chatting pleasantly to her murderer.

'Mr Errington lives abroad now. He is about to marry. I don't think any of his real friends for a moment believed that he committed the dastardly crime. The police think they know better. They do know this much, that it could not have been a case of suicide, that if the man who undoubtedly travelled with Mrs Hazeldene on that fatal afternoon had no crime upon his conscience he would long ago have come forward and thrown what light he could upon the mystery.

'As to who that man was, the police in their blindness have not the faintest doubt. Under the unshakeable belief that Errington is guilty they have spent the last few months in unceasing labour to try and find further and stronger proofs of his guilt. But they won't find them, because there are none. There are no positive proofs against the actual murderer, for he was one of those clever blackguards who think of everything, foresee every eventuality, who know human nature well, and can foretell exactly what evidence will be brought against them, and act accordingly.

'This blackguard from the first kept the figure, the personality, of Frank Errington before his mind. Frank Errington was the dust which the scoundrel threw metaphorically in the eyes of the police, and you must admit that he succeeded in blinding them – to the extent even of making them entirely forget the one simple little sentence, overheard by Mr Andrew Campbell, and which was, of course, the clue to the whole thing – the only slip the cunning rogue made – "Au revoir! Don't be late tonight." Mrs Hazeldene was going that night to the opera with her husband—

'You are astonished?' he added with a shrug of the shoulders, 'you do not see the tragedy yet, as I have seen it before me all along. The frivolous young wife, the flirtation with the friend? – all a blind, all pretence. I took the trouble which the police should have taken immediately, of finding out something about the finances of the Hazeldene *ménage*. Money is in nine cases out of ten the keynote to a crime.

'I found that the will of Mary Beatrice Hazeldene had been proved by the husband, her sole executor, the estate being sworn at fifteen thousand pounds. I found out, moreover, that Mr Edward Sholto Hazeldene was a poor shipper's clerk when he married the daughter of a wealthy builder in Kensington – and then I made note of the fact that the disconsolate widower had allowed his beard to grow since the death of his wife.

'There's no doubt that he was a clever rogue,' added the strange creature, leaning excitedly over the table, and peering into Polly's face. 'Do you know how that deadly poison was injected into the poor woman's system? By the simplest of all means, one known to every scoundrel in southern Europe. A ring – yes! a ring, which has a tiny hollow needle capable of holding a sufficient quantity of prussic acid to have killed two persons instead of one. The man in the tweed suit shook hands with his fair companion – probably she hardly felt the prick, not sufficiently in any case to make her utter a scream. And, mind you, the scoundrel had every facility, through his friendship with Mr Errington, of procuring what poison he required, not to mention his friend's visiting card. We cannot gauge how many months ago he began to try and copy Frank Errington in his style of dress, the cut of his moustache, his general appearance, making the change probably so gradual, that no one in his own entourage would notice it. He selected for his model a man his own height and build, with the same coloured hair.'

'But there was the terrible risk of being identified by his fellow-traveller in the Underground,' suggested Polly.

'Yes, there certainly was that risk; he chose to take it, and he was wise. He reckoned that several days would in any case elapse before that person, who, by the way, was a businessman absorbed in his newspaper, would actually see him again. The great secret of successful crime is to study human nature,' added the man in the corner, as he began looking for his hat and coat. 'Edward Hazeldene knew it well.'

'But the ring?'

'He may have bought that when he was on his honey-moon,' he suggested with a grim chuckle; 'the tragedy was not planned in a week, it may have taken years to mature. But you will own that there goes a frightful scoundrel unhung. I have left you his photograph as he was a year ago, and as he is now. You will see he has shaved his beard again, but also his moustache. I fancy he is a friend now of Mr Andrew Campbell.'

He left Miss Polly Burton wondering, not knowing what to believe.

And that is why she missed her appointment with Mr Richard Frobisher (of the *London Mail*) to go and see Maud Allan dance at the Palace Theatre that afternoon.

Cheese

ETHEL LINA WHITE

* * *

This story begins with a murder. It ends with a mouse-trap.

The murder can be disposed of in a paragraph. An attractive girl, carefully reared and educated for a future which held only a twisted throat. At the end of seven months, an unsolved mystery and a reward of £500.

It is a long way from a murder to a mouse-trap – and one with no finger-posts; but the police knew every inch of the way. In spite of a prestige punctured by the press and public, they had solved the identity of the killer. There remained the problem of tracking this wary and treacherous rodent from his unknown sewer in the underworld into their trap.

They failed repeatedly for lack of the right bait.

And unexpectedly, one spring evening, the bait turned up in the person of a young girl.

Cheese.

Inspector Angus Duncan was alone in his office when her message was brought up. He was a red-haired Scot, handsome in a dour fashion, with the chin of a prize-fighter and keen blue eyes.

He nodded.

'I'll see her.'

It was between the lights. River, government offices and factories were all deeply dyed with the blue stain of dusk. Even in the city, the lilac bushes showed green tips and an occasional crocus cropped through the grass of the public-gardens, like strewn orange-peel. The evening star was a jewel in the pale green sky.

Duncan was impervious to the romance of the hour. He knew that twilight was but the prelude to night and that darkness was a shield for crime.

He looked up sharply when his visitor was admitted. She was young and flower-faced – her faint freckles already fading away into pallor. Her black suit was shabby, but her hat was garnished for the spring with a cheap cowslip wreath.

As she raised her blue eyes, he saw that they still carried the memory of country sweets . . . Thereupon he looked at her more sharply for he knew that of all poses, innocence is easiest to counterfeit.

'You say Roper sent you?' he enquired.

'Yes, Maggie Roper.'

He nodded. Maggie Roper – Sergeant Roper's niece –

75

was already shaping as a promising young Stores' detective.

'Where did you meet her?'

'At the Girls' Hostel where I'm staying.'

'Your name?'

'Jenny Morgan.'

'From the country?'

'Yes. But I'm up now for good.'

For good? . . . He wondered.

'Alone?'

'Yes.'

'How's that?' He looked at her mourning. 'People all dead?'

She nodded. From the lightning sweep of her lashes, he knew that she had put in some rough work with a tear. It prejudiced him in her favour. His voice grew more genial as his lips relaxed.

'Well, what's it all about?'

She drew a letter from her bag.

'I'm looking for work and I advertised in the paper. I got this answer. I'm to be companion-secretary to a lady, to travel with her and be treated as her daughter – if she likes me. I sent my photograph and my references and she's fixed an appointment.'

'When and where?'

'The day after tomorrow, in the First Room in the National Gallery. But as she's elderly, she is sending her nephew to drive me to her house.'

'Where's that?'

She looked troubled.

'That's what Maggie Roper is making the fuss about. First, she said I must see if Mrs Harper – that's the lady's name – had taken up my references. And then she insisted on ringing up the Ritz where the letter was written from. The address was *printed*, so it was bound to be genuine, wasn't it?'

76

'Was it? What happened then?'

'They said no Mrs Harper had stayed there. But I'm sure it must be a mistake.' Her voice trembled. 'One must risk something to get such a good job.'

His face darkened. He was beginning to accept Jenny as the genuine article.

'Tell me,' he asked, 'have you had any experience of life?'

'Well, I've always lived in the country with Auntie. But I've read all sorts of novels and the newspapers.'

'Murders?'

'Oh, I love those.'

He could tell by the note in her childish voice that she ate up the newspaper accounts merely as exciting fiction, without the slightest realisation that the printed page was grim fact. He could see the picture: a sheltered childhood passed amid green spongy meadows. She could hardly cull sophistication from clover and cows.

'Did you read about the Bell murder?' he asked abruptly.

'Auntie wouldn't let me.' She added in the same breath, 'Every word.'

'Why did your aunt forbid you?'

'She said it must be a specially bad one, because they'd left all the bad parts out of the paper.'

'Well, didn't you notice the fact that that poor girl – Emmeline Bell – a well-bred girl of about your own age, was lured to her death through answering a newspaper advertisement?'

'I – I suppose so. But those things don't happen to oneself.'

'Why? What's there to prevent your falling into a similar trap?'

'I can't explain. But if there was something wrong, I should know it.'

'How? D'you expect a bell to ring or a red light to flash "Danger"?'

'Of course not. But if you believe in right and wrong, surely there must be some warning.'

He looked sceptical. That innocence bore a lily in its hand, was to him a beautiful phrase and nothing more. His own position in the sorry scheme of affairs was, to him, proof positive of the official failure of guardian angels.

'Let me see that letter, please,' he said.

She studied his face anxiously as he read, but his expression remained inscrutable. Twisting her fingers in her suspense, she glanced around the room, noting vaguely the three telephones on the desk and the stacked files in the pigeon-holes. A Great Dane snored before the red-caked fire. She wanted to cross the room and pat him, but lacked the courage to stir from her place.

The room was warm, for the windows were opened only a couple of inches at the top. In view of Duncan's weather-tanned colour, the fact struck her as odd.

Mercifully, the future is veiled. She had no inkling of the fateful part that Great Dane was to play in her own drama, nor was there anything to tell her that a closed window would have been a barrier between her and the yawning mouth of hell.

She started as Duncan spoke.

'I want to hold this letter for a bit. Will you call about this time tomorrow? Meantime, I must impress upon you the need of utmost caution. Don't take one step on your own. Should anything fresh crop up, 'phone me immediately. Here's my number.'

When she had gone, Duncan walked to the window. The blue dusk had deepened into a darkness pricked with lights. Across the river, advertisement-signs wrote themselves intermittently in coloured beads.

He still glowed with the thrill of the hunter on the first spoor of the quarry. Although he had to await the report of the expert test, he was confident that the letter which he held had been penned by the murderer of poor ill-starred Emmeline Bell.

Then his elation vanished at a recollection of Jenny's wistful face. In this city were scores of other girls, frail as windflowers too – blossom-sweet and country-raw – forced through economic pressure into positions fraught with deadly peril.

The darkness drew down overhead like a dark shadow pregnant with crime. And out from their holes and sewers stole the rats . . .

At last Duncan had the trap baited for his rat.

A young and pretty girl – ignorant and unprotected. Cheese.

When Jenny, punctual to the minute, entered his office, the following evening, he instantly appraised her as his prospective decoy. His first feeling was one of disappoint-. ment. Either she had shrunk in the night or her eyes had grown bigger. She looked such a frail scrap as she stared at him, her lips bitten to a thin line, that it seemed hopeless to credit her with the necessary nerve for his project.

'Oh, please tell me it's all perfectly right about that letter.'

'Anything but right.'

For a moment, he thought she was about to faint. He wondered uneasily whether she had eaten that day. It was obvious from the keenness of her disappointment that she was at the end of her resources.

'Are you sure?' she insisted. 'It's – very important to me. Perhaps I'd better keep the appointment. If I didn't like the look of things, I needn't go on with it.'

'I tell you, it's not a genuine job,' he repeated. 'But I've something to put to you that is the goods. Would you like to have a shot at £500?'

Her flushed face, her eager eyes, her trembling lips, all answered him.

'Yes, please,' was all she said.

He searched for reassuring terms.

'It's like this. We've tested your letter and know it is written, from a bad motive, by an undesirable character.'

'You mean a criminal?' she asked quickly.

'Um. His record is not good. We want to get hold of him.'

'Then why don't you?'

He suppressed a smile.

'Because he doesn't confide in us. But if you have the courage to keep your appointment tomorrow and let his messenger take you to the house of the supposititious Mrs Harper, I'll guarantee it's the hiding-place of the man we want. We get him – you get the reward. Question is – have you the nerve?'

She was silent. Presently she spoke in a small voice.

'Will I be in great danger?'

'None. I wouldn't risk your safety for any consideration. From first to last, you'll be under the protection of the Force.'

'You mean I'll be watched over by detectives in disguise?'

'From the moment you enter the National Gallery, you'll be covered doubly and trebly. You'll be followed every step of the way and directly we've located the house, the place will be raided by the police.'

'All the same, for a minute or so, just before you can get into the house, I'll be alone with – *him*?'

'The briefest interval. You'll be safe at first. He'll begin with overtures. Stall him off with questions. Don't let him see you suspect – or show you're frightened.'

Duncan frowned as he spoke. It was his duty to society to rid it of a dangerous pest and in order to do so, Jenny's co-operation was vital. Yet, to his own surprise, he disliked the necessity in the case of this especial girl.

'Remember we'll be at hand,' he said. 'But if your nerve goes, just whistle and we'll break cover immediately.'

'Will *you* be there?' she asked suddenly.

'Not exactly in the foreground. But I'll be there.'

'Then I'll do it.' She smiled for the first time. 'You laughed at me when I said there was something inside me which told me – things. But I just know I can trust *you*.'

'Good.' His voice was rough. 'Wait a bit. You've been put to expense coming over here. This will cover your fares and so on.'

He thrust a note into her hand and hustled her out, protesting. It was a satisfaction to feel that she would eat that night. As he seated himself at his desk, preparatory to work, his frozen face was no index of the emotions raised by Jenny's parting words.

Hitherto, he had thought of women merely as 'skirts'. He had regarded a saucepan with an angry woman at the business end of it, merely as a weapon. For the first time he had a domestic vision of a country girl – creamy and fragrant as meadowsweet – in a nice womanly setting of saucepans.

Jenny experienced a thrill which was almost akin to exhilaration when she entered Victoria station, the following day. At the last moment, the place for meeting had been altered in a telegram from 'Mrs Harper'.

Immediately she had received the message, Jenny had gone to the telephone-box in the hostel and duly reported the change of plan, with a request that her message should be repeated to her, to obviate any risk of mistake.

And now – the incredible adventure was actually begun.

The station seemed filled with hurrying crowds as she walked slowly towards the clock. Her feet rather lagged on the way. She wondered if the sinister messenger had already marked the yellow wreath in her hat which she had named as her mark of identification.

Then she remembered her guards. At this moment they

were here, unknown, watching over her slightest move-ment. It was a curious sensation to feel that she was spied upon by unseen eyes. Yet it helped to brace the muscles of her knees when she took up her station under the clock with the sensation of having exposed herself as a target for gun-fire.

Nothing happened. No one spoke to her. She was encouraged to gaze around her . . .

A few yards away, a pleasant-faced smartly dressed young man was covertly regarding her. He carried a yellowish sample-bag which proclaimed him a drummer.

Suddenly Jenny felt positive that this was one of her guards. There was a quality about his keen clean-shaven face – a hint of the eagle in his eye – which reminded her of Duncan. She gave him the beginnings of a smile and was thrilled when, almost imperceptibly, he fluttered one eyelid. She read it as a signal for caution. Alarmed by her indiscretion, she looked fixedly in another direction.

Still – it helped her to know that even if she could not see him, he was there.

The minutes dragged slowly by. She began to grow anxious as to whether the affair were not some hoax. It would be not only a tame ending to the adventure but a positive disappointment. She would miss the chance of a sum which – to her – was a little fortune. Her need was so vital that she would have undertaken the venture for five pounds. Morever, after her years of green country solitude, she felt a thrill at the mere thought of her temporary link with the underworld. This was life in the raw; while screening her as she aided him, she worked with Angus Duncan.

She smiled – then started as though stung.

Someone had touched her on the arm.

'Have I the honour, happiness and felicity of addressing

Miss Jenny Morgan? Yellow wreath in the lady's hat. Red Flower in the gent's buttonhole, as per arrangement.'

The man who addressed her was young and bull-necked, with florid colouring which ran into blotches. He wore a red carnation in the buttonhole of his check overcoat.

'Yes, I'm Jenny Morgan.'

As she spoke, she looked into his eyes. She felt a sharp revulsion – an instinctive recoil of her whole being.

'Are you Mrs Harper's nephew?' she faltered.

'That's right. Excuse a gent keeping a lady waiting, but I just slipped into the bar for a glass of milk. I've a taxi waiting if you'll just hop outside.'

Jenny's mind worked rapidly as she followed him. She was forewarned and protected. But – were it not for Maggie Roper's intervention – she would have kept this appointment in very different circumstances. She wondered whether she would have heeded that instinctive warning and refused to follow the stranger.

She shook her head. Her need was so urgent that, in her wish to believe the best, she knew that she would have summoned up her courage and flouted her fears as nerves. She would have done exactly what she was doing – accompanying an unknown man to an unknown destination.

She shivered at the realisation. It might have been herself. Poor defenceless Jenny – going to her doom.

At that moment she encountered the grave scrutiny of a stout clergyman who was standing by the book-stall. He was ruddy, wore horn-rimmed spectacles and carried the *Church Times*.

His look of understanding was almost as eloquent as a vocal message. It filled her with gratitude. Again she was certain that this was a second guard. Turning to see if the young commercial traveller were following her, she was thrilled to discover that he had preceded her into the station yard. He got into a taxi at the exact moment that her companion flung open the door of a cab which was waiting. It was only this knowledge that Duncan was thus making good his promise which induced her to enter the vehicle. Once again her nerves rebelled and she was rent with sick forebodings.

As they moved off, she had an overpowering impulse to scream aloud for help to the porters – just because all this might have happened to some poor girl who had not her own good fortune.

Her companion nudged her.

'Bit of all right, joy-riding, eh?'

She stiffened, but managed to force a smile.

'Is it a long ride?'

'Ah, now you're asking.'

'Where does Mrs Harper live?'

'Ah, that's telling.'

She shrank away, seized with disgust of his blotched face so near her own.

'Please give me more room. It's stifling here.'

'Now, don't you go taking no liberties with me. A married man I am, with four wives all on the dole.' All the same, to her relief, he moved further away. 'From the country, aren't you? Nice place. Lots of milk. Suit me a treat. Any objection to a gent smoking?'

'I wish you would. The cab reeks of whisky.'

They were passing St Paul's which was the last landmark in her limited knowledge of London. Girls from offices passed on the pavement, laughing and chatting together, or hurrying by intent on business. A group was scattering crumbs to the pigeons which fluttered on the steps of the cathedral.

She watched them with a stab of envy. Safe happy girls.

Then she remembered that somewhere, in the press of traffic, a taxi was shadowing her own. She took fresh courage.

The drive passed like an interminable nightmare in

which she was always on guard to stem the advances of her disagreeable companion. Something seemed always on the point of happening – something unpleasant, just out of sight and round the corner – and then, somehow she staved it off.

The taxi bore her through a congested maze of streets. Shops and offices were succeeded by regions of warehouses and factories, which in turn gave way to areas of dun squalor where gas-works rubbed shoulders with grimed laundries which bore such alluring signs as DEWDROP or WHITE ROSE.

From the shrilling of sirens, Jenny judged that they were in the neighbourhood of the river, when they turned into a quiet square. The tall lean houses wore an air of drab respectability. Lace curtains hung at every window. Plaster pineapples crowned the pillared porches.

'Here's our "destitution".'

As her guide inserted his key in the door of No. 17, Jenny glanced eagerly down the street, in time to see a taxi turn the corner.

'Hop in, dearie.'

On the threshold Jenny shrank back.

Evil.

Never before had she felt its presence. But she knew. Like the fumes creeping upwards from the grating of a sewer, it poisoned the air.

Had she embarked on this enterprise in her former ignorance, she was certain that at this point, her instinct would have triumphed.

'I would never have passed through this door.'

She was wrong. Volition was swept off the board. Her arm was gripped and before she could struggle, she was pulled inside.

She heard the slam of the door.

'Never loiter on the doorstep, dearie. Gives the house a

bad name. This way. Up the stairs. All the nearer to heaven.'

Her heart heavy with dread, Jenny followed him. She had entered on the crux of her adventure – the dangerous few minutes when she would be quite alone.

The place was horrible – with no visible reason for horror. It was no filthy East-end rookery, but a technically clean apartment-house. The stairs were covered with brown linoleum. The mottled yellow wallpaper was intact. Each landing had its marble-topped table, adorned with a forlorn aspidistra – its moulting rug at every door. The air was dead and smelt chiefly of dust.

They climbed four flights of stairs without meeting anyone. Only faint rustlings and whispers within the rooms told of other tenants. Then the blotched-faced man threw open a door.

'Young lady come to see Mrs Harper about the sitooation. Too-tel-oo, dearie. Hope you strike lucky.'

He pushed her inside and she heard his step upon the stairs.

In that moment, Jenny longed for anyone – even her late companion.

She was vaguely aware of the figure of a man seated in a chair. Too terrified to look at him, her eyes flickered around the room.

Like the rest of the house, it struck the note of parodied respectability. Yellowish lace curtains hung at the windows which were blocked by pots of leggy geraniums. A walnut-wood suite was upholstered in faded bottle-green rep with burst padding. A gilt-framed mirror surmounted a stained marble mantelpiece which was decorated with a clock – permanently stopped under its glass case – and a bottle of whisky. On a small table by the door rested a filthy cage, containing a grey parrot, its eyes mere slits of wicked eld between wrinkled lids.

It had to come. With an effort, she looked at the man.

He was tall and slender and wrapped in a once-gorgeous dressing-gown of frayed crimson quilted silk. At first sight, his features were not only handsome but bore some air of breeding. But the whole face was blurred – as though it were a waxen mask half-melted by the sun and over which the Fiend – in passing – had lightly drawn a hand. His eyes drew her own. Large and brilliant, they were of so light a blue as to appear almost white. The lashes were unusually long and matted into spikes.

The blood froze at Jenny's heart. The girl was no fool. Despite Duncan's cautious statements, she had drawn her own deduction which linked an unsolved murder mystery and a reward of £500.

She knew that she was alone with a homicidal maniac – the murderer of ill-starred Emmeline Bell.

In that moment, she realised the full horror of a crime which, a few months ago, had been nothing but an exciting newspaper-story. It sickened her to reflect that a girl – much like herself – whose pretty face smiled fearlessly upon the world from the printed page, had walked into this same trap, in all the blindness of her youthful confidence. No one to hear her cries. No one to guess the agony of those last terrible moments.

Jenny at least understood that first rending shock of realisation. She fought for self-control. At sight of that smiling marred face, she wanted to do what she knew instinctively that other girl had done – precipitating her doom. With a desperate effort she suppressed the impulse to rush madly round the room like a snared creature, beating her hands against the locked door and crying for help. Help which would never come.

Luckily, common sense triumphed. In a few minutes' time, she would not be alone. Even then a taxi was speeding on its mission; wires were humming; behind her was the protection of the Force.

She remembered Duncan's advice to temporise. It was

true that she was not dealing with a beast of the jungle which sprang on its prey at sight.

'Oh, please.' She hardly recognised the tiny pipe. 'I've come to see Mrs Harper about her situation.'

'Yes.' The man did not remove his eyes from her face. 'So you are Jenny?'

'Yes, Jenny Morgan. Is – is Mrs Harper in?'

'She'll be in presently. Sit down. Make yourself at home. What are you scared for?'

'I'm not scared.'

Her words were true. Her strained ears had detected faintest sounds outside – dulled footsteps, the cautious fastening of a door.

The man, for his part, also noticed the stir. For a few seconds he listened intently. Then to her relief, he relaxed his attention.

She snatched again at the fiction of her future employer.

'I hope Mrs Harper will soon come in.'

'What's your hurry? Come closer. I can't see you properly.'

They were face to face. It reminded her of the old nursery story of 'Little Red Riding Hood'.

'What big eyes you've got, Grandmother.'

The words swam into her brain.

Terrible eyes. Like white glass cracked in distorting facets. She was looking into the depths of a blasted soul. Down, down . . . That poor girl. But she must not think of *her*. She must be brave – give him back look for look.

Her lids fell . . . She could bear it no longer.

She gave an involuntary start at the sight of his hands. They were beyond the usual size – unhuman – with long knotted fingers.

'What big hands you've got.'

Before she could control her tongue, the words slipped out.

The man stopped smiling.

But Jenny was not frightened now. Her guards were near. She thought of the detective who carried the bag of samples. She thought of the stout clergyman. She thought of Duncan.

At that moment, the commercial traveller was in an upper room of a wholesale drapery house in the city, holding the fashionable blonde lady buyer with his magnetic blue eye, while he displayed his stock of crêpe-de-Chine underwear.

At that moment, the clergyman was seated in a third-class railway carriage, watching the hollows of the Downs fill with heliotrope shadows. He was not quite at ease. His thoughts persisted on dwelling on the frightened face of a little country girl as she drifted by in the wake of a human vulture.

'I did wrong. I should have risked speaking to her.'

But – at that moment – Duncan was thinking of her.

Jenny's message had been received over the telephone wire, repeated and duly written down by Mr Herbert Yates, shorthand-typist – who, during the absence of Duncan's own secretary, was filling the gap for one morning. At the sound of his chief's step in the corridor outside, he rammed on his hat, for he was already overdue for a lunch appointment with one of the numerous 'only girls in the world'.

At the door he met Duncan.

'May I go to lunch now, sir?'

Duncan nodded assent. He stopped for a minute in the passage while he gave Yates his instructions for the afternoon.

'Any message?' he enquired.

'One come this instant, sir. It's under the weight.'

Duncan entered the office. But in that brief interval, the disaster had occurred.

Yates could not be held to blame for what happened. It

was true that he had taken advantage of Duncan's absence to open a window wide, but he was ignorant of any breach of rules. In his hurry he had also written down Jenny's message on the nearest loose-leaf to hand, but he had taken the precaution to place it under a heavy paper-weight.

It was Duncan's Great Dane which worked the mischief. He was accustomed at this hour to be regaled with a biscuit by Duncan's secretary who was an abject dog-lover. As his dole had not been forthcoming he went in search of it. His great paws on the table, he rooted among the papers, making nothing of a trifle of a letter-weight. Over it went. Out of the window – at the next gust – went Jenny's message. Back to his rug went the dog.

The instant Duncan was aware of what had happened, a frantic search was made for Yates. But that wily and athletic youth, wise to the whims of his official superiors, had disappeared. They raked every place of refreshment within a wide radius. It was not until Duncan's men rang up to report that they had drawn a blank at the National Gallery, that Yates was discovered in an underground dive, drinking coffee and smoking cigarettes with his charmer.

Duncan arrived at Victoria forty minutes after the appointed time.

It was the bitterest hour of his life. He was haunted by the sight of Jenny's flower-face upturned to his. She had *trusted* him. And in his ambition to track the man he had taken advantage of her necessity to use her as a pawn in his game.

He had played her – and lost her.

The thought drove him to madness. Steeled though he was to face reality, he dared not to let himself think of the end. Jenny – country-raw and blossom-sweet – even then struggling in the grip of murderous fingers.

Even then.

Jenny panted as she fought, her brain on fire. The thing had rushed upon her so swiftly that her chief feeling was of sheer incredulity. What had gone before was already burning itself up in a red mist. She had no clear memory afterwards of those tense minutes of fencing. There was only an interlude filled with a dimly comprehended menace – and then this.

And still Duncan had not intervened.

Her strength was failing. Hell cracked, revealing glimpses of unguessed horror.

With a supreme effort she wrenched herself free. It was but a momentary respite, but it sufficed for her signal – a broken tremulous whistle.

The response was immediate. Somewhere outside the door a gruff voice was heard in warning.

'Perlice.'

The killer stiffened, his ears pricked, every nerve astrain. His eyes flickered to the ceiling which was broken by the outline of a trap-door.

Then his glance fell upon the parrot.

His fingers on Jenny's throat, he paused. The bird rocked on its perch, its eyes slits of malicious eld.

Time stood still. The killer stared at the parrot. Which of the gang had given the warning? Whose voice? Not Glass-eye. Not Mexican Joe. The sound had seemed to be within the room.

That parrot.

He laughed. His fingers tightened. Tightened to relax.

For a day and a half he had been in Mother Bargery's room. During that time the bird had been dumb. Did it talk?

The warning echoed in his brain. Every moment of delay was fraught with peril. At that moment his enemies were here, stealing upwards to catch him in their trap. The instinct of the human rodent, enemy of mankind – eternally hunted and harried – prevailed. With an oath, he flung Jenny aside and jumping on the table, wormed through the trap of the door.

Jenny was alone. She was too stunned to think. There was still a roaring in her ears, shooting lights before her eyes. In a vague way, she knew that some hitch had occurred in the plan. The police were here – yet they had let their prey escape.

She put on her hat, straightened her hair. Very slowly she walked down the stairs. There was no sign of Duncan or of his men.

As she reached the hall, a door opened and a white puffed face looked at her. Had she quickened her pace or shown the least sign of fear she would never have left that place alive. Her very nonchalance proved her salvation as she unbarred the door with the deliberation bred of custom.

The street was deserted, save for an empty taxi which she hailed.

'Where to, miss?' asked the driver.

Involuntarily she glanced back at the drab house, squeezed into its strait-waistcoat of grimed bricks. She had a momentary vision of a white blurred face flattened against the glass. At the sight, realisation swept over her in wave upon wave of sick terror.

There had been no guards. She had taken every step of that perilous journey – alone.

Her very terror sharpened her wits to action. If her eyesight had not deceived her, the killer had already discovered that the alarm was false. It was obvious that he would not run the risk of remaining in his present quarters. But it was possible that he might not anticipate a lightning swoop; there was nothing to connect a raw country girl with a preconcerted alliance with a Force.

'The nearest telephone-office,' she panted. 'Quick.'

A few minutes later, Duncan was electrified by Jenny's voice gasping down the wire.

'He's at 17 Jamaica Square, SE. No time to lose. He'll go out through the roof . . . Quick, quick.'

'Right. Jenny, where'll you be?'

'At your house. I mean, Scot – Quick.'

As the taxi bore Jenny swiftly away from the dun outskirts, a shrivelled hag pattered into the upper room of that drab house. Taking no notice of its raging occupant, she approached the parrot's cage.

'Talk for mother, dearie.'

She held out a bit of dirty sugar. As she whistled, the parrot opened its eyes.

'Perlice.'

It was more than two hours later when Duncan entered his private room at Scotland Yard.

His eyes sought Jenny.

A little wan, but otherwise none the worse for her adventure, she presided over a teapot which had been provided by the resourceful Yates. The Great Dane – unmindful of a little incident of a letter-weight – accepted her biscuits and caresses with deep sighs of protest.

Yates sprang up eagerly.

'Did the cop come off, chief?'

Duncan nodded twice – the second time towards the door, in dismissal.

Jenny looked at him in some alarm when they were alone together. There was little trace left of the machine-made martinet of the Yard. The lines in his face appeared freshly re-tooled and there were dark pouches under his eyes.

'Jenny,' he said slowly, 'I've – sweated – blood.'

'Oh, was he so very difficult to capture? Did he fight?'

'Who? That rat? He ran into our net just as he was about to bolt. He'll lose his footing all right. No.'

'Then why are you—'

'*You.*'

Jenny threw him a swift glance. She had just been half-murdered after a short course of semi-starvation, but she commanded the situation like a lion tamer.

'Sit down,' she said, 'and don't say one word until you've drunk this.'

He started to gulp obediently and then knocked over his cup.

'Jenny, you don't know the hell I've been through. You don't understand what you ran into. That man—'

'He was a murderer, of course. I knew that all along.'

'But you were in deadliest peril—'

'I wasn't frightened, so it didn't matter. I knew I could trust you.'

'Don't Jenny. Don't turn the knife. I failed you. There was a ghastly blunder.'

'But it *was* all right, for it ended beautifully. You see, something told me to trust you. I always know.'

During his career, Duncan had known cases of love at first sight. So, although he could not rule them out, he always argued along Jenny's lines.

Those things did not happen to him.

He realised now that it had happened to him – cautious Scot though he was.

'Jenny,' he said, 'it strikes me that I want someone to watch *me*.'

'I'm quite sure you do. Have I won the reward?'

His rapture was dashed.

'Yes.'

'I'm so glad. I'm rich.' She smiled happily. 'So this can't be pity for me.'

'Pity? Oh, Jenny—'

Click. The mouse-trap was set for the confirmed bachelor with the right bait.

A young and friendless girl – homely and blossom-sweet. Cheese.

Crime on the Footplate

FREEMAN WILLS CROFTS

* * *

The August day was stifling as the 11.55 a.m. express from Leeds beat heavily up the grade towards the summit in the foothills of the Pennines. From there the run down to Carlisle would be easy and rapid. The train was on time and travelling at the full thirty miles an hour customary at the place.

On the footplate Driver Deane sat watching the line ahead and occasionally casting an eye over the faceplate, with its maze of dials and gauges and handles. For Fireman Grover, on the other hand, this was the busy time of the run. With a heavy train on a grade like this, firing was practically continuous.

The engine, while a splendid machine, was of one of the older types. The cab was more open than is now usual, having no side windows, an advantage on this day when the heat of the sun vied with that pouring from the steel endplate of the boiler. It was fitted with small doors at each side between engine and tender, and was driven from the right side of the cab.

All seemed well with the train, yet all was not well. On this footplate, as in the great world beyond, human passions were aflame. For many weeks evil had been festering in Fireman Grover's heart. He had not expelled it while he could, and now he was held in its grip. On this very run and before they had gone a dozen miles further he intended to murder his driver, William Deane.

The story of the madness which had overtaken him was commonplace enough. Some three months earlier he had visited his driver's Leeds home on some railway business. There he had met the driver's wife and immediately had fallen for her. He contrived to meet her again and found out that his feeling was returned.

Rosie Deane was a well-meaning young woman who had made an unwise marriage. She had an unhappy home and accepted Deane, who was many years her senior, as a means of escape. But she had not deceived him. Admitting the truth, she had added that while she liked and respected him, she did not love him, though she would do her best to make him happy. Deane had not hesitated and the marriage had taken place.

For several years she had kept her word. But during this time Deane had suffered an increasing disappointment. He had believed that his wife would gradually come to love him, and when he found that, instead of this, the very opposite was taking place he grew bitter. He became sharp-tongued and suspicious. Rosie resented it and her feeling came out in her manner. Relations between the two went from bad to worse.

It was then that Grover had appeared. His love gave him insight and he soon guessed Rosie's unhappiness. Hatred of his driver grew fanatical when he realised that he was at once the cause of her misery and the bar to its alleviation. The thought of murder had not at first entered his mind, but as he brooded the idea became more and more insistent. He began to consider methods, and when he found one which would infallibly guarantee his own safety, Deane's fate was sealed.

One of Grover's friends was a male nurse in a mental home and the two had frequently discussed inmates and work in such places. Among other things Grover had learned that a certain harmless drug was used to calm patients if they became over-excited. His friend had told him about a dose of this being given to the wrong man, with the result that for some time he had become moody, depressed and ill-tempered. Grover had not forgotten the name of the drug.

During a spare hour in London when they were on the St Pancras link, he had changed into his ordinary clothes, which he had taken up in a parcel, and had purchased a small quantity of the drug at a busy chemist's. No interest had been aroused. Thus his first hurdle was taken.

The second depended on the fact that Deane wore a short beard. The man had been a good deal ragged about it, but Grover had learnt that it was to cover a deep scar on his chin. After getting the drug, Grover had gone on to a theatrical supplies shop and bought a false beard of the correct colour 'to amuse the children'. In the security of his room he trimmed it to the shape of Deane's, and practised putting it on till he could do it quickly and without the aid of a mirror.

His third and last essential was to choose a suitable run for the deed. It must be through sparsely populated country, where observation of what took place on the engine would be unlikely. Also as much time as possible was desirable between block posts. This climb up the bleak Pennine foothills exactly met the conditions.

Grover began operations by doctoring the driver's tea. Before taking their engine out Deane went round it, oiling moving parts and looking out for defects. During this time Grover was alone on the footplate, working at the fire. To slip a daily drop or two of the drug into the other's can was simplicity itself.

When by experiment he had learnt the right amount to use, he was overjoyed with the result. Deane reacted perfectly, growing more bitter and morose, while his temper became a byword among the men.

Some six weeks later Grover decided to strike, and now this was the run which was to free Rosie and open a new door of happiness for himself. On the previous day he had given Deane a specially large dose of the drug, and the effect had been clear to all.

They were approaching what might be called the last outpost of civilisation, the little town of Sleet, for here the railway left the green, well-cultivated valley and entered on the open moor. As they laboured through the small station, the powerful beat echoing from the buildings, Grover began firing. By the time this was finished they had passed the signal cabin and sidings. That all was well on the footplate would have been noted by the signalman. Now they were out into the open. On these bare slopes figures stood out clearly. Grover glanced carefully around. There were none.

He laid down his shovel and picked up a heavy spanner which he had secreted in the coal. Stepping over to Driver Deane, he bent down. 'I think I hear a blowing gasket,' he shouted, for the noise was considerable.

Deane sat still, obviously listening. Grover immediately brought his spanner down with force on the man's head. Deane made no sound. He remained for a moment motionless, then pitched slowly forward. He fell on his knees against the end of the boiler, rolled partially back, and lay with head and arms hunched up in the corner of the cab.

Grover was breathless and trembling, but he forced himself to stoop and examine him. That the man was dead there could be no doubt, for the top of the head was driven down, though owing to the cap the skin was not broken. Moreover, the body's position was admirable. It had to be well forward, so as to be screened by the cab from the next signal cabin, and also to leave space on the congested footplate for the act by which Grover intended to secure his safety.

Haste was now the prime essential, for before they reached the next station, Ottershaw, already less than two miles distant, he must be ready to put on his act. Quickly he adjusted the false beard, checking its position in a mirror from his pocket. Then he twisted up his cap to the angle Deane affected and glanced ahead through the cab window.

They were just passing the Ottershaw distant signal, off as it always was. As they approached the platform and signal cabin Grover began dancing, waving his arms and singing drunkenly. While he did so he kept a keen eye on the cabin, some twenty yards away across the sidings. What happened thrilled him. His plan was working out.

He saw the signalman stare at the engine, then swing round and pick something up, slide open his window, lean out, and begin frantically waving a red flag.

For Grover it was a moment of sickening anxiety. If the guard saw the flag and applied the brakes, only the most speedy and skilful action could save him. He danced on lest someone else should see him, but in a cold sweat of fear.

The advanced starting signal had gone to danger in front of him, but he took no notice. It was only another attempt of the signalman to attract the guard's attention. As they left it behind without an application of the brakes, Grover experienced a relief so intense that he feared his nerve would crack. Then he rallied himself fiercely. Though the worst was over, the job was not finished. The least weakness and he was as good as hanged.

Haste again was the ruling factor. He tore off the beard and threw it into the firebox, making sure with his mirror that no traces remained. Then came a horrible part of the affair. With the flat of the spanner he struck a heavy blow on his own left shoulder. It hurt so much that he feared he had done damage. So much the better, he told himself grimly. He dropped the spanner and threw himself forcibly down against the tender. Then taking off his cap, he knocked his head back against the steel plating, again and again till he could endure no more.

Struggling unsteadily to his feet, he glanced once more through the cab window. In a little over a mile they would reach Grammond block post, a signal cabin without any station. At this he was sure they would be checked, as the Ottershaw signalman would certainly have wired on 'Stop and examine train'. This, and the fact that the post was approached by a wide left-hand curve from which cabin and signals could be seen for nearly a mile across the bend of the valley, were features of his plan.

A few seconds later they entered on the curve. Yes, there were the signals, all at danger. Things certainly were going as he had hoped. He had only to carry out one remaining essential and the whole ghastly affair would be done.

Once again he glanced carefully round. Here also no spectator was in sight. He now stooped and pulled off Deane's cap, then seizing the body beneath the armpits, dragged it painfully back to the rear of the footplate. The doors between engine and tender were shut, and using all his strength, he laid the body over the left door, with the head and trunk hanging down outside and the legs within.

He was just in time, for the body was scarcely in position when they passed the Grammond distant signal. Now was the moment! He heaved up the legs and the body shot out, crashed on its head on the ground and rolled on partly down the embankment. The cap he dropped at the same moment. Then, gasping, he staggered back to the faceplate.

By this time they were approaching the home signal and cabin. Grover passed the former without action, intending that his efforts to stop should be seen by the signalman. But just before they reached the cabin the vacuum disappeared on his gauge and the brakes went on. The guard this time had noticed the adverse signal and used his emergency handle. Grover therefore shut off steam, a little earlier than he had intended. Automatically he closed the firebox door and damper and put on the injector, then sank down, shaken and trembling, on one of the cab seats.

The train ground to a standstill, having overshot the home signal by some quarter of a mile. Grover remained seated where he was. No acting was needed to give the impression he desired, for the shock of what he had done added to the blow on his head had left him really weak and dazed. He sat on till a flustered guard climbed on to the footplate. Others followed. To them Grover outlined the story he had prepared. Everyone was sympathetic. His head was bandaged and he was sent home by the first available train.

Next day the police called for a fuller statement. They began by warning him. 'We have to do it, you know,' they told him. 'Matter of form mostly.'

Grover nodded. He had heard that this was their custom. Then he repeated his story: again and again he had polished its every detail. 'Deane had been a bit queer for a few weeks,' he explained. 'Seemed to have something on his mind and was getting worse. You couldn't hardly speak to him about anything: he'd snap the head off you.'

It was a good beginning. To the police the statement had already been attested by many witnesses.

'On this trip he was worse than ever,' went on Grover. 'I was beginning to wonder if I could get a shift to another driver. I signed to him shortly after we left Leeds that the Riglett distant signal was on, and he went off the deep end good and proper: wanted to know if I thought he was blind and that. It never occurred to me his mind was touched, but it settled mine for me. I decided I'd ask for the change.'

The police made encouraging sounds.

'After a while he quieted down. Just sat there and looked ahead same as usual. Then when we got to Sleet the thing happened. I was firing going through the station, but just after we passed it he turned round and threw up his hands and began laughing fit to burst his sides. It was sort of uncanny, him roaring with laughter, but it didn't seem funny to me. At first I didn't interfere, then I asked him what the joke was. That about put the lid on: he jumped up and yelled at me. He looked sort of wild. I knew then that he was mad and I don't deny I was scared stiff. Suddenly he let fly at my head. I twisted and got it on my shoulder. It knocked me back and I hit my head against the tender. Then he went off his rocker altogether. He began to sing and shout and dance about the footplate while I lay there half stunned.'

Grover's belief that the police would have had confirmation of this statement from the Ottershaw signalman was not misplaced. They begged him to continue, and he did so with increasing confidence.

'I can tell you, gentlemen, I was in a proper fix. We're not often checked by signals on this run, but you have to be prepared for it. If we got a check he wouldn't stop and I couldn't.

'Then, easing up on my elbow, I got a peep over the cab door. We were on the big curve coming into Grammond and you can see the signals a mile away across country. They were against us. Well, I had the train to think of as well as my own life, and I hadn't much time to do it in. I don't know whether I was right or wrong, but I gripped a spanner out of the box, and when Deane turned his back, I nipped up and hit him over the head. I only meant to knock him out, but he staggered forward against the door and overbalanced. Before I could catch him he was out over it.'

For this also there was a reasonable amount of corroboration. The signals *could* be seen as described, and they *were* against the train. The place where the body was found worked in with the time element of the story, and Grover bore the bruises which it demanded. Yes, it was a good tale and had confirmation on nearly every point. Grover's self-satisfaction became impressive when the police thanked him politely and withdrew.

He got his first shock, a terrible numbing shock, when the inquest was adjourned. Then for several days nothing happened. But one night the police returned. They were curt and businesslike. Stunned and incredulous, he heard the inconceivable words, 'Arrest . . . charge with murder . . . anything you say . . .'

Though the exact nature of his mistake did not in a way matter, Grover raged against himself in speechless fury when he learned what it was. His scheme was good, indeed masterly, and it would have worked perfectly but for one quite trivial oversight. He had not examined with sufficient care the position into which Deane had fallen. The driver's shoulders and arms were clear of the boiler, but Grover had been in such a hurry that he had looked no further. On the dead man's leg was a huge scorched wound. Some ghastly experiments showed that at least six minutes' contact with the hot steel plate would have been necessary to produce it.

This gave the police something to think about. When the train was passing Sleet, Deane was alive and well: the signalman had seen that conditions on the footplate were normal. Therefore the man could not at that time have received this crippling injury. Some eight minutes later his body fell from the engine near Grammond. For six of those eight minutes, therefore, he must have been lying with his leg against the boiler: and during that time a bearded man was dancing on the footplate. Only impersonation by Grover could explain it.

At the trial the doctor testified to the finding of a debilitating drug in the remains, though the prisoner's responsibility for this could not be proved. But the whole story of Grover's friendship with Rosie Deane came out, together with the purchase of the false beard. The prisoner's failure to account for the latter on legitimate grounds was the factor which finally swayed the jury.

Karmesin The Murderer

GERALD KERSH

IT WAS ROUGH on my poor friend Karmesin. Finding a pound note in his possession for the first time in two months, he rushed out and bought a hundred cigarettes, and received a bad half-crown among the change.

Look,' he said, holding the coin in his fat, white fingers. He pressed: the half-crown bent. 'Lead!' said Karmesin. 'I could make better myself. Swindlers! Tramplers on the faces of the poor!'

'Take it back to the shop,' I suggested, 'and demand another coin.'

'How am I to prove that it was the shopkeeper who gave it to me?' asked Karmesin. Then he laughed, and said 'Bah. It is all in the game. That shopkeeper would probably spit on the name of a pickpocket, a forger, or an utterer of forged notes or coins. Yet let him receive a queer half-crown from a customer, and while that coin remains in his possession he is an enemy of society; his one desire is to pass it off on somebody else. This is the value of the popular conscience: you can buy it for a counterfeit coin. Bah, I say! Let him keep it. He thinks he is smart, but God will punish him. I tell you, my friend: the great wrongdoer who knows good from evil stands a better chance of paradise than the smug citizen who slinks behind the skirts of the law to do petty misdeeds. I could keep this half-crown and pass it to some other unfortunate person. But how am I to know what misery I might cause by so doing? A widow might ultimately receive it; or an old age pensioner. No.'

In spite of his fat and his age, Karmesin must have been as strong as an ox. He grunted, and tore the soft half-crown across, throwing the pieces out of the window.

'I heard a story,' he said, 'about a coin like that. Some men were playing cards. One of them lost everything, and borrowed a silver dollar for his fare home and his breakfast. On the way he was accosted by an unhappy girl in the last stages of despair. He was a good-hearted man, and was touched by her story. In short, he gave her the silver dollar and told her to go in peace. Next morning she was found drowned, a bad dollar clutched in her hand. That bad dollar, you understand, had been the last straw. If it had been a good one, she would have lived on until the dawn . . . and it is God's mercy, my friend, that the daylight always brings new strength. It is the depression of the small hours that kills men, my friend; the horrible seconds when you hear the clock strike three: then you are lost. You see: the man of whom I told you, he was a good man, but Providence used him for a tragic purpose.'

Karmesin became silent. I said, 'Have you ever wanted to commit suicide?'

'No,' said Karmesin. 'Only murder.'

'But I thought you disapproved of murder.'

'I do. Evil-doers should be left in the hands of their destiny, which always destroys them in the end. Nevertheless, I was responsible for the planning of the Perfect Murder.'

'How?'

'Come with me,' said Karmesin, jingling the remains of his pound. 'I have been your guest many times. Now you must be mine.'

He took me to Xavier's Bar and with an air of magnificence that sent the waiter skipping, ordered brandy.

'What is money?' said Karmesin. 'Dross, rubbish. Thank God I have always spent mine as fast as it came!'

He lumbered over to the slot machine in the corner, inserted a shilling, pulled the handle down. The numbered discs whirred round and thudded to a stop . . . 3, 3, 3. Ten shillings dropped out of the machine with a jingle.

'Observe,' said Karmesin. 'There is one thing in the world which no man can resist: the jingle of cash. See – every eye in the bar is upon us. Now, come and drink your brandy, and I will tell you about my murder . . .'

My scheme (said Karmesin) was not unconnected with a slot machine, in a club not unlike this, not many years ago. The victim was a man called Skobeleff, a man who richly deserved to die.

He was a criminal of the worst type, my friend: one who lives upon women. Skobeleff's speciality was blackmail. He had a genius for working his way into the affections of highly respectable women – women with highly placed husbands. You know how it sometimes happens with the wives of great men. Their husbands, preoccupied with affairs, neglect them. They yearn for attention, to be noticed. It is only natural. Then comes an intrigue, possibly an innocent intrigue – a friendship, quite often, with an unworthy man versed in the wiles of the woman-hunter.

Skobeleff was such a man. He moved in good circles; was tolerated, at least, as a friend of people who moved in good circles. Women found it difficult to resist him, for he had a handsome face, a fine Imperial Guardsman's figure, magnificent blue eyes, the flaxen hair of an angel, perfect self-confidence, a boundless experience of women, and a voice more melodious than harp-strings . . . together with a flow of conversation that could make the unhappy laugh, or bring a heartthrob to the bosom of the most nonchalant woman that ever lived.

He struck up friendships with several nice ladies of uncertain age. Then one could see that he was becoming prosperous. He appeared, every day, in a new and elegant suit; marvellous shirts and ties; offered you rare cigars out of a platinum case. He was obviously doing well out of his friendships.

This was his line; he would profess love and the need for spiritual companionship; and then, by devious shifts, manage to get his victim to write him a tender note . . . you know, my friend, 'just to read when you are not here': it is an old trick. And it always worked. It always has and always will, for women are fools with their affection, just like men.

Having his note, he would begin to bleed the victim. She was, you understand, always the wife of a very great man; somebody who could not afford a scandal of any kind, even if she were utterly innocent. He had a heart of ice, that Skobeleff, and bled them dry. Apart from the money, he took a sadistic delight in the writhing of the victim. It was a hideous business.

And when he wanted to have a quiet drink, he always sat in the Maecenas Club near Piccadilly – an elegant drinking-den, with several slot machines in it, at which numerous idiots lost money enough to choke a hippopotamus.

Now it came to pass that I was approached one day by a woman for whom I entertained the deepest affection. I had better not tell you her name, but she was the wife of a very famous French politician. I liked her very much, in a quite platonic and brotherly way. Yes, brotherly is the word for it, for she was twenty years younger than me, and I had bought her an ivory teething-ring with golden bells on it when she was a mere liver-coloured handful of babe in long clothes. She approached me now and told me a sad story.

She was in terrible trouble. She had involved herself with Skobeleff, and had written him letters – which was worse. Now, he demanded twenty thousand pounds. Otherwise, he would place the letters in the hands of her husband's political opposition; ruin him, ruin her, ruin everything. Twenty thousand pounds was his price, and she had not got twenty thousand. By selling some jewels she could raise ten thousand, she told me, but Skobeleff would not take ten thousand. He said, 'Twenty or nothing. I can sell these letters for twenty thousand any way . . .'

Could I help? Could I lend her ten thousand pounds?

I said that I could do better than that: I could get back the letters.

I did so. It is a story of common burglary. I induced my friend to make up a bundle of money, meet Skobeleff at his apartment, and demand the letters in exchange. At a given moment I appeared, heavily disguised, with a large revolver, made him open his safe, took the entire contents of it, together with the letters my friend had written, and having knocked Skobeleff unconscious with the barrel of the gun, quietly made my departure. That was easy.

But when I came to examine the other papers I had taken, I was horrified. I, Karmesin, was disgusted! The man had made indexes and ledgers of dirty crime. He had a whole career of vile blackmail laid out. God knows what a trail of misery he was planning to leave in his wake. I only knew one thing: by stealing his papers, I had held him up only for a little while. Sooner or later he was certain to operate again.

The law could not touch him. If he left this country, he

would operate elsewhere. I decided to take the law into my own hands; play God; kill him.

I approached him with a proposition.

I told him who I was, and he was impressed; he knew of the things Karmesin had done. Then I said, 'Do you know who lives in the flat above the Maecenas Club?'

'Yes,' said Skobeleff, 'old Lord Westerby.'

'Do you know what he keeps in his safe?' I asked.

'No, what?'

'The Westerby Collar.'

'The Westerby Collar!' said Skobeleff. 'A hundred and eighty priceless emeralds, and the Green Devil Emerald in the centre!'

'Yes. Well?'

'Well, what do you say?' he asked.

'You could help me get them. I have an immediate market. We can get at least two hundred thousand. Help me, and I'll split with you fifty-fifty.'

'But how?'

'Now, listen,' I said. 'I will do the work. I will get the emeralds. As for Westerby, leave him to me; I'll handle him.' I grinned ferociously. 'What I am going to suggest is this: I slip upstairs and get the jewels. A diversion is created that draws everybody in the Club into the slot machine room. You slip out on to the balcony in the room behind. That balcony stands directly underneath the servant's bedroom in the Westerby flat. We synchronize our watches. At midnight precisely, you step on to the balcony and I drop the jewels down into your hands. Then you rejoin the crowd in the next room, and nobody will ever know that you have not been there all the time. Next morning you meet me and give me the jewels.'

Even as I spoke to him I could see the idea of a doublecross entering his treacherous mind. I could see it in his eyes. What had he to lose? He had only to stand on a balcony. I was to do all the dirty work, take all the risks.

'But how will you get everybody into the slot machine room?' he asked.

'At ten minutes to twelve,' I said, 'a man will win the jackpot on every machine in the place.'

'If you can arrange that,' he said, 'you must be a wizard.'

'I am a wizard,' I said.

When I left him I looked up a man called Martin, a good little rogue who had had occasions to be thankful to me many a time, especially once when I supported his wife and three children while he spent a year in jail. He was something of a genius in engineering: I mean, very clever with wheels and springs. Would he help me? He would have gone through hell and high water for me. I promised him fifty pounds. His act was simple. At about eleven o'clock he had to come to the Club with a bag, showing the official card of the firm that manufactured the slot machines. Then he was to unlock each machine, and adjust it so that the next revolution of the wheels would bring the total to Three Bars, which wins the jackpot. That is a very simple matter for a man who knows how to handle machinery. Normally, of course, your slot machine engineer sends the wheels flying round six or seven times before leaving the thing, just to see that all is well. But Martin would not do this, of course, and nobody would notice.

I told you: nothing attracts people like the jingle of money. There must have been a dozen machines in the Club. The crash of a dozen jackpots at midnight would bring every member running from the next room: the floor would be knee-deep in silver. Everybody would be pulling handles, or stooping for fallen coins.

Then Skobeleff would come out on the balcony. He thought he ran no risk, for the secretary and commissionaire whom one had to pass before entering or leaving the Club could both swear that he had been in there all the time.

Only I was not going to be on the floor above with a priceless emerald collar. I was to be at the darkened window of the flat across the road. In my hands there was to be a rifle. I was a perfect shot, and still am. From that distance I could not miss. I should put a bullet in the centre of Skobeleff's forehead, and wipe his evil presence from the face of the earth. Martin was waiting in the street with a car. At ten seconds before twelve, as the theatre crowds filled the streets, he would jam the traffic; there would be a chaos of horns. He would make his engine backfire furiously. The sound of my shot would be unheard. It was perfect. And so it turned out.

A young fool called Poppins put a shilling in the slot machine and let out a deluge of coins. Others followed suit. The proprietor of the place came running, white in the face. The machines had gone mad! They were all paying out jackpots! The whole Club poured into the room, eager to put a shilling in, or to see money coming out. Simultaneously, a fearful uproar broke out in the street below. Cars jammed in a black mass, honking like fury. Martin's big automobile banged and thundered, giving out clouds of smoke.

I got Skobeleff's head in line, took a careful aim. He was outlined against the light. I could not miss – I who have knocked the head off a running antelope at five hundred yards. I pressed the trigger.

Skobeleff shrugged his shoulders and walked back into the club. Remembering everything, planning everything, organizing everything so perfectly, *I had forgotten to load my rifle!*

Karmesin laughed. 'Yet he deserved to die,' he said.

'Well?' I asked.

'Yes,' said Karmesin. 'It proves my point. Such men are always punished in the end. Nemesis is always upon them.

They are never more than one jump ahead of vengeance.'

'But *Skobeleff?*

'Skobeleff,' said Karmesin. 'He stayed in the Club until one o'clock in the morning, then went home. Do you remember the big fire in the hosier's shop in Dublin Street, Piccadilly? Skobeleff lived above. He perished that very night. You see, in leaving that blank spot of forgetfulness in my brain, Fate was preserving Skobeleff for something even more terrible. A man cannot run away from his destiny.'

'But one thing more. How did you get into the flat exactly opposite the Club, when you meant to kill Skobeleff?'

'Ha!' said Karmesin. 'I got into it the same way as I got into it before: with a duplicate key. And I knew that the occupant would be on the balcony opposite. *It was Skobeleff's flat!*

'And the fire?'

'Inscrutable Providence,' said Karmesin dryly. 'Later that night I returned to Skobeleff's flat after he had gone to sleep. I took my cigar out of my mouth, and casually flipped it over my shoulder. "Let Providence proceed with the matter," I said. Providence! Fate! Skobeleff perished. It is right and proper that rubbish should be incinerated. So perish all rubbish! Another brandy?'

The Bottle Party

H. C. BAILEY

FEW ARE THE cases which have given Mr Fortune so pure a pleasure.

When Carteret Square was built on a swamp, our ancient aristocracy bid against each other for its mansions and put their horses and carriages into a foul mews on the eastern side. The square is now a colossal quadrangle of flats inhabited by the new rich. The stables of the mews have been rebuilt to make garages for some of them and little houses for those who live upon them and renamed, to preserve the dignity of all, Carteret Place.

It is a narrow, prim street, empty, when the children of the chauffeurs dwelling over the garages have been put to bed, unless some knowing creature has left a car parked in one of the bulges provided to give a turning circle for the chariots of the past. But behind the curtains of the neat houses there is often some noise at night, and policemen stroll by from hour to hour.

About eleven on a misty autumn night a constable was pacing along Carteret Place from the southern end when he heard a police whistle blow at the other. He ran upon the sound and, reaching the northern end, found another breathless officer who had heard the whistle, but no one else. They hunted highways and byways in vain. The neighbourhood is prolific in bright young things who delight to take a rise out of the police.

About one o'clock he came down Carteret Place again. The little houses were quieter than usual. But by one of them a man bumped into him and when rebuked knocked his helmet off. They had a scuffle, the man fell, the constable picked him up and dragged him off, wambling in his walk, to the station, and charged him with assault. The man seemed dazed or drunk. With difficulty the inspector got a name out of him, which was Antony Cray, put him in a cell and sent for a doctor.

At nine o'clock next morning Mr Fortune was, as usual, in his bath. Mrs Fortune opened the door and exhorted him to come out. 'Why?' He sank deeper into the water. 'Why are wives?' She turned on the cold shower. 'Not for that, no,' he moaned.

'A lady has called to see you,' she said severely.

'My dear girl! Have a heart. Not before breakfast.'

'Parker says she wouldn't go away. And she's been here nearly an hour. Her name is Valerie Milburn.'

'Not guilty. Means nothing in my young life.'

'You've seen her. She plays the blondes that gentlemen prefer.'

'An actress? Before nine a.m.? Oh no, Joan.'

'I didn't say she could act,' said Mrs Fortune.

The secret of his eminence, he likes to explain, is a capacity to dress quicker than any man, thus making time for higher things. He ate half a cold partridge before he went to his consulting-room and yet half-past nine had not struck when Valerie Milburn sat down in front of him.

The silly, pretty face of the enchantress of light comedy was not at its best. Without make-up her fair complexion looked insipid. She tried her popular, yearning glance, but the smile on the pale lips was a spasm.

'Oh, Mr Fortune, how kind you are!' She used the drawl of allure with which she spoke all her parts, though her voice could put no life into it.

'Not kind, no. Only curious. Who sent you to me, Miss Milburn?'

'Nobody. I came of myself.'

'Oh! Had a bad night?'

She laughed, rather too long. 'There's nothing the matter with me. It's someone else, Tony Cray, Antony Cray, you know, he's the nephew of Lord Frome.'

'I don't. Is he ill?'

'I believe he is, Mr Fortune. It's like this. I live in Carteret Place, you know the dinky little houses there. I had a bottle party last night, starting ten o'clock. Tony – Mr Cray was there on the dot. I'm sure he shouldn't have come at all. You can back him to be on top of the world at any show, but last night nobody could get a rise out of him. He just sat and gloomed. He owned up, about one, he didn't feel too good, he'd go home. Then the ghastly thing happened. Just outside my door a policeman barged into him, the silly brute, got rough with him, said he was drunk and ran him in. They've kept him at the station, they're going to charge him this morning. But he wasn't drunk, Mr Fortune. He couldn't have been. He wouldn't have a spot. He was sickly sober. But you know what the police are. If they get him convicted it'll break him. He hasn't a bean, except what he gets from Lord Frome. The old man was just going to wangle a Foreign Office job for him. That's right off, suppose Tony's in the news for drunk and scragging policemen. You see?'

'I wonder,' said Mr Fortune.

'You could stop it, you could, couldn't you?' she panted. 'He wasn't drunk, he's never violent. Do help him, do save him.'

'The police won't stop for me. Mustn't count on me to save anybody, Miss Milburn. Feeling this rather a lot, aren't you? However. Curious case. Interestin' case. As you put it. I'll see if they'll let me look it over.'

'Oh, thank you so much,' she started up and ran round the table to clutch his hands.

'Don't do that,' Mr Fortune withdrew them and rang the bell. 'Don't hope too much.' Valerie was shown out gurgling laughter and tears.

Mr Fortune rang up the Chief of the Criminal Investigation Department. 'Fortune speakin', Lomas. Most improperly. To foul the springs of justice. Any objection?'

'I've been pining to catch you at it for years, Reginald. Go on.'

'The woman tempted me. One Valerie Milburn.' He paused for a reply. None came. 'Know her?'

'Not officially,' said Lomas. 'On the stage, yes. The delight of callow youth and aged rips. I thought you had better taste. When did she tempt you? And how? If it's fit for my ears.'

'When? She's only just gone.'

'Good God! Are you talking in your sleep? It's very early for temptation – and for you to be up.'

'I've been up an hour.'

'And fallen for a pretty lady already. Fie!'

'Didn't say fallen. Miss Milburn was woe on the top note. But points did emerge. Her trouble is one Antony Cray. Ever heard of him?'

Again the answer was delayed for some moments. Then Lomas repeated. 'Cray? Do you mean a nephew of old Lord Frome?'

'That's the fellow. Miss Milburn says you've pinched him for drunk and assaulting the constabulary which you didn't ought.' Reggie related precisely all that Valerie had told him. . . .

'Do you believe her, Reginald?'

'What the lady said isn't evidence. However. Statement could be true.'

'Quite,' Lomas admitted. 'Some of these cases are the devil.

It's hard measure to ruin a young fellow's career because he had a rough and tumble with the police. And if this fellow was seedy!'

'As you say,' Reggie murmured, but he contemplated the telephone with a small, satiric smile. 'Very fair, Lomas. Very human. May I look the case over?'

'By all means,' Lomas said heartily. 'You'd like to see the boy before he's charged?'

'Yes, please. And the police doctor. And the policeman.'

'I agree. I'll send Bell to meet you at the police station.' Lomas rang off.

'Well, well,' Reggie sighed to the dead telephone. '"Barkis is willin'."'

Ten minutes later he entered the station and met the solid form of Superintendent Bell. 'This swift attention from the higher powers is gratifyin',' he returned thanks. 'Are you going to tell me things?'

'I don't know any more about the case than you do,' said Bell stolidly. 'But it wants checking up. This way, please.' Reggie was taken to the cell which contained Antony Cray.

He was dirty and tousled and of a yellow pallor, his eyes red rimmed and swollen, his shaking, twitching hands had bled from the knuckles. Yet reason for Valerie's interest in him could be detected. In good condition he might have been a fine fellow, at least a woman's man. He had long legs and a good pair of shoulders, the blurred features of the sickly face were well cut by nature.

'Sorry about this, Mr Cray,' said Reggie. 'I'm a doctor.'

'What do you want?' Cray's voice was hoarse. 'I'm not drunk. I wasn't drunk. The policeman did this,' he held out his damaged hands.

'No drink taken last night?'

'A small whisky at dinner. That's all.'

'Anything besides drink?'

'Yes. I had a splitting headache. I took some phenacetin tablets. They made me all the worse. I couldn't stand the row of the party. When I went out I was dizzy, and stumbled into the policeman, and he said I was drunk and beat me up.'

'Oh. Phenacetin. Often use that?'

'When I get a head.'

Reggie felt his pulse, murmuring: 'Any sickness? No? Rather depressed, what? Did you see things normal last night?'

'With a sick headache? Who does?'

Reggie looked into the swollen eyes and with his fingers on the chin tilted the head back.

Cray jerked it aside. 'Look out! My head's devilish sore.'

'Yes. It would be. That's all, Mr Cray.' Reggie left the cell.

The police doctor, he found, had been told the same tale, and sardonically pronounced it a good story.

'You don't believe it?'

'I never believe 'em. The young rascal wasn't drunk when I saw him, but he smelt of drink. He'd had more than one.'

'That could be, yes. But something else also, what?'

'I dare say. Certainly, I thought him rather down than up.'

'Still is. Not a drunk. No. Nerves all wrong.'

'Well, of course, your opinion is decisive, Mr Fortune,' the doctor was quick to answer. 'If I say neuralgic condition and an overdose of some sedative, that would be about right, I take it?'

'Yes. As near as we can get,' Reggie sighed.

The doctor bustled out.

'Everybody loves me,' Reggie complained to the empty room.

Bell entered. 'The doctor tells me, sir, you and him are agreed Cray was a sick man?'

'Why this kindly joy, Bell?'

'No joy from me one way or the other. I just want things straight.'

'What about the assaulted constable?'

'You want to talk to him, sir? Very good.'

An uncomfortable policeman was brought in. 'This Mr Cray,' Reggie asked, 'How did he collide with you?'

'Sort of staggered into me, sir. But I have to own he wasn't noisy. He caught hold of me, I reproached him. Then he got excited and hit out wild and I had to take him along.'

'Did him proud, didn't you?'

'Sir?' The policeman was aggrieved.

'Bruise under the chin?'

'Then it must have come from his falling down, sir. He did fall heavy. He barked his knuckles proper.'

'Well, well. Nothing more, thanks.'

The constable departed and Bell asked: 'Is that all right, Mr Fortune?'

'My dear Bell. Splendid. Great force, the police force. However. I'd like to see this through.'

'Very good, sir. Come along into court. Cray's case'll be on any minute.'

It went with a rush. The policeman was mild, the doctor masterfully sympathetic. Reggie had just made out the wan face of Valerie watching Cray tell his tale of headache and phenacetin before the magistrate dismissed the charge with soft, paternal words.

'Sort of thing that makes England what she is,' Reggie murmured to Bell as they went out.

'We do know how to be fair,' Bell answered. 'Now would you come along with me? There's a big case turned up.'

Reggie looked up with wide, plaintive eyes. 'Big? What is big? Murder?'

'I want your opinion on that. There's a woman dead.'

'Where?'

'In the Westminster mortuary. Only five minutes' walk.'

'Walk?' Reggie's voice went up. 'My car's here.'

It brought them into the yard of the mortuary. A smaller car stood there, a coupé of class. 'She's inside that,' said Bell.

Reggie gave one glance within and turned. 'Why is she?' he complained.

'I couldn't say, sir.'

'Cautious fellow. Couldn't say whether it was murder! Look again.'

'I leave it to you, Mr Fortune,' Bell recoiled.

The woman's body lay huddled between the seat and the instrument board. Under that her head lolled back, the cheeks, the closed eyes bulged, the nose and lips spread flat. All the face was livid but for purple and yellow marks of bruising. A squirrel coat covered her from bent knees to chin. Reggie drew back its collar. Round the full neck bruises were black to the knot of red bronze hair behind.

He opened the coat wider. Beneath it was a green evening dress. He contemplated that with a pensive gaze which slowly extended to survey the whole of the car's interior before he turned to Bell.

'You don't want to look at her again? Not a cheerin' sight. Not a perfect world. Get your fellows to take her into the mortuary. When she's gone you might bear to look into the car. The higher intelligence could work out a fact or so.'

Bell glowered at him. 'I reckon I'll finish with the car before you're through. If you come back to the station I'll be there.'

Some hours later Reggie entered the bleak room where Bell sat writing, subsided on the only other chair and lit a pipe. 'Not to spoil the story,' he murmured and blew smoke rings. 'Dead woman was forty or so, in good health, well preserved. Married woman as per wedding ring. Cause of death, asphyxia. From throttling with human hands. She died hard. Fought it out.'

'Ah. Clear case of murder,' Bell grunted.

'Oh yes. Not a nice murderer – or murderers. Things are what they seemed. On that point. Hands were almost clenched. Between the fingers of right hand light yellow hairs, from bobbed or shingled woman. On her teeth some scraps of human skin, colour indeterminate, bitten off assailant. Dress and other clothes not torn, not pulled about, but body and legs heavily bruised. She was on her back and somebody knelt on her to kill her. Murder therefore was not committed in the car. Time of murder indefinitely before midnight. That's the medical evidence. How do you like it?'

'Not so bad, Mr Fortune.'

'Always happy to gratify the higher powers. What is the story you're composin'?'

'I was just putting things together in order.'

'Order is a felt want. Yes. Got it?'

'Well, sir, fairly clearly. That car was found at three-fifteen this morning in Carteret Place.'

'Oh! Where Valerie Milburn gave her bottle party. Where Cray had his scrap with the policeman.'

'That's right. At least in a manner of speaking. The car wasn't at Miss Milburn's house but some way up the street, in a little sort of dead end. The constable who arrested Cray says it wasn't there when he went up Carteret Place at eleven p.m. We can fix the time it was left between eleven and three.'

'As near as that! Better than me.'

'Ah! We might get nearer yet,' said Bell. 'At three another constable spotted the car. He didn't bother with it, being no obstruction. He came back about five and it was still there. Thinking that queer he looked in and saw the woman.'

'Oh my Bell!' Reggie protested. 'You haven't put things in order. How did it begin? Who is she?'

'Yes, sir. She's been identified. She's Mrs Arundel, a lady living just by where the car was found, and it's her car.'

Reggie blew one smoke ring inside another. 'Who is Mrs .

Arundel? What is she, that someone strangles her and dumps her in her own car by her own house? Is there a Mr Arundel?'

'Not to my knowledge,' said Bell solemnly, 'but she has had three real husbands.'

'Rather careless with spouses, what?'

'She was no better than she should be, Mr Fortune. A fast woman, half in society, more than half out.'

'The lady's – friends?' Reggie drawled. 'Are they known to the police?'

'She lived in a rackety crowd.'

Reggie smiled. 'Yes, Bell, Carteret Place was having frequent visits from the police at night – eleven, one, three, five. Why?'

'We don't like that street, sir. We have nothing hard, but there is reason to believe it has snow falls. Cocaine, you know.'

'I do. Yes. Though not mentioned when I was introduced to your friend Cray. So Mrs Arundel was suspect of dope dealing?'

'We had her in view. But there have been other reasons for watching Carteret Place, complaints of rowdy parties there and spots of trouble in the neighbourhood. Only last night there was one.' He related the vain pursuit of a police whistle by the eleven o'clock constable.

Reggie sat up. His round face was plaintive and reproachful. 'My Bell! Oh my Bell! Is this puttin' things in order? No. Carteret Place was deprived of the eleven o'clock police inspection. Curious and interestin' fact. Yet I had to pull it out of you with forceps.'

'I'm sorry, sir. It don't signify. The constable went right along the street at eleven and he swears no car was in it. I told you.'

'But he left the street clear. So the car could have been brought along. The woman may have been killed some time before. He didn't come back till one and then he got busy arrestin' Cray. So we don't know whether she and the car were there then. Pity.'

'I grant you there is a look of tricks,' Bell frowned. 'But whistling to get a rise out of the police is a common game with the bright young things round there. I am giving you all the facts, Mr Fortune. When I went over the car I found this –' He displayed a scrap of pale blue silk. 'It was caught on the edge of the door the driver's side. From a woman's dress and not Mrs Arundel's dress. Hers was green.'

'As you say,' Reggie murmured. 'Not her colour. Dress probably worn by a blonde. Same like the hair in the fingers of the deceased. And Valerie of the bottle party is a blonde. Did you get her to look at Mrs Arundel?'

'Why no, sir. Mrs Arundel was recognised by the constable and then identified by her servant – she kept a house man, no maid, that was her style. I have no reason to think Miss Milburn was a special friend.'

'Till this,' Reggie held up the blue silk. 'Further conversation with Miss Milburn is required.'

'I was going to,' said Bell.

'My dear chap, we do agree beautiful.' Reggie stood up and looked at his watch. 'Help! Have you got a car? Mine has to go home.' He strolled out and, with brief instructions, sent his chauffeur away.

Bell joined him. 'We can walk it as quick as drive, sir.'

'Not me,' Reggie protested, hailing a taxi. But he stopped it at the beginning of Carteret Place. 'Walkin' is only justified when you can't get what is wanted otherwise. As now. In this nasty, neat little street. Where you have to show me things. Mrs Arundel's house. Dead end in which Mrs Arundel's car stood. After that, house of Miss Milburn.'

At that hour of the afternoon, the narrow street was a playground and a mixed club. Children of the chauffeurs who lodged over its garages sported across the roadway, chauffeurs and their wives clustered about the garage doors in gossip.

'That's where the car was found.' Bell glanced at a bulge in the roadway which went up between two houses to a blank wall. 'Used to be a turning circle when this was a mews, often used for parking.'

'Handy,' Reggie murmured, 'yet out of the way. Good and dark after dark.'

'That's right,' Bell nodded. 'Now the next house but one is Mrs Arundel's.'

It had an emerald green door and russet window frames and curtains of brown netting. 'Suits her complexion,' Reggie murmured. 'By the way, when did she leave the house yesterday?'

'Ah! You're asking something,' Bell grunted. 'Her man servant don't know. He was taking his weekly day off yesterday, and had leave for the night, he says. He went out at two o'clock, went to see his old dad at Kingston and didn't get back till eight this morning.'

'Do you believe him?'

'I have no reason not to. He hasn't been with Mrs Arundel long – only a month – and he's given us a story we can easily check.'

'Will aged father say son was with him at time of murder? Some check! However. Let's try Miss Milburn.'

'There's her house,' Bell pointed. It was some fifty yards from Mrs Arundel's on the same side, a little larger, double fronted, its door, and everything else that could be painted, white. All the windows had boxes of white flowers, geraniums and petunias.

The door was opened by an oldish maid who glared.

'If you please.' Bell stepped into the hall. 'Tell Miss Milburn I want to see her at once.' He held out his card.

'Madam's not at home.' The maid was shrill.

'Do as you're told,' Bell growled, and she slunk away into

a room on the right and slammed the door, came out again looking malice sideways and went upstairs. She was not gone long. From the landing she beckoned them.

They were taken into a small room on the first floor, which was entirely white and cream but for two people in it. Valerie shimmered silver grey as she glided to meet them. The man behind her had put his lumpy form into bright blue tweeds and a honey-coloured beard and side whiskers grew on his large pink face.

Valerie was flushed out of insipidity. 'Superintendent Bell?' she smiled and the upward glance of allure had a gleam in it.

'Me too, Miss Milburn,' said Reggie.

'Oh, Mr Fortune. How too kind of you. It was splendid about poor old Tony.'

'Has he been here?'

'No, did you want him?'

'I wonder. Let's see. About your party last night, Miss Milburn—' Reggie stopped and glanced at the bearded man.

'I was here, sir.' The man's voice was high.

'You don't know each other,' Valerie giggled. 'How futile! On the left Mr Fortune, on the right Ned Patten.'

'Friend of Mr Cray's?' Reggie asked.

'I think so,' the man answered.

'Seen him since?'

'Since the party? No.'

'Mr Fortune ! ' Valerie cried. 'Has something happened to Tony?'

'What could happen? Charge dismissed. Revertin' to the party—' Valerie was staring at the stolid menace of Bell. 'Please—' Reggie waved her to a chair and sat down beside her. 'You told me it began at ten. When did Cray arrive?'

'With the first bunch,' Patten answered. 'So did I.'

'Many bunches? Lot of people?'

'Quite a crush,' said Patten.

'All in here?' Reggie looked round the little room.

'Heavens no,' Valerie giggled. 'The state apartments are beneath.'

'Oh! Do you mind – like to look at actual scene.'

'Why?' Valerie gasped.

'Want to make sure where Cray was all the time.'

'But – but Tony's out now. You just said so.'

'Yes. He is. However.' Reggie moved to the door.

Valerie sprang up, slid past him downstairs and flung open the doors on either side the hall. Through one was a narrow dining-room of different gold shades, the other opened upon a lounge, with walls, carpet and furniture all white.

'There you are,' she cried. 'Now you know the worst, Mr Fortune. The lily house. Décor by Ned. Spirit by me.' She made him a curtsey, looking up under her eyelashes.

'Charmin' harmony. Yes.' Reggie glanced at the gold room and went into the white lounge. 'Bottle party buzzed about; what? But the main body here. Were you here all the time, Patten?'

'In and out from the gold room. That's where the drinks were.'

'And you, Miss Milburn?'

'I was here in the lounge from start to finish.'

'Where was Cray?'

'Down and dumb in the corner over there,' Patten pointed.

'Poor old Tony,' said Valerie. 'He was sick and hating himself for it.'

'Yet he stayed. Stayed from ten till one.'

'I couldn't shift him,' Valerie cried.

'Silly dam' fool,' said Patten. ' I tried to push him off.'

Reggie looked from one to the other. 'Who else was here?'

Valerie broke out laughing. 'Who wasn't? Hordes! Half my crowd.'

'Mrs Arundel among 'em?' Reggie asked.

That froze them both. Patten spoke first. 'Mrs Arundel was here hours.'

'It seemed like years,' said Valerie. 'She didn't go till after Tony's row with the policeman.'

'Oh. She was still here when he'd been arrested? Quite sure?' Reggie's eyes were set on Valerie.

'Absolutely.' Valerie stared back unflinching. 'She ragged us about it.'

Reggie strolled across the room to a settee. Its rough silk cover showed marks at one end as if it had been scraped by something hard. He bent over it, Bell came to look, they exchanged a glance. Valerie met them as they turned and gasped: 'What, what's the matter?'

'When did she go?' Reggie drawled.

'Mrs Arundel? Some time after Tony.'

'About ten past one,' said Patten.

'How?'

'What do you mean?' Patten scowled at him.

'On her own legs?'

'Of course,' Valerie gasped. 'She didn't have a car. Her house is only a few doors off.'

'I've seen it. So you say Mrs Arundel walked out of your house soon after one. Cray bein' then in the hands of the police. Who remained here?'

Valerie and Patten consulted together with their eyes. 'I did,' said Patten.

'Nobody else?'

'Me of course,' Valerie cried. 'Only me.'

'And then?'

'Then I sat some time with Val and went home,' Patten answered.

'Which way?'

Patten was silent for a moment and grew pale before he answered: 'I live up the street.'

'Beyond Mrs Arundel's house. So you passed it. When did you know Mrs Arundel had been killed?'

'My housekeeper told me this morning.'

'Oh yes. Yes. But passin' Mrs Arundel's house last night, didn't you give an eye to her car?'

'I didn't see any car.'

'Of course we didn't,' Valerie giggled. 'We were only seeing ourselves.'

'Oh. You were with him?'

The giggle faded in a languishing smile. 'It is so hard to say good night. Hasn't anyone ever told you that, Mr Fortune? Give them a chance.'

'I have,' Reggie sighed. 'Good night, Miss Milburn.' He went out.

'You'll be required to make a further statement miss, and you, sir,' Bell told them. 'I warn you what you have said will be tested.'

Reggie had shut the door behind him, and when Bell emerged came from the inner recesses of the hall. 'This bein' thus,' he murmured. 'Passed to you.'

Bell did not answer till they were in the street. 'A pretty couple!'

'As you say.' Reggie stopped and contemplated the house.

'That minx with her goo-goo eyes!'

'Cloyin' damsel. Yes. Cloyin' house. All overdone.' Reggie made a weary gesture. 'Even the side door white.'

'Ah, overdone is right,' Bell chuckled. 'Such silly lying, they didn't know where to stop.'

Reggie looked up at him with pensive wonder. 'That is so. We do agree, Bell.'

'Ah! You got 'em over the car. They knew all about it.'

'One or both. Yes. Lies not so good on that. Smash the rest and all is gas and gaiters. Check the beastly bottle party.' Reggie hailed a taxi and drove off in it.

That night the Chief of the Criminal Investigation Department found him solitary at supper in one of their sprightlier clubs. A bottle of champagne was on his table, he was eating marrow bones.

'Reginald!' Lomas rebuked him. 'And you a married man! Is this domestic virtue?'

'No. Debauch. To preserve sanity. Sufferin' from a public dinner. Mass production food and speeches. On top of your distressful case. The mind was hysterical.'

Lomas sat down with him and ordered a devilled sole and brandy and soda.

Reggie sipped his champagne. 'You may be right. Both equally coarse. Only a wine in name. What's your trouble?'

'Nothing but fatigue. We've done very well. We roped in some of the bottle party and got out of 'em it was an uncomfortable show. Valerie and Mrs Arundel on the edge of a flare up all the time. They've always been cats to each other, but last night well above themselves. They've had Cray in common for a boy friend and he funked both women hard. Mrs Arundel fed the party brimstone scandal about Valerie and Patten. When Cray left he looked dead to the world. On his scrap with the policeman the party broke up. The last of Mrs Arundel comes from a fellow who heard her ragging Valerie and Valerie scolding back. Not too clean, he says. So there's the motive. Then we have the damage to the settee. If the woman was thrown down and strangled there, her heels would have made marks like that.'

'As you say,' Reggie sighed. 'Strikin' and suggestive, the double scrape. Any more evidence?'

'That hair in Mrs Arundel's fingers matches Valerie's. The scrap of pale blue silk in the car was torn from the dress Valerie wore last night. We found finger-prints on the door and window of the car and they're Patten's.'

'Careless animal. Futile liar. So you've taken his prints and searched her lily house. Charged 'em?'

'Not yet,' Lomas smiled. 'We got their prints on statements we handed them to sign. They are detained for enquiries. They'll be charged tomorrow.'

Reggie drank up his champagne. 'End of a perfect day,' he murmured. 'Began by gettin' one rackety fool off a twopenny crime, went on to lag two lying fools for murder. In sweet agreement with the higher intelligence.' He gazed at Lomas with heavy eyes. 'Pleasant dreams. Do you dream? I never could.' He wandered out.

Before eleven next morning Lomas heard his voice again. It came over the telephone. 'I want Bell,' it said. 'Bell in a fast car. With another hefty man or so. At the Oval tube station. Now.'

'Good Gad!' Lomas exclaimed. 'What—'

'I said now,' said Reggie, and rang off.

But when the car stopped by the Oval station, he was not there. Bell fumed for some minutes before a taxi crossed all the traffic lanes and Reggie sprang from it, ran to the police car, slammed the door which Bell opened and thrust himself between the driver and the other man in front. 'Camberwell Road. Let her out.' Between buses and trams the driver did wonders, but Reggie fidgeted and lifted up his voice. 'I asked for a fast car.' The driver flushed and scared all traffic over three busy miles.

Then he was directed into a glum, suburban avenue. 'Slow. Stop,' Reggie ordered. Bell frowned at rows of small houses, each asserting that it was different from the other but of a blinding uniformity.

A man loitering by the corner of a side street turned to look and went on looking.

'Come along, Bell,' Reggie jumped out.

Bell caught him up before he reached the corner, and received a wink from the man standing there. 'My oath!' he muttered, for he knew the man as Reggie's chauffeur. 'What's the idea, Mr Fortune?'

'All present and correct,' said the chauffeur out of the corner of his mouth.

'To see Killarney,' said Reggie. 'Leave your men here.' He turned down the side street.

The houses there were of still bleaker gentility and detached. Scrawny hedges of privet, laurel and aucuba protected each from neighbours and the vulgar world.

Killarney had its name in gold on a red gate. Inside that a monkey puzzler rose over straggling rhododendrons through which a curving path led to the lurid stained glass of the front door. Some noise came out of the house, petulant voices talking together. On a sudden both fell to silence. Reggie took Bell's arm and drew him from the door to a window beyond.

They looked in round aspidistras, upon a dowdy drawing-room and a woman and a man standing close together. Reggie pushed up the window. 'Thanks very much, Cray,' he laughed.

Cray shrank and sagged and stumbled away from the woman. She stood fast. Her purple dress suited the maroon drawing-room, came near matching the mottled flush of her cheeks, but made a cruel discord with the bronze red hair above. She looked from Cray to Reggie and Bell, and they saw her eyes gleam dark.

'Good morning, Mrs Arundel,' Reggie cried, 'this is a pleasure.'

Bell thrust head and shoulders through the window. She clutched the table beside her, a table on which lay some woollen knitting. She looked again at Cray, who was white and dumb.

'Yes, kind of Cray to bring us along,' said Reggie. 'Superintendent Bell did want you.'

She picked up the knitting, she turned and flung herself at

Cray and drove the needles into his face, into his throat.

Bell shouted; Bell clambered into the room. Cray had fallen and she was upon him, stabbing at him with the bestial strength of frenzy.

Bell dragged her off. She kicked and bit, till his men came through the window and mastered her. Reggie was kneeling by Cray. 'Don't be rough,' he said over his shoulder. Handcuffs were put on her, her legs were tied.

'She has done you proud,' he said to Cray, whose throat was welling blood. 'However.' He rose and came to Mrs Arundel. 'Allow me.' He drew her long sleeves back from the handcuffs. On the right arm the skin had been torn and dents showed red. 'Oh yes. Where sister bit you,' he murmured, and the woman shrieked. 'Take her away. Me for the other victim.'

That afternoon he came into Lomas's room dreamy and benign. 'One of your larger cigars is indicated.' He helped himself and sank down in the easiest chair. 'Pleasin' case.'

Lomas took up his telephone. 'Come along, Bell. Mr Fortune's here at last.'

'My dear old thing!' Reggie protested. 'Only paused for a simple lunch.'

'Till half-past three,' Lomas rebuked him.

Bell strode in. 'What about Cray, Mr Fortune? Is he going to come through?'

'He thinks not. I didn't tell him he was wrong.'

'My oath!' Bell muttered.

'Had a confession from him?'

'Yes, sir. Him believing he wouldn't live.'

'Last dying speech,' Reggie smiled. 'Anything like the truth?'

'It's a queer story. He says Mrs Arundel was in the dope business, and broke him down teaching him to take snow. She told him the dead woman was her sister and lived on her, passed her the dope and blackmailed her over it. The trade was bad lately. Money ran short and this sister turned nasty, threatened she'd give the whole game away. She came to Mrs Arundel's house day before yesterday. Mrs Arundel 'phoned him, and when he got there the woman was dead. Mrs Arundel said she'd had to kill her, the only way to stop her mouth; she was going to split on 'em both, but it would be all right if he helped get the body taken for Mrs Arundel's, she'd go off and pass as her sister. But he wouldn't stand for it; he wouldn't do a thing, and he quit. Then this morning he had a telegram: 'Come Killarney,' and he didn't dare not go for fear of her.'

'Fearful fellow. Yes. That's why he's such a brute. He helped to strangle the sister. Hence the bruise under his chin. Any confession from Mrs Arundel?'

'Not a word.'

'There will be. When she hears his. However. Don't matter. Been over Mrs Arundel's house yet?'

'We have, sir. What are you thinking of?'

'Oh my Bell. Settee, divan or bed. Scratches thereon, same like the white settee of Valerie.'

'That's pretty good.' Bell smiled grimly. 'We didn't find anything scratched. But Mrs Arundel's house man says there's an old Persian rug gone from the couch in the drawing-room.'

'Splendid,' Reggie purred. 'Pleasin' case. Subtle female, Mrs Arundel. All clear.'

'Clear!' Lomas exclaimed. 'You flatter yourself, Reginald.'

'Not myself. No.' Reggie sank down in his chair. 'Do I flatter you? Surely not.'

'We can convict these two beauties now, but we don't know how the thing was worked.'

'Oh my Lomas. Think again. Believe the evidence. Cray and the Arundel strangled Mrs Jones and she left her mark on both of 'em, some time before ten. I told you she died earlier than midnight. Cray went off to Valerie's party at ten. The Arundel stripped dead sister and put on the body clothes of her own, evenin' dress matchin' the one she wore herself at the bottle party. Not a nice job. Not a nice woman. Twisted some of Valerie's hair in the dead fingers. Next event. Eleven o'clock constable called out of Carteret Place by a police whistle. No doubt Mrs Arundel blew that from her car. Him being gone, Cray slunk out of Valerie's lily house – I showed you the side door, Bell, it opens on a passage where the cloak room is. The Arundel brought her car round, Cray helped her put the body in the car, covered it with the missin' rug, so it wouldn't show and came back to party via side door and cloak room. The Arundel then arrived by the front door. Either of 'em could easily get a bit torn off Valerie's blue dress to shove in the car, easily scratch the settee like the heels of the woman scratched the rug when they murdered her. When the one o'clock constable was due Cray barged out and got himself arrested, thus fakin' a perfect alibi for the murder of Mrs Arundel, then alive. After puttin' up a row with Valerie to make more evidence against her, the Arundel went off, dressed herself in dead sister's clothes, removed the rug from the body, proceeded to Killarney and became the sister. She is just like sister – to those who haven't had close ups of both. Cray was sweetly confident Valerie would swear he'd never left the party and Patten would back her through hell. Kindly nature, Cray's. Perfect trust in his friends. Patten took his good night walk with Valerie. They saw the car, knew it was Mrs Arundel's. They looked inside, Patten leavin' his fool prints on the door, and saw a dead woman. I should say he didn't recognise her. Not easy to see in the dark, not nice to investigate that face. They wouldn't think of it being Mrs Arundel as she'd only just left 'em. But there was a very dead woman in her car. Cray had behaved queer at the party, funking Valerie, lurking. They knew he might have slunk out and done the kill. They hated Mrs Arundel, they liked him, they knew she had him on a string. All they cared for was to save him. They left the woman for somebody else to find, and fixed up they'd give Cray his alibi, and Valerie came round bright and early to rub it in on me he was a poor, sick fellow under her eye all the time till arrested. Dear fools, Valerie and her Ned. Made for each other. Must have hit 'em cruel hard when they heard the dead woman was Mrs Arundel. And yet they stuck to their story. Very good effort. Bless 'em. Nice people. Hope you haven't charged 'em, Lomas?' Reggie smiled.

'We have not,' said Lomas with dignity. 'They were let go this morning.'

'Splendid. Not a blot on the official scutcheon. Now. I have my uses, Lomas.'

'Confound your impudence.' Lomas made a grimace. 'How did you know the Arundel woman had a sister?'

'By believin' evidence. Try sometime. I told you the dead woman was in good health, well preserved. Too good, too well for a woman who'd led a nasty life, as alleged of the Arundel. She shows wear and tear. Dead face so distorted, identification could only be from general likeness, hair, clothes and what not, and the identification was not made by intimates. So I wondered. I sent my chauffeur, Sam, to browse among the children of Carteret Place. Observant animals girl children. They told him Mrs Arundel wasn't always smart, quite shabby when she went on the buses. Some of 'em spotted her the day before descendin' from a Lewisham bus. Not the first time. Sam tried the Lewisham bus conductors, and heard of a lady like the Arundel who got on in those parts and got off at the stop by Carteret Square. Then the local milkman and postman gave him the glad news she was Mrs Jones, of Killarney. Quite the lady, kept herself to herself, most respectable, though only using a charwoman two days a week. Sam called as a tout and looked her over. Me too, from the adjacent aucubas. On which I 'phoned for the higher powers. There you are. All clear, as I said.'

'Is it?' Lomas put up his eyeglass. 'Why did Cray go to her?'

'My dear old thing!' Reggie stared back with large reproachful eyes. 'Use the evidence. Cray told you in his confession. He got a telegram: "Come Killarney." The Arundel had the wind up. Probably failed to like Sam's face. He will grin.'

'Failed to like Cray when he came,' Lomas answered. 'That's what broke her.'

'It could be,' Reggie murmured. 'Don't suppose he was comfortin'.'

'Who sent the telegram?' Lomas demanded.

'Oh my Lomas! Futile question. Answer obvious. Mrs Arundel.'

'She'll deny it.'

Over Reggie's face came a pensive smile. 'She may, yes. Nobody'll believe her.'

'Why should she telegraph? She was on the telephone.'

'Yet she couldn't get Cray? Nor Cray her? Only wrong numbers. Too bad.'

'The line's broken on the wall of the house, Reginald. Who did that?'

'Take the goods the gods provide. Telegram's all right. Pleasin' case.'

THE LONG DINNER

H. C. Bailey

'I dislike you,' said Mr Fortune. 'Some of the dirtiest linen I've seen.' He gazed morosely at the Chief of the Criminal Investigation Department.

'Quite,' Lomas agreed. 'Dirty fellow. What about those stains?'

'Oh, my dear chap!' Mr Fortune mourned. 'Paint. All sorts of paint. Also food and drink and assorted filth. Why worry me? What did you expect? Human gore?'

'I had no expectations,' said Lomas sweetly.

A certain intensity came into Mr Fortune's blue eyes. 'Yes. I hate you,' he murmured. 'Anything else you wanted to know?'

'A lot of things,' Lomas said. 'You're not useful, Reginald. I want to know what sort of fellow he was, and what's become of him.'

'He was an artist of dark complexion. He painted both in oils and water-colours. He lived a coarse and dissolute life, and had expensive tastes. What's become of him, I haven't the slightest idea. I should say he was on the way to the devil. What's it all about? Why this interest in the debauched artist?'

'Because the fellow's vanished,' said Lomas. 'He is a painter of sorts, as you say. Name—Derry Farquhar. He had a talent and a bit of success years ago, and he's gone downhill ever since. Not altogether unknown to the police—money under false pretences and that sort of thing—but never any clear case. Ten days ago a woman turned up to give information that Mr Derry Farquhar was missing. He had some money out of her—a matter of fifty pounds—three months ago. She don't complain of that. She was used to handing him donations—that kind of woman and that kind of man. What worries her is that, since this particular fifty pounds, he's faded out. And it is a queer case. He's lived these ten years in a rat-hole of a flat in Bloomsbury. He's not been seen there for months. That's unlike him. He's never been long away before. A regular London loafer. And his own money—he's got a little income from a trust—has piled up in the bank. August and September dividends untouched. That's absolutely unlike him. Besides that: one night about a fortnight ago—we can't fix the date—somebody was heard in the flat making a good deal of noise. When Bell went to have a look at things, he found the place in a devil of a mess, and a heap of foul linen. So we sent that to you.'

'Hoping for proof of bloodshed,' Reggie murmured. 'Hopeful fellow. Shirts extremely foul, but affordin' no evidence of foul play. Blood is absent. Almost the only substance that is.'

'So you don't believe there's anything in the case?'

'My dear chap! Oh, my dear chap,' Reggie opened large, plaintive eyes. 'Belief is a serious operation. I believe you haven't found anything. That's all. I should say you didn't look.'

'Thank you,' said Lomas acidly. 'Bell raked it all over' He spoke into the telephone, and Superintendent Bell arrived with a fat folder.

'Mr Fortune thinks you've missed something, Bell,' Lomas smiled.

'If there was anything any use, I have,' Bell said heavily. 'I'll be glad to hear what it is. Here's some photographs of the place, sir. And an inventory.'

'You might pick up a bargain, Reginald,' said Lomas, while Reggie, with a decent solemnity, perused the inventory and contemplated the photographs.

'Four oil paintings, fifteen water-colours. Unframed,' he read, and lifted a gaze of innocent enquiry to Bell.

'I'd call 'em clever, myself,' said Bell. 'Not nice, you know, but very bright and showy. Nudes of ladies, and that sort of thing. I should have thought he could have made a tidy living out of them. But a picture dealer that's seen 'em priced 'em at half a dollar each. Slick rubbish, he called 'em. I'm no hand at art. Anyway—it don't tell us anything.'

'I wouldn't say that. No,' Reggie murmured. 'Builds up the

character of Mr Farquhar for us. Person of no honour, even in his pot-boilin' art. However. Nothing else in the flat?'

'Some letters—mostly bills and duns. Nothing to show what he was up to. Nothing to work on.'

Reggie turned over the correspondence quickly. 'Yes. As you say.' He stopped at a crumpled, stained card. 'Where was this?'

'In a pocket of a dirty old sports coat,' Bell said. 'It's only a menu. I don't know why he kept it. Some faces drawn on the back. Perhaps he fancied 'em. No accounting for taste. Looks like drawing devils to me.'

'Rather diabolical, yes,' Reggie murmurd. 'Conventional devil. Mephistopheles in a flick.' The faces were sketched, in pencil, with a few accomplished strokes, but had no distinction: the same face in variations of grin and scowl and leer: a face of black brows, moustache, and pointed beard. 'Clever craftsman. Only clever.' He turned the card to the menu written on the front. 'My only aunt!' he moaned, and, in a hushed voice of awe read out:

DÎNER
Artichauts à l'Huile
Pommes de Terre à l'Huile
Porc frais froid aux Cornichons
Langouste Mayonnaise
Canard aux Navets
Omelette Rognons
Filet garni
Fromage à la Crème
Fruits, Biscuits

'Good Gad! Some dinner,' Lomas chuckled.

'I don't say I get it all,' Bell frowned. 'But what's it come to? He did himself well some time.'

'Well!' Reggie groaned. 'Oh, my dear chap! Artichokes in oil, cold pork, lobster, duck and turnips—and a kidney omelette and roast beef and trimmings.'

'I've got to own it wants a stomach,' said Bell gloomily. 'What then?'

'Died of indigestion,' said Lomas. 'Or committed suicide in the pangs. Very natural. Very just. There you are, Bell. Mr Fortune has solved the case.'

'I was taking it seriously myself,' Bell glowered at them.

'Oh, my Bell!' Reggie sighed. 'So was I.' He turned on Lomas. 'Incurably flippant mind, your mind. This is the essential fact. Look for Mr Farquhar in Brittany.'

Bell breathed hard. 'How do you get to that, sir?'

'No place but a Brittany inn ever served such a dinner.'

Bell rubbed his chin. 'I see. I don't know Brittany myelf, I'm glad to say. I got to own I never met a dinner like it.' He looked at Lomas. 'That means putting it back on the French.'

'Quite,' Lomas smiled. 'Brilliant thought, Reginald. Would you be surprised to hear that Paris is asking us to look for Mr Derry Farquhar in England?'

'Well, well,' Reggie surveyed him with patient contempt. 'Another relevant fact which you didn't mention. Also indicatin' an association of your Mr Farquhar with France.'

'If you like,' Lomas shrugged. 'But the point is they are sure he's here. Dubois is coming over today. I'm taking him to dine at the club. You'd better join us.'

'Oh, no. No,' Reggie said quickly. 'Dubois will dine with me. You bring him along. Your club dinner would destroy his faith in the English intelligence. If any. And I like Dubois. Pleasant to discuss the case with a serious mind. Good-bye. Half past eight.' . . .

With a superior English smile, Lomas sat back and watched Reggie and Dubois consume that fantasia on pancakes, Crêpes Joan, which Reggie invented as an expression of the way of his wife with her husband. . . .

Dubois wiped his flowing moustaches. 'My homage,' he said reverently.

By way of a devilled biscuit, they came to another claret. Dubois looked and smelt and tasted, and his eyes returned thanks. 'Try it with a medlar,' Reggie purred.

'You are right. There is no fruit better with wine.'

They engaged upon a ritual of ecstasy while Lomas gave himself a glass of port and lit a cigarette. At that, Reggie gave a reproachful stare. 'My only aunt! Forgive him, Dubois. He's mere modern English.'

'I pity profoundly,' Dubois sighed. 'A bleak life. This is a great wine, my friend. Of Pauillac, I think, eh? Of the last century?'

'Quite good, yes,' Reggie purred. 'Mouton Rothschild 1900.'

Dubois's large face beamed. 'Aha. Not so bad for poor old Dubois.'

They proceeded to a duet on claret. . . .

Lomas became restive. 'This unanimity is touching. Now you've embraced each other all over, we might come to business and see if you can keep it up.'

Dubois turned to him with a gesture of deprecation. 'Pardon, my friend. Have no fear. We agree always. But I will not delay you. The affair is, after all, very simple—'

'Quite,' Lomas smiled. 'Tell Fortune. He has his own ideas about it.'

'Aha,' Dubois's eyebrows went up. 'I shall be grateful. Well, I begin, then, with Max Weber. He is what you call a profiteer, but, after all, a good fellow. It is a year ago he married a pretty lady. She was by courtesy an actress, the beautiful Clotilde. One has nothing else against her. They live together very happily in an apartment of luxury. Two weeks ago, they find that some of her jewels, which she had in her bedroom, are gone. Not all that Weber had given her, the most valuable are at the bank, but diamonds worth five hundred thousand francs. Weber comes to the Sûreté and makes a complaint. What do we find? The servants, they have been with Weber many years, they are spoilt, they are careless; but dishonest—I think not. There is no sign of a burglary. But the day before the jewels were missed a man came to the Weber apartment who asked for Madame Weber and was told she was not at home. That was true in fact, but, also, Weber's man did not like his look. A *gouape* of the finest water—that is the description. What you call a blackguard, is it not? The man was shabby but showy; he resembled exactly a loafer in the Quartier Latin, an artist *décavé*—how do you say that.'

'On his uppers. Yes. Still more interesting. But not an identification, Dubois.'

'Be patient still. You see—here is a type which might well have known *la belle* Clotilde before she was Madame Weber. Very well. This gentleman, when he was refused at the Weber door, he did not go far away. We have a *concierge* who saw him loitering till the afternoon at least. In the afternoon the Weber servants take their ease. The man went to a café—he admits it—one woman calls on a friend here, another there. What more easy than for the blackguard artist to enter, to take the jewel case, to hop it, as you say.'

'We do. Yes.'

'Well, then, I begin from a description of Monsieur the Blackguard. It is not so bad. A man who is plump and dark, with little dark whiskers, who has front teeth which stand out, who walks like a bird running, with short steps that go pit pat. He speaks French well enough, but not like a Frenchman. He wears clothes of orange colour, cut very loose, and a soft black hat of wide brim. Then I find that a man like this got into the night train from the Gare St Lazare for Dieppe—that is, you see, to come back to England by the cheap way. Very well. We have worked in the Quartier Latin, we find that a man like this was seen a day or two in some of the cafés. They remember him well, because they knew him ten years ago when he was a student. They are like that, these old folks of the Quartier—it pays. Then his name was Farquhar, Derek Farquhar, an Englishman.' Dubois twirled his moustaches. 'So you see, my friend, I dare to trouble Mr Lomas to find me in England this Farquhar.'

'Yes. Method quite sound,' Reggie mumbled. 'As a method.'

'My poor Reginald,' Lomas laughed. 'What a mournful, reluctant confession! You've hurt him, Dubois. He was quite sure Mr Farquhar was traversing the wilds of Brittany.'

'Aha,' Dubois put up his eyebrows, and made a gesture of respect to Reggie. 'My dear friend, never I consult you but I find you see farther than I. Tell me then.'

'Oh, no. No. Don't see it all,' Reggie mumbled, and told him of the menu of the long dinner.

'Without doubt that dinner was served in Brittany,' Dubois nodded. 'I agree, it is probable he had been there not so long ago. But what of that? He was a painter, he had studied in France, and Brittany is always full of painters.'

'Yes. You're neglectin' part of the evidence. Faces on the back of the menu.' He took out his pocketbook, and sketched the black-browed, black-bearded countenance. 'Like that.'

'The devil,' said Dubois.

'As you say. Devil of opera and fancy ball. The ordinary Mephistopheles. Associated by your Mr Farquhar with Brittany.'

'My dear Fortune!' Dubois's big face twisted into a quizzical smile. 'You are very subtle. Me, I find this is to make too much of little things. After all, drawing devils, it is common sport—you find devils all over our comic papers—a devil and a pretty lady—and he drew pretty ladies often, you say, this Farquhar—and this is a very common devil.'

'Yes, rational criticism,' Reggie murmured, looking at him with dreamy eyes. 'You're very rational, Dubois. However. Any association of the Webers with Brittany?'

'Oh, my friend!' Dubois smiled indulgently. 'None at all. And when they go out of Paris, it is to Monte Carlo, to Aix, not to rough it in Brittany, you may be sure. No. You shall forgive me, but I find nothing in your menu to change my mind. I must look for my Farquhar here.' He shook his head sadly at Reggie. 'I am desolated that you do not agree.' He turned to Lomas. 'But this is the only way, *hein*?'

'Absolutely. There's no other line at all,' said Lomas, with satisfaction. 'Don't let Fortune worry you. He lives to see what isn't there. Wonderful imagination.'

'My only aunt!' Reggie moaned. 'Not me, no. No imagination at all. Only simple faith in facts. You people ignore 'em when they're not rational. Unscientific and superstitious. However. Let's pretend and see what we get. Go your own way.'

'One does as one can,' Dubois shrugged.

'Quite. Fortune is never content with the possible. We must work it out here. I've put things in train for you. We have a copy of Farquhar's photograph. That's been circulated with description, and there's a general warning out for him and the jewels. We're combing out all his friends and his usual haunts.'

'"So runs my dream, but what am I?"' Reggie murmured. '"An infant cryin' in the night. An infant cryin' for the light—" Well, well. Are we downhearted? Yes. A little Armagnac would be grateful and comfortin'.' He turned the conversation imperatively to the qualities of that liqueur, and Dubois was quick with respectful responses. Lomas relapsed upon Olympian disdain and whisky and soda.

When he took Dubois away, 'Fantastic fellow, Fortune, isn't he?' Lomas smiled. 'Mind of the first order, but never content to use it.'

'An artist, my friend,' said Dubois. 'A great artist. He feels life. We think about it.'

'Damme, you don't believe he's right about this Brittany guess?'

'What do I know?' Dubois shrugged. 'It means nothing. Therefore it is nothing for us. However, one must confess, he is disconcerting, your Mr Fortune. He makes one always doubt.'

This, when he heard of it, Reggie considered the greatest compliment which he ever had, except from his wife. He also thinks it deserved. . . .

Some days later he was engaged upon the production in his marionette theatre of the tragedy of *Don Juan*, lyrics by Lord Byron, prose and music by Mr Fortune, when the telephone called him from a poignant passage on the rejection of his hero by hell.

'Yes, Fortune speaking. "Between two worlds life hovers like a star." Perhaps you didn't know that, Lomas. "How little do we know that which we are." Discovery of the late Lord Byron. I'm settin' it to music. Departmental ditty for the Criminal Investigation Department. I—'

'Could you listen for a moment?' said Lomas sweetly. 'You might be interested.'

'Not likely, no. However. What's worryin' you?'

'Nothing, except sympathy for you, Reginald. I'm afraid you'll suffer. To break it gently, we've traced Farquhar. But not in Brittany, Reginald.'

Reggie remained calm. 'No. Of course not,' he moaned. 'You weren't trying. I don't want to hear what you've missed. Takes too long.'

A sound of mockery came over the wire. 'Are you ever wrong, Reginald? No. It's always the other fellow. But the awkward fact is, Farquhar hadn't gone to Brittany, he'd gone to Westshire. So that was the only place we could find him. We have our limitations.'

'You have. Yes. *C'est brutal, mais ça marche.* You're clumsy, but you move—sometimes—like the early cars. What has he got to say for himself?'

'I don't know. We haven't put our hands on him yet. We— what?'

'Pardon me. It was only emotion. A sob of reverence. Oh, my Lomas. You found the only place you could find him, so you haven't found him. The perfect official. No results, but always the superior person.'

'Results quite satisfactory,' Lomas snapped. 'We had a clear identification. He's been staying at Lyncombe. He's bolted again. No doubt found we were on his track. But we shall get him. They're combing out the district. Bell's gone down with Dubois.'

'Splendid. Always shut the stable door when the horse has been removed. I'll go too. I like watching that operation. Raises my confidence in the police force.' . . .

As the moon rose over the sea, Reggie's car drove into Lyncombe. It is a holiday town of some luxury. The affronts to nature of its blocks of hotel and twisting roads of villas for the opulent retired have not yet been able to spoil all the beauty of cliff and cove.

When Reggie saw it, the banal buildings and the headlands were mingled in moonlight to make a dreamland, and the sea was a black mystery with a glittering path on it.

He went to the newest hotel, he bathed well and dined badly, and, as he sat smoking his consolatory pipe on a balcony where the soft air smelt of chrysanthemums and the sea, Dubois came to him with Bell.

'Aha.' Dubois spoke. 'You have not gone to Brittany then, my friend?'

'No. No. Followin' the higher intelligence. I have a humble mind. And where have you got to?'

'We have got to the tracks of Farquhar, there is no doubt of that. What is remarkable, he had registered in his own name at the hotel, and the people there they recognise his photograph—they are sure of it. In fact, it is a face to be sure of, a rabbit face.'

'The identification's all right,' Bell grunted. 'The devil of it is, he's gone again, Mr Fortune. He went in a hurry too. Left all his traps behind, such as they were. The hotel people think he was just bilking them. He'd been a matter of ten days and not paid anything, and his baggage is worth about nothing—a battered old suitcase and some duds fit for the dust-bin.'

'Oh, Peter!' Reggie moaned. 'No, Bell, no. I haven't got to look at his shirts again?'

'I'm not asking you, sir. There's no sort of reason to think there was anything done to him. He just went out and didn't come back. Three days ago. I don't see any light at all. What he was doing here, beats me. You can say he was hiding with the swag he got in Paris. But then, why did he register in his own name? Say he was just a silly ass—you do get that kind of amateur thief. But what has he bolted for? He couldn't have had any suspicions we were on to him. We weren't, at the time he faded out.'

'But, my friend, you go too fast,' said Dubois. 'From you, no, he could not have had any alarm. But there is the other end—Paris. It is very possible that a friend in Paris warned him the police were searching for him.'

'All right,' Bell grunted. 'I give you that. Why would he make the hotel people notice him by bolting without paying his bill? Silly again. Sheer silly. He'd got a pot of money, if he did have the jewels, like you say. Going off without paying 'em just sent them to inform the police quick.'

'That is well argued. You have an insight, a power of mind, my friend.' Dubois's voice was silky. 'But what have we then? It is quite natural that Farquhar should disappear again, it is not natural that he should disappear like this. For me, I confess I do not find myself able to form an idea of Farquhar. That he is the type to rob such a woman as Clotilde, there is evidence enough—he had the knowledge, he had the opportunity. So far, there are a thousand cases like it. But that he should then retire to such a paradise of the bourgeois, that is not like his type at all.'

'That's right,' said Bell. 'No sense in it anyway.'

'No. As you say,' Reggie murmured. 'That struck me. Happy to agree with everybody. We don't know anything about anything.'

'*Bigre!* You go a little strong,' Dubois rumbled. 'Come, there is at least a connection with Clotilde, and her jewels are gone. Be sure of that. Weber is an honest man—except in business. And what, now, is your hypothesis? You said look for him in Brittany. This at least is certain—he had not gone there. What the devil should he have to do with this so correct Lyncombe? As much as with our rough Brittany.'

'Yes. Quite obscure. I haven't the slightest idea what he's been doing. However. Are we downhearted? No. We're in touch with the fundamental problem now. Why does Mr Farquhar deal with Brittany and Clotilde and Lyncombe? First method of solution clearly indicated. Find out what he did do in Lyncombe. That ought to be an easy one, Bell. He must have been noticed. He'd be conspicuous in this correct place. Good night.'

The next day he sat upon the same balcony, spreading the first scone of his tea with clotted cream and blackberry jelly, when the two returned.

'What! Have you not moved since last night?' Dubois made a grimace at him.

'My dear chap! Just walked all along one of the bays. And back. Great big bay. Exercise demanded by impatient and fretful brain. Rest is better. Have a splitter. They're too heavy. But the cream is sound.'

Dubois shuddered. 'Brr! You are a wonderful animal. Me, I am only human. But Bell has news for you. Tell him, old fellow.'

'It's like this,' Bell explained. 'About a week ago—that's three or four days before he disappeared, we can't fix the date nearer—Farquhar went to call at one of the big houses here. There's no doubt about that. It's rather like the Paris case. He was seen loafing round before and after—as you said, he's the sort of chap to get noticed. The house he went to belongs to an old gentleman—Mr Lane Hudson. Lived here for years. Very rich, they say. Made his money in South Wales, and came here when he retired. Well, he's eighty or more; he's half paralysed—only gets about his house and grounds in a wheeled chair. I've seen him; I've had a talk with him. His mind's all right. He looks like a mummy, only a bit plumped out. Sort of yellow, leathery face that don't change or move. Sits in his chair looking at nothing, and talks soft and thick. He tells me he never heard of Farquhar: didn't so much as know Farquhar had been to his house: that's quite in order, it's his rule that the servants tell anybody not known he's not well enough to see people, and I don't blame him. I wouldn't want strangers to come and look at me if I was like he is. I gave him an idea of the sort of fellow Farquhar was, and watched him pretty close, but he didn't turn a hair. He just said again he had no knowledge of any such person, and I believe him. He wasn't interested. He told me the fellow had no doubt come begging for money; he was much exposed to that sort of thing—we ought to stop it—and good day Mr Superintendent. Anyhow, it's certain Farquhar didn't see him. The old butler and the nurse bear that out, and they never heard of Farquhar before. The butler saw him and turned him away—had a spot of bother over it, but didn't worry. Like the old man, he says they do have impudent beggars now and then. So here's another nice old dead end.'

'Yes. As you say. Rather weird isn't it? The flamboyant

debauched Farquhar knockin' at the door—to get to a paralysed old rich man who never heard of him. I wonder. Curious selection of people to call on by our Mr Farquhar. A pretty lady of Paris who's married money and settled down on it; a rich old Welshman who's helpless on the edge of the grave. And neither of 'em sees Mr Farquhar—accordin' to the evidence—neither will admit to knowin' anything about him. Very odd. Yes.' Reggie turned large, melancholy eyes on Dubois. 'Takes your fancy, what? The black-guard artist knockin', knockin', and, upstairs, a mummy of a man helpless in his chair.'

'Name of a name!' Dubois rumbled. 'It is fantasy pure. One sees such things in dreams. This has no more meaning.'

'No. Not to us. But it happened. Therefore it had a cause. Mr Lane Hudson lives all alone, what—except for servants?'

'That's right, sir,' Bell nodded. 'He's been a widower this long time. Only one child—daughter—and there's a grandson, quite a kid. Daughter's been married twice—first to a chap called Tracy, now to a Mr Bernal—son by the first marriage, no other children.'

'You have taken pains, Bell,' Reggie smiled.

'Well, I got everything I could think of,' said Bell, with gloomy satisfaction. 'Not knowing what I wanted. And there's nothing I do want in what I've got. The Bernals come here fairly regular—Mr and Mrs Bernal, not the child—they've been staying with the old man just now. Usual autumn visit. They were there when Far-quhar called, and after—didn't go away till last Wednesday; that's before Farquhar disappeared, you see, the day before. Farquhar didn't ask for the Bernals, and they didn't see him at all, the servants say. So there you are. The Bernals don't link up any way. That peters out, like everything else.'

'Yes. Taken a lot of pains,' Reggie murmured.

'What would you have?' Dubois shrugged. 'To amass useless knowledge—it is our only method; one is condemned to it. Ours is a slow trade, my friend. We gather facts and facts and facts, and so, if we are lucky, eliminate ninety-nine of the hundred and use, at last, one.'

'Yes. As you say,' Reggie mumbled. 'Where do the Bernals live, Bell?'

'In France, sir,' said Bell, and Reggie opened his eyes.

'Aha!' Dubois made a grimace, and pointed a broad finger at him. 'There, my friend. The one grand fact, is it not? In France! And Brittany is in France! But alas, my dear Fortune, they do not live in Brittany! Far from it. They live in the south, near Cannes; they have lived there—what do I know?—since they were married, *hein*?' he turned to Bell.

'That's right,' Bell grunted. 'Lady set up house there with her first husband. He had to live in the south of France—gassed in the war.'

'You see?' Dubois smiled. 'It is still the useless knowledge. And your vision of Brittany, my friend, it has no substance still.'

'I wonder,' Reggie mumbled, and sank deep in his chair. . . .

He is, even without hope, conscientious. That night he examined another set of Farquhar's dirty linen, but neither in that nor the rest of the worthless luggage found any information. Prodded by him, Bell enquired of the Hudson household where the Bernals were to be found, but could obtain only the address of their Cannes villa, for they were reported to be going back by car. Dubois was persuaded to telegraph Cannes and received the reply that the Bernal villa was shut up; monsieur and madame were away motoring, and their boy at school—what school nobody knew.

'Then what?' Dubois summed up. 'Nothing to do.'

'Not tonight, no,' Reggie yawned. 'I'm going to bed.'

'To dream of Brittany, *hein*?'

'I never dream,' said Reggie, with indignation. . . .

But he was waked in the night. He rubbed his eyes and looked up to see Dubois's large face above him. 'Oh, my hat,' he moaned. 'What is it? Why won't it wait?'

'Courage, my friend. They have found him. At least, they think so. Some fishermen, going out yesterday evening, they found a body on the rocks at what they call Granny's Cove. Come. The brave Bell wants you to see.'

'Bless him,' Reggie groaned, and rolled out of bed. 'What is life that one should seek it? I ask you.' And, slipping clothes on him, swiftly he crooned, '"Three fishers went sailin' out into the west, out into the west, as the sun went down"—and incredibly caught the incredible Farquhar.'

'You are right,' Dubois nodded. 'Nothing clear, nothing sure. The more it changes, the more it is the same, this accursed case. It has no shape; there is no reason in it.'

'Structure not yet determined. No,' Reggie mumbled, parting his hair, for he will always be neat. 'We're not bein' very clever. Ought to be able to describe the whole thing from available evidence of its existence. Same like inferrin' the age of reptiles from a fossil or two—"dragons of the prime, tearin' each other in the slime, were mellow music unto him." Yes. The struggle for life of the reptiles might be mellow music compared to the diversions of Mr Farquhar and friends. Progressive world, Dubois.'

'Name of a dog!' Dubois exclaimed. 'When you are philosophic, my stomach turns over. What is in your mind?'

'Feelin' of impotence. Very uncomfortable,' Reggie moaned, and muffled himself to the chin and made haste out.

In the mortuary Bell introduced them to a body covered by a sheet. 'Here you are, sir.' He stepped aside. 'The clothes seem to be Farquhar's clothes all right. Sort of orange tweed and green flannel trousers. But I don't know about the man.'

Reggie drew back the sheet from what was left of a face.

'*Saprelotte!*' Dubois rumbled. 'The fish have bitten.'

'Well, I leave it to you,' said Bell thickly. . . .

Under a sunlit breeze the sea was dancing bright, the mists flying inland from the valleys to the dim bank of the moor, when Reggie came out again.

He drove back to his hotel, and shaved and bathed and rang up the police station. Bell and Dubois arrived to find him in his room, eating with appetite grilled ham and buttered eggs.

'My envy; all my envy,' Dubois pulled a face. 'This is greatness. The English genius at the highest.'

'Oh, no. No,' Reggie protested. 'Natural man. Well. The corpse is that of Mr Farquhar as per invoice. Prominent teeth not impaired by activities of the lobsters. Some other contours still visible. The marmalade—thanks. Yes. Hair, colourin', size and so forth agree. Mr Farquhar's been in the sea three or four days. Correspondin' with date of disappearance. Cause of death, drowning. Severe contusions on head and body, inflicted before death. Possibly by blows, possibly by fall. Might have fallen from cliff; might have been dashed on rocks by sea. No certainty to be obtained. That's the medical evidence.'

'You are talking!' Dubois exclaimed. '*Flute!* There we are again. Whatever arrives, it will mean nothing for us. Here is murder, suicide, accident—what you please.'

'I wonder.' Reggie began to peel an apple. 'Anything in his pockets, Bell?'

'A lot of money, sir. Nothing else. The notes are all sodden, but it's a good wad, and some are fifties. Might be five or six hundred pounds. So he wasn't robbed.'

'And then?' said Dubois. 'It is not enough for all the jewels of Clotilde, but it is something in hand. Will you tell me what the devil he was doing at the door of this paralysed millionaire? It means nothing, none of it.'

'No. Still amassin' useless knowledge, as you were sayin'.' Reggie gazed at Dubois with dreamy eyes. 'I should say that's what we came here for. Don't seem the right place, does it? However. As we are here, let's try and get a little more before departure. Usin' the local talent. Bell—your fishermen—have they got any ideas where a fellow would tumble into the sea to be washed up into Granny's Cove?'

'Ah.' Bell was pleased. 'I have been asking about that, sir. Supposing he got in from the land, they think it would be somewhere round by Shag Nose. That's a bit o' cliff west o' the town. I'm having men search round and enquire. But the scent's pretty cold by now.'

'Yes. As you say,' Reggie sighed. His eyes grew large and melancholy. 'Is it far?' he said, in a voice of fear.

'Matter of a mile or two.'

'Oh, my Bell.' Reggie groaned. He pushed back his chair. He rose stiffly. 'Come on.'

Shag Nose is a headland from which dark cliffs fall sheer. Below them stretches seaward a ridge of rocks, which stand bare some way out at low tide, and in the flood make a turmoil of eddies and broken water.

The top of the headland is a flat of springy turf, in which are many tufts of thrift and cushions of stunted gorse.

'Brr. It is bleak,' Dubois complained. 'Will you tell me why Farquhar should come here? He was not—how do you say?—a man for the great open spaces.'

'Know the answer, don't you?' Reggie mumbled.

'Perfectly. He came to meet somebody in secret who desired to make an end of him. Very well. But who then? Not the paralysed one. Not the son-in-law either. It is in evidence that the son-in-law was gone before Farquhar disappeared.'

'That's right. I verified that,' Bell grunted. 'Bernal and his wife left the night before.'

'There we are again,' Dubois shrugged. 'Nothing means anything. For certain, it is not a perfect alibi. They went by car; they could come back and not be seen. But it is an alibi that will stand unless you have luck, which you have not yet, my dear Bell, God knows.'

'Not an easy case. No,' Reggie murmured. 'However. Possibilities not yet examined. Lyncombe's on the coast. Had you noticed that? I wonder if any little boat from France came in while Farquhar was still alive.'

Dubois laughed. Dubois clapped him on the shoulder. 'Magnificent! How you are resolute, my friend. Always the great idea! A boat from Brittany, *hein*? That would solve everything. The good Farquhar was so kind as to come here and meet it and be killed by the brave Bretons. And the paralysed millionaire, he was merely a diversion to pass the time.'

'Yes. We are not amused,' Reggie moaned. 'You're in such a

hurry. Bell—what's the local talent say about the tide? When was high water on the night Farquhar disappeared?'

'Not till the early morning, sir. Tide was going out from about three in the afternoon onwards.'

'I see. At dusk and after, that reef o' rocks would be comin' out of the water. Assumin' he went over the cliff in the dark or twilight, he'd fall on the rocks.'

'That's right. Of course he might bounce into the sea. But I've got a man or two down there searching the shore and the cliff-side.'

'Good man.' Reggie smiled, and wandered away to the cliff edge.

'Yes. It is most correct,' Dubois shrugged. 'I should do it, I avow. But also I should expect nothing, nothing. After all, we are late. We arrive late at everything.'

Reggie turned and stared at him. 'I know. That's what I'm afraid of,' he mumbled.

He wandered to and fro about the ground near the cliff edge, and found nothing which satisfied him, and at last lay down on his stomach where a jutting of the headland gave him a view of the cliffs on either side.

Two men scrambled about over the rocks below, scanning the cliff face, prying into every crevice they could reach . . . one of them vanished under an overhanging ledge, appeared again, working round it, was lost in a cleft . . . when he came out he had something in his hand.

'Name of a pipe!' Dubois rumbled. 'Is it possible we have luck at last?'

'No.' Reggie stood up. 'Won't be luck, whatever it is. Reward of virtue. Bell's infinite capacity for takin' pains.' . . .

A breathless policeman reached the top of the cliff, and held out a sodden book. 'That's the only perishing thing there is down there, sir,' he panted. 'Not a trace of nothing else.'

Bell gave it to Reggie. It was a sketch-book of the size to slide into a man's pocket. The first leaf bore, in a flamboyant scrawl, the name Derek Farquhar.

'Ah. That fixes it, then,' said Bell. 'He did go over this cliff, and his sketch-book came out of his pocket as he bounced on the ledges.'

'Very well,' Dubois shrugged. 'We know now as much as we guessed. Which means nothing.'

Reggie sat down and began to separate the book's wet pages.

Farquhar had drawn, in pencil, notes rather than sketches at first, scraps of face and figure and scene which took his unholy fancy, a drunken girl, a nasty stage dance, variations of impropriety. Then came some parades of men and women bathing, not less unpleasant, but more studied. 'Aha! Here is something seen at least,' said Dubois.

'Yes, I think so,' Reggie murmured, and turned the page.

The next sketch showed children dancing—small boys and girls. Some touch of cruelty was in the drawing—they were made to look ungainly—but it had power; it gave them an intensity of frail life which was at once pathetic and grotesque. They danced round a giant statue—a block in which the shape of a woman was burlesqued, hideously fat and thin, with a flat, foolish face. There were no clothes on it, but rough lines which might be girdle and necklace.

'What the devil!' Dubois exclaimed. 'This is an oddity. He discovers he had a talent, the animal.'

Reggie did not answer. For a moment more he gazed at the children and the statue, and he shivered, then he turned the other pages of the book. There were some notes of faces, then several satires on the respectability of Lyncombe—the sea front, with nymphs in Bath chairs propelled by satyrs and satyrs propelled by nymphs. He turned back to the dancing children and the giant female statue, and stared at it, and his round face was pale. 'Yes. Farquhar had talent,' he said. 'Played the devil with it all his life. And yet it works on the other side. What's the quickest way to Brittany? London and then Paris by air. Come on.'

Dubois swore by a paper bag and caught him up. 'What, then? How do you find your Brittany again in this?'

'The statue,' Reggie snapped. 'Sort of statue you see in Brittany. Nowhere else. He didn't invent that out of his dirty mind. He'd seen it. It meant something to him. I should say he'd seen the children too.'

'You go beyond me,' said Dubois. 'Well, it is not the first time. A statue of Brittany, eh? You mean the old things they have among the standing stones and the menhirs and dolmens. A primitive goddess. The devil! I do not see our Farquhar interested in antiquities. But it is the more striking that he studied her. I give you that. And the children? I will swear he was not a lover of children.'

'No. He wasn't. That came out in the drawing. Not a nice man. It pleased him to think of children dancin' round the barbarous female.'

'I believe you,' said Dubois. 'The devil was in that drawing.'

'Yes. Devilish feelin'. Yes. And yet it's going to help. Because the degenerate fellow had talent. Not wholly a bad world.'

'Optimist. Be it so. But what can you make the drawing mean, then?'

'I haven't the slightest idea,' Reggie mumbled. 'Place of child life in the career of the late Farquhar very obscure. Only trace yet discovered, the Bernals have a child. No inference justified. I'm going to Brittany. I'm goin' to look for traces round that statue. And meanwhile—Bell has to find out if a French boat has been in to Lyncombe—you'd better set your people findin' the Bernals—with child. Have the Webers got a child?'

'Ah, no.' Dubois laughed. 'The beautiful Clotilde, she is not that type.'

'Pity. However. You might let me have a look at the Webers as I go through Paris.'

'With all my heart,' said Dubois. 'You understand, my friend, you command me. I see nothing, nothing at all, but I put myself in your hand.' He made a grimace. 'In fact there is nothing else to do. It is an affair for inspiration. I never had any.'

'Nor me, no,' Reggie was indignant. 'My only aunt! Inspired! I am not! I believe in evidence. That's all. You experts are so superior.' . . .

Next morning they sat in the *salon* of the Webers. It was overwhelming with the worst magnificence of the Second Empire—mirrors and gilding, marble and malachite and lapis lazuli. But the Webers, entering affectionately arm in arm, were only magnificent in their opulent proportions. Clotilde, a dark full-blown creature, had nothing more than powder on her face, no jewels but a string of pearls, and the exuberance of her shape was modified by a simple black dress. Weber's clumsy bulk was all in black too.

They welcomed Dubois with open arms; they talked together. What had he to tell them? They had heard that the cursed Farquhar had been discovered dead in England—it was staggering; had anything been found of the jewels?

Nothing, in effect, Dubois told them. Only, Farquhar had more money than such an animal ought to have. It was a pity.

Clotilde threw up her hands. Weber scolded.

Dubois regretted—but what to do? They must admit one had been quick, very quick, to trace Farquhar. They would certainly compliment his *confrère* from England—that produced perfunctory bows. What the English police asked—and they were right—it was could one learn anything of who had worked with Farquhar, why had he come to the apartment Weber?

The Webers were contemptuous. What use to ask such a question? One had not an acquaintance with thieves. As to why he came, why he picked out them to rob—a thief must go where there was something to steal—and they—well, one was known a little. Weber smirked at his wife, and she smiled at him.

'For sure. Everyone knows monsieur—and madame.' Dubois bowed. 'But I seek something more.'

They stormed. It was not to be supposed they should know anything of such a down-at-heel.

'Oh, no. No,' said Reggie quickly. 'But in the world of business'—he looked at Weber—'in the world of the theatre'—he looked at Clotilde—'the fellow might have crossed your path, what?'

That was soothing. They agreed the thing was possible. How could one tell? They chattered of the detrimentals they remembered—to no purpose.

Under plaintive looks from Reggie, Dubois broke that off with a brusque departure. When they were outside—'Well, you have met them!' Dubois shrugged. 'And if they are anything which is not ordinary I did not see it.'

Reggie gazed at him with round reproachful eyes. 'They were in mourning,' he moaned. 'You never told me that. Were they in mourning when you saw 'em before?'

'But yes,' Dubois frowned. 'Yes, certainly. What is the matter? Did you think they had put on mourning for the animal Farquhar?'

'My dear chap! Oh, my dear chap,' Reggie sighed. 'Find out why they are in mourning. Quietly, quite quietly. Good-bye. Meet you at the station.' . . .

The night express to Nantes and Quimper drew out of Paris. They ate a grim and taciturn dinner. They went back to the sleeping car and shut themselves in Reggie's compartment. 'Well, I have done my work,' said Dubois. 'The Webers are in mourning for their nephew. A child of ten, whom Weber would have made his heir—his sister's son.'

'A child,' Reggie murmured. 'How did he die?'

'It was not in Brittany, my friend,' Dubois grinned. 'Besides it is not mysterious. He died at Fontainebleau, in August, of diphtheria. They had the best doctors of Paris. There you are again. It means nothing.'

'I wonder,' Reggie mumbled. 'Any news of the Bernals?'

'It appears they have passed through Touraine. If it is they, there was no child with them. Have no fear, they are watched for. One does not disappear in France.'

'You think not? Well, well. Remains the Bernal child. Not yet known to be dead. Of diphtheria or otherwise! I did a job o' work too. Talked to old Huet at the Institut. You know—the prehistoric man. He says Farquhar's goddess is the Woman of Sarn. Recognised her at once. She stands on about the last western hill in France. Weird sort o' place, Huet says. And he can't imagine why

Farquhar thought of children dancin' round her. The people are taught she's of the devil.'

'But you go on to see her?' Dubois made a grimace. 'The fixed idea.'

'No. Rational inference. Farquhar thought of her with children. And there's a child dead—and another child we can't find—belongin' to the people linked with Farquhar. I go on.'

'To the land's end—to the end of the world—and beyond. For your faith in yourself. My dear Fortune, you are sublime. Well, I follow you. Poor old Dubois. Sancho Panza to your Don Quixote, *hein?*' . . .

They came out of the train to a morning of soft sunshine and mellow ocean air. The twin spires of Quimper rose bright among their minarets, its sister rivers gleamed, and the wooded hill beyond glowed bronze. Dubois bustled away from breakfast to see officials. 'Don Quixote is a law to himself, but Sancho had better be correct, my friend.'

'Yes, rather,' Reggie mumbled, from a mouth full of honey. 'Conciliate the authorities. Liable to want 'em.'

'Always the optimist, my Quixote.'

'No. No. Only careful. Don't tell 'em anything.'

'Name of a name!' Dubois exploded. 'That is necessary, that warning. I have so much to tell!'

In an hour, they were driving away from Quimper, up over high moorland of heather and gorse and down again to a golden bay and a fishing village of many boats, then on westward, with glimpses of sea on either hand. There was never a tree, only, about the stone walls which divided the waves of bare land into a draught-board of little fields, thick growth of bramble and gorse. Beyond the next village, with its deep inlet of a harbour, the fields merged into moor again, and here and there rose giant stones, in line, in circle, and solitary.

'Brrr,' Dubois rumbled. 'Tombs or temples, what you please, it was a gaunt religion which put them up here on this windy end of the earth.'

The car stopped, the driver turned in his seat and pointed, and said he could drive no nearer, but that was the Woman of Sarn. 'She is lonely,' Dubois shrugged. 'There is no village near, my lad?'

'There is Sarn.' The driver pointed towards the southern sea. 'But it is nothing.'

Reggie plodded away through the heather. 'Well, this is hopeful, is it not?' Dubois caught him up. 'When we find her, what have we found? An idol in the desert. But you will go on to the end, my Quixote. Forward, then.'

They came to the statue, and stood, for its crude head rose high above theirs, looking up at it. 'And we have found it, one must avow,' Dubois shrugged. 'This is the lady Farquhar drew, devil a doubt. But, *saperlipopette*, she is worse here than on paper. She is real; she is a brute—all that there is of the beast in woman, emerging from the shapeless earth.'

'Inhuman and horrid human, yes,' Reggie murmured. 'Cruelty of life. Yes. He knew about that, the fellow who made her, poor beggar. So did Farquhar.'

'I believe it! But do you ask me to believe little children come and dance round this horror. Ah, no!'

'Oh, no. No. That never happened. Not in our time. Point of interest is, Farquhar thought it fittin' they should. Very interestin' point.' Reggie gave another look at the statue, and walked on towards the highest point of the moor.

From that he could see the tiny village of Sarn, huddled in a cove, the line of dark cliff, a long rampart against the Atlantic. Below the cliff top he made out a white house, of some size, which seemed to stand alone.

His face had a dreamy placidity as he came back to Dubois. 'Well, well. Not altogether desert,' he murmured. 'Something quite residential over there. Let's wander.'

They struck southward towards the sea. As they approached the white house, they saw that it was of modern pattern—concrete, in simple proportions, with more window than wall. Its site was well chosen, in a little hollow beneath the highest of the cliff, sheltered, yet high enough for a far prospect, taking all the southern sun.

'Of the new ugliness, eh?' said Dubois, whose taste is for elaboration in all things. 'All the last fads. It should be a sanatorium, not a house.'

'One of the possibilities, yes.' Reggie went on fast.

They came close above the house. It stood in a large walled enclosure, within which was a trim garden, but most of the space was taken by a paved yard with a roofed platform like a bandstand in the middle. Reggie stood still and surveyed it. Not a creature was to be seen. The acreage of window blazed blank and curtainless.

'The band is not playing.' Dubois made a grimace. 'It is not the season.'

Reggie did not answer. His eyes puckered to stare at a window within which the sun glinted on something of brass. He made a little inarticulate sound, and walked on, keeping above the house. But they saw no one, no sign of life, till they were close to the cliff edge.

Then a cove opened below them in a gleaming stretch of white shell sand, and on the sand children were playing: some of them at a happy-go-lucky game of rounders, some building castles, some tumbling over each other like puppies. On a rock sat, in placid guard over them, a man who had the black pointed beard, the heavy black brows, which Farquhar had sketched on his menu. But these Mephistophelean decorations did not display the leer and sneer of Farquhar's drawing. The owner watched the children with a grave and kindly attention which seemed to be interested in everyone. He called to them cheerily, and had gay answers. He laughed jovial satisfaction at their laughter.

Reggie took Dubois's arm and walked him away. 'Ah, my poor friend!' Dubois rumbled chuckles. 'There we are at last. We arrive. We have the brute goddess, we have the children, we have even the devil of our Farquhar. And behold! he is a genial paternal soul, and all the children love him. Oh, my poor friend!'

'Yes. Funny isn't it?' Reggie snapped. 'Dam' funny. Did you say the end? Then God forgive us. Which He wouldn't. He would not!'

Dubois gave him a queer look—something of derision, something of awe, and a good deal of doubt. 'When you talk like that'— a shrug, a wave of the hands—'it is outside reason, is it not? An inspiration of faith.'

'Faith that the world is reasonable. That's all,' Reggie snarled. 'Come on.'

'And where?'

'Down to this village.'

The huddled cottages of Sarn were already in sight. Then odours, a complex of stale fish and the filth of beast and man, could be smelt. Women clattered in sabots and laboured. Men lounged against the wall above the mess of the beach. A few small and ancient boats lay at anchor in the cove, and one of a larger size, and better condition, which had a motor engine.

They found a dirty *estaminet* and obtained from the landlord a bottle of nameless red wine. He said it was old, it was marvellous, but, being urged to share it, preferred a glass of the apple spirit, Calvados. 'Marvellous, it is the world,' Dubois grinned. 'You are altogether right. Calvados for us also, my friend. It is more humane.'

The landlord was slow of speech, and a pessimist. Even with several little glasses of Calvados inside him he would talk only of the hardness of life and the poverty of Sarn and the curse upon the modern sardine. Reggie agreed that life was dear and life was difficult, but, after all, they had still their good boats at Sarn— motor-boats indeed. The landlord denied it with gloomy vehemence: motors—not one—only in the *Badebec*, and that was no fishing-boat, that one. It was M. David's.

'Is it so?'' Reggie yawned, and lit his pipe. He gazed dreamily down the village street to the hideous little church. From that—under a patched umbrella, to keep off the wind, which was high, or the sun, which was grown faint—came a fat and shabby *curé*. 'Well, better luck my friend,' Reggie murmured, left Dubois to pay the bill, and wandered away.

He met the *curé* by the church gate. Was it permitted to visit that interesting church? Certainly, it was permitted, but monsieur would find nothing of interest—it was new; it was, alas! a poor place.

The *curé* was right—it was new; it was garish, it was mean. He showed it to Reggie with an affecting simplicity of diffident pride, and Reggie was attentive. Reggie praised the care with which it was kept. 'You are kind, sir,' the *curé* beamed. 'You are just. In fact they are admirably pious, my poor people, but poor—poor.'

'You will permit the stranger—' Reggie slipped a note into his hand.

'Ah, monsieur! You are generous. It will be rewarded, please God.'

'It is nothing,' said Reggie quickly. 'Do not think of it.' They passed out of the church. 'I suppose this is almost the last place in France?'

'Sometimes I think we are forgotten,' the *curé* agreed. 'Yes, almost the last. Certainly we are all poor folk. There is only M. David, who is sometimes good to us.'

'A visitor?' Reggie said.

'Ah, no. He lives here. The Maison des Iles, you know. No? It is a school for young children—a school of luxury. He is a good man, M. David. Sometimes he will take, for almost a nothing, children who are weakly, and in a little while he has them as strong as the best. I have seen miracles. To be sure it is the best air in the world, here at Sarn. But he is a very good man. He calls his school 'of the islands' because of the islands out there'—the *curé* pointed to what looked like a reef of rocks. 'My poor people call them the islands of the blessed. It is not good religion, but they used to think the souls of the innocent went there. Yes, the Maison des Iles, his school is. But you should see it, sir. The children are charming.'

'If I had time—' said Reggie, and said good-bye.

Dubois was at the gate. Dubois took his arm and marched him off. 'My friend, almost thou persuadest me—' He spoke into Reggie's ear. 'Guess what I have found, will you? That motor-yacht, the yacht of M. David, she was away a week ten days ago.

161

And M. David on board. You see? It is possible she went over to England. A guess, yes, a chance, but one must avow it fits devilish well, if one can make it fit. A connection with all your fantasy—M. David over in England when Farquhar was drowned. Is it possible we arrive at last?'

'Yes, it could be. Guess what I've heard. M. David keeps school. That wasn't a bandstand. Open-air class-room. M. David is a very good man, and he uses his beautiful school to cure the children of the poor. He does miracles. The old *curé* has seen 'em.'

'The devil!' said Dubois. 'That does not fit at all. But a priest would see miracles. It is his trade.'

'Oh, no. No. Not unless they happen,' Reggie murmured.

'My friend, you believe more than any man I ever knew,' Dubois rumbled. 'Come, I must know more of this David. The sooner we were back at Quimper the better.'

'Yes. That is indicated. Quimper and telephone.' He checked a moment, and gazed anguish at Dubois. 'Oh, my hat, how I hate telephones.'

Dubois has not that old-fashioned weakness. Dubois, it is beyond doubt, enjoyed the last hours of that afternoon, shut into privacy at the post office with its best telephone, stirring up London and Paris and half France till sweat dripped from his big face and the veins of his brow dilated into knotted cords.

When he came into Reggie's room at the hotel it was already past dinner-time. Reggie lay on his bed, languid from a bath. 'My dear old thing,' he moaned sympathy. 'What a battle! You must have lost pounds.'

'So much the better,' Dubois chuckled. 'And also I have results. Listen. First. I praise the good Bell. He has it that a French boat—cutter rig with motor—was seen by fishermen in the bay off Lyncombe last week. They watched her, because they had suspicions she was poaching their lobsters and crabs, which they unaccountably believe is the habit of our honest French fishermen. She was lying in the bay the night of Tuesday—you see, the night that Farquhar disappeared. In the morning she was gone. They are not sure of the name, but they thought it was *Badboy*. That is near enough to Badebec, *hein*? In fact, myself, I do not understand the name Badebec.'

'Lady in Rabelais,' Reggie murmured. 'Rather interestin'. Shows the breadth of M. David's taste.'

'Aha. Very well. Here is a good deal for M. David to explain. Second, M. David himself. He is known: there is nothing against him. In fact he is like you, a man of science, a biologist, a doctor. He was brilliant as a student, which was about the same time that Farquhar studied art—and other things—in the Quartier Latin. David had no money. He served in hospitals for children; he set up his school here—a school for delicate children—four years ago. Its record is very good. He has medical inspection by a doctor from Quimper each month. But, third, Weber's nephew was at this school till July. He went home to Paris, they went out to Fontainebleau, and—piff!' Dubois snapped his fingers. 'He is dead like that. There is no doubt it was diphtheria. Do you say fulminating diphtheria? Yes, that is it.'

'I'd like a medical report,' Reggie murmured.

'I have asked for it. However—the doctors are above suspicion, my friend. And now, fourth—the Bernals are found. They are at Dijon. They have been asked what has become of their dear little boy, and, they reply, he is at school in Brittany. At the school of M. David, Maison des Iles, Quimper.'

'Yes. He would be. I see.'

'Name of a name! I think you have always seen everything.'

'Oh, no. No. Don't see it now,' Reggie mumbled. 'However. We're workin' it out. You've done wonderfully.'

'Not so bad.' Dubois smiled. 'My genius is for action.'

'Yes. Splendid. Yes. Mine isn't. I just went and had a look at the museum.'

'My dear friend,' Dubois condescended. 'Why not? After all, the affair is now for me.'

'Thanks, yes. Interestin' museum. Found a good man on the local legends there. Told me the Woman of Sarn used to have children sacrificed to her. That'll be what Farquhar had in his nice head. Though M. David is so good to children.'

'Aha. It explains, and it does not explain,' Dubois said. 'In spite of you, M. David remains an enigma. Let poor old Dubois try. I have all these people under observation—the Webers, the Bernals—they cannot escape me now. And there are good men gone out to watch over M. David in his Maison des Iles. Tomorrow we will go and talk to him, *hein?*'

'Pleasure,' Reggie murmured. 'You'd better go and have a bath now. You want it. And I want my dinner.' . . .

When they drove out to Sarn in the morning a second car followed them. In a blaze of hot sunshine they started, but they had not gone far before a mist of rain spread in from the sea, and by the time they reached the Maison des Iles they seemed to be in the clouds.

'An omen, *hein?*' Dubois made a grimace. 'At least it may be inconvenient—if he is alarmed; if he wishes to play tricks. We have

163

no luck in this affair. But courage, my friend. Poor old Dubois, he is not without resource.'

Their car entered the walled enclosure of the Maison des Iles, the second stopped outside. When Dubois sent in his card to M. David, they were shown to a pleasant waiting-room, and had not long to wait.

David was dressed with a careless neatness. He was well groomed and perfectly at ease. His full red lips smiled; his dark eyes quizzed them. 'What a misery of a morning you have found, gentlemen. I apologise for my ocean. M. Dubois?' he made a bow.

'Of the Sûreté.' Dubois bowed. 'And M. Fortune, my distinguished *confrère* from England.'

David was enchanted. And what could he do for them?

'We make some little enquiries. First, you have here a boy— Tracy, the son of Mme Bernal. He is in good health?'

'Of the best.' David lifted his black brows. 'You will permit me to know why you ask.'

'Because another boy who was here is dead. The little nephew of M. Weber. You remember him?'

'Very well. He was a charming child. I regret infinitely. But you are without doubt aware that he fell ill on the holidays. It was a tragedy for his family. But the cause is not here. We have had no illness, no infection at all. I recommend you to Dr Lannion, at Quimper. He is our medical inspector.'

'Yes. So I've heard,' Reggie murmured. 'Have you had other cases of children who went home for the holidays and died?'

'It is an atrocious question!' David cried.

'But you are not quite sure of the answer?' said Dubois.

'If that is an insinuation, I protest,' David frowned. 'I have nothing to conceal, sir. It is impossible, that must be clear, I should know what has become of every child who has left my school. But, I tell you frankly, I do not recall any death but that of the little nephew of Weber, poor child.'

'Very well. Then you can have no objection that my assistant should examine your records,' said Dubois. He opened the window, and whistled and lifted a hand.

'Not the least in the world. I am at your orders.' David bowed. 'Permit me, I will go and get out the books,' and he went briskly.

'Now if we had luck he would try to run away,' Dubois rumbled. 'But do not expect it.'

'I didn't,' Reggie moaned.

And David did not run away. He came back and took them to his office, and there Dubois's man was set down to work at registers. 'You wish to assist?' David asked.

'No, thanks. No,' Reggie murmured. 'I'd like to loook at your school.'

'An inspection!' Dubois smiled. 'I shall be delighted. I dare to hope for the approval of a man of science so eminent.'

They inspected dormitories and dining-room and kitchen, class-rooms and workshop and laboratory. M. David was expansive and enthusiastic, yet modest. Either he was an accomplished actor, or he had a deep interest in school hygiene, and his arrangements were beyond suspicion. In the laboratory Reggie lingered. 'It is elementary,' David apologised. 'But what would you have? Some general science, that is all they can do, my little ones: botany for the most part; as you see, a trifle of chemistry to amuse them.'

'Yes. Quite sound. Yes. I'd like to see the other laboratory.'

'What?' David stared. 'There is only this.'

'Oh, no. Another one with a big microscope,' Reggie murmured. 'North side of the house.'

'Oh, la, la,' David laughed. 'you have paid some attention to my poor house. I am flattered. You mean my own den, where I play with marine biology still. Certainly you shall see it. But a little moment. I must get the key. You will understand. One must keep one's good microscope locked up. These imps, they play every-where.' He hurried out.

'*Bigre!* How the devil did you know there was another laboratory?' said Dubois.

'Name of a dog! Is there anything you do not see?' Dubois complained. 'Well, if we have any luck he has run away this time.'

They waited some long while, and Dubois's face was flattened against the window to peer through the rain at the man on watch. But David had not run away, he came back at last, and apologised for some delay with a fool of a master, heaven given him patience! He took them briskly to the other laboratory, his den.

It was not pretentious. There were some shelves of bottles, and a bench with a sink, and a glass cupboard which stood open and empty. On the broad table in the window was a microscope of high power, and some odds and ends.

Reggie glanced at the bottles of chemicals and came to the microscope. 'I play at what I worked at. That is middle age,' David smiled. 'Here is something a little interesting.' He slipped a slide into the microscope and invited Reggie to look.

'Oh, yes. One of the diatoms. Pretty one,' Reggie murmured, and was shown some more. 'Thanks very much.' A glance set Dubois in a hurry to go. David was affably disappointed. He had hoped they would lunch with him. The gentleman with the registers could hardly have finished his investigations. He desired an investigation the most complete.

'I will leave him here,' Dubois snapped, and they got away. 'Nothing, my friend?' Dubois muttered.

'No. That was the point,' Reggie said. '"When they got there the cupboard was bare."'

As their car passed the gate, a man signalled to them out of the rain. They stopped just beyond sight of the house, and he joined them. 'Bouvier has held someone,' he panted. 'A man with a sack.' They got out of the car and Dubois waved him on.

Through the blinding rain-clouds they came to the back of the house, and, on the way up to the cliffs, found Bouvier with his hand on the collar of a sullen, stupefied Breton. A sack lay on the ground at their feet.

'He says it is only rubbish,' Bouvier said, 'and he was taking it to throw into the sea, where they throw their waste. But I kept him.'

'Good. Let us see.' Dubois pulled the sack open. 'The devil, it is nothing but broken glass!'

Reggie grasped the hand that was going to turn it over. 'No, you mustn't do that,' he said sharply. 'Risky.'

'Why? What then? It is broken glass and bits of jelly.'

'Yes. As you say. Broken glass and bits of jelly. However.' Over Reggie's wet face came a slow benign smile. 'Just what we wanted. Contents of cupboard which was bare. I'll have to do some work on this. I'm going to the hospital. You'd better collect David—in the other car. Good-bye.' . . .

Twenty-four hours, later, he came into a grim room of the *gendarmerie* at Quimper. There Dubois and David sat with a table between them, and neither man was a pleasant sight. David's florid colour was gone, he had become untidy, he sagged in his chair, unable to hide fatigue and pain. Dubois also was dishevelled, and his eyes had sunk and grown small, but the big face wore a look of hungry cruelty. He turned to Reggie. 'Aha. Here you are at last. And what do you tell M. David?'

'Well, we'll have a little demonstration.' Reggie set down a box on the table and took from it a microscope. 'Not such a fine instrument as yours, M. David, but it will do.' He adjusted a slide. 'You showed me some beautiful marine diatoms in your laboratory. Let me show you this. Also from your laboratory. From the sackful of stuff you tried to throw into the sea.'

David dragged himself up and looked, and stared at him, and dropped back in his chair.

'Oh, that's not all, no.' Reggie changed the slide. 'Try this one.'

Again, and more wearily, David looked. He sat down again. His full lips curled back to show his teeth in a grin. 'And then?' he said.

'What have you?' Dubois came to the microscope. 'Little chains of dots, eh?' Reggie put back the first slide. 'And rods with dots at the end.'

'Not bad for a layman, is it, M. David?' Reggie murmured. 'Streptococcus pyogenes, and the diphtheria bacillus. I've got some more—'

'Indeed?' David sneered.

'Oh, yes. But these will do. Pyogenes was found in poor little Weber: accountin' for the virulence of the diphtheria. Very efficient and scientific murder.'

'And the others?' Dubois thundered. 'The other children who went home for their holidays and died. Two, three, four, is it, David?'

David laughed. 'What does it matter? Yes, there are others who have gone to the isles of the blessed. But, also, there are many who have been made well and strong. I mock at you.'

'You have cause, Herod,' Dubois cried. 'You have grown rich on the murder of children. But it is we who laugh last. We deliver you to justice now.'

'Justice! Ah, yes, you believe that.' David laughed again. 'You are primitive, you are barbarous. Me, I am rational, I am a man of science. I sacrifice one life that a dozen may live well and happy. These who stand in the way of the rich, their deaths are paid for, and with the money I heal many. What, if life is valuable, is not this wisdom and justice? Let one die to save many—it is in all the religions, that. But no one believes his religions now. I—I believe in man. Well, I am before my time. But some day the world will be all Davids. With me it is finished.'

'Not yet, name of God!' Dubois growled.

'Oh yes, my friend. I am sick to death already. I have made sure of that.' He waved his hand at Reggie. 'You will not save me—no, not even you, my clever *confrère*. Good night! Go chase the Weber and the Bernal and the rest. David, he is gone into the infinite.' He fell back, a hand to his head.

Reggie went to him, and looked close and felt at him. 'Better take him away,' he pronounced. 'Hospital, under observation.'

Dubois gave the orders. . . . 'Play-acting, my friend,' he shrugged.

'Oh, no. No. That kind of man. Logical and drastic. He's ill all right. There was the diplococcus of meningitis in his collection. Might be that.' And it was. . . .

Ten days afterwards Dubois came to London with Reggie and gave Lomas a lecture on the case. 'I am desolated that I cannot offer you anyone to hang, my friend. But what can one do? The wretched Farquhar—I have no doubt he was murdered between David and Bernal. But there is no evidence. And, after all, David, he is dead, and we have Bernal for conspiracy to murder his stepson. That will do. It was, in fact, a case profoundly simple, like all the great crimes. To make a trade of arranging the deaths of unwanted children, that is very old. The distinction of David was to organise it scientifically, that is all. The child who was an heir to fortune, with a greedy one waiting to succeed, that was the child for him. Weber's nephew stood in the way of the beautiful Clotilde to Weber's fortune. Mrs Bernal's little boy was in the way of her second husband to the fortune of her father, the old millionaire. And the others! Well here is a beautiful modern school for delicate children, nine out of ten of them thrive marvellously. But, for the tenth, there is David's bacteriological laboratory, and a killing disease to take home with him when he goes for his holidays. Always at home, they die; always a disease of infection they could pick up anywhere. *Bigre!* It was a work of genius. And it would have gone on for ever but that this worthless Farquhar blunders into Brittany upon it, and begins to blackmail the beautiful Clotilde, the Bernal. Clotilde pays with her jewels, and has to pretend a robbery. Bernal will not pay—cannot, perhaps. Farquhar approaches the old grandfather, and Bernal calls in David, and the blackmailer is killed. The oldest story in the world. Rascals fall out, justice comes in. There is your angel of justice.' He bowed to Reggie. 'Dear master. You have shown me the way. Well, I am content to serve. Does he serve badly, poor old Dubois?'

'Oh, no. No. Brilliant,' Reggie murmured. 'Queer case, though. I believe David myself. He wanted to be a god. Make lives to his desire. And he did. Cured more than he killed. Far more. Then this fellow, who never wanted to be anything but a beast, blows in and beats him. Queer world. And David might have been a kindly, human fellow, if he hadn't had power. Dangerous stuff, science. Lots of us not fit for it.'

A Mystery of the Underground

JOHN OXENHAM

The underground station at Charing Cross was the scene of considerable excitement on the night of Tuesday, the fourth of November. As the 9.17 London and North-Western train rumbled up the platform, a lady was seen standing at the door of one of the first-class carriages, frantically endeavouring to get out, and screaming wildly.

The station inspector ran up to the carriage, and pulled open the door, when the lady literally sprang into his arms. She was in a state of violent hysterics, and it was with difficulty that he assisted her across the platform to a seat.

Meanwhile, a small crowd gathered round the open carriage door. The guard of the train had come up, elbowed his way through, and entered the carriage. The spectators could see a man sitting in the further corner, apparently asleep, his hat over his eyes, his head sunk forward.

'Drunken brute! he's frightened the lydy!'

'Pitch him out, guard, and we'll jump on 'im!'

The guard shook the man roughly, his hat rolled off, and the crowd jeered.

Then, suddenly, the guard came back to the door, waved his flag to a porter, and said hurriedly:

'Block the line behind – quick – and send the inspector.'

The porter hurried off, shouted to the inspector, and ran down the train to the signal-box.

The inspector left his charge in care of some ladies, and pushed his way into the carriage. The guard said a word to him, and they bent over the man in the corner. Then, with startled faces and compressed lips, after a momentary hesitation, they stopped and lifted him out of the carriage. The head fell back as they carried him awkwardly across the platform, and the crowd shrank away, silent and scared, at sight of the ghastly limpness and the stains of blood.

'Where to?' said the guard.

'Upstairs, I suppose,' said the inspector; and then added:

'Best thing would be to take him right on to Westminster. It's a Scotland Yard job, is this!'

'That's so!' said the guard. 'And her, too?' nodding towards the hysterical lady on the seat.

'Yes. Put him in again, and lock the door. I'll see to her. Tell Bob to keep the line blocked till they get the word from Westminster.'

They put the body back into the carriage, locked the door, and the guard went off to the signal-box, while the inspector took in hand the more difficult task of getting the lady, still in a state of hysterics, back into a carriage.

Finally, he had to have her carried in; he stepped in himself, and the train rolled off through the fog, past the line of scared faces on the platform, into the darkness which led towards Westminster; and the red stern light blinked ghoulishly back at the crowd, and tremulously disappeared up the tunnel like a great clot of blood.

Within seven minutes of the arrival of the train at Westminster, Scotland Yard was in possession of the facts, and of the chief factors in the case – the body – and the lady – by this time in a state of extreme nervous prostration. A couple of detectives were minutely examining the carriage as it sped on its journey, and the traffic on the Underground resumed its normal course.

The morning papers contained a brief announcement of the discovery. The evening papers imaginatively worked up all the details they had been able to obtain, and promoted the item to a prominent position among the day's news, in large type, well spaced out. But with the inquest, held next day, the excitement increased. Briefly, all that was learned was this:

From letters and papers found upon the deceased, the body was identified as that of Conrad Grosheim, a financier and speculator in the City. The identification was confirmed by Grosheim's clerk, and by the landlady of the room he occupied in King's Road, Chelsea.

The station inspector at Charing Cross and the guard of the train spoke to the finding of the body.

Maud Jones stated that she had had a race to catch the train at Temple station. She was running up towards the second-class carriages when the train started and the inspector flung open the door of a first-class and assisted her in, telling her to change at the next station. She had not noticed anything wrong with the gentleman in the corner – thought he was asleep – remembered his cigarette had slipped from his fingers, and was still smoking on the floor, when suddenly her eyes caught sight of blood dripping from his coat, and it flashed upon her that he was dead. She was so horrified that she nearly lost her senses. Was positive the cigarette on the floor was smoking when she got in. No, she did not smell anything like powder – nothing but the cigarette. The window next to the dead man was up. She touched nothing in the carriage, and got out of it as soon as she could. She was a waitress at Belloni's Restaurant, in the Strand. She had never seen the gentleman before, and was only sorry she had ever set eyes on him at all.

The inspector at Temple station confirmed Miss Jones's story as to her being put into the carriage.

The ticket porter at Temple station swore positively that no one whatever got out of the train. He had watched the young lady helped into the first-class carriage by the inspector, and there was not a single person on the platform when the train went out, except the inspector. Nobody could possibly have got up the stairs while he was watching. He had snapped the ingress gate as the lady passed through, and had not opened the egress one.

Dr Mortimer stated that he had examined the body, and was of the opinion that death had taken place not more than fifteen minutes, certainly not more than half an hour, before his examination. Cause of death was a bullet through the heart. It had entered the body level and straight, passed through the heart, causing instant death, and was found inside the ribs on the right side of the body. Bullet produced. It was of an unusually conical shape, and by impact with the ribs had been slightly flattened. In its natural shape it would be sharper, almost pointed. There were no signs of singeing or burning on deceased's clothing. The bullet made a clean cut through coat and vest, and did its work. If, as he understood, deceased was sitting in the corner of the carriage facing slightly towards the corner which Miss Jones occupied, the shot must have been fired from the seat exactly opposite where deceased sat.

'Or through the window?' queried the coroner.

'Or through the window,' granted the doctor. 'The exact spot from which the shot was fired would depend upon the angle at which deceased was sitting, but I understood the window was found closed.'

'Could the wound have been self-inflicted?'

'It could, of course, but not without singeing the clothing.'

'Could deceased have shot himself, thrown the revolver out of the window, and raised the window?'

'Absolutely impossible; death was instantaneous.'

Miss Jones, recalled, stated that the window was up when she entered the carriage. She was quite certain of that. It was a close, muggy night, and she felt half-suffocated. The window nearest her was jammed, and she could not let it down. She had looked across at the other, and thought of trying to open it. Then she saw the cigarette smoking on the floor, and then she saw the blood, and then she remembered screaming.

Detective-Sergeant Doane, of Scotland Yard, stated that the case had been placed in his hands; that he had taken possession of the carriage within a few minutes of the discovery of the body. It had been examined most minutely by himself and a colleague, both inside and out. Beyond the cigarette, trampled flat, probably in the removal of the body, and a few drops of blood on the floor, nothing whatever had been found. There was no weapon, no sign of a struggle. The contents of deceased's pockets, including a valuable watch and chain, had not been touched. He had questioned the passengers in the next compartments, but no one had heard a shot, or any sound whatever, except the screams of Miss Jones. Further stated that if Miss Jones was correct in stating that the cigarette was still burning on the floor when she entered, and he had no reason to doubt it, he judged that the deed was committed in the tunnel between Mansion House and Blackfriars, and he arrived at it thus. A cigarette of that brand would burn on the floor for five minutes; the train took one and a half minutes to travel from Temple to Charing Cross, half a minute's stoppage at Temple; two minutes from Blackfriars to Temple, half a minute's stoppage at Blackfriars took them into the tunnel between Mansion House and Blackfriars, and there the shot must have been fired. That tunnel had been searched inch by inch, so had the others, but nothing whatever had been found. He had his own ideas on the subject, but declined at present to make them public. Deceased's ticket was from Mansion House to Sloane Square.

The jury returned a verdict of wilful murder against some person or persons unknown; and so one more was added to the long list of undiscovered crimes of the Metropolis.

(From the *Link*, 12 November 1894)
ANOTHER MURDER ON THE UNDERGROUND
THE *LINK* MAN ON THE SPOT, AS USUAL

At 9.21 exactly, last night, as the weary *Link* man, having finished his appointed tasks, was patiently travelling in an Underground train to his humble abode at Chelsea, a piece of great good fortune befell him.

Great good fortune to one man generally means corresponding bad fortune to some other man, and so it was in this case. Without desiring to appear over-presumptuous, it does seem providential, that is, to the readers of the *Link*, that the *Link* man was right on the spot, and is therefore able to give an eye-witness's account of the very strange occurrence which took place at St James's Park station on the Underground railway last night.

Our contemporaries have published more or less garbled versions of the matter. They have done their best. The *Link*, however, was the only paper actually represented, and able, therefore, to give an absolutely exact account of what happened.

The *Link* man entered the train at Blackfriars, travelling third-class, as usual. He always travels third – not, as you might imagine, from necessity, but from choice. He thereby sees and feels, and, in every sense of the word, comes so much more in contact with his fellows, than is possible in the cold, refined, varnish-and-saddlebag atmosphere of the first-class. After standing patiently past three stations, the *Link* man had just managed to gently insinuate his person into the sixth place on a seat intended for five, and was jocularly remarking to his scowling neighbours, upon portions of whom he was sitting, that the tighter you sat the less you joggled, when a series of piercing screams from the next carriage forward rent the darkness of the tunnel, and heated all the *Link* man's professional instincts to boiling point. He sprang to the door. Something was happening – something untoward and out of the common. Such screams – off the stage – were an outrage, or implied one.

His first intention was to climb along the footboard till he arrived at the screams. But thoughts of Mrs *Link*-man and all the little *Link* men and women deterred him, and he decided not to risk his precious life, but to be first on the scene, all the same.

The screams had ceased. The silence seemed even more pregnant. While the screams continued something was happening. With their cessation, it – whatever it was – had happened. As the train slowed up at St James's Park, the *Link* man dashed forward to the next carriage – the rearmost first-class – and this is what he saw on opening the door – a lady lying apparently lifeless in the corner seat nearest the platform, and on the floor face downwards, the body of a man.

A crowd rushed to the door almost as soon as the *Link* man, but his were the first eyes that witnessed the scene. The station inspector came up, and was for ordering the *Link* man away, but, upon the latter disclosing his identity, became the courteous official the *Link* man has always found him, except upon that one unfortunate occasion when he (the inspector) found him (the *Link* man) riding first with a third-class ticket, and only let him off imprisonment for life with a reprimand, which still tingles in the *Link* man's ears, on the *Link* man's proving to him by ocular demonstration that every third-class carriage was carrying thirty per cent more humanity than it had any right to do.

The guard came up, too, and *ex officio*, the *Link* man was privileged to share the labours and cogitations of these officials.

By virtue of her sex, the lady claimed their first attention. She was in a dead faint, and was carefully carried through a double line of curious faces by the *Link* man and the guard to one of the station seats.

The *Link* man left the guard in charge, and hurried back to the carriage.

The inspector was stooping over the prostrate man, and as the *Link* man stepped in, he looked up with scared face, and said, 'It's another murder!'

'Good God!' said the *Link* man, involuntarily, for this was getting exciting. Then he saw blood on the inspector's hands.

'Better block the line behind, and wire to Scotland Yard, hadn't you?' he suggested.

'It blocks itself,' said the inspector; 'but we'll make doubly sure. Stop here in charge, will you, and I'll wire Scotland Yard at same time.' And he went off at a run, leaving the *Link* man in full charge.

Notebook and pencil came out of their own accord, with the following results: 'First-class carriage No. 32. London and North-Western train, St James's Park; time 9.25 p.m. Body dressed in dark grey overcoat with velvet collar – dark trousers – black diagonal coat and vest – patent leather shoes – Lincoln and Bennet hat, bruised from a fall. Face, so far as visible, dark and pale – age about forty-five – four-coil snake ring, with ruby and diamond in head, on third finger of left hand. In vest, exactly over heart, small, clean-cut hole, no singeing or burning, no smell of powder – no signs of struggle – window furthest from platform closed. Note – Exactly a week, to the minute almost, since discovery of the murder at Charing Cross last week. Is this accident or horrible intention?'

Link man acknowledges to creepy feeling. Door opens. Inspector returns, and a few minutes later, Scotland Yard, in the person of quiet, stern-faced Detective-Sergeant Doane, who has the previous case in hand, arrives with a colleague. They examine carriage minutely, inside and out, rear-side and off-side, under and over. They say little, but make many notes.

Carriage is locked up, and train sent on. *Link* man notices that most carriages are about half as full as when train came in, as though many had conceived sudden distaste for underground travel – that no single travellers are to be seen – general mistrustful gregariousness observable. *Link* man feels himself that sooner than travel in a carriage alone, or with only one other person, he would stop on the platform all night, and sleep on Smith's bookstall.

Body is carried to ambulance. Lady, now reviving, is placed in cab, and all drive off to Scotland Yard.

The unfortunate victim of this second outrage has since been identified as George Villars, commercial traveller, residing at West Kensington. The lady is Mrs Corbett, manageress of the ABC shop in Albert Street, Westminster.

Her account is simply that she entered the train at Westminster, and had barely got seated when the gentleman opposite lurched forward in his seat, presumably with the shaking of the carriage, and then fell prone on the floor. She saw blood on the floor, and screamed, and then fainted.

What may be the meaning of this exact repetition of the murder at Charing Cross exactly a week ago it is impossible to say. The time, the manner, the general conditions, are as nearly as possible identical.

Are both murders the act of the same hand; or is Number Two but one more proof of the epidemic nature of abnormal crimes – the result, in fact, of the action of Crime Number One on some weak intellect, with a morbid craving for notoriety?

One thing is certain: travel on the Underground is less attractive than of yore, and the homely 'bus is rising in public estimation.

(From the *Daily Telephone*, 19 November 1894)
A THIRD MURDER ON THE UNDERGROUND

The appalling discovery last night at Ealing Broadway station, on the District Railway, places beyond possibility of doubt the fact that a cold-blooded murderer is at large in our midst, and that travellers on that at all times depressing line are completely at his mercy. The police, we are willing to believe, are doing their best in the matter, but so far their efforts have apparently been fruitless. Every Tuesday night for the last three weeks, at, as near as can be told, exactly the same time to the minute, the mysterious death-dealer has chosen his victim, fired his fatal shot, and vanished. Whatever his motive and whatever his method, he has succeeded in instilling such a sense of dread into the public mind that the District Railway is beginning to be shunned by all persons of nervous temperament.

This curious state of things recalls to mind a similar series of crimes perpetrated on the Ceinture Railway, in Paris, about seven years ago. There, too, the victims were smitten down by an undiscoverable hand, and it was only when the seventh had fallen that the slaughter stopped. If it had not, the traffic on that line would have ceased, for the excitement was indescribable, and travellers shunned the Ceinture Railway as they would a pest-house.

Much the same feeling is growing in the minds of travellers by the District Railway, and especially so on Tuesday nights, which is the time fixed by the mysterious one for his horrible work. Last Tuesday night the trains ran nearly empty. Numbers of people, so curious is the hankering of the morbid mind after sensation, gathered in the stations most likely to afford the chance of a thrill. The platforms at Charing Cross, Westminster, St James's Park and Victoria were crowded with sensation-seekers, who had taken tickets which they had no intentions of using, but simply with the idea of being on the spot in case anything happened. And a very curious study those platforms were.

Throngs of people, waiting silently, in a damp fog, peering into carriage after carriage as the almost empty trains rolled slowly, like processions of funeral cars, in and out of the stations. In one carriage a party of young roughs had ensconced themselves, and endeavoured to make things lively by chaffing and jeering the silent crowds on the platforms as they passed through. They met with no encouragement, however, and had things all their own way. We wonder how those lively youths feel now when they know that, beyond a doubt, the mysterious murderer looked in on them, and could, had he so chosen, have launched his deadly bullet into their midst. But, as usual, his fatal choice fell upon a solitary wayfarer occupying a corner seat in a carriage by himself, and within three compartments of one occupied by the rowdy gang referred to.

Many of the crowd on the stations remarked on the temerity of the occupant of that corner seat. He might well sit so quiet. The fatal bullet was in his heart before he reached Victoria, at all events. But he journeyed peacefully on until he reached Ealing Broadway station, the terminus of the line. There, one of the principal duties of the porters is to arouse all the passengers who have succumbed to the monotony of the journey from the City and there John Small, the Ealing porter, tried in vain to arouse Carl Groeb, the occupant of the corner seat in the rear compartment of one of the first-class carriages, and found him dead – murdered, in the same way, and, beyond all doubt, by the same hand which struck down Conrad Grosheim, at, or about, 9.15 on the evening of Tuesday, the fourth inst., at Charing Cross, and which struck down George Villars, at 9.15 on the evening of Tuesday, the eleventh inst., at St James's Park.

The crowds at the stations up the line had dispersed with a sigh of disappointment, or let us take a charitable view, and say of relief. But the tragedy was there all the same, and the victim had passed beneath their eyes, though the public had to wait till Wednesday morning to get its thrill.

It is a terrible fact, but one that has to be faced that, in the greatest city in the world, in this year of grace 1894, such an appalling series of crimes can be perpetrated with impunity.

The police seem powerless. We give them credit for doing their utmost, but, up to now, nothing, so far as they let it be known, has resulted from their efforts.

One thing is certain, if the criminal cannot be brought to justice the directors of the District Railway can close up their line. It would pay them to run the electric light through every tunnel, and to line the route and sprinkle the carriages with detectives, in the style of an Imperial progress in Russia. The matter is really too gruesome for a jest, but *Punch* certainly hit the case off admirably in Bernard Partidge's clever sketch of the young City man attracting all the attentions of all the beauties in the drawing-room by the simple assertion that he had travelled from town by the District Railway, in a first-class carriage, *all by himself*, while the season's lions scowl at him from a distance, and twirl their moustaches, and growl in their neglected corners.

While, in another portion of the same journal, Mr Anstey's 'Voces Populi', describing the scene at Victoria station on Tuesday night, while the crowds waited for what they feared, and made simple bets on the basis of murder or no murder, and more complicated ones as to the age and nationality of the expected victim, the station where the discovery would be made, and so on, is immensely clever, but grim in the extreme. It proves the identity of one of the crowd at all events, and it will afford matter for much wondering comment on the part of readers of this year's *Punch* twenty years hence.

To return to the facts which confront us, however.

Murder, grim, cold, calculating, glides unchecked in our midst. No man's life is safe. You yourself, reading this, may be the next victim – that is, if you are so unwise as to trust yourself alone in a carriage on the District Railway. And this in London, AD 1894! What a satire on our boasted civilisation!

The official report of this latest crime is, with the necessary alterations of names, places, and dates, a mere duplication of the previous ones.

Carl Groeb took ticket at Mansion House for Victoria on the evening of Tuesday, the twenty-fifth inst., at 9.20. Before he reached Victoria he was dead – shot through the heart, in identically the same manner as the previous victims, and not a trace of the murderer is discoverable.

It is beyond belief, and yet it is horrible fact.

(From the *Daily Telephone*, 23 November 1894)

More light has been thrown on the dark corners of the Underground railway during the last few days than at any period of its existence, and yet the mystery remains unsolved. Travellers between 9 and 10.30 p.m. have been few and far between. Indeed, between those hours the service has been almost suspended, not more than one train in ten being run, and that running practically empty. But such hardy voyagers as have ventured, at risk of their lives, to run the passage from the City to Earl's Court, have travelled through a torchlight procession. Every tunnel has been filled with men with flare-lights, and the grotesque effects of the continuous blaze and the weird gigantic shadows are things to be remembered for a lifetime.

Not only is traffic on the Underground disorganised – business and pleasure alike are interrupted in their regular courses. Never, during the last twenty years, has London worked itself up into such a state of excitement as it has done over these mysterious crimes on the Underground. Suburban residents find words even of the most cerulean hue quite inadequate to express the annoyance and inconvenience they are being put to.

Scotland Yard has had a detective patrolling the footboard of every train. This, however, is to be stopped. The sensation of suddenly finding a strange face peering in at your ear as you sit harmlessly reading your evening paper in your favourite corner seat, is enough to startle any man. It has given rise to some most ludicrous scenes. Going home in a Richmond train last night, the writer sat opposite to a quiet, nervous-looking old gentleman. He happened to raise his eyes from his paper just as the patrol on the footboard passed the window. The old gentleman made up his mind at once that he had been selected as the murderer's next victim, and that the deadly bullet was just about to be launched. He instinctively sheltered his head behind his newspaper, and sank suddenly off his seat, and remained flat on the floor, nor could he be induced to rise till the next station was reached. Many ladies have been driven into hysterics in the same way, and the patrols are to be abolished.

In connection with the murder of Carl Groeb, it is now proved beyond doubt that the murderer has added to his other crime the meaner one of robbery. Groeb's pockets were empty when he was discovered – money, watch, chain, all were gone, though the evidence is conclusive that, when he left his office in Houndsditch, he carried a good round sum, and wore a good gold watch and chain. There is more hope of catching the murderer if he is driven by the exigencies of want, or the desire for gain, to unite the functions of footpad with those of self-constituted executioner. At all events, he descends from the sphere of the supernatural, into which popular credulity has been inclined to elevate him, and becomes a mere murderous thief.

(From the *Daily Telephone*, 25 November 1894)

We have received the following letter:
    To the Editor of the *Daily Telephone*.
SIR, – You are wrong. I never touched the money or effects of Carl Groeb, or any other of my victims. I kill; I do not rob. – Yours truly,
    The Underground Murderer.

The letter is post-marked 'London, SE, 24 November, 1894'. Is it a grim jest, or is it a genuine document? We give it for what it is worth.

(From the *Daily Telephone*, 26 November, 1894)

    To the Editor of the *Daily Telephone*.
SIR, – The Underground Murderer has enough on his conscience. He did *not* rob Carl Groeb of his watch, chain and money. I did. I entered the carriage at Sloane Square. The attitude of the figure in the corner startled me. When we had passed South Kensington I spoke to him. He did not answer. I touched him. He did not move. I saw he was dead. I was stone-broke myself. I had bilked the ticket-man at Sloane Square, and intended doing the same at Earl's Court. The opportunity was too good to be missed. The man in the corner had no further use for his money. I had. I relieved him of it, and also of his watch and chain. The latter I pawned in Liverpool, and I enclose you the ticket. I am a bad lot, but, thank Heaven, I am
    (Signed) Not the Underground Murderer.

The above letter was received by us two days ago, post-marked 'Liverpool'. We sent the pawn-ticket on to Liverpool. The watch and chain, recovered from the pawnbroker, have been sent to London, and have been identified beyond all doubt as Carl Groeb's!

Both letters are in possession of the police.

(From the *Daily Telephone*, 27 November 1894)

What, in Heaven's name, is this monstrous thing that is waging cruel, remorseless and indiscriminate warfare with that section of London that travels by the Underground? Is it against the Underground railway itself, as a system or as a corporation, that this foul fiend is fighting? Or is it some lunatic registering in this gruesome fashion his protest against the influx of foreigners into English business life? – for it is a noticeable fact that three out of the four victims have been foreigners.

Last night was 'Murder Night', as Tuesday night has come to be grimly dubbed on the Underground, and two more victims fell to the assassin's bullet – one in the usual neat and finished style to which we are becoming accustomed, but with a change of locality, necessitated, no doubt, by the close and incessant watch kept on every corner of the murderer's old haunts; the other was a gratuitous slap in the face – or, to be precise, bullet in the leg – of one of the guardians of the public safety in charge of the tunnel between Victoria and Sloane Square.

As the train which left Mansion House at 9.16, and left Victoria at 9.31, was running through the tunnel between Victoria and Sloane Square, it passed an up-line train proceeding to Mansion House.

The flare-light men are mostly concentrated between Victoria and Mansion House, in the tunnels of which section all the murders have hitherto been committed. As a precautionary measure, however, half a dozen men have been told off for duty each night in the tunnel between Victoria and Sloane Square. As the two trains passed, one of the flare-men standing in the six-foot fell to the ground, shot through the leg. No report was heard. Nothing but the rattle of the passing trains, which drowned the man's groans as he sank to the ground. His mate down the line saw a blaze of light as his flare fell over, and the oil caught fire and spread along the ground. Running up, he dragged the wounded man away from the flames, and yelled to the other men further down the tunnel.

Among them they carried this latest victim up to Victoria station, where their arrival caused a stampede of all except the officials.

The men's accounts of the matter are confused.

The bullet, of course, came from one of the passing trains, but which they cannot say. Even the wounded man is not certain how he was standing when the bullet struck him, but in any case only the very promptest action could have thrown any light on the matter. Had the men promptly wired to the next stations, both up and down the line, at which both trains would stop, strict search might have led to some discovery. But their wounded mate absorbed all their attention, and the chance, such as it was, was lost. We may, however, conclude, without doubt, that the shot came from the down train. That train reached Baker Street at 9.58, and four minutes later the murderer's fifth victim was discovered in a first-class carriage at Gower Street, in the person of John Stern, merchant, of Jewin Street, who was discovered shot through the heart, in exactly the same way as all the previous victims of the Underground fiend.

How much longer this state of matters is to continue depends, apparently, entirely on the will of the mysterious and bloodthirsty perpetrator of these atrocious crimes. The arm of the law seems powerless. It only remains now for the Underground fiend to shoot down an engine driver and his mate to bring about a catastrophe too horrible to contemplate. The bare possibility of an Underground train deprived of its natural controllers, and crashing madly along at its own sweet will, is enough to make one forswear for ever the delights of travel on that much-maligned line.

(From the *Link*, 4 December 1894)
ANOTHER OUTRAGE ON THE UNDERGROUND
THE *LINK* MAN THE SIXTH VICTIM

To all intents and purposes, I am a dead man.

To all intents and purposes, I am victim No. Six of the Underground Demon.

That I am here alive to tell the tale is no fault of his, but is due to a little precautionary measure of my own.

I have passed through a very strange experience.

I have done what no other man has done. I have looked Death in the face – the Death of the Underground. I have looked down the barrel of the weapon with which the Underground Death-dealer slaughters his victims.

I myself was the victim.

I am free to confess that I am shaken in nerves and sorely bruised in body.

After the detailed account given below of my experiences last 'Murder Night' I have done with the matter. I have had enough of it. My constitution cannot stand the exigencies of up-to-date travel on the Underground. The facts I am about to relate are so passing strange, that I may state at once that they are vouched for by the one man who has had more to do with the Underground Murders (except, of course, the chief actor of all) than anyone else – Detective-Sergeant Doane, of Scotland Yard. Sergeant Doane, into whose hands, from the first, has been entrusted the discovery of the mysterious murderer, has been greatly exercised by the failure of all the ingenious plans laid for his capture, and the apparent impossibility of coming to grips with the invisible one.

It is obviously impossible to have a detective on the step of every carriage of every train on the Underground railway. It is impossible to line the whole length of the system with flare-light men, even on 'Murder Night'. As a matter of fact, since the shooting of John Cran, the flare-man, in Sloane Square tunnel, it is not easy to induce the men to undertake the duty at all, for every one of them feels that he takes his life in his hand when he picks up his lamp. Every man of them knows that, as like as not, he may be the next victim.

I came into contact with Sergeant Doane over the second murder, the one at St James's Park, as readers of the *Link* will remember. I have met him many times since, and we have discussed the matter from many points of view.

On Saturday last I laid before him a scheme which seemed to me to offer at least the chance of a solution of the mystery.

My proposition was this: I offered to take my place, alone, in a first-class compartment in the train leaving Mansion House at 9.12 on 'Murder Night,' and to afford the Underground Fiend every facility for selecting me as his next victim. As a precaution, I was to wear inside my waistcoat a breastplate of solid steel; I was to have the company of an armed detective beneath the opposite seat within reach of a kick, and on top of the carriage, lying flat on the roof, directly over each window of my compartment, were to be two other detectives.

Sergeant Doane turned this idea over in his mind before cautiously venturing the remark that it might do – might do for me, in any case, he grimly added.

The idea was carried out precisely as given above, and 9.13 last Tuesday night found me comfortably ensconced, steel breastplate and all, in the rear first-class compartment of the London and North-Western train from Mansion House to Willesden, gliding through brilliant tunnel after tunnel into the comparative obscurity of the stations, and patiently waiting to be shot at. Beneath the opposite seat, within easy reach of my toe, was one of Doane's trusty followers, armed with a revolver. Flat on the roof, feet to engine, and head over my window, with the cold night wind ploughing up his back hair, was Sergeant Doane himself and over the opposite window another of his men, both armed with revolvers. A slight iron framework had been fixed to the top of the carriage to prevent their rolling off.

Now, a scheme of this kind – I speak from experience – is all very well in the heat of inception and preliminary discussion, but, in the carrying out of it, one's temperature is apt to fall.

I must confess to feeling distinctly nervous as I took my seat in the carriage, and, as the train rumbled along through the weird, irregular illumination of the flare-light men, an odd idea grew upon me that the compartment I was sitting in was somehow unpleasantly familiar to me.

The sensation grew, and the feelings of discomfort increased in proportion. It was likely enough I had ridden in that same carriage dozens of times, for I use the Underground freely, and occasionally go 'first' when, in my opinion, the 'thirds' are full. I was arguing myself into the idea that it was just the natural nervousness incidental to the job I had in hand, when my eye, roving around, caught the number of the carriage – No. 32 – on the small enamelled plate above the door, and I experienced all the sensation of a cold douche down the spine.

'Nonsense!' said I to myself. 'Don't be an idiot!'

But I sat and stared at that small enamelled plate till it began to hypnotise me.

To prove myself a fool, and disperse the blue devils, I hauled out my notebook, and turned over the pages till I came to what was in my mind. And then – I had a strong inclination to get out of the carriage, and have done with the business.

I was sitting in the exact spot of the very compartment of the very carriage in which George Villars was shot exactly five weeks ago to the day, and almost to the minute. As readers of the *Link* will remember, I was the first to discover his body at St James's Park station. It was distinctly unpleasant, but it could not be helped.

For companionship's sake, I landed a kick on a tender portion of the recumbent detective under the seat opposite, and he grunted wakefully. Then, feeling deucedly uncomfortable, I sank my head down into the pose of a tired man, drew my hat down over my brow, and turned my eyes almost upside down in the endeavour to keep a bright look-out from under the brim of it.

Blackfriars, Temple, Charing Cross, Westminster, St James's, Victoria, Sloane Square: I heaved a sigh of relief. We were through the original murder zone, and looked like drawing blank this time. Still, as the murderer had broken fresh ground at Baker Street last week, there was no knowing where he might strike this time. And so the train rumbled on.

Earl's Court, and tickets; Addison Road, Uxbridge Road, Shepherd's Bush, and we were rushing across the wilds of Wormwood Scrubs, when my eyes, wearied almost to blindness with the unnatural strain, closed for a moment's rest.

When I opened them, to my amazement, the window on my left, which I had carefully closed, was down, and wind and rain were pouring in. It sank to the bottom. Every drop of blood in me was tingling with excitement. My heart was going like a sledge-hammer. I wanted to kick the man under the seat, but could not move a toe.

As I glanced at the window, along the polished framework of the part that slides down, there came gently and silently into view a shining steel barrel, pointing straight for my heart. I caught just one vague glimpse of a face beyond it, then – without any report, or any warning, an awful shock – and – blank.

They tell me that I was lifted out at Willesden, and that I was unconscious for upwards of four hours.

I take their word for it; at present I will take anybody's word for anything. As far as I am personally concerned, I have done with the Underground Murders. I hold a season ticket on that abnormal line from Blackfriars to Sloane Square. Anyone who wants it, and will take it with all risks, including its non-transferability, is welcome to it. I would suggest that whoever takes it, should also take out a £10,000 Life Policy for the benefit of his widow and children.

For myself, as I said at the beginning. Underground travel is not adapted to my peculiar constitution. I now go home by 'bus.

As this story is passing strange, and may, in some quarters, be received with incredulity, Sergeant Doane has very kindly offered to add a few words concerning his experiences on Tuesday night.

If any of my fellow-journalists desire ocular demonstration of the truth of my story, and will call at St Bartholomew's Hospital, they can see for themselves the documents in the case, viz.: one steel shield, and one journalist, with a bruise, of the dimensions of a soup-plate, round about the spot where his heart is supposed to be.

Sergeant Doane's account is as follows:—

'I have read the foregoing statement, and endorse it in every particular which came under my own knowledge. Journeying on one's stomach, stern foremost, on top of the Underground train, is not a mode of locomotion that

I can recommend. The motion of the train, much more violent up there than in the body of the carriage, the peculiar position, and the horrible atmosphere, produced a feeling of nausea to such an extent that my colleague, on the other side of the roof, when he descended at Willesden, was white as a sheet, and was practically in the throes of sea-sickness.

'Nothing happened on our journey till we reached Wormwood Scrubs. It was blowing half a gale. The heavy rain stung like pellets, and, combined with the rattle of the train, drowned every other sound.

'Half-way between Wormwood Scrubs station and Willesden Junction, the gale seemed to seize the train and shake it, and it was all we could do to hang on by main force. It was at that moment that I heard a shout in the carriage below; then my colleague, Detective Trevor, who had been hidden under the seat, put his head through the window, shouting, "Doane, Doane, he is shot." Half a minute more, and we ran into Willesden station. Mr Lester was insensible from the impact of the bullet, which was flattened on the shield like a shilling. I heard no report, and feel sure there was none. Trevor confirms this fact. Beyond the "ping" of the bullet on the shield, he heard nothing. On hearing that, however, he crawled out, found Mr Lester with all the breath knocked out of him, and yelled for me.'

(From the *Daily Telephone*, 10 December 1894)

We feel like accessories before the fact – like partners in the horrible work of the Underground Murderer.

Ten days ago we hinted in these columns at the appalling catastrophe which might result from the massacre of an Underground engine driver and his mate by the Underground Murderer.

Last night, William Johnson, driver of the 9.1 Outer

Circle train, was shot at and wounded, fortunately not fatally, as the train ran through the tunnel beyond South Kensington station.

When the train steamed into Gloucester Road station, it was seen at once that something was wrong. Charles Jones, the fireman, was hanging on to the brake lever, white as a sheet, shouting for help. As the train came to a stand, and the inspectors and guard ran up, Driver Johnson was found lying in a heap on the floor of the cab.

Jones explained hurriedly that, as they ran through the tunnel Johnson suddenly clapped his hand to his side, and cried, 'My God! I'm shot!' and fell all of a heap.

'I'm off,' said Jones, when he had finished his story. I'll have no more o' this – a man's life isn't safe.' Neither threats nor persuasion availed to induce him to resume his place on the engine. Another driver and fireman were eventually procured from Mansion House, and traffic was resumed.

Matters, however, have come to a pretty pass when such an occurrence is possible, and something has got to be done, and at once, to put an end to this unheard-of state of affairs.

The following proclamation has been posted broadcast over the Metropolis. May it have some effect:—

£1,000 REWARD

WHEREAS, on the night of Tuesday, 4 November 1894, Conrad Grosheim was murdered in a first-class carriage on the Underground railway between Mansion House and Charing Cross stations; and

WHEREAS on the night of Tuesday, 11 November 1894, George Villars was murdered in a first-class carriage on the Underground railway between Mansion House and Westminster Stations; and

WHEREAS, on the night of Tuesday, 18 November Carl

Groeb was murdered in a first-class carriage on the Underground railway between Mansion House and Victoria stations; and

WHEREAS, on the night of Tuesday, 25 November John Cran was shot in the leg in the tunnel between Victoria and Sloane Square stations on the Underground railway; and, on the same night, John Stern was found murdered, in a first-class carriage at Baker Street station; and

WHEREAS, on the night of Tuesday, 2 December Charles Lester was shot at and wounded, with intent to murder, while travelling in a first-class carriage between Wormwood Scrubs and Willesden; and

WHEREAS, on the night of Tuesday, 9 December William Johnson, engine-driver, was shot at and wounded, with intent to murder, while travelling on his engine, between South Kensington and Gloucester Road station on the Underground railway:

The sum of ONE THOUSAND POUNDS (£1,000) will be paid to any person or persons (not being the actual murderer or murderers) who shall give such information as shall lead to the detection of the perpetrator of the above deeds.

The above emanated from Scotland Yard. The chairman of the District Railway Company authorises us to state that his company will double the government reward for information.

(From the *Link*. Third Edition. Wednesday, 12 December 1894)

The £1,000 reward seems to have had its effect. Last night was 'Murder Night' on the Underground, and, for the first time in six weeks, we have no murder to chronicle.

Is the Underground Fiend sated with blood – or,

having accomplished the magical number 'Seven', has he retired, satisfied with his work?

Time will show. The terrible chain, however, is broken, and from this we may draw some slight hope that the reign of terror on the Underground is over – until such time as the Death-dealer chooses to resume his self-imposed duties.

Receiving a tip-off that a man believed to be the Underground Murderer is about to flee the country on a boat sailing for Australia, the Link *man Charles Lester joins the vessel, the* Bendigo. *During the following weeks at sea two more murders are committed before Lester finally narrows down the suspects to the most unlikely passenger on board: an old man named Hood who is travelling with his pretty young grand-daughter. When the murderer strikes a third time, however, and tries to kill the ship's doctor, Shannon, who has also become increasingly suspicious of the old fellow, the medical man defends himself with an iron bar and causes his adversary to fall down a stairway to his death. As soon as the news of the old man's death is conveyed to his grand-daughter she is overwhelmed with relief, having apparently been an unwitting accomplice to the reign of terror on the London subway and at sea. After Hood's body has been committed to the ocean, Charles Lester is summoned by Miss Hood to the cabin that had been occupied by her grandfather and there he finally learns the secret of the Underground mystery . . .*

The girl was kneeling on the floor, amid piles of books, papers, clothing, etc., which she had taken from his boxes.

She beckoned me inside, and bade me close the door.

'You have a right to see some of these things, Mr Lester,' she said. 'When you have seen all you care to, will you help me to get rid of them? I only learned this morning from Captain Joram that you were the Mr Lester who—' She faltered, and the large eyes, turned pathetically up to mine, were swimming with tears.

'Try and forget all about it,' I said, 'and let me help you.'

She stooped hurriedly, and picked up a bundle of papers.

'Read those – and those – and look at these,' putting into my hand some strange steel instruments, quite unlike anything I had ever seen before. One had a horse-shoe clutch at the end, and, at the other extremity, it was pinned on to another long, thin steel rod, one end of which terminated in four fine sharp teeth, like the prongs of a fork.

I turned it over in my hand, but could make nothing of it, so proceeded to look over the papers. And, reading them, I arrived at old Hood's story.

A mechanical engineer, of quite unique powers, he had patented a number of inventions, and offered them to the District Railway Company, in whose employment he had spent the best part of his life. Nothing had come of them, however, and I gathered from some of the company's letters in reply that the old man had accused them of using his ideas, but giving him no benefit of them. Then he left the company's service, with his brain bursting with grievances, and it was easy to conceive that he determined to strike at them in a way that was as horribly effective as it was, for him, easy of accomplishment.

I was puzzling over the strange implements, and trying to get at their use. In thought, I went back to one of the murderer's journeys along the swinging footboards, and suddenly it all flashed upon me. A long steel rod, with curved top – that hitched on to the edge of the carriage roof, and had enabled him to pass rapidly along, without troubling to grasp each handle. That spidery implement, with the curved horse-shoe clutch and the pronged lever – I could see the sharp teeth inserted quietly into the window sash, the clutch fitted to the bottom outside frame, the pressing of the lever – and my closed window was sliding quietly down, the wind and rain of Wormwood Scrubs were beating in on me again, and my paralysed eyes were looking once more down the deadly death-tube. I could see myself lying bruised and stunned in the corner, and, in imagination, could follow the murderer as he rapidly made his way back to the carriage he had issued from, and, perhaps, concealed himself under the seat, or, riding between two carriages, dropped quietly off as the train began to slow up to the station.

There were other curious contrivances, whose meaning I could not fathom, but had no doubt they all tended to the same end – the boarding of, or hanging on to, trains in motion.

I looked up at the girl.

'What do you want me to do with all these things?'

'Throw them all overboard – clothes – books – papers – everything. I have kept the only papers I need. Please get rid of them all for me.'

I did. Shannon, however, claimed the air-gun, and certainly no one who wanted it had a better right to it.

It was a wonderful weapon, the only remaining monument to the old engineer's skill. With two twists it came into three pieces, and was easily stowed in one's ordinary pockets. The first day Shannon appeared on deck, Miss Hood being below, he tried that demon air-gun on the main-mast with a bullet of his own making. It buried itself out of sight, and a three-inch probe failed to reach it.

'No wonder it knocked the wind out of you, old man,' he said; 'if you hadn't had that breastplate on, you wouldn't be here now.'

We cleaned our memories of Old Man Hood as far as we could, as we had cleaned the ship of himself and his belongings, and Mary Hood grew brighter every day. Her burden lay behind her at the bottom of the Indian Ocean, and her sweet face was set bravely and hopefully towards

the new life that awaited her in the unknown land that lay
beneath the rising sun.

The Elusive Bullet

JOHN RHODE

'BY THE WAY, professor, there's something in the evening papers that might interest you,' said Inspector Hanslet, handing over as he spoke the copy he had been holding in his hand. 'There you are, "Prominent City Merchant found dead". Read it, it sounds quite interesting.'

Dr Priestley adjusted his spectacles and began to read the paragraph. The professor and myself, Harold Merefield, who had been his secretary for a couple of years, had been sitting in the study of Dr Priestley's house in Westbourne Terrace, one fine June evening after dinner, when Inspector Hanslet had been announced. The inspector was an old friend of ours, who availed himself of the professor's hobby, which was the mathematical detection of crime, to discuss with him any investigations upon which he happened to be engaged. He had just finished giving the professor an outline of a recent burglary case, over which the police had confessed themselves puzzled, and had risen to go, when the item in the newspaper occurred to him.

'This does not appear to me to be particularly interesting,' said the professor. 'It merely states that on the arrival of the 3.20 train this afternoon at Tilbury station a porter, in examining the carriages, found the dead body of a man, since identified as a Mr Farquharson, lying in a corner of a first-class carriage. This Mr Farquharson appears to have met his death through a blow on the side of the head although no weapon capable of inflicting such a blow has so far been found. I can only suggest that if the facts are as reported, there are at least a dozen theories which could be made to fit in with them.'

'Such as?' inquired Hanslet tentatively.

The professor frowned. 'You know perfectly well, inspector, that I most strongly deprecate all conjecture,' he replied severely. 'Conjecture, unsupported by a thorough examination of facts, has been responsible for more than half the errors made by mankind throughout the ages. But, to demonstrate my meaning, I will outline a couple of theories which fit in with all the reported facts. Mr Farquharson may have been struck by an assailant who left the train before its arrival at Tilbury, and who disposed of the weapon in some way. On the other hand, he may have leant out of the window, and been struck by some object at the side of the line, or even by a passing train, if he was at the right-hand side of the carriage, looking in the direction in which the train was going. Of course, as I wish to emphasize, a knowledge of *all* the facts, not only those contained in this brief paragraph, would probably render both these theories untenable.'

Hanslet smiled. He knew well enough from experience the professor's passion for facts and his horror of conjecture.

'Well, I don't suppose the case will come my way,' he said

as he turned towards the door. 'But if it does I'll let you know what transpires. I shouldn't wonder if we know the whole story in a day or two. It looks simple enough. Well good night, sir.'

The professor waited till the front door had closed behind him. 'I have always remarked that Hanslet's difficulties are comparatively easy of solution, but that what he calls simple problems completely baffle his powers of reasoning. I should not be surprised if we heard from him again very shortly.'

As usual, the professor was right. Hanslet's first visit had been on Saturday evening. On the following Tuesday, at about the same time, he called again, with a peculiarly triumphant expression on his face.

'You remember that Farquharson business, don't you, professor?' he began without preliminary. 'Well, it did come my way, after all. The Essex police called Scotland Yard in, and I was put on to it. I've solved the whole thing in under forty-eight hours. Not a bad piece of work eh? Mr Farquharson was murdered by—'

Dr Priestley held up his hand protestingly. 'My dear inspector, I am not the least concerned with the murderer of this Mr Farquharson. As I have repeatedly told you my interest in these matters is purely theoretical, and confined to the processes of deduction. You are beginning your story at the wrong end. If you wish me to listen to it, you must first tell me the full facts, then explain the course of your investigations, step by step.'

'Very well, sir,' replied Hanslet, somewhat crestfallen. 'The first fact I learnt was how Farquharson was killed. It appeared at first sight that he had been struck a terrific blow by some weapon like a pole-axe. There was a wound about two inches across on the right side of his head. But, at the post-mortem, this was found to have been caused by a bullet from an ordinary service rifle, which was found embedded in his brain.'

'Ah!' remarked the professor. 'A somewhat unusual instrument of murder, surely? What position did the body occupy in the carriage when it was found?'

'Oh, in the right-hand corner, facing the engine, I believe,' replied Hanslet impatiently. ' But that's of no importance, as you'll see. The next step, obviously, was to find out something about Farquharson, and why any one should want to murder him. The discovery of a motive is a very great help in an investigation like this. Farquharson lived with his daughter in a biggish house near a place called Stanford-le-Hope, on the line between Tilbury and Southend. On Saturday last he left his office, which is close to Fenchurch Street station, about one o'clock. He lunched at a restaurant near by, and caught the 2.15 at Fenchurch Street. As this was the train in which his dead body was found, I need hardly detail the inquiries by which I discovered these facts.'

The professor nodded. 'I am prepared to take your word for them,' he said.

'Very well, now let us come to the motive,' continued Hanslet. 'Farquharson was in business with his nephew, a rather wild young fellow named Robert Halliday. It seems that this young man's mother, Farquharson's sister, had a good deal of money in the business, and was very anxious that her son should carry it on after Farquharson's death. She died a couple of years ago, leaving rather a curious will, by which all her money was to remain in her brother's business, and was to revert to her son only at her brother's death.'

The professor rubbed his hands. 'Ah, the indispensable motive begins to appear!' he exclaimed with a sarcastic smile. 'I am sure that you feel that no further facts are necessary, inspector. It follows, of course, that young Halliday murdered his uncle to secure the money. You described him as a wild young man, I think? Really, the evidence is most damning!'

'It's all very well for you to laugh at me, professor,' replied

Hanslet indignantly. 'I'll admit that you've given me a line on things that I couldn't find for myself often enough. But in this case there's no possible shadow of doubt about what happened. What would you say if I told you that Halliday actually travelled in the very train in which his uncle's body was found?'

'Speaking without a full knowledge of the facts, I should say that this rather tended to establish his innocence,' said the professor gravely.

Hanslet winked knowingly. ' Ah, but that's by no means all,' he replied. 'Halliday is a Territorial, and he left London on Saturday afternoon in uniform, and carrying a rifle. It seems that, although he's very keen, he's a shocking bad marksman, and a member of a sort of awkward squad which goes down occasionally to Purfleet ranges to practise. Purfleet is a station between London and Tilbury. Halliday got out there, fired a number of rounds, and returned to London in the evening.'

'Dear, dear, I'm sorry for that young man,' remarked the professor. 'First we have a motive, then an opportunity. Of course, he travelled in the same carriage as his uncle, levelled his musket at his head, inflicted a fearful wound, and decamped. Why, there's hardly a weak link in the whole chain.'

'It wasn't quite as simple as that,' replied Hanslet patiently. 'He certainly didn't travel in the same carriage as his uncle, since that very morning they had quarrelled violently. Farquharson, who was rather a strict old boy, didn't approve of his nephew's ways. Not that I can find out much against him, but he's a bit of a young blood, and his uncle didn't like it. He travelled third class, and swears that he didn't know his uncle was on the train.'

'Oh, you have interviewed him already, have you?' said the professor quietly.

'I have,' replied Hanslet. 'His story is that he nearly missed the train, jumped into it at the last moment, in fact. Somewhere after Barking he found himself alone, and that's all he told me. When I asked him what he was doing scrambling along the footboard outside the train between Dagenham and Rainham, he became very confused, and explained that on putting his head out of the window he had seen another member of the awkward squad a few carriages away, and made up his mind to join him. He gave me the man's name, and when I saw him he confirmed Halliday's story.'

'Really, inspector, your methods are masterly,' said the professor. 'How did you know that he had been on the footboard?'

'A man working on the line had seen a soldier in uniform, with a rifle slung over his back, in this position,' replied Hanslet triumphantly.

'And you immediately concluded that this man must be Halliday,' commented the professor. 'Well, guesses must hit the truth sometimes, I suppose. What exactly is your theory of the crime?'

'It seems plain enough,' replied Hanslet. 'Halliday had watched his uncle enter the train, then jumped into a carriage close to his. At a predetermined spot he clambered along with his loaded rifle, shot him through the window, then, to avert suspicion, joined his friend, whom he had also seen enter the train, a little further on. It's as plain as a pikestaff to me.'

'So it appears,' remarked the professor dryly. 'What steps do you propose to take in the matter?'

'I propose to arrest Halliday at the termination of the inquest,' replied Hanslet complacently.

The professor made no reply to this for several seconds. 'I think it would be to everybody's advantage if you consulted me again before doing so,' he said at last.

A cloud passed for an instant over Hanslet's face. 'I will, if you think it would do any good,' he replied. 'But you must see for yourself that I have enough evidence to secure a conviction from any jury.'

'That is just what disquiets me,' returned the professor quickly. 'You cannot expect the average juryman to have an intelligence superior to yours, you know. I have your promise?'

'Certainly, if you wish it,' replied Hanslet rather huffily. He changed the subject abruptly, and a few minutes later he rose and left the house.

In the course of our normal routine I forgot the death of Mr Farquharson entirely. It was not until the following afternoon, when Mary the parlourmaid entered the study with the announcement that a Miss Farquharson had called and begged that she might see the professor immediately, that the matter recurred to me.

'Miss Farquharson!' I exclaimed. 'Why, that must be the daughter of the fellow who was murdered the other day. Hanslet said he had a daughter, you remember.'

'The balance of probability would appear to favour that theory,' replied the professor acidly. 'Yes, I'll see her. Show Miss Farquharson in, please, Mary.'

Miss Farquharson came in, and the professor greeted her with his usual courtesy. 'To what do I owe the pleasure of this visit?' he inquired.

Miss Farquharson hesitated a moment or two before she replied. She was tall and fair, dressed in deep mourning with an elusive prettiness which I, at least, found most attractive. And even before she spoke, I guessed something of the truth from the flush which suffused her face at the professor's question.

'I'm afraid you may think this an unpardonable intrusion,' she said at last. ' The truth is that Bob – Mr Halliday – who is my cousin, has heard of you and begged me to come and see you.'

The professor frowned. He hated his name becoming known in connection with any of the investigations which he undertook, but in spite of all his efforts, many people had come to know of his hobby. Miss Farquharson took his frown for a sign of disapproval, and continued with an irresistible tone of pleading in her voice.

'It was only as a last hope I came to you,' she said. 'It's all so awful that I feel desperate. I expect you know that my father was found dead last Saturday in a train at Tilbury, while he was on his way home?'

The professor nodded. 'I am aware of some of the facts,' he replied non-committally. 'I need not trouble you to repeat them. But in what way can I be of assistance to you?'

'It's too terrible!' she exclaimed with a sob. 'The police suspect Bob of having murdered him. They haven't said so, but they have been asking him all sorts of dreadful questions. Bob thought perhaps you might be able to do something—'

Her voice tailed away hopelessly under the professor's unwinking gaze.

'My dear young lady, I am not a magician,' he replied. 'I may as well tell you that I have seen Inspector Hanslet who has what he considers a convincing case against your cousin.'

'But you don't believe it, do you, Doctor Priestley?' interrupted Miss Farquharson eagerly.

'I can only accept the inspector's statements as he gave them to me,' replied the professor. 'I know nothing of the case beyond what he has told me. Perhaps you would allow me to ask you a few questions?'

'Of course!' she exclaimed. 'I'll tell you everything I can.'

The professor inclined his head with a gesture of thanks. 'Was your father in the habit of travelling by the 2.15 train from Fenchurch Street on Saturday afternoons?'

'No,' replied Miss Farquharson with decision. 'Only when he was kept later than usual at the office. His usual custom was to come home to a late lunch.'

'I see. Now, can you tell me the reason for the quarrel between him and your cousin?'

This time Miss Farquharson's reply was not so prompt. She lowered her head so that we could not see her face, and kept silence for a moment. Then, as though she had made up her mind, she spoke suddenly.

'I see no harm in telling you. As a matter of fact, Bob and I have been in love with one another for a long time, and Bob decided to tell my father on Saturday morning. Father was rather old-fashioned, and he didn't altogether approve of Bob. Not that there was any harm in anything he did, but father couldn't understand that a young man liked to amuse himself. There was quite a scene when Bob told him, and father refused to hear anything about it until Bob had reformed, as he put it. But I know that Bob didn't kill him,' she concluded entreatingly. 'It's impossible for anybody who knew him to believe he could. You don't believe it, do you?'

'No, I do not believe it,' replied the professor slowly. 'If it is any consolation to you and Mr Halliday, I may tell you in confidence that I never have believed it. When is the inquest to be?'

A look of deep thankfulness overspread her features. 'I am more grateful to you than I can say, Doctor Priestley,' she said earnestly. ' The inquest? On Saturday morning. Will you be there?'

The professor shook his head. 'No, I shall not be there,' he replied. 'You see, it is not my business. But I shall take steps before then to make certain inquiries. I do not wish to raise your hopes unduly, but it is possible that I may be able to divert suspicion from Mr Halliday. More than that I cannot say.'

Tears of thankfulness came to her eyes. 'I can't tell you what this means to Bob and me,' she said. 'He has been terribly distressed. He quite understands that things look very black against him, and he cannot suggest who could have wanted to kill my father. Father hadn't an enemy in the world, poor dear.'

'You are sure of that?' remarked the professor.

'Quite,' she replied positively. 'I knew every detail of his life, he never hid the smallest thing from me.'

And after a further short and unimportant conversation she took her leave of us.

The professor sat silent for some minutes after her departure. 'Poor girl!' he said at last. 'To lose her father so tragically, and then to see the man she loves accused of his murder! We must see what we can do to help her, Harold. Get me the one-inch map of the country between London and Tilbury, and a time-table of the Southend trains.'

I hastened to obey him, and for an hour or more he pored over the map, working upon it with a rule and a protractor. At the end of this period he looked up and spoke abruptly.

'This is remarkably interesting, more so than I imagined at first it would be. Run out and buy me the sheets of the six-inch survey which cover Rainham and Purfleet. I think we shall need them.'

I bought the maps he required and returned with them. For the rest of the day he busied himself with these, and it was not until late in the evening that he spoke to me again.

'Really, my boy, this problem is beginning to interest me,' he said. 'There are many points about it which are distinctly baffling. We must examine the country on the spot. There is a train to Purfleet, I see, at 10.30 tomorrow morning.'

'Have you formed any theory, sir?' I inquired eagerly. The vision of Miss Farquharson, and her conviction of her cousin's innocence, had impressed me in her favour.

The professor scowled at me. 'How often am I to tell you that facts are all that matter?' he replied. 'Our journey tomorrow will be for the purpose of ascertaining facts. Until we know these, it would be waste of time to indulge in conjecture.'

He did not mention the subject again until the next morning, when we were seated in the train to Purfleet. He had chosen an empty first-class carriage, and himself took the right-hand corner facing the engine. He said nothing until the train was travelling at a good speed, and then he addressed me suddenly.

'You are a good shot with a rifle, are you not?' he inquired.

'I used to be pretty fair,' I replied in astonishment. 'But I don't think I've had a rifle in my hand since the war.'

'Well, take my stick, and hold it as you would a rifle. Now go to the far end of the carriage and lean against the door. That's right. Point your stick at my right eye, as though you were going to shoot at it. Stand like that a minute. Thank you, that will do.'

He turned away from me, took a pair of field-glasses from a case he was carrying, and began to survey the country through the window on his side. This he continued to do until the train drew up at Purfleet and we dismounted on to the platform.

'Ah, a lovely day!' he exclaimed. 'Not too warm for a little walking. We will make our first call at Purfleet ranges. This was where young Halliday came to do his shooting, you remember.'

We made our way to the ranges, and were lucky enough to find the warden at home. Dr Priestley had, when he chose, a most ingratiating way with him, and he and the warden were very shortly engaged in an animated conversation.

'By the way,' inquired the professor earnestly, 'was there any firing going on here between half-past two and three on Saturday last?'

The range-warden scratched his head with a thoughtful expression on his face. 'Let me see, now, last Saturday afternoon? We had a squad of Territorials here on Saturday afternoon, but they didn't arrive till after three. Lord, they was queer hands with a rifle, some of them. Much as they could do to hit the target at all at three hundred. They won't never make marksmen, however hard they try.'

'Isn't it rather dangerous to allow such wild shots to fire at all?' suggested the professor.

'God bless your heart, sir, it's safe enough,' replied the range-warden. 'There's never been an accident the whole time I've been here. They can't very well miss the butts, and even if they did, there's nobody allowed on the marshes when firing's going on.'

'That is comforting, certainly,' said the professor. 'Apart from this squad, you had nobody else?'

The range-warden shook his head. 'No, sir, they was the only people on the range that day.'

'I suppose it is part of your duty to issue ammunition?' inquired the professor.

'As a rule, sir. But, as it happens, this particular squad always brings their own with them.'

The professor continued his conversation for a little longer, then prepared to depart.

'I'm sure I'm very much obliged to you,' he said as he shook hands. 'By the way, I believe there are other ranges about here somewhere?'

'That's right, sir,' replied the range-warden. 'Over yonder, beyond the butts. Rainham ranges, they're called.'

'Is there any objection to my walking across the marshes to them?'

'Not a bit, sir. There's no firing today. Just keep straight on past the butts, and you'll come to them.'

The professor and I started on our tramp, the professor pausing every hundred yards or so to look about him through his field-glasses and to verify his position on the map. We reached the Rainham ranges at last, discovered the warden, who fell under the influence of the professor's charm as readily as his colleague at Purfleet had done, and opened the conversation with him in much the same style.

'On Saturday afternoon last, between half-past two and three?' replied the warden to the professor's inquiry. 'Well, sir, not what you might call any shooting. There was a party from Woolwich, with a new sort of light machine-gun, something like a Lewis. But they wasn't shooting, only testing.'

'What is the difference?' asked the professor.

'Well, sir, by testing I mean they had the thing held in a clamp, so that it couldn't move. The idea is to keep it pointing in exactly the same direction, instead of wobbling about as it might if a man was holding it. They use a special target, and measure up the distance between the various bullet-holes on it when they've finished.'

'I see,' replied the professor. 'I wonder if you would mind showing me where they were firing from?'

'Certainly, sir, it's close handy.' The range-warden led us to a firing-point near by, and pointed out the spot on which the stand had been erected.

'That's the place, sir. They were firing at number 10 target over yonder. A thousand yards it is, and wonderful accurate the new gun seemed. Shot the target to pieces they did.'

The professor made no reply, but took out his map and drew a line upon it from the firing-point to the butts. The line, when extended, led over a tract of desolate marshes until it met the river.

'There is very little danger on these ranges, it appears,' remarked the professor, with a note of annoyance in his voice. 'If a shot missed the butts altogether, it could only fall into the river, far away from any frequented spot.'

'That's what they were laid out for,' replied the range-warden. 'You see, on the other side there's a house or two, to say nothing of the road and the railway. It wouldn't do to have any stray rounds falling among them.'

'It certainly would not,' replied the professor absently. 'I see by the map that Rainham station is not far beyond the end of the ranges. Is there any objection to my walking to it past the butts?'

'None at all, sir, it's the best way to get there when there's no firing on. Thank you, sir, it's been no trouble at all.'

We started to walk down the ranges, a puzzled frown on the professor's face. Every few yards he stopped and examined the country through his glasses, or pulled out the map and stared at it with an absorbed expression. We had reached the butts before he said a word, and then it was not until we had climbed to the top of them that he spoke.

'Very puzzling, very!' he muttered. 'There must, of course, be some explanation. A mathematical deduction from facts can never be false. But I wish I could discover the explanation.'

He was looking through his field-glasses as he spoke, and suddenly his attention became riveted upon an object in front of him. Without waiting for me he hurried down the steep sides of the butts, and almost ran towards a flagstaff standing a couple of hundred yards on the far side of them. When he arrived at the base of it, he drew a couple of lines on the map, walked half round the flagstaff and gazed intently through his glasses. By the time I had caught up with him he had put the glasses back in their case, and was smiling benevolently.

'We can return to town by the next train, my boy,' he said cheerfully. 'I have ascertained everything I wished to know.'

He refused to say a word until our train was running into Fenchurch Street station. Then suddenly he turned to me.

'I am going to the War Office,' he said curtly. 'Will you go to Scotland Yard, see Inspector Hanslet, and ask him to come to Westbourne Terrace as soon as he can?'

I found Hanslet, after some little trouble, and gave him the professor's message.

'Something to do with the Farquharson business, I suppose?' he replied. ' Well, I'll come if the professor wants to see me. But I've got it all fixed up without his help.'

He turned up, true to his promise, and the professor greeted him with a pleasant smile.

'Good evening, inspector, I'm glad you were able to come. Will you be particularly busy tomorrow morning?'

'I don't think so, professor,' replied Hanslet in a puzzled voice. 'Do you want me to do anything?'

'Well, if you can spare the time, I should like to introduce you to the murderer of Mr Farquharson,' said the professor casually.

Hanslet lay back in his chair and laughed. 'Thanks very much, professor, but I've met him already,' he replied. 'It would be a waste of your time, I'm afraid.'

'Never mind,' said the professor, with a tolerant smile. ' I assure you that it will be worth your while to spend the morning with me. Will you meet me by the bookstall at Charing Cross at half-past ten?'

Hanslet reflected for a moment. The professor had never yet led him on a wild-goose chase, and it might be worth while to humour him.

'All right,' he replied reluctantly. 'I'll come. But I warn you it's no good.'

The professor smiled, but said nothing. Hanslet took his leave of us, and the professor appeared to put all thought of the Farquharson case out of his head.

We met again at Charing Cross the next day. The professor had taken tickets to Woolwich, and we got out of the train there and walked to the gates of the arsenal. The professor took an official letter out of his pocket, which he gave to the porter. In a few minutes we were led to an office, where a young officer rose to greet us.

'Good morning, Doctor Priestley,' he said. 'Colonel Conyngham rang me up to say that you were coming. You want to see the stand we use for testing the new automatic rifle? It happens to be in the yard below, being repaired.'

'Being repaired?' repeated the professor quickly. 'May I ask what is the matter with it?'

'Oh, nothing serious. We used it at Rainham the other day, and the clamp broke just as we were finishing a series. We had fired ninety-nine rounds out of a hundred, when the muzzle of the gun slipped up. I don't know what happened to the round. I suppose it went into the river somewhere. Beastly nuisance, we shall have to go down and start all over again.'

'Ah!' exclaimed the professor, in a satisfied tone. 'That explains it. But I wouldn't use number 10 target again, if I were you. Can we see this stand?'

'Certainly,' replied the officer. 'Come along.'

He led us into the yard, where a sort of tripod with a clamp at the head of it was standing. The professor looked at it earnestly for some moments, then turned to Hanslet.

'There you see the murderer of Mr Farquharson,' he said quietly.

Of course Hanslet, the officer, and myself bombarded him with questions, which he refused to answer until we had returned to London and were seated in his study. Then, fixing his eyes upon the ceiling and putting the tips of his fingers together, he began.

'It was, to any intelligent man, perfectly obvious that there are half a dozen reasons why young Halliday could not have shot his uncle. In the first place, he must have fired at very close range, from one side or other of the carriage, and a rifle bullet fired at such a range, although it very often makes a very extensive wound of entry, does not stay in a man's brain. It travels right through his head, with very slightly diminished velocity. Next, if Halliday fired at his uncle at all, it must have been from the left-hand side of the carriage. Had he fired from the right-hand side, the muzzle of the weapon would have been almost touching his victim, and there would have been signs of burning or blackening round the wound. Do you admit this, inspector?'

'Of course,' replied Hanslet. 'My theory always has been that he fired from the left-hand side.'

'Very well,' said the professor quickly. 'Now Halliday is notoriously a very bad shot, hence his journey to Purfleet. Harold, on the contrary, is a good shot. Yet, during our expedition of yesterday, I asked him to aim at my right eye with a stick while the train was in motion. I found that never for an instant could he point the stick at it. I find it impossible to believe that a bad shot, firing from the footboard and therefore compelled to use one hand at least to retain his hold, could shoot a man on the far side of the carriage exactly on the temple.'

The professor paused, and Hanslet looked at him doubtfully.

'It all sounds very plausible, professor, but until you can produce a better explanation I shall continue to believe that my own is the correct one.'

'Exactly. It was to verify a theory which I had formed that I carried out my investigations. It was perfectly obvious to me, from your description of the wound, that it had been inflicted by a bullet very near the end of its flight, and therefore possessing only enough velocity to penetrate the skull without passing through it. This meant that it had been fired from a considerable distance away. Upon consulting the map, I discovered that there were two rifle ranges near the railway between London and Tilbury. I could not help feeling that the source of the bullet was probably one of these ranges. It was, at all events, a possibility worth investigating.

'But at the outset I was faced with what seemed an insuperable objection. I deduced from the map, a deduction subsequently verified by examination of the ground, that a round fired at any of the targets on either range would take a direction away from the railway. I also discovered that the only rounds fired while the train in which Mr Farquharson's body was found was passing the ranges were by an experimental party from the arsenal. This party employed a special device which eliminated any inaccuracy due to the human element. At this point it occurred to me that my theory was incapable of proof, although I still adhered to my view that it was correct.'

The professor paused and Hanslet ventured to remark:

'I still do not see how you can prove that the breakage of the clamp could have been responsible,' he said. 'The direction of the bullet remained the same, and only its elevation was affected. By your own showing, the last shot fired from the machine must have landed in the marshes or the river.'

'I knew very well that notwithstanding the apparent impossibility, this must have been the bullet which killed Mr Farquharson,' replied the professor equably. 'I climbed the butts behind the target at which the arsenal party had been firing, and while there I made an interesting discovery which solved the difficulty at once. Directly in line with number 10 target and some distance behind it was a flagstaff. Further, upon examination of this flagstaff I discovered that it was made of steel.

'Now the map had told me that there was only a short stretch of line upon which a train could be struck by a bullet deflected by this flagstaff. If this had indeed been the case, I knew exactly where to look for traces, and at my first inspection I found them. High up on the staff is a scar where the paint has recently been removed. To my mind the cause of Mr Farquharson's death is adequately explained.'

Hanslet whistled softly. ' By Jove, there's something in it!' he exclaimed. 'Your theory, I take it, is that Farquharson was struck by a bullet deflected by the flagstaff?'

'Of course,' replied the professor. 'He was sitting on the right-hand side of the carriage, facing the engine. He was struck on the right side of the head, which supports the theory of a bullet coming through the open window. A bullet deflected in this way usually turns over and over for the rest of its flight, which accounts for the size of the wound. Have you any objection to offer?'

'Not at the moment,' said Hanslet cautiously. 'I shall have to verify all these facts, of course. For one thing, I must take the bullet to the arsenal and see if it is one of the same type as the experimental party were using.'

'Verify everything you can, certainly,' replied the professor. 'But remember that facts, not conjecture, are what should guide you.'

Hanslet nodded. 'I'll remember, professor,' he said. And with that he left us.

Two days later Mary announced Miss Farquharson and Mr Halliday. They entered the room, and Halliday walked straight up to the professor and grasped his hand.

'You have rendered me the greatest service one man can render to another, sir!' he exclaimed. ' Inspector Hanslet tells me that all suspicion that I murdered my uncle has been cleared away, and that this is due entirely to your efforts.'

Before the professor could reply, Miss Farquharson ran up to him and kissed him impulsively. 'Doctor Priestley, you're a darling!' she exclaimed.

The professor beamed at her through his spectacles. 'Really, my dear, you make me feel quite sorry that you are going to marry this young man,' he said.

The Border-line Case

MARGERY ALLINGHAM

IT WAS SO hot in London that night that we slept with the wide skylight in our city studio open and let the soot-blacks fall in on us willingly, so long as they brought with them a single stirring breath to move the stifling air. Heat hung on the dark horizons and beneath our particular bowl of sky the city fidgeted, breathless and uncomfortable.

The early editions of the evening papers carried the story of the murder. I read it when they came along about three o'clock on the following afternoon. My mind took in the details lazily, for my eyelids were sticky and the printed words seemed remote and unrelated to reality.

It was a straightforward little incident, or so I thought it, and when I had read the guarded half-column I threw the paper over to Albert Campion, who had drifted in to lunch and stayed to sit quietly in a corner, blinking behind his spectacles, existing merely, in the sweltering day.

The newspapers called the murder the 'Coal Court Shooting Case', and the facts were simple.

At one o'clock in the morning, when Vacation Street, N.E., had been a deserted lane of odoriferous heat, a policeman on the beat had seen a man stumble and fall to the pavement. The intense discomfort of the night being uppermost in his mind, he had not unnaturally diagnosed a case of ordinary collapse and, after loosening the stranger's collar, had summoned the ambulance.

When the authorities arrived, however, the man was pronounced to be dead and the body was taken to the mortuary, where it was discovered that death had been due to a bullet wound neatly placed between the shoulder-blades. The bullet had made a small blue hole and, after perforating the left lung, had furrowed the heart itself, finally coming to rest in the body structure of the chest.

Since this was so, and the fact that the police constable had heard no untoward sound, it had been reasonable to believe that the shot had been fired at some little distance from a gun with a silencer.

Mr Campion was only politely interested. The afternoon certainly was hot and the story, as it then appeared, was hardly original or exciting. He sat on the floor reading it patiently, his long thin legs stretched out in front of him.

'Someone died at any rate,' he remarked at last and added after a pause: 'Poor chap! Out of the frying-pan . . . Dear me, I suppose it's the locality which predisposes one to think of that. Ever seen Vacation Street, Margery?'

I did not answer him. I was thinking how odd it was that a general irritant like the heat should make the dozens of situations arising all round one in the great city seem suddenly almost personal. I found I was desperately sorry for the man who had been shot, whoever he was.

It was Stanislaus Oates who told us the real story behind the half-column in the evening paper. He came in just after four, looking for Campion. He was a Detective-Inspector in those days and had just begun to develop the habit of chatting over his problems with the pale young man in the horn-rimmed spectacles. Theirs was an odd relationship. It was certainly not a case of the clever amateur and the humble policeman: rather the irritable and pugnacious policeman taking it out on the inoffensive, friendly representative of the general public.

On this occasion Oates was rattled.

'It's a case right down your street,' he said briefly to Campion as he sat down. 'Seems to be impossible, for one thing.'

He explained after a while, having salved his conscience by pointing out that he had no business to discuss the case and excusing himself most illogically on grounds of the heat.

'It's "low-class" crime,' he went on briskly. 'Practically gang-shooting. And probably quite uninteresting to all of you who like romance in your crimes. However, it's got me right down on two counts: the first because the man who shot the fellow who died couldn't possibly have done so, and second because I was wrong about the girl. They're so true to type, these girls, that you can't even rely on the proverbial exception.'

He sighed as if the discovery had really grieved him.

We heard the story of Josephine as we sat round in the paralysingly hot studio and, although I never saw the girl then or afterwards, I shall not forget the scene; the three of us listening, breathing rather heavily, while the Inspector talked.

She had been Donovan's girl, so Oates said, and he painted a picture of her for us: slender and flat-chested, with black hair and eyes like a Russian madonna's in a transparent face. She wore blouses, he said, with lace on them and gold ornaments, little chains and crosses and frail brooches whose security was reinforced by gilt safety-pins. She was only twenty, Oates said, and added enigmatically that he would have betted on her, but that it served him right and showed him there was no fool like an old one.

He went on to talk about Donovan, who, it seemed, was thirty-five and had spent ten years of his life in gaol. The Inspector did not seem to think any the less of him for that. The fact seemed to put the man in a definite category in his mind and that was all.

'Robbery with violence and the R.O. boys,' he said with a wave of his hand and smiled contentedly as though he had made everything clear. 'She was sixteen when he found her and he's given her hell ever since.'

While he still held our interest he mentioned Johnny Gilchick. Johnny Gilchick was the man who was dead.

Oates, who was never more sentimental than was strictly reasonable in the circumstances, let himself go about Josephine and Johnny Gilchick. It was love, he said – love, sudden, painful and ludicrous; and he admitted that he liked to see it.

'I had an aunt once who used to talk about the Real Thing,' he explained, 'and embarrassingly silly the old lady sounded, but after seeing those two youngsters meet and flame and go on until they were a single fiery entity – youngsters who were pretty ordinary tawdry material without it – I find myself sympathizing with her if not condoning the phrase.'

He hesitated and his smooth grey face cracked into a deprecating smile.

'Well, we were both wrong, anyway,' he murmured, 'my aunt and I. Josephine let her Johnny down just as you'd expect her to and after he had got what was coming to him and was lying in the mortuary he was born to lie in she upped and perjured her immortal soul to swear his murderer an alibi. Not that her testimony is of much value as evidence. That's beside the point. The fact remains that she's certainly done her best. You may think me sentimental, but it depresses me. I thought that girl was genuine and my judgement was out.'

Mr Campion stirred.

'Could we have the details?' he asked politely. 'We've only seen the evening paper. It wasn't very helpful.'

Oates glared at him balefully.

'Frankly, the facts are exasperating,' he said. 'There's a little catch in them somewhere. It must be something so simple that I missed it altogether. That's really why I've come to look for you. I thought you might care to come along and take a glance at the place. What about it?'

There was no general movement. It was too hot to stir. Finally the Inspector took up a piece of chalk and sketched a rough diagram on the bare boards of the model's throne.

'This is Vacation Street,' he said, edging the chalk along a crack. 'It's the best part of a mile long. Up this end, here by the chair, it's nearly all wholesale houses. This sandbin I'm sketching in now marks the boundary of two police divisions. Well, here, ten yards to the left, is the entrance to Coal Court, which is a cul-de-sac composed of two blank backs of warehouse buildings and a café at the far end. The café is open all night. It serves the printers from the two big presses farther down the road. That's its legitimate trade. But it is also a sort of unofficial headquarters for Donovan's mob. Josephine sits at the desk downstairs and keeps an eye on the door. God knows what hours she keeps. She always seems to be there.'

He paused and there came into my mind a recollection of the breathless night through which we had all passed, and I could imagine the girl sitting there in the stuffy shop with her thin chest and her great black eyes.

The Inspector was still speaking,

'Now,' he said, 'there's an upstairs room in the café. It's on the second floor. That's where our friend Donovan spent most of his evening. I expect he had a good few friends with him and we shall locate them all in time.'

He bent over the diagram.

'Johnny Gilchick died here,' he said, drawing a circle about a foot beyond the square which indicated the sandbin. 'Although the bobby was right down the road, he saw him pause under the lamp post, stagger and fall. He called the Constable from the other division and they got the ambulance. All that is plain sailing. There's just one difficulty. Where was Donovan when he fired the shot? There were two policemen in the street at the time, remember. At the moment of the actual shooting one of them, the Never Street man, was making a round of a warehouse yard, but the other, the Phyllis Court chap, was there on the spot, not forty yards away, and it was he who actually saw Johnny Gilchick fall, although he heard no shot. Now I tell you, Campion, there's not an ounce of cover in the whole of that street. How did Donovan get out of the café, where did he stand to shoot Johnny neatly through the back, and how did he get back again without being seen? The side walls of the cul-de-sac are solid concrete backs of warehouses, there is no way round from the back of the café, nor could he possibly have gone over the roofs. The warehouses tower over the café like liners over a tug. Had he come out down the road one or other of the bobbies must have been certain to have seen him. How did he do it?'

'Perhaps Donovan didn't do it,' I ventured and received a pitying glance for my temerity.

'That's the one fact,' said the Inspector heavily. 'That's the one thing I do know. I know Donovan. He's one of the few English mob boys who carry guns. He served five years with the gangs in New York and has the misfortune to take his liquor in bouts. After each bout he has a period of black depression, during which he may do anything. Johnny Gilchick used to be one of Donovan's mob and when Johnny fell for the girl he turned in the gang, which was adding insult to injury where Donovan was concerned.'

He paused and smiled.

'Donovan was bound to get Johnny in the end,' he said. 'It was never anything but a question of time. The whole mob expected it. The neighbourhood was waiting for it. Donovan had said openly that the next time Johnny dropped into the café would be his final appearance there. Johnny called last night, was ordered out of the place by the terrified girl, and finally walked out of the cul-de-sac. He turned the corner and strolled down the road. Then he was shot by Donovan. There's no way round it, Campion. The doctors say that death was as near instantaneous as may be. Johnny Gilchick could not have walked three paces with the bullet in his back. As for the gun, that was pretty obviously Donovan's too. We haven't actually picked it up yet, but we know he had one of the type we are after. It's a clear case, a straightforward case, if only we knew where Donovan stood when he fired the shot.'

Mr Campion looked up. His eyes were thoughtful behind his spectacles.

'The girl gave Donovan an alibi?' he inquired.

Oates shrugged his shoulders. 'Rather,' he said. 'She was passionate about it. He was there the whole time, every minute of the time, never left the upper room once in the whole evening. I could kill her and she would not alter her story; she'd take her dying oath on it and so on. It didn't mean anything either way. Still, I was sorry to see her doing it, with her boy friend barely cold. She was sucking up to the mob, of course; probably had excellent reasons for doing so. Yet, as I say, I was sorry to hear her volunteering the alibi before she was asked.'

'Ah! she volunteered it, did she?' Campion was interested.

Oates nodded and his small eyes widened expressively.

'Forced it on us. Came roaring round to the police station with it. Threw it off her chest as if she were doing something fine. I'm not usually squeamish about that sort of thing, but it gave me a distinct sense of distaste, I don't mind telling you. Frankly, I gave her a piece of my mind. Told her to go and look at the body, for one thing.'

'Not kind of you,' observed Mr Campion mildly. 'And what did she do?'

'Oh, blubbered herself sick, like the rest of 'em.' Oates was still disgruntled. 'Still, that's not of interest. What girls like Josephine do or don't do doesn't really matter. She was saving her own skin. If she hadn't been so enthusiastic about it I'd have forgiven her. It's Donovan who is important. Where was Donovan when he fired?'

The shrill chatter of the telephone answered him and he glanced at me apologetically.

'I'm afraid that's mine,' he said. 'You don't mind, do you? I left the number with the Sergeant.'

He took off the receiver and as he bent his head to listen his face changed. We watched him with an interest it was far too hot to dissemble.

'Oh,' he said flatly after a long pause. 'Really? Well, it doesn't matter either way, does it? . . . Still, what did she do it for? . . . What? . . . I suppose so . . . Yes? . . . Really?'

He seemed suddenly astounded as his informant at the other end of the wire evidently came out with a second piece of information more important than the first.

'You can't be certain . . . you are? . . . What?'

The faraway voice explained busily. We could hear its steady drone. Inspector Oates's exasperation grew.

'Oh, all right, all right,' he said at last. 'I'm crackers . . . we're all crackers . . . have it your own damned way.'

With which vulgar outburst he rang off.

'Alibi sustained?' inquired Mr Campion.

'Yes.' The Inspector grunted out the word. 'A couple of printers who were in the downstairs room swear he did not go through the shop all the evening. They're sound fellows. Make good witnesses. Yet Donovan shot Johnny. I'm certain of it. He shot him clean through the concrete angle of a piano warehouse as far as I can see.' He turned to Campion almost angrily. 'Explain that, can you?'

Mr Campion coughed. He seemed a little embarrassed.

'I say, you know,' he ventured, 'there are just two things that occur to me.'

'Then out with them, son.' The Inspector lit a cigarette and wiped his face. 'Out with them. I'm not proud.'

Mr Campion coughed again. 'Well, the – er – heat, for one thing, don't you know,' he said with profound uneasiness. 'The heat, and one of your concrete walls.'

The Inspector swore a little and apologized.

'If anyone could forget this heat he's welcome,' he said. 'What's the matter with the wall, too?'

Mr Campion bent over the diagram on the boards of the throne. He was very apologetic.

'Here is the angle of the warehouse,' he said, 'and here is the sandbin. Here to the left is the lamp post where Johnny Gilchick was found. Farther on to the left is the P.C. from Never Street examining a courtyard and temporarily off the scene, while to the right, on the other side of the entrance to Coal Court, is another constable, P.C. someone-or-other, of Phyllis Court. One is apt to – er – think of the problem as though it were contained in four solid walls, two concrete walls, two policemen.'

He hesitated and glanced timidly at the Inspector.

'When is a policeman not a concrete wall, Oates? In – er well, in just such heat . . . do you think, or don't you?'

Oates was staring at him, his eyes narrowed.

'Damn it!' he said explosively. 'Damn it, Campion, I believe you're right. I knew it was something so simple that it was staring me in the face.'

They stood together looking down at the diagram. Oates stooped to put a chalk cross at the entrance to the cul-de-sac.

'It was *that* lamp post,' he said. 'Give me that telephone. Wait till I get hold of that fellow.'

While he was carrying on an excited conversation we demanded an explanation from Mr Campion and he gave it to us at last, mild and apologetic as usual.

'Well, you see,' he said, 'there's the sandbin. The sandbin marks the boundary of two police divisions. Policeman A, very hot and tired, sees a man collapse from the heat under a lamp post on his territory. The man is a little fellow and it occurs to Policeman A that it would be a simple matter to move him to the next lamp post on the other side of the sandbin, where he would automatically become the responsibility of Policeman B, who is even now approaching. Policeman A achieves the change and is bending over the prostrate figure when his colleague comes up. Since he knows nothing of the bullet wound, the entrance to the cul-de-sac, with its clear view to the café, second-floor room, has no significance in his mind. Today, when its full importance must have dawned upon him, he evidently thinks it best to hold his tongue.'

Oates came back from the phone triumphant.

'The first bobby went on leave this morning,' he said. 'He was an old hand. He must have spotted the chap was dead, took it for granted it was the heat, and didn't want to be held up here by the inquest. Funny I didn't see that in the beginning.'

We were all silent for some moments.

'Then – the girl?' I began at last.

The Inspector frowned and made a little grimace of regret.

'A pity about the girl,' he said. 'Of course it was probably an accident. Our man who saw it happen said he couldn't be sure.'

I stared at him and he explained, albeit a little hurriedly.

'Didn't I tell you? When my sergeant phoned about the alibi he told me. As Josephine crossed the road after visiting the mortuary this morning she stepped under a bus . . . Oh yes, instantly.'

He shook his head. He seemed uncomfortable.

'She thought she was making a gesture when she came down to the station, don't you see? The mob must have told her to swear that no one had been in the upstairs room; that must have been their first story until they saw how the luck lay. So when she came beetling down to us she must have thought she was risking her life to give her Johnny's murderer away, while instead of that she was simply giving the fellow an alibi . . . Funny the way things happen, isn't it?'

He glanced at Campion affectionately.

'It's because you don't get your mind cluttered up with the human element that you see these things so quickly,' he said. 'You see everything in terms of A and B. It makes all the difference.'

Mr Campion, the most gentle of men, made no comment at all.

Dangerous Game

MICHAEL GILBERT

'THEY BURNED HIM to death,' said Elfe. He said it without any attempt to soften the meaning of what he was saying. 'He was almost certainly alive when they dumped him in the car and set fire to it.'

Deputy Assistant Commissioner Elfe had a long sad face and grey hair. In the twenty years that he had been head of the Special Branch he had seen more brutality, more treachery, more fanaticism, more hatred than had any of his predecessors in war or in peace. Twice he had tried to retire, and twice had been persuaded to stay.

'He couldn't have put up much of a fight,' said Mr Calder, 'only having one arm and one and a half legs.'

They were talking about Michael Finnegan, whose charred carcass had been found in a burned-out stolen car in one of the lonelier parts of Hampstead Heath. Finnegan had been a lieutenant in the Marines until he had blown off his right arm and parts of his right leg while defusing a new type of anti-personnel mine. During his long convalescence his wife

Sheilagh had held the home together, supplementing Michael's disability pension by working as a secretary. Then Finnegan had taught himself to write left-handed, and had gained a reputation and a reasonable amount of cash for his articles; first only in service journals, but later in the national press, where he had emerged as a commentator on men and affairs.

'It's odd,' as Mr Behrens once observed, 'you'd think that he'd be a militant chauvinist. Actually he seems to be a moderate and a pacifist. It was Finnegan who started arguing that we ought to withdraw our troops from Ireland. That was long before the I.R.A. made it one of the main planks in their platform.'

'You can never tell how a serious injury will affect a man,' said Mr Calder.

This was, of course, before he had become professionally involved with Michael Finnegan.

'For the last year you've been acting as his runner, haven't you?' said Elfe. 'You must have got to know him well.'

'Him and his wife,' said Mr Calder. 'They were a great couple.' He thought about the unremarkable house at Banstead with its tiny flower garden in front and its rather larger kitchen garden in the rear, both of which Michael Finnegan tended one-armed, hobbling down between times for a pint at the local. A respected man with many friends and acquaintances, none of whom knew he was playing a lonely, patient, dangerous game. His articles in the papers, his casual contacts, his letters to old friends in Ireland and conversations with new friends in the pub, all had been slanted toward a predetermined end.

The fact was that the shape of the I.R.A.'s activities was changing, a change which had been forced on them by the systematic penetration of their groups in England. Now, when an act of terrorism was planned, the operators came from Ireland to carry it out, departing as soon as it was done. They travelled a roundabout route, via Morocco or Tunis, entering England from France or Belgium and returning by the same way. Explosives, detonators, and other material for the job came separately, and in advance. Their one essential requirement was an operational base where materials could be stored and the operators could lodge for the few days needed for the job.

It was to hold out his house as such a safe base that every move in Michael Finnegan's life had been planned.

'We agreed,' said Mr. Calder, 'that as far as possible Michael should have no direct contacts of any sort with the security forces. What the Department did was to lease a house which had a good view, from its front windows, of Michael's back gate. They installed one of their pensioners in it, old Mrs Lovelock—'

'Minnie Lovelock?' said Elfe. 'She used to type for me forty years ago. I was terrified of her, even then.'

'All she had to do was to keep Michael's kitchen window sill under observation at certain hours. There was a simple code of signals. A flower pot meant the arrival of explosives or arms. One or more milk bottles signalled the arrival of that number of operators. And the house gave us one further advantage. Minnie put it about that she had sublet a room on the ground floor to a commercial gentleman who kept his samples there, and occasionally put up there for the night. For the last year the commercial gent was me. I was able to slip out, after dark, up the garden path and in at the back door of Michael's house. I tried to do it at least once a month. My ostensible job was to collect any information Michael might have for us. In fact, I believe my visits kept him sane. We used to talk for hours. He liked to hear the gossip, all about the interdepartmental feuds, and funny stories about the Minister.'

'And about the head of the Special Branch?'

'Oh, certainly. He particularly enjoyed the story of how

two of your men tried to arrest each other.'

Elfe grunted, and said, 'Go on.'

'And there was one further advantage. Michael had a key to this room. In a serious emergency he could deposit a message – after dark, of course – or even use it as an escape hatch for Sheilagh and himself.'

'Did his wife know what he was up to?'

'She had to be told something, if only to explain my visits. Our cover story was that Michael was gathering information about subversion in the docks. This was plausible, as he'd done an Intelligence job in the Marines. She may have suspected that it was more than that. She never interfered. She's a grand girl.'

Elfe said, 'Yes,' and after a pause, 'Yes. That's really what I wanted to tell you. I've had a word with your chief. He agrees with me. This is a job we can't use you in.'

'Oh,' said Mr Calder coldly. 'Why not?'

'Because you'd feel yourself personally involved. You'd be unable to be sufficiently dispassionate about it. You knew Finnegan and his wife far too well.'

Mr Calder thought about that. If Fortescue had backed the prohibition it would be little use kicking. He said, 'I suppose we *are* doing something about it.'

'Of course. Superintendent Outram and Sergeant Fallows are handling it. They're both members of the A.T. squad, and very capable operators.'

'I know Tom Outram,' said Mr Calder. 'He's a sound man. I'll promise not to get under his feet. But I'm already marginally involved. If he wants to question Sheilagh he'll have to do it at my cottage. I moved her straight down there as soon as I heard the news. Gave her a strong sleeping pill and put her to bed.'

'They wondered where she'd disappeared to. I'll tell them she's living with you.'

'If you put it quite like that,' said Mr Calder, 'it might be misunderstood. She's being chaperoned, by Rasselas.'

'I think,' said Superintendent Outram, 'that we'd better see Mrs Finnegan alone. That is, if you don't mind.'

He and Sergeant Fallows had driven out to Mr Calder's cottage, which was built on a shoulder of the North Downs above Lamperdown in Kent.

'I don't mind,' said Mr Calder. 'But you'll have to look out for Rasselas.'

'Your dog?'

'Yes. Mrs Finnegan's still in a state of shock, and Rasselas is very worried about it. The postman said something sharp to her – not meaning any harm at all – and he went for him. Luckily I was there and I was able to stop him.'

'Couldn't we see her without Rasselas?'

'I wouldn't care to try and shift him.'

Outram thought about it. Then he said, 'Then I think you'd better sit in with us.'

'I think that might be wise,' said Mr Calder gravely.

Sheilagh Finnegan had black hair and a white face out of which looked eyes of startling Irish blue. Her mouth was thin and tight and angry. It was clear that she was under stress. When Outram and Fallows came in she took one look at them and jerked as though an electric shock had gone through her.

Rasselas, who was stretched out on the floor beside her, raised his head and regarded the two men thoughtfully.

'Just like he was measuring us for a coffin,' said Fallows afterward.

Mr Calder sat on the sofa, and put one hand on the dog's head.

It took Outram fifteen minutes of patient, low-keyed questioning to discover that Mrs Finnegan could tell him very little. Her husband, she said, had suggested that she needed a vacation, and had arranged for her to spend a week in a small private hotel at Folkestone. She wasn't sorry to agree because she hadn't had a real holiday in the last three or four years.

Outram nodded sympathetically. Had the holiday been fixed suddenly? Out of the blue, like? Sheilágh gave more attention to this than she had to some of the earlier questions. She said, 'We'd often talked about it before. Michael knew I had friends at Folkestone.'

'But on this occasion it was your husband who suggested it? How long before you left?'

'Two or three days.'

'Then it *was* fairly sudden.'

'Fairly sudden, yes.'

'Did he give any particular reason? Had he had an unexpected message? Something like that?'

'He didn't say anything about a message. I wouldn't have known about it, anyway. I was out at work all day.'

Outram said, 'Yes, of course.'

There was nothing much more she could tell them. A quarter of an hour later the two men drove off. As their car turned down the hill they passed Mr Behrens, who was walking up from Lamperdown. Mr Behrens waved to the Superintendent.

'Looks a genial old cove,' said Sergeant Fallows.

'That's what he looks like,' agreed Outram.

When Mr Behrens reached the cottage he found Mr Calder and Sheilagh making coffee in the kitchen. They added a third cup to the tray and carried it back to the sitting room where Rasselas was apparently asleep. By contrast with what had gone before it was a relaxed and peaceful scene.

Mr Calder tried the coffee, found it still too hot, put the cup carefully back on its saucer, and said, 'Why were you holding out on the Superintendent?'

'How did you know I was holding out?'

'Rasselas and I both knew it.'

Hearing his name the great dog opened one brown eye, as though to confirm what Mr Calder had said, and then shut it again.

'If I tell you about it,' said Sheilagh, 'you'll understand why I was holding out.'

'Then tell us at once,' said Mr Behrens.

'Of course I knew something was in the wind. I didn't know exactly what Michael was up to. He was careful not to tell me any details. But whatever it was he was doing, I realized it was coming to a head. That was why he sent me away. He said it shouldn't be more than two or three days. He'd get word to me as soon as he could. That was on the Friday. I had a miserable weekend, you can imagine. Monday came, and Tuesday, and still no word. By Wednesday I couldn't take it any longer. What I did was wrong, I know, but I couldn't help myself.'

'You went back,' said Mr Calder. He said it sympathetically.

'That's just what I did. I planned it all carefully. I wasn't going to barge in and upset all Michael's plans. I just wanted to see he was all right and go away again. He'd given me a key to that room in Mrs Lovelock's house. I got there after dark. There's a clear view from the window straight into our kitchen. The light was on and the curtains weren't drawn.'

As she talked she was living the scene. Mr Behrens pictured her, crouched in the dark, like an eager theatre-goer in the gallery staring down on to the lighted stage.

She said, 'I could see Michael. He was boiling a kettle on the stove and moving about, setting out cups and plates. There were two other people in the room. I could see the legs of a man who was sitting at the kitchen table. Once, when he leaned forward, I got a glimpse of him. All I could tell you was he was young and had black hair. The other was a girl. I saw her quite plainly. She was dark, too. Medium height and rather thin. The sort of girl who could dress as a man and get away with it.

'I got the impression, somehow, that they'd just arrived, and Michael was bustling about making them at home. The girl still had her outdoor coat on. Maybe that's what gave me the idea. Just then I saw another man coming. He was walking along the road which runs behind our kitchen garden, and when he stopped, he was right under the window where I was sitting. When he opened the gate I could see that he was taking a lot of trouble not to make any noise. He shut the gate very gently, and stood there for a moment, looking at the lighted kitchen window. Then he tiptoed up the garden path and stood, to one side of the kitchen window, looking in. That's when I saw his face clearly for the first time.'

Sheilagh was speaking more slowly now. Mr Calder was leaning forward with his hands on his knees. Rasselas was no longer pretending to be asleep. Mr Behrens could feel the tension without understanding it.

'Then he seemed to make up his mind. He went across to the kitchen door, opened it without knocking, and went in quickly, as though he was planning to surprise the people inside. Next moment someone had dragged the curtains across. From the moment I first saw that man I knew he meant harm to Michael. But once the curtains were shut I couldn't see what was happening.'

'You couldn't see,' said Mr Calder. 'But could you hear?'

'Nothing. On account of Mrs Lovelock's television set in the room just above me. She's deaf and keeps it on full strength. All I could do was sit and wait. It must have been nearly an hour later when I saw the back door open. All the lights in the house had been turned out and it was difficult to see, but Michael was between the two men. They seemed to be supporting him. The girl was walking behind. They came out and turned up the road. Then I noticed there was a car parked about twenty yards farther up. They all got into it. And I went on sitting there. I couldn't think what to do.'

There was a moment of silence. Neither of the men wanted to break it. Sheilagh said, 'I do realize now that I should have done something. I should have run down, screamed – anything to stop them taking Michael away like that. But I didn't know what was happening. Going with them might all have been part of his plan.'

'It was an impossible situation,' said Mr Calder.

'When you thought about it afterwards,' said Mr Behrens, 'am I right about this? You got the impression that things had been going smoothly until that other man arrived, and that he was the one who upset things.'

'He was the one who gave Michael away,' said Sheilagh. 'I'm sure of it.' There was a different note in her voice now. Something hard and very cold.

'I agree with Calder,' said Mr Behrens. 'You couldn't have done anything else at the time. But as soon as you knew that things had gone wrong for Michael, why didn't you tell the police everything that you've just told us? Time was vital. You could give a good description of two of the people involved. Surely there wasn't a moment to lose.'

Sheilagh said, 'I didn't go to the police because I recognized the man, the one who arrived on foot. I'd seen his photograph. Michael had pointed it out to me in the paper. I only saw him clearly as he stood outside the lighted window, but I was fairly certain I was right.' She paused, then added, 'Now I'm quite certain.'

Both men looked at her.

She said, 'It was Sergeant Fallows.'

The silence that followed was broken unexpectedly. Rasselas gave a growl at the back of his throat, got up, stalked to the door, pushed it open with his nose, and went out. They heard him settling down again outside.

'That's where he goes when he's on guard,' said Mr Calder. There was another silence.

'I know what you're thinking,' said Sheilagh. 'You both think I'm crazy, but I'm not. It *was* Fallows.'

'Not an easy face to forget,' agreed Mr Calder, 'and it would explain something that has been puzzling me. We'd taken such tight precautions over Michael that I didn't see how they could suddenly have known that he was a plant. He might eventually have done something, or said something, which gave him away. They might have got suspicious. But not certain. Not straight away. It could only have happened like that if he was betrayed, and the only person who could have betrayed him was someone working in the Squad.'

Mr Behrens' mind had been moving on a different line. He said, 'When they got into the car, and turned the lights on, you'd have been able to see the number plate at the back, I take it.'

'That's right. I saw it and wrote it down. I've put it here. LKK 910 P.'

'Good girl. Now think back. When you were talking about the last man to arrive you called him 'the one who came on foot'. What made you say that?'

Sheilagh said, 'I'm not sure. I suppose because he came from the opposite direction to where the car was parked. So I assumed—'

'I'm not disputing it. In fact, I'm sure you were right. Fallows wouldn't have driven up in a police car. He wouldn't even have risked taking his own car. He'd have gone by bus or train to the nearest point and walked the rest of the way.'

Mr Calder said, 'Then the car belongs to the Irish couple. Of course they might have stolen it, like the one they left on the Heath.'

'They might. But why risk it? It would only draw attention to them, which was the last thing they wanted. My guess is that they hired it. Just for the time they were planning to be here.'

'If you're right,' said Mr Calder, 'there's a lot to do and not much time to do it. You'd better trace that car. And remember, we've been officially warned off, so you can't use the police computer.'

'LKK's a Kent number. I've got a friend in County Hall who'll help.'

'I'll look into the Fallows end of it. It'll mean leaving you alone here for a bit, Sheilagh, but if anyone should turn up and cause trouble, Rasselas will attend to him.'

'In case there might be two of them,' said Mr Behrens, 'you'd better take this. It's loaded. That's the safety catch. You push it down when you want to fire.'

The girl examined the gun with interest. She said, 'I've never used one, but I suppose, if I got quite close to the man, pointed it at his stomach, and pulled the trigger—'

'The results should be decisive,' said Mr Behrens.

Fallows was whistling softly to himself as he walked along the carpeted corridor to the door of his flat. It was on the top floor of a new block on the Regent's Park side of Albany Street and seemed an expensive pad for a detective sergeant. He opened the door, walked down the short hall into the living room, switched on the light, and stopped.

A middle-aged man, with greying hair and steel-rimmed glasses, was standing by the fireplace regarding him benevolently. Fallows recognized him, but had no time to be surprised. As he stepped forward something soft but heavy hit him on the back of the neck.

When he came round, about five minutes later, he was seated in a heavy chair. His arms had been attached to the arms of the chair and his legs to the chair's legs by yards of elastic bandage, wound round and round. Mr Behrens was examining the contents of an attaché case which he had brought with him. Mr Calder was watching him. Both men were in their shirtsleeves and were wearing surgical gloves.

'I think our patient is coming round,' said Mr Calder.

'What the bloody hell are you playing at?' said Fallows.

Mr Behrens said, 'First, I'm going to give you these pills. They're ordinary sleeping pills. I think four should be sufficient. We don't want him actually to go to sleep. Just to feel drowsy.'

'Bloody hell you will.'

'If you want me to wedge your mouth open, hold your nose, and hit you on the throat each time until you swallow, I'm quite prepared to do it, but it would be undignified and rather painful.'

Fallows glared at him, but there was an implacable look behind the steel spectacles which silenced him. He swallowed the pills.

Mr Behrens looked at his watch and said, 'We'll give them five minutes to start working. What we're trying' – he turned courteously back to Fallows – 'is an experiment which has often been suggested but never, I think, actually performed. We're going to give you successive doses of scopolamine dextrin to inhale, while we ask you some questions. In the ordinary way I have no doubt you would be strong enough to resist the scopolamine until you became unconscious. There are men who have sufficient resources of will power to do that. That's why we first weaken your resistance with a strong sedative. Provided we strike exactly the right balance, the results should be satisfactory. About ready now, I think.'

He took a capsule from a box on the table and broke it under Fallows' nose.

'The snag about this method,' Mr Behrens continued, in the

same level tones of a professor addressing a class of students, 'is that the interreaction of the sedative and the stimulant would be so sharp that it might, if persisted with, affect the subject's heart. You'll appreciate therefore – head up, Sergeant – that by prolonging our dialogue you may be risking your own life. Now then. Let's start with your visit to Banstead—'

This produced a single, sharp obscenity.

Fifty minutes later Mr Behrens switched off his tape recorder. He said, 'I think he's gone. I did warn him that it might happen if he fought too hard.'

'And my God, did he fight,' said Mr Calder. He was sweating. 'We'd better set the scene. I think he'd look more convincing if we put him on his bed.'

He was unwinding the elastic bandages and was glad to see that, in spite of Fallows' struggles, they had left no mark. The nearly empty bottle of sleeping pills, a half-empty bottle of whiskey, and a tumbler were arranged on the bedside table. Mr Behrens closed Fallows' flaccid hand round the tumbler, then knocked it on to the floor.

'Leave the bedside light on,' said Mr Calder. 'No one commits suicide in the dark.'

'I've done a transcript of the tape for you,' said Sheilagh. 'I've cut out some of the swearing, but otherwise it's all there. There's no doubt now that he betrayed Michael, is there?'

'None at all,' said Mr Behrens. 'That was something he seemed almost proud of. The trouble was that when we edged up to one of the things we really wanted to know, an automatic defence mechanism seemed to take over, and when we fed him a little more scopolamine to break through it, he started to ramble.'

'All the same,' said Mr Calder, 'we know a good deal. We know what they're planning to do, and roughly when. But not how.'

Mr Behrens was studying the neatly typed paper. He said, 'J. J. That's clear enough. Jumping Judas. It's their name for Mr Justice Jellicoe. That's their target, all right. They've been gunning for him ever since he sent down the Manchester bombers. I've traced their car. It was hired in Dover last Friday, for ten days. The man they hired it from told them he had another customer who wanted it on Monday afternoon. They said that suited them because they were planning to let him have it back by one o'clock that day, Monday. Which means that whatever they're going to do is timed to be done some-time on Monday morning, and they aim to be boarding a cross-Channel ferry by the time it happens.'

'They might have been lying to the man,' said Sheilagh.

'Yes. They might have been. But bear in mind that if they brought the car back on Saturday afternoon or Sunday the hire firm would be shut for the weekend and they'd have to leave the car standing about in the street, which would call attention to it. No. I think they've got a timetable, and they're sticking to it.'

'Which gives us three days to find out what it is,' said Mr Calder. 'If the payoff is on Monday there are two main possi-bilities. Jellicoe spends his weekends at his country house at Witham, in Essex. He's pretty safe there. He's got a permanent police guard and three boxer dogs that are devoted to him. He comes up to court on Monday by car, with a police driver. All right, that's one chance. They could arrange some sort of ambush. Detonate one of their favourite long-distance mines. Not easy, though, because there are three different routes the car can take. This isn't the Ulster border. They can't go round laying minefields all over Essex.'

'The alternative,' said Mr Behrens, 'is to try something in or around the Law Courts. We'll have to split this. You take the Witham end. Have a word with the bodyguard. They may not know that we've been warned off, so they'll probably cooperate. I'll tackle the London end.'

'Isn't there something I could do?' said Sheilagh.

'Yes,' said Mr Calder. 'There is. Play that tape over and over again. Twenty times. Until you know it by heart. There was something inside Fallows' muddled brain, something trying to get out. It may be a couple of words. Even a single word. If you can interpret it, it could be the key to the whole thing.'

So Friday was spent by Mr Calder at Witham, making friends with a police sergeant and a police constable; by Sheilagh Finnegan listening to the drug-induced ramblings of the man who had been responsible for her husband's death; and by Mr Behrens investigating the possibility of blowing up a judge in court.

As a first step Mr Behrens introduced himself to Major Haines. The Major, after service in the Royal Marines, had been given the job of supervising security at the Law Courts. He had known Michael Finnegan, and was more than willing to help.

He said, 'It's a rambling great building. I think the chap who designed it had a Ruritanian palace in mind. Narrow windows, heavy doors, battlements and turrets, and iron gratings. The judges have a private entrance, which is inside the car park. Everyone else, barristers, solicitors, visitors, all have to use the front door in the Strand, or the back door in Carey Street. They're both guarded, of course. Teams of security officers, good men. Mostly ex-policemen.'

'I was watching them for a time, first thing this morning,' said Mr Behrens. 'Most people had to open their bags and cases, but there were people carrying sort of blue-and-red washing bags. They let them through uninspected.'

'They'd be barristers, or barristers' clerks, and they'd let them through because they knew their faces. But I can assure you of one thing. When Mr Justice Jellicoe is on the premises everyone opens everything.'

'Which court will he be using?'

Major Haines consulted the printed list. 'On Monday he's in Court Number Two. That's one of the courts at the back. I'll show you.'

He led the way down the vast entrance hall. Mr Behrens saw what he meant when he described it as a palace. Marble columns, spiral staircases, interior balconies, and an elaborately tessellated floor.

'Up these stairs,' said Haines. 'That's Number Two Court. And there's the rear door, straight ahead of you. It leads out into Carey Street.'

'So that anyone making for Court Number Two would be likely to come this way.'

'Not if they were coming from the Strand.'

'True,' said Mr Behrens. 'I think I'll hang around for a bit and watch the form.'

He went back to the main hall and found himself a seat, which commanded the front entrance.

It was now ten o'clock and the flow of people coming in was continuous. They were channelled between desks placed lengthways, and three security guards were operating. They did their job thoroughly. Occasionally, when they recognized a face, a man was waved through. Otherwise everyone opened whatever they were carrying and placed it on top of the desk. Suitcases, briefcases, even women's handbags were carefully examined. The red-and-blue bags which, Mr Behrens decided, must contain law books, were sometimes looked into, sometimes not. But they would all be looked into on Monday morning.

'It looked pretty watertight to me,' said Mr Behrens to Sheilagh and Mr Calder, as they compared notes after supper. 'Enough explosive to be effective would be bulky and an elaborate timing device would add to the weight and bulk. They might take a chance and put the whole thing in the bottom of one of those book bags and hope it wouldn't be looked at, but they don't seem to me to be people who would take chances of that sort.'

'Could the stuff have been brought in during the weekend and left somewhere in the Court?'

'I put it to Haines. He said No. The building is shut on Friday evening and given a thorough going-over on Saturday.'

'Sheilagh and I have worked one thing out,' said Mr Behrens. 'There's a reference, towards the end, to "fields". In the transcript it's been reproduced as "in the fields", and the assumption was that the attempt was going to be made in the country, when Jellicoe was driving up to London. But if you listen very carefully it isn't "in the fields". It's "in fields" with the emphasis on the first word, and there's a sort of crackle in the tape before it which makes it difficult to be sure; but I think what he's saying is "Lincoln's Inn Fields".'

They listened once more to the tape.

Mr Calder said, 'I think you're right.'

'And it does explain one point,' said Mr Behrens. 'When I explored the area this morning it struck me how difficult it was to park a car. But Lincoln's Inn Fields could be ideal – there are parking spaces all down the South and East sides, and the South East corner is less than two hundred yards from the rear entrance to the Courts.'

'Likely enough,' said Mr Calder, 'but it still doesn't explain how they're going to get the stuff in. Did you get anything else out of the tape, Sheilagh?'

'I made a list of the words and expressions he used most often. Some were just swearing, but apart from that his mind seemed to be on the subject of time. He said "midday" and "twelve o'clock" a dozen times at least. And he talks about a "midday special". That seemed to be some sort of joke. He doesn't actually use the word "explosion", but he talks once or twice about a report, or reports.'

'Report?' said Mr Calder thoughtfully. 'That sounds more like a shot from a gun than a bomb.'

'It's usually in the plural. Reports.'

'Several guns.'

'Rather elaborate, surely. Hidden rifles, trained on the Bench, and timed to go off at midday?'

'And it still doesn't explain how he gets the stuff past the guards,' said Mr Behrens.

He took the problem down the hill with him to his house in Lamperdown village and carried it up to bed. He knew, from experience, that he would get little sleep until he had solved it. The irritating thing was that the answer was there. He was sure of it. He had only to remember what he had seen and connect it up with the words on the tape, and the solution would appear, as inevitably as the jackpot came out of the slot when you hit three lemons in a row.

Visualize the people, pouring through the entrance into the building, carrying briefcases, book bags, handbags. One man had had a camera slung over his shoulder. The guard had called his attention to a notice prohibiting the taking of photographs in Court. This little episode had held up the queue for a moment. The young man behind, a barrister's clerk Mr Behrens guessed, had been in a hurry, and had pushed past the camera owner. He had not been searched, because he hadn't been carrying a case. But he had been carrying *something*. When Mr Behrens reached this point he did, in fact, doze off, so that the solution must have reached him in his sleep.

Next morning, after breakfast, he telephoned his solicitor, catching him before he set out for the golf course. He said, 'When you go into Court and have to tell the judge what another judge said in another case—'

'Quote a precedent, you mean.'

'That's right. Well, do you take the book with you, or is it already in Court?'

'Both. There's a complete set of Reports in Court. Several sets, in fact. They're for the judges. And you bring your own with you.'

'That might mean lugging in a lot of books.'

'A trolleyful sometimes.'

'Suppose you had, say, five or six sets of Reports to carry. How would you manage?'

'I'd get my clerk to carry them.'

'All right,' said Mr Behrens patiently, 'how would he manage?'

'If it was just half a dozen books, he's got a sort of strap affair, with a handle.'

'That's what I thought I remembered seeing,' said Mr Behrens. 'Thank you very much.'

'I suppose you've got some reason for asking all these questions?'

'An excellent reason.'

His solicitor, who knew Mr Behrens well, said no more.

'We'll get there early,' said Mr Calder, 'and park as close as we can to the South East corner. There's plenty of cover in the garden and we can watch both lines of cars. As soon as one of us spots LKK 910P he tips off the others using one of these pocket radios. Quite easy, Sheilagh. Just press the button and talk. Then let it go, and listen.'

'That doesn't sound too difficult,' said Sheilagh. 'What then?'

'Then Henry gets busy.'

'Who's Henry?'

'An old friend of mine who'll be coming with us. His job is to unlock the boot of their car as soon as they're clear of it. By my reckoning he'll have ten minutes for the job, which will be nine and a half minutes more than he needs.'

The man and girl walked up Searle Street, not hurrying, but not wasting time, crossed Carey Street, climbed the five shallow steps, and pushed through the swing doors and into the Court building.

Mr Behrens had got there before them. He was standing on the far side of the barrier. A little queue had already formed and he had plenty of time to observe them.

They had dressed for the occasion with ritual care. The man in a dark suit, cream shirt, and dark red tie. The girl in the uniform of a female barrister, black dress, black shoes and stockings, with a single touch of colour, the collar points of a yellow shirt showing at the throat.

As he watched them edge forward to the barrier, Mr Behrens felt a prickle of superstitious dread. They may have been nervous, but they showed no sign of it. They looked serious and composed, like the young crusaders who, for the more thorough purging of the holy places, mutilated the living bodies of their pagan prisoners; like the novices who watched impassively at the auto-da-fé where men and women were burned to the greater glory of God.

Now they were at the barrier. The girl was carrying a book bag and a satchel. She opened them both. The search was thorough and took time. The man showed very slight signs of impatience.

Mr Behrens thought, they've rehearsed this very carefully.

When it came to the man's turn, he placed the six books, held together in a white strap, on the counter and opened his briefcase. The guard searched the briefcase, and nodded. The man picked up the books and the briefcase and walked down the short length of corridor to where the girl was standing. He ignored her, turned the corner, and made for Court Number 2.

Although it was not yet ten o'clock there were already a number of people in the courtroom. Two elderly barristers were standing by the front bench discussing something.

Behind them a girl was arranging a pile of books and papers. The young man placed his six books, still strapped together, on the far end of the back bench, and went out as quietly as he had come in. No one took any notice of him.

A minute later Mr Behrens appeared, picked up the books, and left. No one took any notice of him either.

When the young man came out he joined the girl and they moved off together. Having come in by the back entrance it was evidently their intention to leave by the front. They had gone about ten paces when a man stopped them. He said, 'Excuse me, but have you got your cards?'

'Cards?' said the young man. He seemed unconcerned.

'We're issuing personal identity cards to all barristers using the court. Your clerk should have told you. If you'd come with me I'll give you yours.'

The girl looked at her companion, who nodded slightly, and they set off after their guide. He led the way down a long empty passage toward the western annex to the Courts.

The young man closed up behind the guide. He put his hand into a side pocket, pulled out a leather cosh, moved a step closer, and hit the man on the head. The guide fell forward on to his knees and rolled over on to his face.

The young man and the girl had swung round and were moving back the way they had come.

'Walk, don't run,' said the young man.

They turned a corner and went down a spiral staircase which led to the main hall and the front entrance.

When they were outside, and circling the Court building, the girl said, 'That man. Did you notice?'

'Notice what?'

'When you hit him. He was expecting it.'

'What do you mean?'

'He started to fall forward just before you hit him. It must have taken most of the force out of the blow.'

Without checking his pace the young man said, 'Do you think he was a plant? Holding us up so they could get to the car ahead of us?'

'I thought it might be.'

The young man put one hand on the shoulder holster inside his coat and said, 'If that's right, you'll see some fireworks.'

There was no one waiting for them by the car. The nearest person to the car was a small man, with a face like a friendly monkey, who was sitting on a bench inside the garden reading the *Daily Mirror*.

No one tried to stop them as they drove out of Lincoln's Inn Fields and turned south toward the Embankment. 'Twenty past ten,' said the young man, 'good timing.'

They were five miles short of Dover, on the bare escarpment over Bridge, before he spoke again. He said, 'Twelve o'clock. Any time now.'

Either his watch was fast or the timing mechanism was slow. It was fully five minutes later when their car went up in a searing sheet of white flame.

The Girl Who Loved Graveyards

P. D. JAMES

SHE COULDN'T REMEMBER anything about the day in the hot August of 1956 when they first brought her to live with her Aunt Gladys and Uncle Victor in the small east London house at 49 Alma Terrace. She knew that it was three days after her tenth birthday and that she was to be cared for by her only living relations now that her father and grandmother were dead, killed by influenza within a week of each other. But those were just facts which someone, at some time, had briefly told her. She could remember nothing of her previous life. Those first ten years were a void, insubstantial as a dream which had faded but which had left on her mind a scar of unarticulated childish anxiety and fear. For her, memory and childhood both began with that moment when, waking in the small unfamiliar bedroom with the kitten, Sambo, still curled asleep on a towel at the foot of her bed, she had walked bare-foot to the window and drawn back the curtain.

And there, stretched beneath her, lay the cemetery, luminous and mysterious in the early morning light, bounded by iron railings and separated from the rear of Alma Terrace only by a narrow path. It was to be another warm day, and over the serried rows of headstones there lay a thin haze pierced by the occasional obelisk and by the wing tips of marble angels whose disembodied heads seemed to be floating on particles of shimmering light. And as she watched, motionless in an absorbed enchantment, the mist began to rise and the whole cemetery was revealed to her, a miracle of stone and marble, bright grass and summer-laden trees, flower-bedecked graves and intersection paths stretching as far as her eyes could see. In the far distance she could just make out the top of the Victorian chapel gleaming like the spire of some magical castle in a long-forgotten fairy tale. In those moments of growing wonder she found herself shivering with delight, an emotion so rare that it stole through her thin body like a pain. And it was then, on that first morning of her new life with the past a void and the future unknown and frightening, that she made the cemetery her own. Throughout her childhood and youth it was to remain a place of delight and mystery, her habitation and her solace.

It was a childhood without love, almost without affection. Her uncle Victor was her father's elder half-brother; that, too, she had been told. He and her aunt weren't really her relations. Their small capacity for love was expended on each other, and even here it was less a positive emotion than a pact of mutual support and comfort against the threatening world which lay outside the trim curtains of their small claustrophobic sitting room.

But they cared for her as dutifully as she cared for the cat Sambo. It was a fiction in the household that she adored Sambo, her own cat, brought with her when she arrived, her one link with the past, almost her only possession. Only she knew that she disliked and feared him. But she brushed and fed him with conscientious care as she did everything and in return he gave her a slavish allegiance, hardly ever leaving her side, slinking through the cemetery at her heels and only turning back when they reached the main gate. But he wasn't her friend. He didn't love her and he knew that she didn't love him. He was a fellow conspirator, gazing at her through slits of azure light, relishing some secret knowledge which was her knowledge too. He ate voraciously yet he never grew fat. Instead his sleek black body lengthened until, stretched in the sunlight along her window sill, his sharp nose turned always to the cemetery, he looked as sinister and unnatural as a furred reptile.

It was lucky for her that there was a side gate to the cemetery from Alma Terrace and that she could take a short cut to and from school across the graveyard avoiding the dangers of the main road. On her first morning her uncle had said doubtfully: 'I suppose it's all right. But it seems wrong somehow, a child walking every day through rows of the dead.'

Her aunt had replied: 'The dead can't rise from their graves. They lay quiet. She's safe enough from the dead.'

Her voice had been unnaturally gruff and loud. The words had sounded like an assertion, almost a defiance. But the child knew that she was right. She did feel safe with the dead, safe and at home.

The years in Alma Terrace slipped by, bland and dull as her aunt's blancmange, a sensation rather than a taste. Had she been happy? It wasn't a question which it had ever occurred to her to ask. She wasn't unpopular at school, being neither pretty nor intelligent enough to provoke much interest either from the children or the staff; an ordinary child, unusual only because she was an orphan but unable to capitalize even on that sentimental advantage. Perhaps she might have found friends, quiet unenterprising children like herself who might have responded to her unthreatening mediocrity. But something about her repelled their timid advances, her self-sufficiency, the bland uncaring gaze, the refusal to give anything of herself even in casual friendship. She didn't need friends. She had the graveyard and its occupants.

She had her favourites. She knew them all, when they had died, how old they had been, sometimes how they had died. She knew their names and learned their memorials by heart. They were more real to her than the living, those rows of dearly loved wives and mothers, respected tradesmen, lamented fathers, deeply mourned children. The new graves hardly ever interested her although she would watch the funerals from a distance then creep up later to read the mourning cards. But what she liked best were the old neglected oblongs of mounded earth or chipped stones, the tilted crosses, the carved words almost erased by time. It was round the names of the long dead that she wove her childish fantasies.

Even the seasons of the year she experienced in and through the cemetery. The gold and purple spears of the first crocuses thrusting through the hard earth. April with its tossing daffodils. The whole graveyard *en fête* in yellow and white as mourners dressed the graves for Easter. The smell of mown grass and the earthy tang of high summer as if the dead were breathing the flower-scented air and exuding their own mysterious miasma. The glare of sunlight on stone and marble as the old women in their stained cotton dresses shuffled with their vases to fill them at the tap behind the chapel. Seeing the cemetery transformed by the first snow of winter, the marble angels grotesque in their high bonnets of glistening snow. Watching at her window for the thaw, hoping to catch that moment when the edifice would slip and the shrouded shapes become themselves again.

Only once had she asked about her father and then she had known as children do that this was a subject which, for some mysterious adult reason, it was better not to talk about. She had been sitting at the kitchen table with her homework while her aunt busied herself cooking supper. Looking up from her history book she had asked: 'Where is Daddy buried?'

The frying pan had clattered against the stove. The cooking fork dropped from her aunt's hand. It had taken her a long time to pick it up, wash it, clean the grease from the floor. The child had asked again: 'Where is Daddy buried?'

'Up north. At Creedon outside Nottingham with your mum and gran. Where else?'

'Can I go there? Can I visit him?'

'When you're older, maybe. No sense is there, hanging about graves. The dead aren't there.'

'Who looks after them?'

'The graves? The cemetery people. Now get on with your homework, do, child. I'll be wanting the table for supper.'

She hadn't asked about her mother, the mother who had died when she was born. That desertion had always seemed to her wilful, a source of secret guilt. 'You killed your mother.' Someone, some time, had spoken those words to her, had laid on her that burden. She wouldn't let herself think about her mother. But she knew that her father had stayed with her, had loved her, hadn't wanted to die and leave her. Some day, secretly, she would find his grave. She would visit it, not once but every week. She would tend it and plant flowers on it and clip the grass as the old ladies did in the cemetery. And if there wasn't a stone she would pay for one, not a cross but a gleaming obelisk, the tallest in the graveyard, bearing his name and an epitaph which she would choose. She would have to wait until she was older, until she could leave school and work, and save enough money. But one day she would find her father. She would have a grave of her own to visit and tend. There was a debt of love to be paid.

Four years after her arrival in Alma Terrace her aunt's only brother came to visit from Australia. Physically he and his sister were alike, the same stolid short-legged bodies, the same small eyes set in square pudgy faces. But Uncle Ned had a brash assurance, a cheerful geniality which was so alien to his sister's unconfident reserve that it was hard to believe that they were siblings. For the two weeks of his visit he dominated the little house with his strident alien voice and assertive masculinity. There were unfamiliar treats, dinners in the West End, a visit to a greyhound stadium, a show at Earls Court. He was kind to the child, tipping her lavishly, even walking through the cemetery with her one morning to buy his racing paper. And it was that evening, coming silently down the stairs to supper, that she overheard disjointed scraps of conversation, adult talk, incomprehensible at the time but taken into her mind and stored there.

First the harsh boom of her uncle's voice: 'We were looking at this grave stone together, see. Beloved husband and father. Taken from us suddenly on 14 March 1892. Something like that. Marble chips, cracked urn, bloody great angel pointing upwards. You know the kind of thing. Then the kid turned to me. "Daddy's death was sudden, too." That's what she said. Came out with it cool as you please. Now what in God's name made her say that? I mean, why then? Christ, it gave me a turn I can tell you. I didn't know where to put my face. And what a place to choose, the bloody cemetery. I'll say one thing for coming out to Sydney. You'll get a better view. I can promise you that.'

Creeping closer, she strained her ears vainly to catch the indistinct mutter of her aunt's reply.

Then came her uncle's voice again: 'That bitch never forgave him for getting Helen pregnant. No one was good enough for her precious only daughter. And then when Helen died having the kid she blamed him for that too. Poor sod, he bought a packet of trouble when he set eyes on that girl. Too soft, too romantic. That was always Martin's trouble.'

Again the murmur of indistinguishable voices, the sound of her aunt's footsteps moving from table to stove, the scrape of a chair. Then her Uncle Ned's voice again.

'Funny kid, isn't she? Old-fashioned. Morbid you might say. Seems to live in that bone yard, she and that damned cat. And the split image of her dad. Christ, it turned me up I can tell you. Looking at me with his eyes and then coming out with it. "Daddy's death was sudden, too." I'll say it was! Influenza? Well, it's as good a name for it as any if you can get away with it. Helps having such an ordinary name, I suppose.

People don't catch on. How long ago is it now? Four years? It seems longer.'

Only one part of this half-heard, incomprehensible conversation had disturbed her. Uncle Ned was trying to persuade them to join him in Australia. She might be taken away from Alma Terrace, might never see the cemetery again, might have to wait for years before she could save enough money to return to England and find her father's grave. And how could she visit it regularly, how could she tend and care for it from the other side of the world? After Uncle Ned's visit ended it was months before she could see one of his rare letters with the Australian stamp drop through the letter box without the cold clutch of fear at the heart.

But she needn't have worried. It was October 1966 before they left England and they went alone. When they broke the news to her one Sunday morning at breakfast it was apparent that they had never even considered taking her with them. Dutiful as ever, they had waited to make their decision until she had left school and was earning her living as a shorthand typist with a local firm of estate agents. Her future was assured. They had done all that conscience required of them. Hesitant and a little shame-faced they justified their decision as if they believed that it was important to her, that she cared whether they left or stayed. Her aunt's arthritis was increasingly troublesome; they longed for the sun; Uncle Ned was their only close relation and none of them was getting any younger. Their plan, over which they had agonized for months in whispers behind closed doors, was to visit Sydney for six months and then, if they liked Australia, to apply to emigrate. The house in Alma Terrace was to be sold to pay the air fare. It was already on the market. But they had made provision for her. When they told her what had been arranged, she had to bend her face low over her plate in case the flood of joy should be too apparent. Mrs Morgan, three doors down, would be glad to take her as a lodger if she didn't mind having the small bedroom at the back overlooking the cemetery. In the surging tumult of relief she hardly heard her aunt's next words. There was one small problem. Everyone knew how Mrs Morgan was about cats. Sambo would have to be put down.

She was to move into 43 Alma Terrace on the afternoon of the day on which her aunt and uncle flew from Heathrow. Her two cases, holding all that she possessed in the world, were already packed. In her handbag she carefully stowed the meagre official confirmations of her existence: her birth certificate, her medical card; her Post Office savings book showing the £103 painstakingly saved towards the cost of her father's memorial. And, the next day, she would begin her search. But first she took Sambo to the vet to be destroyed. She made a cat box from two cartons fitted together, pierced it with holes, then sat patiently in the waiting room with the box at her feet. The cat made no sound and this patient resignation touched her, evoking for the first time a spasm of pity and affection. But there was nothing she could do to save him. They both knew it. But then, he had always known what she was thinking, what was past and what was to come. There was something they shared, some knowledge, some common experience which she couldn't remember and he couldn't express. Now with his destruction even that tenuous link with her first ten years would go for ever.

When it was her turn to go into the surgery she said: 'I want him put down.'

The vet passed his strong experienced hands over the sleek fur. 'Are you sure? He seems quite healthy still. He's old, of course, but he's in remarkably good condition.'

'I'm sure. I want him put down.'

And she left him there without a glance or another word.

She had thought that she would be glad to be free of the

pretence of loving him, free of those slitted accusing eyes. But as she walked back to Alma Terrace she found herself crying; tears, unbidden and unstoppable, ran like rain down her face.

There was no difficulty in getting a week's leave from her job. She had been husbanding her holiday entitlement. Her work, as always, was up to date. She had calculated how much money she would need for her train and bus fares and for a week's stay in modest hotels. Her plans had been made. They had been made for years. She would begin her search with the address on her birth certificate, Cranstoun House, Creedon, Nottingham, the house where she had been born. The present owners might remember her and her father. If not, there would be neighbours or older inhabitants of the village who would be able to recall her father's death, where he was buried. If that failed she would try the local undertakers. It was, after all, only ten years ago. Someone locally would remember. Somewhere in Nottingham there would be a record of burials. She told Mrs Morgan that she was taking a week's holiday to visit her father's old home, packed a hold-all with overnight necessities and, next morning, caught the earliest-possible fast train from St Pancras to Nottingham.

It was during the bus ride from Nottingham to Creedon that she felt the first stirrings of anxiety and mistrust. Until then she had travelled in calm confidence, but strangely without excitement, as if this long-planned journey was as natural and inevitable as her daily walk to work, an inescapable pilgrimage ordained from that moment when a bare-footed child in her white nightdress had drawn back her bedroom curtains and seen her kingdom spread beneath her. But now her mood changed. As the bus lurched through the suburbs she found herself shifting in her seat as if mental unease were provoking physical discomfort. She had expected green countryside, small churches guarding neat domestic graveyards patterned with yew trees. These were graveyards she had visited on holidays, had loved almost as much as she loved the one she had made her own. Surely it was in such bird-loud sanctified peace that her father lay. But Nottingham had spread during the past ten years and Creedon was now little more than an urban village separated from the city by a ribbon development of brash new houses, petrol stations and parades of shops. Nothing in the journey was familiar, and yet she knew that she had travelled this road before and travelled it in anxiety and pain.

But when, thirty minutes later, the bus stopped at its terminus at Creedon she knew at once where she was. The Dog and Whistle still stood at one corner of the dusty litter-strewn village green with the same bus shelter outside it. And with the sight of its graffiti-scrawled walls memory returned as easily as if nothing had ever been forgotten. Here her father used to leave her when he brought her to pay her regular Sunday visits to her grandmother. Here her grandmother's elderly cook would be waiting for her. Here she would look back for a final wave and see her father patiently waiting for the bus to begin its return journey. Here she would be brought at six-thirty when he arrived to collect her. Cranstoun House was where her grandmother lived. She herself had been born there but it had never been her home.

She had no need to ask her way to the house. And when, five minutes later, she stood gazing up at it in appalled fascination, no need to read the name painted on the shabby padlocked gate. It was a square built house of dark brick standing in incongruous and spurious grandeur at the end of a country lane. It was smaller than she now remembered, but it was still a dreadful house. How could she ever have forgotten those ornate overhanging gables, the high pitched roof, the secretive oriel windows, the single forbidding turret at the east end? There was an estate agent's board wired to the gate and it was apparent that the house was empty. The paint on the front door was peeling, the lawns were overgrown, the boughs of the rhododendron bushes were broken and the gravel path was studded with clumps of weed. There was no one here who could help her to find her father's grave. But she knew that she had to visit, had to make herself pass again through that intimidating front door. There was something the house knew and had to tell her, something that Sambo had known. She couldn't escape her next step. She must find the estate agent's office and get a permit to view.

She had missed the returning bus and by the time the next one had reached Nottingham it was after three o'clock. She had eaten nothing since her early breakfast but she was too driven now to be aware of hunger. But she knew that it would be a long day and that she ought to eat. She turned into a coffee bar and bought a toasted cheese sandwich and a mug of coffee, grudging the few minutes which it took to gulp them down. The coffee was hot but almost tasteless. Flavour would have been wasted on her, but she realised as the hot liquid stung her throat how much she had needed it.

The girl at the cash desk was able to direct her to the house agent's office. It seemed to her a happy augury that it was within ten minutes' walk. She was received by a sharp featured young man in an over-tailored pin-stripe suit who, in one practised glance at her old blue tweed coat, the cheap hold-all and bag of synthetic leather, placed her precisely in his private category of client from whom little can be expected and to whom less need be given. But he found the particulars for her and his curiosity sharpened as she merely glanced at them, then folded the paper away in her bag. Her request to view that afternoon was received, as she expected, with politeness but without enthusiasm. But this was familiar territory and she knew why. The house was unoccupied. She would have to be escorted. There was nothing in her respectable drabness to suggest that she was a likely purchaser. And when he briefly excused himself to consult a colleague and returned to say that he could drive her to Creedon at once she knew the reason for that too. The office wasn't particularly busy and it was time that someone from the firm checked up on the property.

Neither of them spoke during the drive. But when they reached Creedon and he turned down the lane to the house the apprehension she had felt on her first visit returned, but deeper and stronger. Yet now it was more than the memory of an old wretchedness. This was childish misery and fear re-lived, but intensified by a dreadful adult foreboding. As the house agent parked his Morris on the grass verge she looked up at the blind windows and was seized by a spasm of terror so acute that, momentarily, she was unable to speak or move. She was aware of the man holding open the car door for her, of the smell of beer on his breath, of his face, uncomfortably close, bending on her a look of exasperated patience. She wanted to say that she had changed her mind, that the house was totally wrong for her, that there would be no point in viewing it, that she would wait for him in the car. But she willed herself to rise from the warm seat and scrambled out under his supercilious eyes, despising herself for her gracelessness. She waited in silence as he unlocked the padlock and swung open the gate.

They passed together between the neglected lawns and the spreading rhododendron bushes towards the front door. And suddenly the feet shuffling the gravel beside her were different feet and she knew that she was walking with her father as she had walked in childhood. She had only to stretch out her hand to feel the grasp of his fingers. Her companion was saying something about the house but she didn't hear. The meaningless chatter faded and she heard a different voice, her father's voice, heard for the first time in over ten years.

'It won't be for always, darling. Just until I've found a job. And I'll visit you every Sunday for lunch. Then, afterwards,

we'll be able to go for a walk together, just the two of us.
Granny has promised that. And I'll buy you a kitten. I'll bring
it next weekend. I'm sure Granny won't mind when she sees
him. A black kitten. You've always wanted a black kitten.
What shall we call him? Little black Sambo? He'll remind you
of me. And then, when I've found a job, I'll be able to rent a
little house and we'll be together again. I'll look after you, my
darling. We'll look after each other.'

She dared not look up in case she should see again those
desperately pleading eyes, begging her to understand, to make
things easy for him, not to despise him. She knew now that
she ought to have helped him, to have told him that she
understood, that she didn't mind living with Granny for a
month or so, that everything would be all right. But she hadn't
managed so adult a response. She remembered tears, desperate
clingings to his coat, her grandmother's old cook, tight-lipped,
pulling her away from him and bearing her up to bed. And
the last memory was of watching him from her room above
the porch, of his drooping defeated figure making its way
down the lane to the bus stop.

As they reached the front door she looked up. The window
was still there. But, of course, it was. She knew every room in
this dark house.

The garden was bathed in a mellow October sunlight, but
the hall struck cold and dim. The heavy mahogany staircase
led up from gloom to a darkness which hung above them like
a pall. The estate agent felt along the wall for the light switch.
But she didn't wait. She felt again the huge brass door knob
which her childish fingers had hardly encompassed and moved
unerringly into the drawing room.

The smell of the room was different. Then there had been
a scent of violets overlaid with furniture polish. Now the air
smelt cold and musty. She stood in the darkness shivering but
perfectly calm. It seemed to her that she had passed through a

267

barrier of fear as a tortured victim might pass through a pain barrier into a kind of peace. She felt a shoulder brush against her as the man went across to the window and swung open the heavy curtains.

He said: 'The last owners have left it partly furnished. Looks better that way. Easier to get offers if the place looks lived in.'

'Has there been an offer?'

'Not yet. It's not everyone's cup of tea. Bit on the large size for a modern family. And then, there's the murder. Ten years ago, but people still talk in the neighbourhood. There's been four owners since then and none of them stayed long. It's bound to affect the price. No good thinking you can hush up murder.'

His voice was carefully nonchalant, but his gaze never left her face. Walking to the empty fire grate, he stretched one arm along the mantelpiece and followed her with his eyes as she moved as if in a trance about the room.

She heard herself asking: 'What murder?'

'A sixty-four-year-old woman. Battered to death by her son-in-law. The old cook came in from the back kitchen and found him with the poker in his hand. Come to think of it, it could have been one like that.'

He nodded down to a collection of brass fire-irons resting against the fender. He said: 'It happened right where you're standing now. She was sitting in that very chair.'

She said in a voice so gruff and harsh that she hardly recognized it: 'It wasn't this chair. It was bigger. Her chair had an embroidered seat and back and there were armrests edged with crochet and the feet were like lions' claws.'

His gaze sharpened. Then he laughed warily. The watchful eyes grew puzzled, then the look changed into something else. Could it have been contempt?

'So you know about it. You're one of those.'

'One of those?'

'They aren't really in the market for a place. Couldn't afford one this size anyway. They just want a thrill, want to see where it happened. You get all sorts in this game and I can usually tell. I can give you all the gory details if you're interested. Not that there was much gore. The skull was smashed but most of the bleeding was internal. They say there was just a trickle falling down her forehead and dripping on to her hands.'

It came out so pat that she knew that he had told it all before, that he enjoyed telling it, this small recital of horror to titillate his clients and relieve the boredom of his day. She wished that she wasn't so cold. If only she could get warm again her voice wouldn't sound so strange.

She said through her dry and swollen lips: 'And the kitten. Tell me about the kitten.'

'Now that was something! That was a touch of horror if you like. The kitten was on her lap, licking up the blood. But then you know, don't you? You've heard all about it.'

'Yes,' she lied. 'I've heard all about it.'

But she had done more than that. She knew. She had seen it. She had been there.

And then the outline of the chair altered. An amorphous black shape swam before her eyes, then took form and substance. Her grandmother was sitting there, squat as a toad, dressed in her Sunday black for morning service, gloved and hatted, prayer book in her lap. She saw again the glob of phlegm at the corner of the mouth, the thread of broken veins at the side of the sharp nose. She was waiting to inspect her grandchild before church, turning on her again that look of querulous discontent. The witch was sitting there. The witch who hated her and her daddy, who had told her that he was useless and feckless and no better than her mother's murderer. The witch who was threatening to have Sambo put down because he had torn her chair, because Daddy had given him

269

to her. The witch who was planning to keep her from Daddy for ever.

And then she saw something else. The poker was there, too, just as she remembered it, the long rod of polished brass with its heavy knob.

She seized it as she had seized it then and, with a high scream of hatred and terror, brought it down on her grandmother's head. Again and again she struck, hearing the brass thudding against the leather, blow on splitting blow. And still she screamed. The room rang with the terror of it. But it was only when the frenzy passed and the dreadful noise stopped that she knew from the pain of her torn throat that the screaming had been hers.

She stood shaking, gasping for breath. Beads of sweat stood out on her forehead and she felt the stinging drops seeping into her eyes. Looking up she was aware of the man's eyes, wide with terror, staring into hers, of a muttered curse, of footsteps running to the door. And then the poker slid from her moist hands and she heard it thud softly on the rug.

He had been right, there was no blood. Only the grotesque hat knocked forward over the dead face. But as she watched a sluggish line of deep red rolled from under the brim, zigzagged down the forehead, trickled along the creases of the cheeks and began to drop steadily on to the gloved hands. And then she heard a soft mew. A ball of black fur crept from behind the chair and the ghost of Sambo, azure eyes frantic, leapt as he had leapt ten years earlier delicately up to that unmoving lap.

She looked at her hands. Where were the gloves, the white cotton gloves which the witch had always insisted must be worn to church? But these hands, no longer the hands of a nine-year-old child, were naked. And the chair was empty. There was nothing but the split leather, the burst of horsehair stuffing, a faint smell of violets fading on the quiet air.

She walked out of the front door without closing it behind her as she had left it then. She walked as she had walked then, gloved and unsullied, down the gravel path between the rhododendrons, out of the ironwork gate and up the lane towards the church. The bell had only just started ringing; she would be in good time. In the distance she had glimpsed her father climbing a stile from the water meadow into the lane. So he must have set out early after breakfast and had walked to Creedon. And why so early? Had he needed that long walk to settle something in his mind? Had it been a pathetic attempt to propitiate the witch by coming with them to church? Or, blessed thought, had he come to take her away, to see that her few belongings were packed and ready by the time the service was over? Yes, that was what she had thought at the time. She remembered it now, that fountain of hope soaring and dancing into glorious certainty. When she got home all would be ready. They would stand there together and defy the witch, would tell her that they were leaving together, the two of them and Sambo, that she would never see them again. At the end of the road she looked back and saw for the last time the beloved ghost crossing the lane to the house towards that fatally open door.

And after that? The vision was fading now. She could remember nothing of the service except a blaze of red and blue shifting like a kaleidoscope then fusing into a stained glass window, the Good Shepherd gathering a lamb to his bosom. And afterwards? Surely there had been strangers waiting in the porch, grave concerned faces, whispers and sidelong glances, a woman in some kind of uniform, an official car. And after that, nothing. Memory was a blank.

But now, at last, she knew where her father was buried. And she knew why she would never be able to visit him, never make that pious pilgrimage to the place where he lay because of her, the shameful place where she had put him. There could

271

be no flowers, no obelisk, no loving message carved in marble for those who lay in quicklime behind a prison wall. And then, unbidden, came the final memory. She saw again the open church door, the trickle of the congregation filing in, enquiring faces turning towards her as she arrived alone in the porch. She heard again that high childish voice speaking the words which more than any others had slipped that rope of hemp over his shrouded head.

'Granny? She isn't very well. She told me to come on my own. No, there's nothing to worry about. She's quite all right. Daddy's with her.'

Aces High

PETER CHEYNEY

LORD PRIORTON – A perfect replica of the stage nobleman – rose from the desk and advanced to meet Callaghan. His face was long, lean, distinguished; his drooping but well-trimmed grey moustache gave him the appearance, Callaghan thought, of an unhappy seal.

He said: 'Sit down please, Mr Callaghan.' He opened a silver box of cigarettes, handed it to Callaghan. He went on: 'Like most other people of my class, Mr Callaghan, I've very little money. In fact I've nothing except this house, my cottage in the country, and, when I've paid my taxes, a few hundreds a year to live on. But I have one thing – my pride. And I'm afraid it has received a severe shock.'

Callaghan said: 'That's too bad! And you think I can do something to help about it?'

The peer nodded. 'It's not only a matter of pride, but of reputation,' he said, 'and also –' he paused for a second – 'of some money.'

'I see,' said Callaghan. 'Supposing you tell me about it.'

Priorton said: 'As you probably know, Mr Callaghan, I used to be a great gambler. Well, I still gamble a little. From time to time I have a few friends in here, give them dinner and we play cards. Such a party was held here last week.' He sighed. 'Little did I realize when I arranged it,' he went on, 'what the results were to be.'

Callaghan said: 'So the results weren't so good, hey? I suppose you knew the people you were playing cards with?'

Lord Priorton nodded. 'I know them all very well,' he said. 'The party consisted of two men, a woman and myself. We were playing poker. One of the men was a rich American – George Vandeler – who is over here on business; the other man – a young man of thirty – Eustace Willhaven, the eldest son of my old friend Hubert Willhaven; the lady, a charming widow – Mrs Melody Vazeley – is the sister of another good friend of mine, Charles Venning. Last, there was, of course, myself. In other words,' continued the peer gloomily, 'there was no one who is not very well known to me. You understand?'

'I understand perfectly,' said Callaghan. 'Go on, Lord Priorton. And who did what to who?'

The other nodded. He said: 'Exactly! You've put it very succinctly, Mr Callaghan. Who did what to who! To cut a long story short, I was very lucky, and when the settlement came I had won just over three thousand pounds. The upshot of it was that Eustace Willhaven owed me three thousand five hundred – a very nice sum.'

'Did he mind losing the money?' asked Callaghan.

'Good heavens, no,' said Priorton. 'Anyway, he knew his father would pay – his father always does pay. He's a rich man and even if he does keep Eustace short of money he's only too glad to settle his gambling debts when he loses and even more delighted when his son wins.'

Callaghan asked: 'And did Eustace settle?'

'Not then,' said Priorton. 'He said laughingly that he

couldn't give me a cheque on his own bank because he'd only a few pounds in his account, but that if I wouldn't mind he would arrange things with his father and send a cheque round to me in the course of the next day. Well . . . he did so.'

'I see. And what happened?' asked Callaghan.

Priorton took a cigarette from the silver box on the table. He lit it. Callaghan noticed that the hand that held the lighter was shaking a little.

Priorton said: 'The cheque was an open cheque. I went round to Eustace's bank to cash it. Well, they wouldn't cash it. They marked it "Orders not to pay" and gave it back to me.'

Callaghan nodded. 'Not so good,' he said. 'So Eustace Willhaven had stopped payment of the cheque. Why?'

Priorton shook his head. 'I don't know,' he said gloomily.

Callaghan asked: 'I suppose Eustace's father – Hubert Willhaven – isn't hard up?'

Priorton smiled. 'Don't worry about that,' he said. 'Willhaven is practically a millionaire. Three thousand five hundred means nothing to him. That's what I can't understand.'

Callaghan said: 'I see. You mean that Eustace must have a really serious reason for stopping payment of this cheque?'

'Precisely,' said Priorton.

Callaghan drew on his cigarette. He said: 'It's odd, isn't it? I suppose Willhaven knew his son had been playing cards here?'

'Good heavens, yes,' said Priorton. 'Young Willhaven plays here at least once a month. Several times his father's been here and played with him, or stood by and watched the game.'

Callaghan said: 'What do you want me to do?'

'First of all,' said the peer. 'I'm fearfully worried about Willhaven having stopped that cheque. Quite obviously, he or his father must *think* they've got a good reason for doing so. They may think that I'm going to tell people that Eustace stopped payment of a cheque for a debt of honour, and he'll naturally want to defend himself against such an accusation. He may say things that will react against my character.

'Secondly, I want the money, Mr Callaghan. Three thousand five hundred pounds is a lot to me.'

Callaghan asked casually: 'Lord Priorton, did it ever occur to you to ring up Eustace Willhaven and ask him why he'd stopped payment of that cheque?'

Priorton nodded his head. 'It did occur to me,' he said. 'I rang up Eustace, and he said that he was fearfully sorry about it, but that he did it because his father *ordered* him to stop payment – he didn't know why.'

'I see,' said Callaghan. 'You didn't speak to the father?'

'No,' said Priorton. 'I think it's his business to explain his action to *me!*'

Callaghan said: 'You're quite right.' He got up. 'Well, I'll do my best,' he said.

Priorton asked: 'What are you going to do, Mr Callaghan?'

Callaghan grinned. He said: 'Perhaps it would be better if I didn't tell you. What people don't know can't hurt 'em.'

Priorton nodded. He said: 'About your fee. You know I'm pretty hard up.'

Callaghan said: 'I'll take a chance on you, Lord Priorton. I think you've told me the truth. If I get that cheque paid, I'll take the odd five hundred. If I don't, I'll charge you nothing. How's that?'

'Very sportin'!' said the peer.

Callaghan stopped Eustace Willhaven on his way out of the Berkeley Buttery. He said: 'Excuse me, Mr Willhaven, my name's Callaghan. I'm a private detective. I'm trying to clear up a small point that's worrying a client of mine – Lord Priorton. It's about that cheque you gave him in settlement of your gambling losses.'

Eustace Willhaven said: 'Well, really! Do you think this is a good place to discuss it?'

'It's as good as any other, isn't it?' retorted Callaghan. 'Do you know why your father told you to stop that cheque?'

Willhaven adjusted his eyeglass. He looked seriously at Callaghan. He said: 'To tell you the truth, Mr Callaghan, I don't. I don't know why my father told me to stop that cheque. But if you knew anything about my father, you'd know he's not likely to do a thing like that without good reason. Good-day to you!'

Hubert Willhaven – tall, distinguished, ascetic looking – listened attentively to what Callaghan had to say. When the detective had finished talking, Willhaven smoked silently for a few seconds. Then he said: 'What you have to say interests me very much, Mr Callaghan. And I appreciate your explanation as to why Lord Priorton should have employed you to try and settle this matter.' Callaghan said: 'Let's not become confused about the issues at stake, Mr Willhaven. The position, to my mind, is quite simple.'

Willhaven raised his eyebrows. 'Is it?' he queried.

Callaghan said: 'To my mind, yes. A settlement was arrived at when this poker game was over – a general settlement. On this general settlement your son had to pay three thousand five hundred pounds to Lord Priorton. Quite obviously, when he left that house he intended to pay that debt. The proof of that is that he asked you for the money. The fact that *you* thought he owed it is proved by you having given him the money to put into his bank so that he could send a cheque to Lord Priorton.' Callaghan grinned. 'After that, of course,' he said, 'there's a snag.'

Willhaven smiled. He thought that Callaghan's grin was infectious.

'The snag being that I told Eustace to stop the cheque.

Perhaps you can tell me something about that too, Mr Callaghan,' he suggested.

Callaghan said: 'I think I can. To my mind there is only one reason why you should have done that. There *could* only be one reason; that is that one of the other people who took part in that game besides Lord Priorton and your son have influenced you to have the payment of that cheque stopped. Lord Priorton *wanted* to receive the money. You *intended* it should be paid. Something made you alter your mind. My guess is, it was one of those two other people, and I'm going to find out. Either you tell me or I'll find some means of making them talk.'

Willhaven said: 'They might not *want* to talk, Mr Callaghan.'

Callaghan said: 'Whenever I want somebody to talk I find a means of making 'em talk.' He grinned. 'You'd be surprised,' he said.

Willhaven said: 'I probably shouldn't be. But I'll save them the inconvenience. You're quite right in your supposition, because one of the other parties who took part in that game gave me some information which merited the payment being stopped.'

Callaghan said: 'One of the other parties? That would be Mr Vandeler or Mrs Vazeley.'

'Exactly,' said Willhaven. 'Mrs Vazeley wrote me a note and informed me that in her opinion the game had been crooked from start to finish.'

Callaghan said: 'Do you know Mrs Vazeley well?'

Willhaven shook his had. 'Not *very* well,' he said. 'I've met her.'

Callaghan nodded. 'You were prepared to accept this accusation from a woman who is merely an acquaintance, against the reputation of a man – Lord Priorton – whom you've known for years?'

Willhaven said: 'The point doesn't arise, Mr Callaghan. She was able to prove what she said!'

Mrs Vazeley was a delightful woman of about thirty-eight. Her clothes were simple but marvellous. She had *chic* and an extraordinary allure. Callaghan thought he could fall for Mrs Vazeley very easily. He said: 'You know, Mrs Vazeley, you're in rather a jam.'

She said airily: 'Am I, Mr Callaghan? How exciting! My life is so uneventful that the idea of being in a jam almost appeals to me. Another thing, I ought to tell you that I'm absolutely *thrilled* at meeting a private detective. Please have a cigarette. And would you like a drink?'

Callaghan said he would. Whilst he was drinking the brandy and soda, she said:

'Do tell me about the jam I'm in. I think I ought to know, don't you?'

Callaghan said: 'You wrote a note to Hubert Willhaven, and you afterwards talked to him, either personally or on the telephone, and told him that the poker game at Lord Priorton's house was crooked. Quite obviously, as Willhaven told his son to stop payment of the cheque after that conversation with you, the suggestion was that Lord Priorton was the crook. Have you ever heard of the law of libel and slander, Mrs Vazeley? If you can't prove that Lord Priorton was responsible for that game being crooked you will be in a jam, and it might cost you a lot of money.'

She said: 'I know. I knew that when I told Mr Willhaven. But what else could I do? You see I *knew* that game was crooked, Mr Callaghan.'

Callaghan said: 'May I know how you knew?'

She said: 'It's fearfully simple. *I* had no reason to complain about the game. I won about fifty pounds. I won fifty pounds from Mr Vandeler, and he settled that in bank-notes before the general settlement was made between the others. So you'll agree that I've no cause for complaint.'

Callaghan said: 'That's agreed. But how can you prove that that game was crooked and that Priorton was responsible?'

She said: 'I'll tell you. I was rather elated at winning fifty pounds, and when the game broke up I left my cigarette case behind. It's rather a valuable case. I'd left it on a little table by the side of my chair whilst I was playing. Next morning I had a very early appointment to leave London for Bangor on a train at seven-twenty, and I thought that on my way to the station I'd call in at Lord Priorton's house – I thought that possibly the servants would be up – and get my cigarette case. When I arrived at the house, the boot-boy let me in. I told him what I wanted and he said he'd go and look for my cigarette case. He seemed a rather stupid boy, so I told him not to bother but to go on with his work and I'd go and get the cigarette case because I knew exactly where it was. So I went up to the room on the first floor where we'd played, and there was my cigarette case. I picked it up. The card table was just as we'd left it the night before with the cards still lying on the table.

'The early morning sunlight was coming through the windows. It reflected on the glazed backs of the cards, and I saw something that gave me rather a shock.'

Callaghan asked: 'What did you see?'

'Every one of those cards was marked,' said Mrs Vazeley. 'They'd been beautifully marked – cleverly marked – with a pin. Once you knew where to look you could see the little tiny pin-points, and if you were dealing you could tell the value of the card by the touch. Needless to say I was shocked. But I wanted to make quite certain. I examined all the cards. They were all marked. I took three or four of them and I showed them to Mr Willhaven when I talked to him about it. If that isn't proof, what is?'

Callaghan said: 'It looks as if there isn't a great deal of argument.' He picked up his hat. 'I'm afraid you won't have to worry about that action for slander.'

She said: 'No, I didn't think I should. Must you be going, Mr Callaghan?

Hubert Willhaven put down his newspaper as Callaghan was shown into the room. He said: 'Good morning, Mr Callaghan. What can I do for you?'

Callaghan lit a cigarette. He said casually: 'I think the easiest thing for you to do, Willhaven, would be to give me a cheque for three thousand five hundred pounds, and we'll call this business quits.'

Willhaven said: 'You're being funny, aren't you? I'm not in a frame of mind for humour this morning.'

Callaghan said: 'I'm not being funny. Just listen to me for a moment. When I'm handling a case I never look for clues. I leave that to the detectives in fiction. Usually I'm only interested in people. If I can find that somebody in a case has done something that seems to me incongruous, I wonder why.' Callaghan grinned. 'It usually gets me somewhere,' he said.

Willhaven said: 'It would have to be a hell of an incongruity to get you three thousand five hundred pounds from me, Callaghan.'

'I'll get it all right,' said Callaghan. 'Because it was a hell of an incongruity. Listen. I wondered why it was that Mrs Vazeley had to telephone *you* and tell *you* that that game was crooked. Why didn't she telephone your son? She knows him. He's a man. He's thirty years of age. The obvious thing for her to have done was to have telephoned to *him*. She didn't do it.'

Willhaven said: 'I don't see the point.'

'Of course you don't,' said Callaghan. 'I'll tell you what the point was. It was necessary for the success of your son's little plot that there should seem to be no connection between Mrs Vazeley and himself. That's why she telephoned you.'

Willhaven said: 'Are you suggesting that this is a put-up job between my son and Mrs Vazeley?'

'I'm not suggesting anything. I'm *telling* you,' said Callaghan. 'Lord Priorton told me that you'd paid your son's gambling debts before. You're a rich man and you aren't going to have people saying that his debts of honour are unpaid. But quite obviously your son is often short of money – you keep him so because of his extravagance – otherwise he wouldn't have to go to you to pay money into his bank in order to give a cheque that would be met for a gambling debt.' He grinned. 'Not only has he been doing it on the people that he and Mrs Vazeley have played cards with, but he's also been doing it on *you.*'

Willhaven said: 'I think you're talking nonsense. I still don't understand what you mean.'

Callaghan said: 'I'll tell you what I mean. Your son and Mrs Vazeley went into that poker game at Lord Priorton's as partners. If they both won, it was going to be all right, but on this occasion Mrs Vazeley won fifty pounds, and your son dropped three thousand five hundred. So Mrs Vazeley leaves her cigarette case behind. The next morning, before anybody's up, she goes round to the house, rings the bell and asks for her cigarette case. She says she knows where she's left it. She probably tells the boot-boy to get on with his business and not bother to take her upstairs. While she was up there she very quickly marked the cards with a pin. That was easy. She's used to doing it, and it would take her five or six minutes. Then she went off, taking four or five of the cards with her. She rang you up. She knew you'd tell your son; that he'd stop the cheque. And she also knew, as *he* knew, that you wouldn't ask him to return the three thousand five hundred pounds. Get it?'

Willhaven said: 'I see. You might be wrong, mightn't you?'

Callaghan said: 'I *might* be. But unfortunately for herself Mrs Vazeley told me that she got up early that morning in order to catch a train for Bangor in North Wales – the seven-twenty. Well, there wasn't a seven-twenty. That substantiates it a little bit, doesn't it?'

Willhaven nodded.

'The other thing is this,' said Callaghan, 'I understand from Lord Priorton that the last person to shuffle and deal the cards was your son. Therefore his thumb-prints should have been superimposed on practically every card in the pack. But that wasn't so. The most recent thumb-prints on every card in the pack were Mrs Vazeley's.' Callaghan grinned. 'I think that clinches it, don't you?' he said.

Willhaven said: 'I'm not going to argue. Anyway, I'll give you the cheque.'

He went to the desk, got his cheque book.

Lord Priorton handed Callaghan a large whisky and soda. He said: 'Very nice work, Mr Callaghan. I shall be delighted to pay you your fee. I congratulate you on your brilliant idea of checking the finger-prints on the back of the cards. I didn't know you had done that. That really was first class.'

Callaghan said: 'You can save your congratulations. I didn't check *any* finger-prints on *any* cards. I had a hunch and I played it.'

The Bones of the Case

R. AUSTIN FREEMAN

PART I

MR PERCIVAL BLAND was a somewhat uncommon type of criminal. In the first place he really had an appreciable amount of common-sense. If he had only had a little more, he would not have been a criminal at all. As it was, he had just sufficient judgment to perceive that the consequences of unlawful acts accumulate as the acts are repeated; to realize that the criminal's position must, at length, become untenable; and to take what he considered fair precautions against the inevitable catastrophe.

But in spite of these estimable traits of character and the precautions aforesaid, Mr Bland found himself in rather a tight place and with a prospect of increasing tightness. The causes of this uncomfortable tension do not concern us, and may be dismissed with the remark, that, if one perseveringly distributes flash Bank of England notes among the money-changers of the Continent, there will come a day of reckoning when those notes are tendered to the exceedingly knowing old lady who lives in Threadneedle Street.

Mr Bland considered uneasily the approaching storm-cloud as he raked over the 'miscellaneous property' in the Sale-rooms of Messrs Plimpton. He was a confirmed frequenter of auctions, as was not unnatural; for the criminal is essentially a gambler. And criminal and auction-frequenter have one quality in common; each hopes to get something of value without paying the market price for it.

So Percival turned over the dusty oddments and his own difficulties at one and the same time. The vital questions were: When would the storm burst? And would it pass by the harbour of refuge that he had been at such pains to construct? Let us inspect that harbour of refuge.

A quiet flat in the pleasant neighbourhood of Battersea bore a name-plate inscribed, Mr Robert Lindsay; and the tenant was known to the porter and the charwoman who attended to the flat, as a fair-haired gentleman who was engaged in the book trade as a travelling agent, and was consequently a good deal away from home. Now Mr Robert Lindsay bore a distinct resemblance to Percival Bland; which was not surprising seeing that they were first cousins (or, at any rate, they said they were; and we may presume that they knew). But they were not very much alike. Mr Lindsay had flaxen, or rather sandy, hair; Mr Bland's hair was black. Mr Bland had a mole under his left eye; Mr Lindsay had no mole under his eye – but carried one in a small box in his waistcoat pocket.

At somewhat rare intervals the cousins called on one another; but they had the very worst of luck, for neither of them ever seemed to find the other at home. And what was even more odd was that whenever Mr Bland spent an evening at home in his lodgings over the oil shop in Bloomsbury, Mr Lindsay's flat was empty; and as sure as Mr Lindsay was at home in his flat so surely were Mr Bland's lodgings vacant for the time being. It was a queer coincidence, if anyone had noticed it; but nobody ever did.

However, if Percival saw little of his cousin, it was not a case of 'out of sight, out of mind'. On the contrary; so great was his solicitude for the latter's welfare that he not only had made a will constituting him his executor and sole legatee, but he had actually insured his life for no less a sum than three thousand pounds; and this will, together with the insurance policy, investment securities and other necessary documents, he had placed in the custody of a highly respectable solicitor. All of which did him great credit. It isn't every man who is willing to take so much trouble for a mere cousin.

Mr Bland continued his perambulations, pawing over the miscellaneous raffle from sheer force of habit, reflecting on the coming crisis in his own affairs, and on the provisions that he had made for his cousin Robert. As for the latter, they were excellent as far as they went, but they lacked definiteness and perfect completeness. There was the contingency of a 'stretch', for instance; say fourteen years penal servitude. The insurance policy did not cover that. And, meanwhile, what was to become of the estimable Robert?

He had bruised his thumb somewhat severely in a screw-cutting lathe, and had abstractedly turned the handle of a bird-organ until politely requested by an attendant to desist, when he came upon a series of boxes containing, according to the catalogue, 'a collection of surgical instruments the property of a lately deceased practitioner'. To judge by the appearance of the instruments, the practitioner must have commenced practice in his early youth and died at a very advanced age. They were an uncouth set of tools, of no value whatever excepting as testimonials to the amazing tenacity of life of our ancestors; but Percival fingered them over according to his wont, working the handle of a complicated brass syringe. and ejecting a drop of greenish fluid on to the shirtfront of a dressy Hebrew (who requested him to 'point the damn thing at thomeone elth nectht time'), opening musty leather cases, clicking off spring scarifiers and feeling the edges of strange, crooked-bladed knives. Then he came upon a largish black box, which, when he raised the lid, breathed out an ancient and fish-like aroma and exhibited a collection of bones, yellow, greasy-looking and spotted in places with mildew. The catalogue described them as 'a complete set of human osteology'; but they were not an ordinary 'student's set', for the bones of the hands and feet, instead of being strung together on cat-gut, were united by their original ligaments and were of an unsavoury brown colour.

'I thay, misther,' expostulated the Hebrew, 'shut that bocth. Thmellth like a blooming inquetht.'

But the contents of the black box seemed to have a fascination for Percival. He looked in at those greasy remnants of mortality, at the brown and mouldy hands and feet and the skull that peeped forth eerily from the folds of a flannel wrapping; and they breathed out something more than that stale and musty odour. A suggestion – vague and general at first, but rapidly crystallizing into distinct shape – seemed to steal out of the black box into his consciousness; a suggestion that somehow seemed to connect itself with his estimable cousin Robert.

For upwards of a minute he stood motionless, as one immersed in reverie, the lid poised in his hand and a dreamy eye fixed on the half-uncovered skull. A stir in the room roused him. The sale was about to begin. The members of the knock-out and other habitués seated themselves on benches around a long, baize-covered table; the attendants took possession of the first lots and opened their catalogues as if about to sing an introductory chorus; and a gentleman with a waxed moustache and a striking resemblance to his late Majesty, the third Napoleon, having ascended to the rostrum bespoke the attention of the assembly by a premonitory tap with his hammer.

How odd are some of the effects of a guilty conscience! With what absurd self-consciousness do we read into the minds of others our own undeclared intentions, when those intentions are unlawful! Had Percival Bland wanted a set of human bones for any legitimate purpose – such as anatomical study – he would have bought it openly and unembarrassed. Now, he found himself earnestly debating whether he should not bid for some of the surgical instruments, just for the sake of appearances; and there being little time in which to make up his mind – for the deceased practitioner's effects came first in the catalogue – he was already the richer by a set of cupping-glasses, a tooth-key, and an instrument of unknown use and diabolical aspect, before the fateful lot was called.

At length the black box was laid on the table, an object of obscene mirth to the knockers-out, and the auctioneer read the entry:

'Lot seventeen; a complete set of human osteology. A very useful and valuable set of specimens, gentlemen.'

He looked round at the assembly majestically, oblivious of sundry inquiries as to the identity of the deceased and the verdict of the coroner's jury, and finally suggested five shillings.

'Six,' said Percival.

An attendant held the box open, and, chanting the mystic word 'Loddlemen!' (which, being interpreted, meant 'Lot, gentlemen'), thrust it under the rather bulbous nose of the smart Hebrew; who remarked that 'they 'ummed a bit too much to thoot him' and pushed it away.

'Going at six shillings,' said the auctioneer, reproachfully; and as nobody contradicted him, he smote the rostrum with his hammer and the box was delivered into the hands of Percival on the payment of that modest sum.

Having crammed the cupping-glasses, the tooth-key and the unknown instrument into the box, Percival obtained from one of the attendants a length of cord, with which he secured the lid. Then he carried his treasure out into the street, and, chartering a four-wheeler, directed the driver to proceed to Charing Cross Station. At the station he booked the box in the cloak-room (in the name of Simpson) and left it for a couple of hours; at the expiration of which he returned, and, employing a different porter, had it conveyed to a hansom, in which it was borne to his lodgings over the oil-shop in Bloomsbury. There he, himself, carried it, unobserved, up the stairs, and, depositing it in a large cupboard, locked the door and pocketed the key.

And thus was the curtain rung down on the first act.

The second act opened only a couple of days later, the office of call-boy – to pursue the metaphor to the bitter end –

being discharged by a Belgian police official who emerged from the main entrance to the Bank of England. What should have led Percival Bland into so unsafe a neighbourhood it is difficult to imagine, unless it was that strange fascination that seems so frequently to lure the criminal to places associated with his crime. But there he was within a dozen paces of the entrance when the officer came forth, and mutual recognition was instantaneous. Almost equally instantaneous was the self-possessed Percival's decision to cross the road.

It is not a nice road to cross. The old-fashioned horse-driver would condescend to shout a warning to the indiscreet wayfarer. Not so the modern chauffeur, who looks stonily before him and leaves you to get out of the way of Juggernaut. He knows his 'exonerating' coroner's jury. At the moment, however, the procession of Juggernauts was at rest; but Percival had seen the presiding policeman turn to move away and he darted across the fronts of the vehicles even as they started. The foreign officer followed. But in that moment the whole procession had got in motion. A motor omnibus thundered past in front of him; another was bearing down on him relentlessly. He hesitated, and sprang back; and then a taxi-cab, darting out from behind, butted him heavily, sending him sprawling in the road, whence he scrambled as best he could back on to the pavement.

Percival, meanwhile, had swung himself lightly on to the footboard of the first omnibus just as it was gathering speed. A few seconds saw him safely across at the Mansion House, and in a few more, he was whirling down Queen Victoria Street. The danger was practically over, though he took the precaution to alight at St Paul's, and, crossing to Newgate Street, board another west-bound omnibus.

That night he sat in his lodgings turning over his late experience. It had been a narrow shave. That sort of thing mustn't happen again. In fact, seeing that the law was undoubtedly about to be set in motion, it was high time that certain little plans of his should be set in motion, too. Only, there was a difficulty; a serious difficulty. And as Percival thought round and round that difficulty his brows wrinkled and he hummed a soft refrain.

'Then is the time for disappearing.
Take a header – down you go—'

A tap at the door cut his song short. It was his landlady, Mrs Brattle; a civil woman, and particularly civil just now. For she had a little request to make.

'It was about Christmas Night, Mr Bland,' said Mrs Brattle. 'My husband and me thought of spending the evening with his brother at Hornsey, and we were going to let the maid go home to her mother's for the night, if it wouldn't put you out.'

'Wouldn't put me out in the least, Mrs Brattle,' said Percival.

'You needn't sit up for us, you see,' pursued Mrs Brattle, 'if you'd just leave the side door unbolted. We shan't be home before two or three, but we'll come in quiet not to disturb you.'

'You won't disturb me,' Percival replied with a genial laugh. 'I'm a sober man in general; but "Christmas comes but once a year." When once I'm tucked up in bed, I shall take a bit of waking on Christmas Night.'

Mrs Brattle smiled indulgently. 'And you won't feel lonely, all alone in the house?'

'Lonely!' exclaimed Percival. 'Lonely! With a roaring fire, a jolly book, a box of good cigars and a bottle of sound port – ah, and a second bottle if need be. Not I.'

Mrs Brattle shook her head. 'Ah,' said she, 'you bachelors! Well, well. It's a good thing to be independent,' and with this profound reflection she smiled herself out of the room and descended the stairs.

As her footsteps died away Percival sprang from his chair and began excitedly to pace the room. His eyes sparkled and his face was wreathed with smiles. Presently he halted before the fireplace, and, gazing into the embers, laughed aloud.

'Damn funny!' said he. 'Deuced rich! Neat! Very neat! Ha! Ha!' And here he resumed his interrupted song:

'When the sky above is clearing
When the sky above is clearing
Bob up serenely, bob up serenely,
Bob up serenely from below!'

Which may be regarded as closing the first scene of the second act.

During the few days that intervened before Christmas, Percival went abroad but little; and yet he was a busy man. He did a little surreptitious shopping, venturing out as far as Charing Cross Road; and his purchases were decidedly miscellaneous. A porridge saucepan, a second-hand copy of *Gray's Anatomy*, a rabbit skin, a large supply of glue and upwards of ten pounds of shin of beef seems a rather odd assortment; and it was a mercy that the weather was frosty, for otherwise Percival's bedroom, in which these delicacies were deposited under lock and key, would have yielded odorous traces of its wealth.

But it was in the long evenings that his industry was most conspicuous; and then it was that the big cupboard with the excellent lever lock, which he himself had fixed on, began to fill up with the fruits of his labours. In those evenings the porridge saucepan would simmer on the hob with a rich lading of good Scotch glue, the black box of the deceased practitioner would be hauled forth from its hiding-place, and the well-thumbed *Gray* laid open on the table.

It was an arduous business though; a stiffer task than he had bargained for. The right and left bones were so confoundedly alike, and the bones that joined were so difficult to fit together. However, the plates in *Gray* were large and very clear, so it was only a question of taking enough trouble.

His method of work was simple and practical. Having fished a bone out of the box, he would compare it with the illustrations in the book until he had identified it beyond all doubt, when he would tie on it a paper label with its name and side – right or left. Then he would search for the adjoining bone, and, having fitted the two together, would secure them with a good daub of glue and lay them in the fender to dry. It was a crude and horrible method of articulation that would have made a museum curator shudder. But it seemed to answer Percival's purpose – whatever that may have been – for gradually the loose 'items' came together into recognizable members such as arms and legs, the vertebrae – which were, fortunately, strung in their order on a thick cord – were joined up into a solid backbone, and even the ribs, which were the toughest job of all, fixed on in some semblance of a thorax. It was a wretched performance. The bones were plastered with gouts of glue and yet would have broken apart at a touch. But, as we have said, Percival seemed satisfied, and as he was the only person concerned, there was nothing more to be said.

In due course, Christmas Day arrived. Percival dined with the Brattles at two, dozed after dinner, woke up for tea, and then, as Mrs Brattle, in purple and fine raiment, came in to remove the tea-tray, he spread out on the table the materials for the night's carouse. A quarter of an hour later, the side-door slammed, and, peering out of the window, he saw the shopkeeper and his wife hurrying away up the gas-lit street towards the nearest omnibus route.

Then Mr Percival Bland began his evening's entertainment; and a most remarkable entertainment it was, even for a solitary bachelor, left alone in a house on Christmas Night. First, he took off his clothing and dressed himself in a fresh suit. Then, from the cupboard, he brought forth the reconstituted 'set of osteology', and, laying the various members on the table, returned to the bedroom, whence he presently reappeared with a large, unsavoury parcel which he had disinterred from a trunk. The parcel, being opened, revealed his accumulated purchases in the matter of shin of beef.

With a large knife, providently sharpened beforehand, he cut the beef into large, thin slices which he proceeded to wrap around the various bones that formed the 'complete set'; whereby their nakedness was certainly mitigated though their attractiveness was by no means increased. Having thus 'clothed the dry bones', he gathered up the scraps of offal that were left, to be placed presently inside the trunk. It was an extraordinary proceeding, but the next was more extraordinary still.

Taking up the newly clothed members one by one, he began very carefully to insinuate them into the garments that he had recently shed. It was a ticklish business, for the glued joints were as brittle as glass. Very cautiously the legs were separately inducted, first into underclothing and then into trousers, the skeleton feet were fitted with the cast-off socks and delicately persuaded into the boots. The arms, in like manner, were gingerly pressed into their various sleeves and through the arm-holes of the waistcoat; and then came the most difficult task of all – to fit the garments on the trunk. For the skull and ribs, secured to the back-bone with mere spots of glue, were ready to drop off at a shake; and yet the garments had to be drawn over them with the arms enclosed in the sleeves. But Percival managed it at last by resting his 'restoration' in the big, padded arm-chair and easing the garments on inch by inch.

It now remained only to give the finishing touch; which

was done by cutting the rabbit-skin to the requisite shape and affixing it to the skull with a thin coat of stiff glue; and when the skull had thus been finished with a sort of crude, makeshift wig, its appearance was so appalling as even to disturb the nerves of the matter-of-fact Percival. However, this was no occasion for cherishing sentiment. A skull in an extemporized wig or false scalp might be, and in fact was, a highly unpleasant object; but so was a Belgian police officer.

Having finished the 'restoration', Percival fetched the water-jug from his bedroom, and, descending to the shop, the door of which had been left unlocked, tried the taps of the various drums and barrels until he came to the one which contained methylated spirit; and from this he filled his jug and returned to the bedroom. Pouring the spirit out into the basin, he tucked a towel round his neck and filling his sponge with spirit, proceeded very vigorously to wash his hair and eyebrows and as, by degrees, the spirit in the basin grew dark and turbid, so did his hair and eyebrows grow lighter in colour until, after a final energetic rub with a towel, they had acquired a golden or sandy hue indistinguishable from that of the hair of his cousin Robert. Even the mole under his eye was susceptible to the changing conditions, for when he had wetted it thoroughly with spirit, he was able with the blade of a penknife, to peel it off as neatly as if it had been stuck on with spirit-gum. Having done which, he deposited it in a tiny box which he carried in his waistcoat pocket.

The proceedings which followed were unmistakable as to their object. First he carried the basin of spirit through into the sitting-room and deliberately poured its contents on to the floor by the arm-chair. Then, having returned the basin to the bedroom, he again went down to the shop, where he selected a couple of galvanised buckets from the stock, filled them with paraffin oil from one of the great drums and carried them upstairs. The oil from one bucket he poured over the arm-chair and its repulsive occupant; the other bucket he simply emptied on the carpet, and then went down to the shop for a fresh supply.

When this proceeding had been repeated once or twice the entire floor and all the furniture were saturated, and such a reek of paraffin filled the air of the room that Percival thought it wise to turn out the gas. Returning to the shop, he poured a bucketful of oil over the stack of bundles of firewood, another over the counter and floor and a third over the loose articles on the walls and hanging from the ceiling. Looking up at the latter he now perceived a number of greasy patches where the oil had soaked through from the floor above, and some of these were beginning to drip on to the shop floor.

He now made his final preparations. Taking a bundle of 'Wheel' firelighters, he made a small pile against the stack of firewood. In the midst of the firelighters he placed a ball of string saturated in paraffin; and in the central hole of the ball he stuck a half-dozen diminutive Christmas candles. This mine was now ready. Providing himself with a stock of firelighters, a few balls of paraffined string and a dozen or so of the little candles, he went upstairs to the sitting-room, which was immediately above the shop. Here, by the glow of the fire, he built up one or two piles of firelighters around and, partly under the arm-chair, placed the balls of string on the piles and stuck two or three bundles in each ball. Everything was now ready. Stepping into the bedroom, he took from the cupboard a spare overcoat, a new hat and a new umbrella – for he must leave his old hats, coat and umbrella in the hall. He put on the coat and hat, and, with the umbrella in his hand, returned to the sitting-room.

Opposite the arm-chair he stood awhile, irresolute, and a pang of horror shot through him. It was a terrible thing that he was going to do; a thing the consequences of which no one could foresee. He glanced furtively at the awful shape that sat huddled in the chair, its horrible head all awry and its rigid limbs sprawling in hideous grotesque deformity. It was but a dummy, a mere scarecrow; but yet, in the dim firelight, the grisly face under that horrid wig seemed to leer intelligently, to watch him with secret malice out of its shadowy eye-sockets, until he looked away with clammy skin and a shiver of half-superstitious terror.

But this would never do. The evening had run out, consumed by these engrossing labours; it was nearly eleven o'clock, and high time for him to be gone. For if the Brattles should return prematurely he was lost. Pulling himself together with an effort, he struck a match and lit the little candles one after the other. In a quarter of an hour or so, they would have burned down to the balls of string, and then—

He walked quickly out of the room; but, at the door, he paused for a moment to look back at the ghastly figure, seated rigidly in the chair with the lighted candles at its feet, like some foul fiend appeased by votive fires. The unsteady flames threw flickering shadows on its face that made it seem to mow and gibber and grin in mockery of all his care and caution. So he turned and tremblingly ran down the stairs – opening the staircase window as he went. Running into the shop, he lit the candles there and ran out again, shutting the door after him.

Secretly and guiltily he crept down the hall, and opening the door a few inches peered out. A blast of icy wind poured in with a light powdering of dry snow. He opened his umbrella, flung open the door, looked up and down the empty street, stepped out, closed the door softly and strode away over the whitening pavement.

PART II

IT WAS ONE of the axioms of medico-legal practice laid down by my colleague, John Thorndyke, that the investigator should be constantly on his guard against the effect of suggestion. Not only must all prejudices and preconceptions be avoided, but when information is received from outside, the actual, undeniable facts must be carefully sifted from the inferences which usually accompany them. Of the necessity for this precaution our insurance practice furnished an excellent instance in the case of the fire at Mr Brattle's oil-shop.

The case was brought to our notice by Mr Stalker of the 'Griffin' Fire and Life Insurance Society a few days after Christmas. He dropped in, ostensibly to wish us a Happy New Year, but a discreet pause in the conversation on Thorndyke's part elicited a further purpose.

'Did you see the account of that fire in Bloomsbury?' Mr Stalker asked.

'The oil-shop? Yes. But I didn't note any details, excepting that a man was apparently burnt to death and that the affair happened on the twenty-fifth of December.'

'Yes, I know,' said Mr Stalker. 'It seems uncharitable, but one can't help looking a little askance at these quarter-day fires. And the date isn't the only doubtful feature in this one; the Divisional Officer of the Fire Brigade, who has looked over the ruins, tells me that there are some appearances suggesting that the fire broke out in two different places – the shop and the first-floor room over it. Mind you, he doesn't say that it actually did. The place is so thoroughly gutted that very little is to be learned from it; but that is his impression; and it occurred to me that if you were to take a look at the ruins, your radiographic eye might detect something that he had overlooked.'

'It isn't very likely,' said Thorndyke. 'Every man to his trade. The Divisional Officer looks at a burnt house with an expert eye, which I do not. My evidence would not carry much weight if you were contesting the claim.'

'Perhaps not,' replied Mr Stalker, 'and we are not anxious

to contest the claim unless there is manifest fraud. Arson is a serious matter.'

'It is wilful murder in this case,' remarked Thorndyke.

'I know,' said Stalker. 'And that reminds me that the man who was burnt happens to have been insured in our office, too. So we stand a double loss.'

'How much?' asked Thorndyke.

'The dead man, Percival Bland, had insured his life for three thousand pounds.'

Thorndyke became thoughtful. The last statement had apparently made more impression on him than the former ones.

'If you want me to look into the case for you,' said he, 'you had better let me have all the papers connected with it, including the proposal forms.'

Mr Stalker smiled. 'I thought you would say that – know you of old, you see – so I slipped the papers in my pocket before coming here.'

He laid the documents on the table and asked: 'Is there anything that you want to know about the case?'

'Yes,' replied Thorndyke. 'I want to know all that you can tell me.'

'Which is mighty little,' said Stalker; 'but such as it is, you shall have it.

'The oil-shop man's name is Brattle and the dead man, Bland, was his lodger. Bland appears to have been a perfectly steady, sober man in general; but it seems that he had announced his intention of spending a jovial Christmas Night and giving himself a little extra indulgence. He was last seen by Mrs Brattle at about half-past six, sitting by a blazing fire, with a couple of unopened bottles of port on the table and a box of cigars. He had a book in his hand and two or three newspapers lay on the floor by his chair. Shortly after this, Mr and Mrs Brattle went out on a visit to Hornsey, leaving him alone in the house.'

'Was there no servant?' asked Thorndyke.

'The servant had the day and night off duty to go to her mother's. That, by the way, looks a trifle fishy. However, to return to the Brattles; they spent the evening at Hornsey and did not get home until past three in the morning, by which time their house was a heap of smoking ruins. Mrs Brattle's idea is that Bland must have drunk himself sleepy, and dropped one of the newspapers into the fender, where a chance cinder may have started the blaze. Which may or may not be the true explanation. Of course, a habitually sober man can get pretty mimsey on two bottles of port.'

'What time did the fire break out?' asked Thorndyke.

'It was noticed about half-past eleven that flames were issuing from one of the chimneys, and the alarm was given at once. The first engine arrived ten minutes later, but, by that time, the place was roaring like a furnace. Then the water-plugs were found to be frozen hard, which caused some delay; in fact, before the engines were able to get to work the roof had fallen in, and the place was a mere shell. You know what an oil-shop is, when once it gets a fair start.'

'And Mr Bland's body was found in the ruins, I suppose?'

'Body!' exclaimed Mr Stalker; 'there wasn't much body! Just a few charred bones, which they dug out of the ashes next day.'

'And the question of identity?'

'We shall leave that to the coroner. But there really isn't any question. To begin with, there was no one else in the house; and then the remains were found mixed up with the springs and castors of the chair that Bland was sitting in when he was last seen. Moreover, there were found, with the bones, a pocket-knife, a bunch of keys and a set of steel waistcoat buttons, all identified by Mrs Brattle as belonging to Bland. She noticed the cut steel buttons on his waistcoat when she wished him good-night.'

'By the way,' said Thorndyke,' was Bland reading by the light of an oil lamp?'

'No,' replied Stalker. 'There was a two-branch gasalier with a porcelain shade to one burner, and he had that burner alight when Mrs Brattle left.'

Thorndyke reflectively picked up the proposal form, and, having glanced through it, remarked: 'I see that Bland is described as unmarried. Do you know why he insured his life for this large amount?'

'No; we assumed that it was probably in connection with some loan that he had raised. I learn from the solicitor who notified us of the death, that the whole of Bland's property is left to a cousin – a Mr Lindsay, I think. So the probability is that this cousin had lent him money. But it is not the life claim that is interesting us. We must pay that in any case. It is the fire claim that we want you to look into.'

'Very well,' said Thorndyke; 'I will go round presently and look over the ruins, and see if I can detect any substantial evidence of fraud.'

'If you would,' said Mr Stalker, rising to take his departure, 'we should be very much obliged. Not that we shall probably contest the claim in any case.'

When he had gone, my colleague and I glanced through the papers, and I ventured to remark: 'It seems to me that Stalker doesn't quite appreciate the possibilities of this case.'

'No,' Thorndyke agreed. 'But, of course, it is an insurance company's business to pay, and not to boggle at anything short of glaring fraud. And we specialists, too,' he added with a smile, 'must beware of seeing too much. I suppose that, to a rhinologist, there is hardly such a thing as a healthy nose – unless it is his own – and the uric acid specialist is very apt to find the firmament studded with dumb-bell crystals. We mustn't forget that normal cases do exist, after all.'

'That is true,' said I; 'but, on the other hand, the rhinologist's business is with the unhealthy nose, and our concern is with abnormal cases.'

Thorndyke laughed. '"A Daniel come to judgment,"' said he. 'But my learned friend is quite right. Our function is to pick holes. So let us pocket the documents and wend Bloomsbury way. We can talk the case over as we go.'

We walked at an easy pace, for there was no hurry, and a little preliminary thought was useful. After a while, as Thorndyke made no remark, I reopened the subject.

'How does the case present itself to you?' I asked.

'Much as it does to you, I expect,' he replied. 'The circumstances invite inquiry, and I do not find myself connecting them with the shopkeeper. It is true that the fire occurred on quarter-day; but there is nothing to show that the insurance will do more than cover the loss of stock, chattels and the profits of trade. The other circumstances are much more suggestive. Here is a house burned down and a man killed. That man was insured for three thousand pounds, and, consequently, some person stands to gain by his death to that amount. The whole set of circumstances is highly favourable to the idea of homicide. The man was alone in the house when he died; and the total destruction of both the body and its surroundings seems to render investigation impossible. The cause of death can only be inferred; it cannot be proved; and the most glaring evidence of a crime will have vanished utterly. I think that there is a quite strong *prima facie* suggestion of murder. Under the known conditions, the perpetration of a murder would have been easy, it would have been safe from detection, and there is an adequate motive.

'On the other hand, suicide is not impossible. The man might have set fire to the house and then killed himself by poison or otherwise. But it is intrinsically less probable that a man should kill himself for another person's benefit than that he should kill another man for his own benefit.

'Finally, there is the possibility that the fire and the man's death were the result of accident; against which is the official opinion that the fire started in two places. If this opinion is correct, it establishes, in my opinion, a strong presumption of murder against some person who may have obtained access to the house.'

This point in the discussion brought us to the ruined house, which stood at the corner of two small streets. One of the firemen in charge admitted us, when we had shown our credentials, through a temporary door and down a ladder into the basement, where we found a number of men treading gingerly, ankle deep in white ash, among a litter of charred wood-work, fused glass, warped and broken china, and more or less recognisable metal objects.

'The coroner and the jury,' the fireman explained; 'come to view the scene of the disaster.' He introduced us to the former, who bowed stiffly and continued his investigations.

'These,' said the other fireman, 'are the springs of the chair that the deceased was sitting in. We found the body – or rather the bones – lying among them under a heap of hot ashes; and we found the buttons of his clothes and the things from his pockets among the ashes, too. You'll see them in the mortuary with the remains.'

'It must have been a terrific blaze,' one of the jurymen remarked. 'Just look at this, sir,' and he handed to Thorndyke what looked like part of a gas-fitting, of which the greater part was melted into shapeless lumps and the remainder encrusted into fused porcelain.

'That,' said the fireman, 'was the gasalier of the first-floor room, where Mr Bland was sitting. Ah! you won't turn that tap, sir; nobody'll ever turn that tap again.'

Thorndyke held the twisted mass of brass towards me in silence, and, glancing up the blackened walls, remarked: 'I think we shall have to come here again with the Divisional

Officer, but meanwhile, we had better see the remains of the body. It is just possible that we may learn something from them.'

He applied to the coroner for the necessary authority to make the inspection, and, having obtained a rather ungracious and grudging permission to examine the remains when the jury had 'viewed' them, began to ascend the ladder.

'Our friend would have liked to refuse permission,' he remarked when we had emerged into the street, 'but he knew that I could and should have insisted.'

'So I gathered from his manner,' said I. 'But what is he doing here? This isn't his district.'

'No; he is acting for Bettsford, who is laid up just now; and a very poor substitute he is. A non-medical coroner is an absurdity in any case, and a coroner who is hostile to the medical profession is a public scandal. By the way, that gas-tap offers a curious problem. You noticed that it was turned off?'

'Yes.'

'And consequently that the deceased was sitting in the dark when the fire broke out. I don't see the bearing of the fact, but it is certainly rather odd. Here is the mortuary. We had better wait and let the jury go in first.'

We had not long to wait. In a couple of minutes or so the 'twelve good men and true' made their appearance with a small attendant crowd of ragamuffins. We let them enter first, and then we followed. The mortuary was a good-sized room, well lighted by a glass roof, and having at its centre a long table on which lay the shell containing the remains. There was also a sheet of paper on which had been laid out a set of blackened steel waistcoat buttons, a bunch of keys, a steel-handled pocket-knife, a steel-cased watch on a partly-fused rolled-gold chain and a pocket corkscrew. The coroner drew the attention of the jury to these objects, and then took possession of them, that they might be identified by witnesses. And meanwhile the jurymen gathered round the shell and stared shudderingly at its gruesome contents.

'I am sorry, gentlemen,' said the coroner, 'to have to subject you to this painful ordeal. But duty is duty. We must hope, as I think we may, that this poor creature met a painless, if in some respects a rather terrible death.'

At this point, Thorndyke, who had drawn near to the table, cast a long and steady glance down into the shell; and, immediately his ordinarily rather impassive face seemed to congeal; all expression faded from it, leaving it as immovable and uncommunicative as the granite face of an Egyptian statue. I knew the symptom of old and began to speculate on its present significance.

'Are you taking any medical evidence?' he asked.

'Medical evidence!' the coroner repeated, scornfully. 'Certainly not, sir! I do not waste the public money by employing so-called experts to tell the jury what each of them can see quite plainly for himself. I imagine,' he added, turning to the foreman, 'that you will not require a learned doctor to explain to you how that poor fellow mortal met his death?' And the foreman, glancing askance at the skull, replied, with a pallid and sickly smile, that 'he thought not'.

'Do you, sir,' the coroner continued, with a dramatic wave of the hand towards the plain coffin, 'suppose that we shall find any difficulty in determining how that man came by his death?'

'I imagine,' replied Thorndyke, without moving a muscle, or, indeed, appearing to have any muscles to move, 'I imagine you will find no difficulty whatever.'

'So do I,' said the coroner.

'Then,' retorted Thorndyke, with a faint, inscrutable smile, 'we are, for once, in complete agreement.'

As the coroner and jury retired, leaving my colleague and me alone in the mortuary, Thorndyke remarked:

'I suppose this kind of farce will be repeated periodically so long as these highly technical medical inquiries continue to be conducted by lay persons.'

I made no reply, for I had taken a long look into the shell, and was lost in astonishment.

'But my dear Thorndyke!' I exclaimed; 'what on earth does it mean? Are we to suppose that a woman can have palmed herself off as a man on the examining medical officer of a London Life Assurance Society?'

Thorndyke shook his head. 'I think not,' said he. 'Our friend, Mr Bland, may conceivably have been a woman in disguise, but he certainly was not a negress.'

'A negress!' I gasped. 'By Jove! So it is. I hadn't looked at the skull. But that only makes the mystery more mysterious. Because, you remember, the body was certainly dressed in Bland's clothes.'

'Yes, there seems to be no doubt about that. And you may have noticed, as I did,' Thorndyke continued dryly, 'the remarkably fire-proof character of the waistcoat buttons, watch-case, knife-handle, and other identifiable objects.'

'But what a horrible affair!' I exclaimed. 'The brute must have gone out and enticed some poor devil of a negress into the house, have murdered her in cold blood, and then deliberately dressed the corpse in his own clothes! It is perfectly frightful!'

Again Thorndyke shook his head. 'It wasn't as bad as that, Jervis,' said he, 'though I must confess that I feel strongly tempted to let your hypothesis stand. It would be quite amusing to put Mr Bland on trial for the murder of an unknown negress, and let him explain the facts himself. But our reputation is at stake. Look at the bones again and a little more critically. You very probably looked for the sex first; then you looked for racial characters. Now carry your investigations a step further.'

'There is the stature,' said I. 'But that is of no importance, as these are not Bland's bones. The only other point that I notice is that the fire seems to have acted very unequally on the different parts of the body.'

'Yes,' agreed Thorndyke, 'and that is *the* point. Some parts are more burnt than others; and the parts which are burnt most are the wrong parts. Look at the back-bone, for instance. The vertebrae are as white as chalk. They are mere masses of bone ash. But, of all parts of the skeleton, there is none so completely protected from fire as the back-bone, with the great dorsal muscles behind, and the whole mass of the viscera in front. Then look at the skull. Its appearance is quite inconsistent with the suggested facts. The bones of the face are bare and calcined and the orbits contain not a trace of the eyes or other structures; and yet there is a charred mass of what may or may not be scalp adhering to the crown. But the scalp, as the most exposed and the thinnest covering, would be the first to be destroyed, while the last to be consumed would be the structures about the jaws and the base, of which, you see, not a vestige is left.'

Here he lifted the skull carefully from the shell, and, peering in through the great foramen at the base, handed it to me.

'Look in,' he said, 'through the Foramen Magnum' – you will see better if you hold the orbits towards the skylight – and notice an even more extreme inconsistency with the supposed conditions. The brain and membranes have vanished without leaving a trace. The inside of the skull is as clean as if it had been macerated. But this is impossible. The brain is not only protected from the fire; it is also protected from contact with the air. But without access of oxygen, although it might become carbonized, it could not be consumed. No, Jervis; it won't do.'

I replaced the skull in the coffin and looked at him in surprise.

'What is it that you are suggesting?' I asked.

'I suggest that this was not a body at all, but merely a dry skeleton.'

'But,' I objected, 'what about those masses of what looks like charred muscle adhering to the bones?'

'Yes,' he replied, ' I have been noticing them. They do, as you say, look like masses of charred muscle. But they are quite shapeless and structureless; I cannot identify a single muscle or muscular group; and there is not a vestige of any of the tendons. Moreover, the distribution is false. For instance, will you tell me what muscle you think that is?'

He pointed to a thick, charred mass on the inner surface of the left tibia or shin-bone. 'Now this portion of the bone – as many a hockey-player has had reason to realize – has no muscular covering at all. It lies immediately under the skin.'

'I think you are right, Thorndyke,' said I. 'That lump of muscle in the wrong place gives the whole fraud away. But it was really a rather smart dodge. This fellow Bland must be an ingenious rascal.'

'Yes,' agreed Thorndyke; 'but an unscrupulous villain too. He might have burned down half the street and killed a score of people. He'll have to pay the piper for this little frolic.'

'What shall you do now? Are you going to notify the coroner?'

'No; that is not my business. I think we will verify our conclusions and then inform our clients and the police. We must measure the skull as well as we can without callipers, but it is, fortunately, quite typical. The short, broad, flat nasal bones, with the 'Simian groove', and those large, strong teeth, worn flat by hard and gritty food, are highly characteristic.' He, once more, lifted out the skull, and, with a spring tape, made a few measurements, while I noted the lengths of the principal long bones and the width across the hips.

'I make the cranial-nasal index 55.1,' said he, as he replaced the skull, 'and the cranial index about 72, which are quite representative numbers; and, as I see that your notes show the usual disproportionate length of arm and the characteristic curve of the tibia, we may be satisfied. But it is fortunate that the specimen is so typical. To the experienced eye, racial types have a physiognomy which is unmistakable on mere inspection. But you cannot transfer the experienced eye. You can only express personal conviction and back it up with measurements.

'And now we will go and look in on Stalker, and inform him that his office has saved three thousand pounds by employing us. After which it will be Westward Ho! for Scotland Yard, to prepare an unpleasant little surprise for Mr Percival Bland.'

There was joy among the journalists on the following day. Each of the morning papers devoted an entire column to an unusually detailed account of the inquest on the late Percival Bland – who, it appeared, met his death by misadventure – and a verbatim report of the coroner's eloquent remarks on the danger of solitary, fireside tippling, and the stupefying effects of port wine. An adjacent column contained an equally detailed account of the appearance of the deceased at Bow Street Police Court to answer complicated charges of arson, fraud and forgery; while a third collated the two accounts with gleeful commentaries.

Mr Percival Bland, *alias* Robert Lindsay, now resides on the breezy uplands of Dartmoor, where, in his abundant leisure, he, no doubt, regrets his misdirected ingenuity. But he has not laboured in vain. To the Lord Chancellor he has furnished an admirable illustration of the danger of appointing lay coroners; and to me an unforgettable warning against the effects of suggestion.

The Adventure of the First-Class Carriage

RONALD A. KNOX,
after SIR ARTHUR CONAN DOYLE

The general encouragement extended to my efforts by the public is my excuse, if excuse were needed, for continuing to act as chronicler of my friend Sherlock Holmes. But even if I confine myself to those cases in which I have had the honour of being personally associated with him, I find it difficult to make a selection among the large amount of matter at my disposal.

As I turn over my records, I find that some of them deal with events of national or even international importance; but the time has not yet come when it would be safe to disclose (for instance) the true facts about the recent change of government in Paraguay. Others (like the case of the Missing Omnibus) would do more to gratify the modern craving for sensation; but I am well aware that my friend himself is the first to deplore it when I indulge what is, in his own view, a weakness.

My preference is for recording incidents whose bizarre features gave special opportunity for the exercise of that analytical talent which he possessed in such a marked degree. Of these, the case of the Tattooed Nurseryman and that of the Luminous Cigar-Box naturally suggest themselves to the mind. But perhaps my friend's gifts were even more signally displayed when he had occasion to investigate the disappearance of Mr Nathaniel Swithinbank, which provoked so much speculation in the early days of September, five years back.

Mr Sherlock Holmes was, of all men, the least influenced by what are called class distinctions. To him the rank was but the guinea stamp; a client was a client. And it did not surprise me, one evening when I was sitting over the familiar fire in Baker Street – the days were sunny but the evenings were already falling chill – to be told that he was expecting a visit from a domestic servant, a woman who 'did' for a well-to-do, childless couple in the southern Midlands.

'My last visit,' he explained, 'was from a countess. Her

mind was uninteresting, and she had no great regard for the truth; the problem she brought was quite elementary. I fancy Mrs John Hennessy will have something more important to communicate.'

'You have met her already, then?'

'No, I have not had the privilege. But anyone who is in the habit of receiving letters from strangers will tell you the same – handwriting is often a better form of introduction than hand-shaking. You will find Mrs Hennessy's letter on the mantelpiece; and if you care to look at her j's and her w's, in particular, I think you will agree that it is no ordinary woman we have to deal with. Dear me, there is the bell ringing already; in a moment or two, if I mistake not, we shall know what Mrs Hennessy, of the Cottage, Guiseborough St Martin, wants of Sherlock Holmes.'

There was nothing in the appearance of the old dame who was shown up, a few minutes later, by the faithful Mrs Hudson to justify Holmes's estimate. To the outward view she was a typical representative of her class; from the bugles on her bonnet to her elastic-sided boots everything suggested the old-fashioned caretaker such as you may see polishing the front doorsteps of a hundred office buildings any spring morning in the city of London. Her voice, when she spoke, was articulated with unnecessary care, as that of the respectable working-class woman is apt to be. But there was something precise and businesslike about the statement of her case which made you feel that this was a mind which could easily have profited by greater educational advantages.

'I have read of you, Mr Holmes,' she began, 'and when things began to go wrong up at the Hall it wasn't long before I thought to myself, if there's one man in England who will be able to see light here, it's Mr Sherlock Holmes. My husband was in good employment, till lately, on the railway at Chester; but the time came when the rheumatism got hold of him, and after that nothing seemed to go well with us until he had thrown up his job, and we went to live in a country village not far from Banbury, looking out for any odd work that might come our way.

'We had only been living there a week when a Mr Swithinbank and his wife took the old Hall, that had long been standing empty. They were newcomers to the district, and their needs were not great, having neither chick nor child to fend for; so they engaged me and Mr Hennessy to come and live in the lodge, close by the house, and do all the work of it for them. The pay was good and the duties light, so we were glad enough to get the billet.'

'One moment!' said Holmes. 'Did they advertise, or were you indebted to some private recommendation for the appointment?'

'They came at short notice, Mr Holmes, and were directed to us for temporary help. But they soon saw that our ways suited them, and they kept us on. They were people who kept very much to themselves, and perhaps they did not want a set of maids who would have followers, and spread gossip in the village.'

'That is suggestive. You state your case with admirable clearness. Pray proceed.'

'All this was no longer ago than last July. Since then they have once been away in London, but for the most part they have lived at Guiseborough, seeing very little of the folk round about. Parson called, but he is not a man to put his nose in where he is not wanted, and I think they must have made it clear they would sooner have his room than his company. So there was more guessing than gossiping about them in the countryside. But, sir, you can't be in domestic employment without finding out a good deal about how the land lies; and it wasn't long before my husband and I were certain of two things. One was that Mr and Mrs Swithinbank were deep in debt. And the other was that they got on badly together.'

'Debts have a way of reflecting themselves in a man's

correspondence,' said Holmes, 'and whoever has the clearing of his waste-paper basket will necessarily be conscious of them. But the relations between man and wife? Surely they must have gone very wrong indeed before there is quarrelling in public.'

'That's as may be, Mr Holmes, but quarrel in public they did. Why, it was only last week I came in with the blancmange, and he was saying, "The fact is, no one would be better pleased than you to see me in my coffin." To be sure, he held his tongue after that, and looked a bit confused; and she tried to put a brave face on it. But I've lived long enough, Mr Holmes, to know when a woman's been crying. Then last Monday, when I'd been in drawing the curtains, he burst out just before I'd closed the door behind me, "The world isn't big enough for both of us." That was all I heard, and right glad I'd have been to hear less. But I've not come round here just to repeat servants'-hall gossip.

'Today, when I was cleaning out the waste-paper basket, I came across a scrap of a letter that tells the same story, in his own handwriting. Cast your eye over that, Mr Holmes, and tell me whether a Christian woman has the right to sit by and do nothing about it.'

She had dived her hand into a capacious reticule and brought out, with a triumphant flourish, her documentary evidence. Holmes knitted his brow over it, and then passed it on to me. It ran: 'Being of sound mind, whatever the numbskulls on the jury may say of it.'

'Can you identify the writing?' my friend said.

'It was my master's,' replied Mrs Hennessy. 'I know it well enough; the bank, I am sure, will tell you the same.'

'Mrs Hennessy, let us make no bones about it. Curiosity is a well-marked instinct of the human species. Your eye having lighted on this document, no doubt inadvertently, I will wager you took a look round the basket for any other fragments it might contain.'

'That I did, sir; my husband and I went through it carefully together, for who knew but the life of a fellow-creature might depend on it? But only one other piece could we find written by the same hand, and on the same note-paper. Here it is.' And she smoothed out on her knee a second fragment, to all appearances part of the same sheet, yet strangely different in its tenor. It seemed to have been torn away from the middle of a sentence; nothing survived but the words 'in the reeds by the lake, taking a bearing at the point where the old tower hides both the middle first-floor windows'.

'Come,' I said, 'this at least gives us something to go upon. Mrs Hennessy will surely be able to tell us whether there are any landmarks in Guiseborough answering to this description.'

'Indeed there are, sir; the directions are plain as a pikestaff. There is an old ruined building which juts out upon the little lake at the bottom of the garden, and it would be easy enough to hit on the place mentioned. I daresay you gentlemen are wondering why we haven't been down to the lake-side ourselves to see what we could find there. Well, the plain fact is, we were scared. My master is a quiet-spoken man enough at ordinary times, but there's a wild look in his eye when he's roused, and I for one should be sorry to cross him. So I thought I'd come to you, Mr Holmes, and put the whole thing in your hands.'

'I shall be interested to look into your little difficulty. To speak frankly, Mrs Hennessy, the story you have told me runs on such familiar lines that I should have been tempted to dismiss the whole case from my mind. Dr Watson here will tell you that I am a busy man, and the affairs of the Bank of Mauritius urgently require my presence in London. But this last detail about the reeds by the lake-side is piquant, decidedly piquant, and the whole matter shall be gone into. The only difficulty is a practical one. How are we to explain my presence at Guiseborough without betraying

316

to your employers the fact that you and your husband have been intruding on their family affairs?'

'I have thought of that, sir,' replied the old dame, 'and I think we can find a way out. I slipped away today easily enough because my mistress is going abroad to visit her aunt, near Dieppe, and Mr Swithinbank has come up to town with her to see her off. I must go back by the evening train, and had half thought of asking you to accompany me. But no, he would get to hear of it if a stranger visited the place in his absence. It would be better if you came down by the quarter past ten train tomorrow, and passed yourself off for a stranger who was coming to look at the house. They have taken it on a short lease, and plenty of folks come to see it without troubling to obtain an order-to-view.'

'Will your employer be back so early?'

'That is the very train he means to take; and to speak truth, sir, I should be the better for knowing that he was being watched. This wicked talk of making away with himself is enough to make anyone anxious about him. You cannot mistake him, Mr Holmes,' she went on; 'what chiefly marks him out is a scar on the left-hand side of his chin, where a dog bit him when he was a youngster.'

'Excellent, Mrs Hennessy; you have thought of everything. Tomorrow, then, on the quarter past ten for Banbury without fail. You will oblige me by ordering the station fly to be in readiness. Country walks may be good for health, but time is more precious. I will drive straight to your cottage, and you or your husband shall escort me on my visit to this desirable country residence and its mysterious tenant.' With a wave of his hand, he cut short her protestations of gratitude.

'Well, Watson, what did you make of her?' asked my companion when the door had closed on our visitor.

'She seemed typical of that noble army of women whose hard scrubbing makes life easy for the leisured classes. I could not see her well because she sat between us and the window, and her veil was lowered over her eyes. But her manner was enough to convince me that she was telling the truth, and that she is sincere in her anxiety to avert what may be an appalling tragedy. As to its nature, I confess I am in the dark. Like yourself, I was particularly struck by the reference to the reeds by the lake-side. What can it mean? An assignation?'

'Hardly, my dear Watson. At this time of the year a man runs enough risk of cold without standing about in a reed-bed. A hiding-place, more probably, but for what? And why should a man take the trouble to hide something, and then obligingly litter his waste-paper basket with clues to its whereabouts? No, these are deep waters, Watson, and we must have more data before we begin to theorise. You will come with me?'

'Certainly, if I may. Shall I bring my revolver?'

'I do not apprehend any danger, but perhaps it is as well to be on the safe side. Mr Swithinbank seems to strike his neighbours as a formidable person. And now, if you will be good enough to hand me the more peaceful instrument which hangs beside you, I will try out that air of Scarlatti's, and leave the affairs of Guiseborough St Martin to look after themselves.'

I often had occasion to deprecate Sherlock Holmes's habit of catching trains with just half a minute to spare. But on the morning after our interview with Mrs Hennessy we arrived at Paddington station no later than ten o'clock – to find a stranger, with a pronounced scar on the left side of his chin, gazing out at us languidly from the window of a first-class carriage.

'Do you mean to travel with him?' I asked, when we were out of earshot.

'Scarcely feasible, I think. If he is the man I take him for, he has secured solitude all the way to Banbury by the simple process of slipping half a crown into the guard's hand.'

And, sure enough, a few minutes later we saw that functionary shepherd a fussy-looking gentleman, who had been vigorously assaulting the locked door, to a compartment further on. For ourselves, we took up our post in the carriage next but one behind Mr Swithinbank. This, like the other first-class compartments, was duly locked when we had entered it; behind us the less fortunate passengers accommodated themselves in seconds.

'The case is not without its interest,' observed Holmes, laying down his paper as we steamed through Burnham Beeches. 'It presents features which recall the affairs of James Phillimore, whose disappearance (though your loyalty may tempt you to forget it) we investigated without success. But this Swithinbank mystery, if I mistake not, cuts even deeper. Why, for example, is the man so anxious to parade his intention of suicide, or fictitious suicide, in the presence of his domestic staff? It can hardly fail to strike you that he chose the moment when the good Mrs Hennessy was just entering the room, or just leaving it, to make those remarkable confidences to his wife. Not content with that, he must leave evidence of his intentions lying about in the waste-paper basket. And yet this involved the risk of having his plans foiled by good-natured interference. Time enough for his disappearance to become public when it became effective! And why, in the name of fortune, does he hide something only to tell us where he has hidden it?'

Amid a maze of railway tracks, we came to a standstill at Reading. Holmes craned his neck out of the window, but reported that all the doors had been left locked. We were not destined to learn anything about our elusive travelling companion until, just as we were passing the pretty hamlet of Tilehurst, a little shower of paper fragments fluttered past the window on the right-hand side of the compartment, and two of them actually sailed in through the space we had dedicated to ventilation on that bright morning of autumn. It may easily be guessed with what avidity we pounced on them.

The messages were in the same handwriting with which Mrs Hennessy's find had made us familiar; they ran, respectively, 'Mean to make an end of it all' and 'This is the only way out.' Holmes sat over them with knitted brows, till I fairly danced with impatience.

'Should we not pull the communication cord?' I asked.

'Hardly,' answered my companion, 'unless five pound notes are more plentiful with you than they used to be. I will even anticipate your next suggestion, which is that we should look out of the windows on either side of the carriage. Either we have a lunatic two doors off, in which case there is no use in trying to foresee his next move, or he intends suicide, in which case he will not be deterred by the presence of spectators, or he is a man with a scheming brain who is sending us these messages in order to make us behave in a particular way. Quite probably, he wants to make us lean out of the windows, which seems to me an excellent reason for not leaning out of the windows. At Oxford we shall be able to read the guard a lesson on the danger of locking passengers in.'

So indeed it proved; for when the train stopped at Oxford there was no passenger to be found in Mr Swithinbank's carriage. His overcoat remained, and his wide-awake hat; his portmanteau was duly identified in the guard's van. The door on the right-hand side of the compartment, away from the platform, had swung open; nor did Holmes's lens bring to light any details about the way in which the elusive passenger had made his exit.

It was an impatient horse and an injured cabman that awaited us at Banbury, when we drove through golden woodlands to the little village of Guiseborough St Martin, nestling under the shadow of Edge Hill. Mrs Hennessy met us at the door of her cottage, dropping an old-fashioned curtsy; and it may easily be imagined what wringing of hands, what wiping of eyes with her apron, greeted the announcement of her master's disappearance. Mr Hennessy, it seemed, had gone off to a neighbouring farm upon some errand, and it was the old dame herself who escorted us up to the Hall.

'There's a gentleman there already, Mr Holmes,' she informed us. 'Arrived early this morning and would take no denial; and not a word to say what business he came on.'

'That is unfortunate,' said Holmes. 'I particularly wanted a free field to make some investigation. Let us hope that he will be good enough to clear off when he is told that there is no chance of an interview with Mr Swithinbank.'

Guiseborough Hall stands in its own grounds a little way outside the village, the residence of a squire unmistakably, but with no airs of baronial grandeur. The old, rough walls have been refaced with pointed stone, the mullioned windows exchanged for a generous expanse of plate-glass, to suit a more recent taste, and a portico has been thrown out from the front door to welcome the traveller with its shelter. The garden descends at a precipitous slope from the main terrace, and a little lake fringes it at the bottom, dominated by a ruined eminence that serves the modern owner for a gazebo.

Within the house, furniture was of the scantiest, the Swithinbanks having evidently rented it with what fittings it had, and introduced little of their own. As Mrs Hennessy ushered us into the drawing-room, we were not a little surprised to be greeted by the wiry figure and melancholy features of our old rival, Inspector Lestrade.

'I knew you were quick off the mark, Mr Holmes,' he said, 'but it beats me how you ever heard of Mr Swithinbank's little goings-on; let alone that I didn't think you took much stock in cases of common fraud like this.'

'Common fraud?' repeated my companion. 'Why, what has he been up to?'

'Drawing cheques, and big ones, Mr Holmes, when he

knew that his bank wouldn't honour them; only little things of that sort. But if you're on his track I don't suppose he's far off, and I'll be grateful for any help you can give me to lay my hands on him.'

'My dear Lestrade, if you follow out your usual systematic methods, you will have to patrol the Great Western line all the way from Reading to Oxford. I trust you have brought a drag-net with you, for the line crossed the river no less than four times in the course of the journey.' And he regaled the astonished inspector with a brief summary of our investigations.

Our information worked like a charm on the little detective. He was off in a moment to find the nearest telegraph office and put himself in touch with Scotland Yard, with the Great Western Railway authorities, with the Thames Conservancy. He promised, however, a speedy return, and I fancy Holmes cursed himself for not having dismissed the jarvey who had brought us from the station, an undeserved windfall for our rival.

'Now, Watson!' he cried, as the sound of the wheels faded away into the distance.

'Our way lies to the lake-side, I presume.'

'How often am I to remind you that the place where the criminal tells you to look is the place not to look? No, the clue to the mystery lies, somehow, in the house, and we must hurry up if we are to find it.'

Quick as a thought, he began turning out shelves, cupboards, escritoires, while I, at his direction, went through the various rooms of the house to ascertain whether all was in order, and whether anything suggested the anticipation of a hasty flight. By the time I returned to him, having found nothing amiss, he was seated in the most comfortable of the drawing-room armchairs, reading a book he had picked out of the shelves – it dealt, if I remember right, with the aborigines of Borneo.

'The mystery, Holmes!' I cried.

'I have solved it. If you will look on the bureau yonder, you will find the household books which Mrs Swithinbank has obligingly left behind. Extraordinary how these people always make some elementary mistake. You are a man of the world, Watson; take a look at them and tell me what strikes you as curious.'

It was not long before the salient feature occurred to me. 'Why, Holmes,' I exclaimed, 'there is no record of the Hennessys being paid any wages at all!'

'Bravo, Watson! And if you will go into the figures a little more closely, you will find that the Hennessys apparently lived on air. So now the whole facts of the story are plain to you.'

'I confess,' I replied, somewhat crestfallen, 'that the whole case is as dark to me as ever.'

'Why, then, take a look at that newspaper I have left on the occasional table; I have marked the important paragraph in blue pencil.'

It was a copy of an Australian paper, issued some weeks previously. The paragraph to which Holmes had drawn my attention ran thus:

ROMANCE OF RICH MAN'S WILL

The recent lamented death of Mr John Macready, the well-known sheep-farming magnate, has had an unexpected sequel in the circumstance that the dead man, apparently, left no will. His son, Mr Alexander Macready, left for England some years back, owing to a misunderstanding with his father – it was said – because he announced his intention of marrying a lady from the stage. The young man has completely disappeared, and energetic steps are being taken by the lawyers to trace his whereabouts. It is estimated that the fortunate heirs, whoever they be, will be the richer by not far short of a hundred thousand pounds sterling.

Horse-hoofs echoed under the archway, and in another

minute Lestrade was again of our party. Seldom have I seen the little detective looking so baffled and ill at ease.

'They'll have the laugh of me at the Yard over this,' he said. 'We had word that Swithinbank was in London, but I made sure it was only a feint, and I came racing up here by the early train, instead of catching the quarter past ten and my man in it. He's a slippery devil, and he may be half-way to the Continent by this time.'

'Don't be downhearted about it, Lestrade. Come and interview Mr and Mrs Hennessy, at the lodge; we may get news of your man down there.'

A coarse-looking fellow in a bushy red beard sat sharing his tea with our friend of the evening before. His greasy waistcoat and corduroy trousers proclaimed him a manual worker. He rose to meet us with something of a defiant air; his wife was all affability.

'Have you heard any news of the poor gentleman?' she asked.

'We may have some before long,' answered Holmes. 'Lestrade, you might arrest John Hennessy for stealing that porter's cap you see on the dresser, the property of the Great Western Railway Company. Or, if you prefer an alternative charge, you might arrest him as Alexander Macready, alias Nathaniel Swithinbank.' And while we stood there literally thunder-struck, he tore off the red beard from a chin marked with a scar on the left-hand side.

'The case was difficult,' he said to me afterwards, 'only because we had no clue to the motive. Swithinbank's debts would almost have swallowed up Macready's legacy; so it was necessary for the couple to disappear, and take up the claim under a fresh alias. This meant a duplication of personalities, but it was not really difficult. She had been an actress; he had really been a railway porter in his hard-up days. When he got out at Reading, and passed along the six-foot way to take his place in a third-class carriage, nobody marked the circumstance, because on the way from London he had changed into a porter's clothes; he had the cap, no doubt, in his pocket. On the sill of the door he left open, he had made a little pile of suicide messages, hoping that when it swung open these would be shaken out and flutter into the carriages behind.'

'But why the visit to London? And, above all, why the visit to Baker Street?'

'That is the most amusing part of the story; we should have seen through it at once. He wanted Nathaniel Swithinbank to disappear finally, beyond all hope of tracing him. And who would hope to trace him, when Mr Sherlock Holmes, who was travelling only two carriages behind, had given up the attempt? Their only fear was that I should find the case uninteresting; hence the random reference to a hiding-place among the reeds, which so intrigued you. Come to think of it, they nearly had Inspector Lestrade in the same train as well. I hear he has won golden opinions with his superiors by cornering his man so neatly. *Sic vos non vobis*, as Virgil said of the bees; only they tell us nowadays the lines are not by Virgil.'

DINNER FOR TWO

Roy Vickers

Today, if you were to mention the Ennings mystery, you would be assured that 'everyone knows' that Dennis Yawle murdered Charles Ennings. In this case, 'everyone' happens to be right, though for the wrong reasons. The public of the day decided that he was guilty because he denounced an attractive young woman of pleasing manners and assumed respectability. And 'everyone knows' that nice young women don't commit murder, whatever their walk in life, and that self-centred, solitary, aggressive little men sometimes do.

Charles Ennings was a patent agent. He lived in a flat on the third floor at Barslade Mansions, Westminster, the kind of flats that are occupied by moderately successful professional men and junior directors. A bachelor, with a promiscuous impulse freely indulged, he nevertheless managed to avoid scandalising his neighbours.

His dead body was found in his sitting-room by the daily help at eight-thirty. Death, which had occurred upwards of ten hours previously, had been caused by a knife—thrust in the throat—an ordinary pocket knife such as could then be bought in any cutler's for a few shillings. The news, of course, did not appear before the lunchtime editions.

Dennis Yawle, the murderer, was a prematurely embittered man of thirty-two. He had taken a science degree in chemistry and had been employed by a well-known firm of soap manufacturers for the last nine years at a modest salary. His personality, rather than his science, had precluded him from promotion. The firm had given him a chance as manager of their depot in the Balkans; but he disappointed them in everything except his routine work. Incidentally, it was in the Balkans that he had learned how to use a knife for purposes other than the cutting of string.

In chemistry alone he was enterprising. He had worked out some useful little compounds, unconnected with soap, and had patented them through Ennings. His income had been substantially increased, but not to the point where he could prudently resign his job.

He believed that Ennings had tricked him over his patents, which was true. He believed that he had lost Aileen Daines because he had insufficient money—which may have been true. Hysteria was added to grievance by the further belief that Ennings himself had enjoyed the lady's favours for a brief period before discarding her for another, which was probably an exaggeration. By that particular exaggeration many a man has been flicked from hatred to murderous intent.

Daily at lunchtime he would emerge from the laboratory in North London with his colleague, Holldon. Holldon had his daily bet on the races, and always bought a paper from a stand outside the restaurant. He would prop it up during lunch, while Yawle generally read a book. But on January 18th, 1933, he brought no book, because he had to stage a little pantomime with Holldon's paper.

First, he must eat his lunch, which was not too easy. When the coffee arrived he delivered his line, which began with a yawn:

'Any news in that thing?'

'No. They've had to plug a murder to fill space.'

Holldon was doing everything right, even to pushing the paper across the table. Yawle's stage business with the paper was easy enough.

'Good—*lord!*' He shot it out, and Holldon was sufficiently startled to attend. 'I know this chap who's been murdered. I say, Holldon, this is pretty ghastly for me! I was with him last evening—I must ring the police.'

'I'd keep out of it, if I were you. You have to turn up at court day after day in case they want you to give evidence.'

'But they've called in Scotland Yard, which means that the local police can't produce a suspect.' Yawle kept it up until the other professed himself convinced.

Five minutes later he was speaking on the telephone to Chief

Inspector Karslake, giving particulars of himself.

'I was at that flat last night between seven and half-past. I don't suppose I can tell you anything you don't know but I thought I'd better give you a ring.'

Karslake thanked him with some warmth, and said he would send a man to Mr Yawle's office.

'Well-l, I have rather a crowded afternoon in front of me. I could make Scotland Yard in about twenty minutes. If you could see me then, we could get my little bit tidied up right away.'

In his pocket was a crystal of cyanide to complete the tidying-up process if necessary.

To walk up to the tiger and stoke it was a desperate improvisation, necessitated by the blunders of an ill-designed murder. Indeed, it is doubtful whether his plans had ever emerged from the fantasy stage, until he struck the blow—if we except the solitary precaution of observing the porter's movements.

For three nights previously he had strolled past the flats on the opposite side of the road, noting that between seven and eight the porter was extremely busy—with three entrances and forty-five flats, most of whose tenants were arriving or departing by taxi or car. It would be child's play to slip in—and out again—without being seen.

In the fantasy, he eluded the porter, passed through an empty hall, ascended an empty staircase.

In actuality, he did elude the porter. But the hall was not empty. In the miniature lounge, consisting of one palm, a radiator, and three chairs, stood a girl who, as he fancied, bore some resemblance to Aileen Daines. That is, she was neither tall nor short; she was slim and dark, with regular features and liberal eyebrows. She glanced at the electric clock, sat down and began to sort her shopping parcels. Yawle looked straight into her eyes, but she took no notice of him, which, irrationally, inflamed his sense of the loss of Aileen.

The staircase, too, contributed its quota of trouble. Most people used the automatic elevator—that was why he had chosen the staircase. On the first turn, between floors, he all but crashed into an elderly lady from behind: it was such a near thing that she dropped a parcel.

He was himself startled and at a loss. The woman, small but imposing, fiftyish, glared at him with an indignation that had a quality of voraciousness—to his nerve-racked fancy, she looked as if she wanted to pounce upon him, spiderwise, and eat him.

'I'm most awfully sorry, madam! Very careless of me! I hope I didn't frighten you.'

The voracious, spiderlike quality vanished from a face which was ordinary enough and even pleasing. She accepted the parcel with a graceful, old-fashioned bow and the kind of smile that used to go with the bow.

He hurried on to the first floor—up the next flight, to the second.

'I say! Do you know you really *lose* time when you do two stairs at once?'

The thin, piping treble had come from a boy of about ten.

'Do I? Pr'aps you're right. I'll take your advice.'

This was a nightmare journey. The murder, still in part a fantasy, receded. Funny how that girl had reminded him of Aileen! Must have been like her, in a way. But that girl was sure of herself and happy. If only he could tell what had happened to Aileen!

The device of writing to her parents to inquire had not occurred to him. By the time he reached the third floor Aileen's present condition was deplorable and even unmentionable—as a result of the general behaviour of Charles Ennings.

When Ennings opened the door he was wearing a dinner jacket, which somehow made everything worse. He seemed younger than his fifty years, the heavy lips had become masterful, he had pulled himself in, probably with corsets. He looked successful, confident, insolent.

'I want to talk to you, Ennings.'

'By all means!' Ennings was unenthusiastic, if not positively damp. 'Between ourselves, I don't do business at home, but— come in, won't you?'

The hall was but a bulge in the corridor of the flat. Opposite were two doors some ten feet apart. Ennings opened one and Yawle entered the kind of near-luscious sitting-room he had expected, littered with cabinet photographs of the current inamorata—not even attractive, in Yawle's eyes.

The telephone rang, as if to emphasise that Yawle's presence was an intrusion.

'No, it was a washout,' said Ennings into the receiver. 'I got home at the usual time after all, and I'm taking an evening off. Can't talk now. I have a client who's in a hurry.'

Ennings cut off. He pointed to an armchair, but Yawle remained standing. Ennings sat in the other armchair.

'Gronston's,' said Yawle, 'have put my Cleanser in every grocer's, and every oil shop and every hardware store in the country. And it's selling.'

'Of course it's selling! It's a damn fine fluid, old man. Who's saying it isn't!'

'Why do I get such measly royalties? Why is the contract signed by Lanberry's instead of by Gronston's?'

'So that's what's biting you!' Ennings had had this conversation, in one form or another, with a good many inventors. 'Between ourselves, Lanberry's is a holding company, if you know what that means—'

'I know that Lanberry's *holds* one desk in one room in a back street off Holborn. And I know that the Chairman is a clerk employed by you. I've been there.'

'You've been there!' snorted Ennings. 'So it only remains for the bloodsucking financier to burst into tears and disgorge the loot! My good young man, you're poking your nose into things you don't understand—and you're making an infernal fool of yourself.'

The main purpose, of course, was to talk about Aileen. Yawle had given no detailed thought to the matter of the royalties. Ennings and his dinner jacket—successful, confident, insolent— was riding him.

'I shall take it up with Gronston's! There's another thing—'

'Good! I hope you'll be fool enough to do just that. In the meantime you can take yourself and your business to the devil. Your business! Your *invention!* Between ourselves, there are a good few others who've rediscovered that old formula, or copied it out of a back number—'

So, in the end, Aileen's name hadn't even been mentioned.

The skill of the Balkan bandits with their short knives—very like our pocket knives—is based on a knowledge of how to hold the knife. If you hold it properly, as Yawle did, in the palm of the hand, you leave no fingerprints on the haft. Your index finger lies along the back of the blade, slides down it as the blade impacts with an upward sweep: so there's no detectable fingerprint there, either. If your aim is accurate, as Yawle's was, there is neither bother nor noise in the killing.

Ennings remained sitting in his armchair as he had sat in life.

If all the movements were performed correctly, there should be no stains. Yawle studied himself in the mirror. There were no stains. The brainstorm, the moment of hysteria, had passed, leaving him cool, tingling with a sense of achievement and well-being. He felt successful, confident, insolent.

He noted that Ennings's electric clock registered seven twenty-three. He had been in the flat for less than six minutes, all told.

He shut the door of the sitting-room. He was halfway to the front door when he heard footsteps on the landing. He backed away from the front door, found himself opposite the room next to that of the sitting-room. The dining-room. He opened the door.

The footsteps died away. The light from the corridor of the flat had fallen on a white tablecloth. Using his sleeve, he switched on the room light.

The table was laid for two, and the food was on the table. Cold food. Smoked salmon; chicken; trifle in fairy glasses, with a peach on top—canned peach! So Ennings had been expecting a girl! Who might turn up at any minute!

Yawle was in the act of opening the front door, was reaching forward for the latch, when he again heard footsteps approaching. This time he did not panic. He merely stood back, so that his shadow should not fall on the glass panel.

This time the footsteps stopped outside the door. The knocker was lifted and discreetly applied. Yawle kept still. In due course, people go away when there is no response to a knock.

But this caller did not go away. There came the unmistakable sound of a latchkey being inserted.

There was no time to rush back to the dining-room. He slipped into the sitting-room, locked himself in with the dead man, turning the key with his handkerchief.

He did not hear the outer door of the flat being shut. For a moment he was ready to believe that his over-taut nerves had tricked him—that there had been no footsteps and no latchkey.

Some ten seconds later there came a light knock on the door of the sitting-room. Then the handle was turned. Yawle held his breath.

'*Char*-lie! It's *me*-e!'

A full throated, middle-contralto Aileen had a middle contralto voice, too. But that voice was not—could not be—Aileen's voice. If it were Aileen, would she hand him over to the police?

As, by hypothesis, it was not Aileen, there was a danger amounting to certainty that the owner of the voice *would* hand him over to the police.

Seconds passed without any sound to give him a clue as to what was happening.

Then the sound of the front door being shut.

Within a minute or so he had evolved a feasible theory of his predicament. The girl has been given a latchkey, so she's one of Ennings's harem. She thinks he's cut a date with her, so she's gone off in a huff. If she's waiting for him on the landing—but she won't be! She's on latchkey terms and would curl herself up in the flat. Give her a couple of minutes to get clear.

When the two minutes had passed he slipped out of the flat, pausing only to shut the outer door as silently as possible. The main thing was to avoid being seen or heard leaving the flat.

No footsteps. No one on the staircase. By the time he reached the second floor, his confidence returned.

That table spread with a meal for two was nothing less than a first-class alibi, provided the body were not discovered in the next ten minutes or so. No man, he could point out, would be such a fool as to murder another in a flat when he knew that a guest was momentarily expected.

He had merely to pretend that he had seen the table when he entered the flat, and he could add that Ennings had explained that he was expecting a girl friend. He need not even bother to dodge the porter.

When Yawle reached the ground floor, the porter was not there to be dodged or not dodged, being occupied with a tenant who had arrived with luggage at another entrance. Yawle strode on.

In the miniature lounge the girl who resembled Aileen Daines was adjusting her make-up. Unaware of his presence, she snapped her bag, gathered up her shopping parcels and went out of the building.

Might be Ennings's girl friend, he reflected—but without deep interest, for his ego was fully inflated. He had done what he had done—he had turned deadly peril to positive advantage. He would top it off by making use of the porter.

Luckily, he had a pen on him. He began to write a noncommital message for Ennings, but found to his surprise that his hand was shaking. Never mind! His resourcefulness was equal to any emergency.

He found the porter at the third entrance.

'I've just left Mr Ennings and I find that I've absent-mindedly pocketed his fountain pen.' It was a standard model, unidentifiable. He gave it to the porter, with a florin. 'If I were you, I wouldn't return it until the morning. The fact is, porter, he is entertaining—well, let's say a *friend!*'

By bedtime, Yawle's confidence had ebbed. Again and again he reviewed his movements, with increasing alarm. He had got clean away, but could he be dragged back? He ticked off the items.

The first person to see him enter the block had been the girl, but she obviously had not noticed him and could be ignored. Then the old lady who had looked at him like a spider. She might or might not remember him enough to give a description.

Then there was that wretched boy—almost certainly a Boy Scout obsessed with stairs and footsteps, who would love telling the police everything.

With that sterling alibi of the dinner table it would be safe to come forward, unsafe to hang back.

'There's the boy, the middle-aged woman, and the girl—all three saw you entering the building at about seven-ten, Mr Yawle?' Chief Inspector Karslake was making notes as he spoke. 'Can you remember what they looked like?'

'The boy I didn't notice—an ordinary boy of about ten or so. The woman, smallish, about fifty, old-fashioned, but not exactly old, round sort of face. The girl—middle twenties, about my height, dark, good looking, well-marked eyebrows, slim, quietly dressed. But I'm sure she didn't know I was there—if you're thinking of asking these people whether they saw me.'

'It's only for checking up with others,' Karslake assured him. 'Please go on, Mr Yawle.'

'I went to the flat. Ennings opened the door. He was in a dinner jacket and told me he was expecting a friend to dinner. The way he said it, I guessed it was a girl. He showed me the dining-room—I suppose so that I shouldn't think he was stalling me—cold supper set for two. I said I would only keep him a few minutes. As soon as we got into his sitting-room the phone rang. He answered briefly and cut off.'

Yawle waited while Karslake wrote. He had not anticipated that everything he said would be noted.

'And then you both sat down and discussed your business?'

'If we are to be literal, I didn't sit down—wanted to make it clear that I wasn't going to stick around.'

The next bit was tricky. In the night he had worked out that the porter might have noticed when Ennings' guest went upstairs—that must have been while he was in the flat.

'We were about halfway through our business when his girl turned up.

'And he got up to let her in?'

Confound the man with his passion for footling little details! Be careful to tell no unnecessary lies.

'She let herself in with a latchkey. I said I'd just write out a note and then—'

'Half a minute. Don't think I'm niggling, Mr Yawle. The fact is, we use everything an honest witness tells us to check on the people who are not public spirited and may be hiding something. How did you know some one had come in with a latchkey if you were shut up in a room talking business?'

'Ennings had one ear listening for that latchkey.' Yawle managed a realistic snigger. 'He got up, spoke to her, said he would be with her in a few minutes.'

Karslake passed him a chart of Ennings's sitting-room.

'Will you show me on that chart where you were standing when he went to speak to the girl?'

There was only one spot where one could stand to talk to a man sitting as Ennings had sat.

'Oh the hearth rug— here.'

'Could you identify the girl, Mr Yawle?'

'Oh, no—no! Certainly not!'

'But you must have seen her if you were standing there!' It was a statement rather than a question, and Yawle shrank from contradicting.

'Well—yes—but—in these circumstances, Inspector, I simply can't make a statement involving someone else unless I'm sure of what I say.'

'You couldn't put it better, Mr Yawle. All I want you to tell me now is what you saw. To begin with, you saw it was a girl and not a man. Tall or short? Fair or dark?'

'I don't think we need winkle it out that way. I can go as far as this—she was of the same physical type as the girl I noticed in the hall when I was coming in. But I cannot state that she was the same girl.'

It would be better, he had decided, not to add that he had also seen the girl when he was leaving the building.

'From your description of the girl in the hall the thing a man would notice first would be those eyebrows,' persisted Karslake.

'Y-yes. But—'

'Was she in evening dress?'

'No.'

'Same sort of clothes as the girl in the hall, eh?' As Yawle did not deny it, 'Very natural that you won't state it's the same girl, because you aren't quite positive. Very proper attitude, if I may say so. Where did Ennings park the girl in the flat?'

'I don't know. He came back to me. I wanted to make that note. I'd forgotten my pen and he lent me his. I went on talking a minute or so and absent-mindedly pocketed his pen. When I got downstairs—which I suppose was about half-past seven—I looked for the porter and asked him to return the fountain pen—' Yawle repeated the snigger '—in the morning.'

Karslake had the air of an inspector who is not only satisfied but even grateful.

'I think that's about all, Mr Yawle. We shall round up the boy and the woman on the stairs so that you can identify each other. The local police will probably want you for the inquest. Otherwise, I don't suppose we shall trouble you—' he pressed a bell push '—if you'll be good enough to give us your fingerprints before you go.'

A junior entered with a frame and Yawle obliged.

'As far as I know,' he said when the process had been completed, 'I didn't leave any fingerprints in the flat. Don't think I touched anything except that fountain pen.'

'But look at it from our point of view, Mr Yawle.' Karslake was urbane and even confidential. 'Until we've taken your prints we can't prove that it wasn't you who had dinner with Ennings.'

'Dinner with Ennings?' echoed Yawle, genuinely puzzled.

'Well, supper if you like, as it was cold stuff. There were prints other than those of the deceased on the cutlery, the plates, the glasses, some of the dishes—someone who doesn't take salt or pepper but fairly shovels the sugar on a sweet.'

'D'you mean that meal was eaten?' gasped Yawle.

'You bet it was! Look here, I'm not supposed to show this, but you'll see it at the inquest tomorrow.'

Karslake displayed photographs of the dining-room and of the table, of the débris of a meal consumed by two persons. Yawle observed particularly the fairy glasses that had held the trifle. The glasses in the photograph were opaque, with nothing showing above the rims. Before consumption the trifle had topped the rim and the canned peach had topped the trifle.

Yawle left Scotland Yard, dazed to the point of being but barely aware of his surroundings. That dinner had been untouched when he left the flat. As Ennings was dead, he could not possibly have had dinner with the girl. Therefore, somebody else had dinner with the girl—which was absurd.

Alternatively, the flat had been burgled after the girl had gone. The burglars, notwithstanding the presence of a corpse in the flat, had sat down to a meal—which was even more absurd.

Which all proved that the dinner had not been eaten when, in point of fact, it had been eaten.

That it removed all danger from himself was scarcely heeded. That photograph gave him a creeping doubt of his own sanity. He had read of eye-witnesses making wholly false statements in wholly good faith. In some amazing way he must have seen an untouched meal when he was really looking at the débris of a meal.

That meal cropped up again at the inquest. One of the jurymen, unsupported by the others, challenged Yawle's evidence in a question to the Coroner.

'How do we know that this meal was eaten after Mr Yawle had left the flat? It might have been eaten before—I mean, it might have been lunch or anything. I'm not suggesting it was but as it's important evidence I think we ought to have that point cleared up.'

'I think I can help there, sir,' said Yawle. 'When the deceased took me into his dining-room I happened to notice particularly two fairy glasses containing trifle, with a canned peach on the top. If the police can confirm that statement I think it must prove that I saw the meal laid out before it was consumed.'

The police could confirm that statement. The jury returned a verdict of murder against a person unknown, with a rider indicating the young woman who had entered the flat with a latchkey at approximately seven-twenty.

The boy was found some six weeks later. He had spent a couple of nights with an uncle, one of the tenants, who suddenly remember that fact and reported it with profuse apologies. The boy had gone back to board in school at Brighton: the incident had utterly passed from his mind, and he failed to identify Yawle.

The elderly lady with the parcel was another unexpected stumbling block. When appeals through press and radio failed to solicit response, the Yard was ready to believe that she was an invention of Yawle's, prompted by a desire to tie the time of his presence at the flat at both ends. Innocent people often did that kind of thing.

The porter was interviewed again and again. His story remained sufficiently consistent. It was his busy time, dodging from one of the three entrances to another. There had never been any trouble with the police—they weren't that kind of tenant, and he was not given to observing their actions. He had not seen Mr Yawle until he made his request concerning the fountain pen—which was close to seven-thirty.

He had certainly noticed a young woman sitting in the hall-lounge round about ten past seven. That was nothing unusual. He had only noticed her because, as he passed, she was fiddling with her bag and dropped something, but picked it up before he could do it for her. He mentioned her eyebrows and her dress, which was not the expensive kind.

The dragnet went out through the West End, though from the description of the porter and of Yawle, she was not likely to be found in any of the bars or night clubs. The search became intensive, was carried to the theatres, including the dress circles and stalls, with the result that, some six weeks after the inquest, Yawle was asked to accompany a plainclothes man and wait outside a City office about lunch time.

Out of the office came Aileen Daines.

'Hullo, Dennis!' She shook hands with frank friendliness. 'I'm so glad to see you—I was going to write. You see, Leonard and I— yes, at Easter.'

When she had gone, Yawle rejoined the plainclothes man.

'You saw her speak to me. She is not the one we want. I know her very well indeed.'

The porter, at the same time on the next day, was not so positive. By a majority vote, as it were, of his muddled recollections, he decided that he did not think this young lady was that young lady.

'All the same, there's the bare possibility that this young lady *is* that young lady,' said Karslake when he was discussing the report with his staff. 'Used to be Yawle's girl, eh? There might be some tangled sex stuff there. We haven't enough to sail in with a request for her dabs. Now, if one of you boys could manage to watch her eating—when she isn't with her young man—we might get a line.'

None of them did see her eating, but one of them obtained her fingerprints without her knowledge. And that dropped her out of the case—and dropped the case itself into the Department of Dead Ends.

As weeks lengthened into months, Yawle ceased to worry about his sanity in the matter of the dinner which could not possibly have been—but had been—eaten. He still carried the crystal of cyanide in a dummy petrol lighter, but it had become a talisman rather than a menace.

Learning that Ennings's estate had been proved at £60,000 he went to see Gronston's, who gladly gave him details of the royalties paid to Lanberry's. Yawle brought an action against the estate for balance of royalties withheld by a fraudulent device.

The action was heard in the following Spring. Detective Inspector Rason was present, not because he expected to find in the public gallery the girl who had murdered Ennings, but because it was a routine duty to keep contact with the principals in an unsolved crime.

The hearing was very brief, for there was in effect no defence. Yawle obtained judgement for some four thousand pounds and his costs. The judge remarked that the deceased had behaved as an unscrupulous scoundrel and that Hendricks, his shabby little clerk who survived him, would do well to examine his own conscience.

Rason decided to do a little examining of the clerk's conscience himself, for he had the glimmer of an idea. Over a pint of beer and a sandwich Hendricks was willing to talk.

'I knew there was going to be a rumpus when Mr Yawle turned up at my room,' said Hendricks. 'I gave the guv'nor the wire, but he only laughed at me.'

'When did Mr Yawle turn up at your room?' asked Rason.

'I dunno—not the date anyhow. Must've been about a week before the guv'nor copped out.'

That was the sort of thing Rason was hoping for. What business had Yawle transacted with Ennings when he knew that Ennings had been cheating him? No business. He had gone to demand restitution. And had he borrowed Ennings's fountain pen to make a note of it? Rats!

Barking up the wrong tree, muttered Rason. Proving that Yawle quarrelled with Ennings and killed him, when the job is to find the girl and prove she did.

Back in the office he was reluctant to admit that he had wasted his morning. He tried hard to squeeze a bit into the discovery that Yawle had known that Ennings was swindling him. No link-up.

Start with the girl, now! She comes in with a latchkey, has her dinner and then knifes him. Why? She must've expected him to get free. Can't pull the dewy innocent with that latchkey in her bag. Suppose she was an inventor, too? In the sitting-room she finds something, proving that Ennings has been buying her the stockings out of her own money?

The next morning he paddled back to Hendricks.

'Have you got on your books a girl middle twenties, height about five six, thickish eyebrows—'

'I've never seen any of 'em except Mr Yawle. And we got no girls. Only a couple o' widows, legatees of course.'

'Let's have the widows!'

Mrs Siegman lived in Hampstead, was middle-aged and had virtually no eyebrows. Mrs Deaker lived in Surbiton, which was an hour's drive out of London, allowing for traffic. With some difficulty Rason found a small house with a brick wall surrounding the garden on the outskirts of the suburb.

The door was opened by a good-looking girl in the middle twenties, height about five-six, dark, with well-defined eyebrows.

'Are you Mrs Deaker?'

'No. Mrs Deaker is in town. I'm her companion and at the moment her domestic staff too. Do you want to leave a message?'

Rason presented his official card.

'Oh!' said the girl, and Rason decided to spring it on her.

'What were you doing in Barslade Manions, Westminster, the night Charles Ennings was killed?'

'Oh!' said the girl again. 'I'm not going to tell you anything until I have a lawyer.'

'In that case I'm afraid you'll have to come with me to Scotland Yard,' said Rason.

He was with her while she packed a suitcase and left a note for her employer, kept her within arm's reach while he telephoned the Yard. On the journey the only admission she made was that her name was Margaret Halling. On arrival at the Yard she made no objection to having her fingerprints taken.

Some three hours later Dennis Yawle turned up at Scotland Yard in response to a request by telephone. Some five minutes previously Margaret Halling's employer had arrived with a lawyer. All three, with some half a dozen others, were enduring time in a waiting-room.

Detective Inspector Rason thanked Yawle profusely, took him along a corridor behind the waiting-room.

'I want you to look through this little panel, Mr Yawle—they can't see you—and tell me if there's anybody in the room you recognise.'

Yawle looked through the panel. A smile broadened.

'Yes,' he said. 'I shall never forget that face! That is the elderly lady whose parcel I picked up on the stairs.'

'Well, I'm—' Rason was more astonished than he had been for a long time. 'Excuse me, Mr Yawle.' In his agitation he pushed Yawle back to the panel, put his hand on the crown of Yawle's head, and gently twisted until Yawle could be presumed to have a view of the seat in the window.

This time there was no broad smile. Rason had the impression that he saved Yawle from subsiding to the floor.

'That's the girl with the eyebrows—the girl I saw in the hall.'

'And she's the girl you saw when she let herself in with the latchkey?'

'I don't know. I said at the time I couldn't be sure the girls were the same.'

'That's all right, Mr Yawle—we never lead a witness,' said Rason unblushingly. He was now in extremely high spirits, for he had had another glimmer. 'Your statement in my file says they were of similar type. That passes the buck to us.'

They went to Chief Inspector Karslake's room. The chair at the roll-top desk was placed at Rason's disposal, with Karslake on his left, for this was Rason's case, and his own room was too much of a museum for interviews.

'Well, I suppose the first thing to do,' hinted Karslake, when he had heard the news, 'is to have the girl in for a formal identification.'

'No, it isn't, sir,' said Rason, picking up Karslake's house telephone.

'Mrs Deaker, in the waiting-room—ask her if she would like to see me. If so, bring her in.'

'Mr Yawle,' said Rason. 'This old girl has given Mr Karslake a good deal of trouble, one way and another.' Karslake's surprise change to profound disapproval, as Rason went on: 'If she hands us anything you know to be phoney, I'd be grateful if you'd chip in and flatten her out.'

Yawle assented politely. The 'old woman' presented no problem. She could do nothing but confirm his statement.

Mrs Deaker chose to brave the detective without the support of the lawyer, who was earmarked for Margaret Halling.

'I think you have seen this gentleman before, Mrs Deaker?' Rason indicated Yawle.

'Not to my recollection,' answered Mrs Deaker. 'Perhaps if you were to tell me his name—?'

'At Barslade Mansions, Westminster, on the evening of January 17th 1933, this gentleman retrieved a parcel you had dropped on the staircase.

'Did he! Then it was very kind of him, and it is ungracious of me to forget.'

'We advertised in the press and on the radio, asking you to come forward, Mrs Deaker,' said Rason severely.

'I remember those advertisements, I didn't realise you meant me!' She glared at Yawle. 'Did you describe me as an *elderly* woman? That's what the advertisement said!' Before Yawle could excuse himself, she went on: 'I suppose I do seem elderly to a man of your age. However, if we may consider the incident of the parcel is closed I would like to tell the police about Margaret Halling, my companion. She was there solely because my taxi brought her there. I was dining with a friend. Her train home from Waterloo was not until eight-ten. It was a cold night and I told her to sit in the lounge by the radiator until it was time to leave.'

'Who was the friend with whom you were dining, Mrs Deaker?'

'The man who was murdered. Mr Ennings. But of course, you must know all about him, as you're still looking for the murderer. Now that we have mentioned the subject, you may wish me to account for my own movements, though they are of no significance, or I would have reported them.

'Mr Ennings was a friend—a very intimate friend—before I married, somewhat injudiciously, the man who invented the Deaker commutator. He handled my husband's affairs. In recent years, after his death, Mr Ennings and I—Mr Ennings and I resumed our friendship, which was cemented by the fact that my husband had made him trustee.

'Mr Ennings telephoned me in the morning that he might be detained at some special meeting or other. As I was doing a day's shopping, I was to come—he would have a cold meal prepared—

and I was not to wait dinner for him after seven-thirty.

'As to the parcel incident, I never enter an elevator unless there is a responsible-looking man in charge. I selected the staircase—which took a long time—no doubt because I am *elderly*! I duly waited until seven-thirty, and then I sat down to dinner by myself. I waited in the flat until a little after nine-thirty and then caught the ten-five home.'

Rason had taken from the dossier the photographs of the débris of the meal.

'When did you see Mr Ennings?'

'Obviously, I didn't see him at all.'

'How did you obtain entry to the flat?'

'I lifted the knocker, as there was a light in the hall.' Her words were laboured as she went on: 'I thought I had sufficiently emphasised the fact of our friendship. I have a latchkey. Here it is.' She took it from her bag and gave it to Rason. 'I went to the sitting-room, but the door was locked. I knocked, then called his name. Then I looked about the flat, shut the front door and went into the dining-room to wait for him. Once, I thought I heard the front door being closed, but it was a false alarm, so I sat down and had my dinner.'

Yawle had reached forward and snatched from Rason's desk the photograph of the débris of the meal.

'I don't think so, Mrs Deaker!' cried Yawle. 'Look at this photograph. Two persons ate that dinner!'

They were glaring at each other.

'Half a minute, Mr Yawle!' interposed Rason. 'I thought Mr Karslake had told you everything! Did he forget to tell you that there was *only one set of fingerprints on those dishes*?'

'Then they must be mine!' sighed Mrs Deaker. 'I had hoped to escape this public humiliation. The degrading truth is that I can eat—and I often do—as much as two men! By nine, I concluded that Mr Ennings must have had his dinner. So I—I—I really *did*—'

Rason left Mrs Deaker floundering in a whirlpool of social shame.

'Well, Yawle, let's get back to that young girl you saw in the flat, whom you can't *quite* identify with the young girl you saw in the hall. Eyebrows an' all, too! Or would you rather ask Mrs Deaker some questions about that sitting-room door *that was locked on the inside*? At about twenty past seven, as near as makes no matter to you, Yawle!'

But Yawle possessed a talisman in a dummy petrol lighter that warded off all further assaults on his dignity.

The Funspot-Street Affair

THOMAS BURKE

ONCE A MONTH Morton passed that street. The business of the firm for which he worked as a collector took him once a month to an office just beyond the limits of the recent spread of the City; an office which called itself City; but was, indeed, North-East.

To reach that office from the Tube station he had to pass that street, and after passing it once a month for two years he found that it had grown upon him and become part of his imaginative life. Every time he passed it, its name, in conjunction with its dark, dishevelled aspect, struck him as bizarre.

After a while he was wanting to do something about it: write a song about it or a paragraph about it, or somehow get it into the news. He wished he knew some newspaper man, who could make it known. He wanted to see it in headlines; he thought it would look well – 'Funspot-street'. It seemed to him to cry for dramatization, and he wished it were possible for him to give it celebrity and immortality.

Funspot-street: he saw it on newspaper bills and he heard the radio announcer mentioning it in news-bulletins, and heard the giggles which the name would arouse in a million homes.

He wondered sometimes why it never had been in the news. It was surely made for it. By the look of it, it was the sort of street whose people would be fairly regular guests of the police-courts, and whose name, when they gave it as an address, would give great chances to the men who write those facetious stories about other people's troubles, which have taken the place of serious police-court reporting.

Constantly thinking about it, and seeing it in many connections, comic and dramatic, he decided finally that it would look most apt in type as:

THE FUNSPOT-STREET MURDER

He could see the sub-heads and cross-heads. Shocking Murder in Funspot-street . . . Early this morning the police were called to a house in Funspot-street . . . Detectives working on the Funspot-street tragedy are in possession of an important clue which is likely . . . Funspot Tragedy Arrest . . . No Reprieve for Funspot Murderer . . . And so on.

No; comedy wouldn't do. It called for tragedy, and the more squalid and grotesque the tragedy the more fitting. Something out of the inkwell of Baudelaire or Poe, or De Nerval. He could half see the kind of thing that would fit, and on each monthly visit to that district the fascination of the name and of fitting it with the right story provided him with entertainment for several evenings. He would add extra details to the half-formed idea in his mind, discarding those of last week in favour of some with a keener edge of the bizarre.

He wasn't a writer, and found it difficult to write two paragraphs in sequence, but the name of that street became almost a muse to him; a spur to do what he couldn't do, and write it into prominence.

He never did write it; but after long brooding there came a

time when Funspot-street and its Horrible Tragedy were so clear in his mind that in abstracted moments he could hardly believe that it hadn't happened.

He could locate the house, the room, the time (it would be midnight, of course), and he could visualize the act itself as though he had been an eye-witness. He could see the room and its flimsy, shabby furniture. He could smell the stale, unopened reek of it. He could see the gas-bracket and its incandescent mantle, which would be broken and the flame spluttering.

He could see the violently flowered wallpaper, discoloured in places, and elsewhere peeling off. He could see the strip of cheap carpet, with holes at the points where feet had constantly rested. And he could see the man who had somehow, by some aberration, got into this squalid hole, away from his regular, decent surroundings: a slim, neatly-dressed fellow, something like himself.

And he could see the blowsy woman, the fitting châtelaine of such a house. He could hear the violent noises, and he could see the man turning in fury and disgust and striking the woman and rushing from the room.

And then the midday papers, with Funspot-street front-paged. And then the daily and hourly hunt for this decent young chap, just as it might be himself, who, for all his previous decency and integrity, would leave his name in certain records, and be exhibited at Madame Tussaud's as 'The Funspot-street Murderer'. Not even complete tragedy to mark his sudden fall, but tragedy streaked with the ridiculous . . . Funspot-street.

In building the story he attributed to the man, at the moment of walking to the scaffold, a burning grievance. Not at his fate, not at the irresponsible moment which had led him to his fate, or at his capture, when many men who have committed that act have escaped capture. But at the fact that it didn't happen in some other street – in Cavendish- street or Jermyn-street, or Kingsway. Over-riding remorse and resignation and the natural horror of the situation would stand this crowning indignity to a man's *finis* – Funspot-street. He felt that it was a good story, if only he could write it.

The salary which his firm considered an adequate balance to the services he rendered did not permit him much evening entertainment; a theatre or music-hall once a month, perhaps, and the movies once a week. Other evenings he spent in wandering about London, getting for nothing an entertainment superior to anything for which one pays money; the entertainment of the streets and the crowds.

On these walks, while observing the pageant, he let his mind play round his Funspot-street Tragedy, going over it again and again, detail for detail. He wished, whimsically, that somebody would put it into action; that there really would be a murder in Funspot-street, just like that, and that the evening-paper contents bills would flash it at him. But they never did.

It was on one of these walks, when he was wandering round the strange, lost byways of Islington, and playing with the trial in the Funspot-street Tragedy and the duel between prisoner and counsel, that something thick touched him softly on the forehead. For one moment he was aware that he was looking closely at a puddle in the road, and that above his head was the number-plate of a taxi and the wheels of a motor-bus. He was aware also of disturbed voices, and then of a babble; and then, through the babble, a firm voice which said: 'All right . . . we know him . . . we'll look after him.'

That was all he heard in that moment. Next moment, it seemed, he heard a voice saying, in a low growl: 'See if he's got the day's collection on him.' And then another voice saying: ' 'm! Here it is.'

His eyelids seemed of iron, but he managed to open them. They gave his eyes a sight of a strip of cheap carpet, with holes here and there. Above him he saw a gas-bracket, with the flame spluttering. Then he saw a violently flowered wallpaper, and places where it was peeling off.

Over him stood a large, heavy man. Just behind the man stood a blowsy woman wearing a flashy, stained frock which he thought he had seen before. In the woman's hands was a bundle of Treasury notes secured with a rubber band.

At the sight of them, and the memory of the words he had heard, his brain began to move. He realized that he had been robbed. The other details passed back into dream, but the fact that he had been robbed remained as a fact. Somehow or other he managed to scramble to his feet and to make a fierce lunge at the woman.

The midday papers of next afternoon had Funspot-street well on their bills and on their front pages. But Morton never saw them. The last thing he saw was a poker in the hand of the blowsy woman.

The Murder on the
Okehampton Line

VICTOR L. WHITECHURCH

The solution of the murder on the Okehampton line was, at best, only partial, and yet there can be no doubt whatever that Godfrey Page penetrated the mystery as deeply as it could be penetrated and that his theory was correct; in fact, though some links in the chain of evidence were missing, there was quite sufficient to prove that my brother-in-law had fathomed the leading points.

He was not pressed into the investigation, but took it up out of sheer curiosity.

I had been dining at his house one night and he had sent out for the last edition of the evening paper. I think there was a railway strike or something of the kind going on that interested him. But however that might be, his attention was caught directly he opened the paper with the following paragraph, which he handed me to read:

MURDER ON THE OKEHAMPTON LINE!
(A Railway Mystery)

On the arrival of the last train from Exeter to Okehampton at the latter station last night, a gruesome discovery was made. A porter on the platform noticed a gentleman seated in the corner of a third-class compartment and, as he made no attempt to get out of the carriage, opened the door to wake him, thinking he might be asleep. To his horror he discovered that the man was dead and a subsequent examination revealed the fact that he had been stabbed in the heart with some sharp instrument. There were signs of a struggle in the carriage.

The murdered man was dressed in a dark blue suit with a soft felt hat, but there was absolutely nothing on him to lead to his identification – not a scrap of paper of any sort.

That robbery was not the object is proved by the fact that some five or six pounds in gold and silver and his watch and chain were still on him.

Although the police were communicated with at once

nothing further has been ascertained up to going to press. The body has been removed to the White Hart Hotel and there awaits identification.

'Here's a mystery if you like,' said Godfrey Page. 'Let me see, the last down train arrives at Okehampton at ten-fifty. It's the one that leaves Waterloo at five-fifty and Exeter, St David's, at ten-thirty. Of course, the great question is – where did he get into the train and whereabouts on the journey was he murdered?'

'And who he was?' I added.

'Exactly. Do you know, I've half a mind to run down tomorrow and have a look at things. Would you care to come?'

'Well,' I said, 'I think I could spare the day.'

'It means two days. We'll go down tomorrow morning by the ten-thirty express from Paddington. I've been wanting to have a run on that train for a long time.'

'But Okehampton is on the L & SW Railway,' I ventured to suggest.

'I fancy I'm aware of that,' he replied snappishly, 'but I tell you I want a run on the Great Western. I've got a friend at Paddington, too, who'll give me a leg up. I'll write to him tonight. Meet me at Paddington at ten-fifteen under the clock.'

I found him waiting for me when I arrived, holding in his hand a newspaper and a letter.

'It's all right,' he said; 'I've got a line of introduction to the officials at St David's in case I want information. And there's a whole column about the case in this morning's paper. We'll read it as we go down.'

He spent the rest of the time before starting in noting the name of the engine, the number of the coaches, and other details of the express, and then we found ourselves in a comfortable carriage, speeding westward.

'Now,' he said, when we had read the paper, 'you see,

there are several new points in the case. Let's try and sum them up.

'First of all, the identity of the murdered man is still unknown. Secondly, you see, the crime must have been committed between Exeter and Okehampton, because the guard of the train remembers speaking to the man at Exeter. It appears that the guard put his head in the window just before the train started and said: "Where are you for, sir?" To which the man made a singular reply. He answered: "Where does this train go to?" Upon the guard saying "Okehampton," he simply replied, "All right." Now this seems to show that he was in a train *the destination of which he didn't know.*'

'And the next point evidently touches the murderer,' I said.

'Yes; I think so, too. Two men got off the train at Yeoford junction, telling the ticket-collector that there had been no time for them to get a ticket at St David's and paying him the fare. These two men seem to have disappeared. They could not have got away by train, for that was the last one at the junction that night. But it's only a seven or eight miles' walk back to Exeter, and that's probably how they've eluded search.

'Now, you see, this gives us two more points. First, if these two men committed the crime, they did it between Exeter and Yeoford; and secondly, the fact of their having no tickets proves our theory correct that the murdered man was in a train that was strange to him.'

'How so?'

'Because *they* didn't know where they were going either. They must have been following him. They saw him get into the Okehampton train and they got in after him.'

'But the guard said he was alone when he saw him at St David's and spoke to him.'

'Very likely. But the train had not quite started. There was time for them to get in – if not in his compartment in another one. And there *is* such a thing as walking along the footboard of a train in motion, and getting into another compartment. I've done it lots of times.

'Now,' he went on, 'acting on these theories, the next question is – what made the murdered man get into the Okehampton train, and where was he before he got in? Perhaps our good friend Bradshaw will help us.' He opened the book and consulted its pages carefully. 'I won't say what I think yet,' he remarked presently, 'but I've a sort of an idea. There's an island platform at St David's.'

'What on earth's that?'

He looked at me scornfully.

'An island platform is one between two lines, so that trains run on either side of it. But now I'm going to enjoy the run.'

I scarcely saw where the enjoyment came in. He was not still for five minutes together. At every station his head went out of the window, once or twice when we slowed down he grew impatient, but brightened up when he timed a mile in fifty-seven and three-fifths seconds. He made notes of all sorts of things and generally fidgeted during the whole journey.

'It's been a glorious run,' he exclaimed as we drew up at St David's. 'One hundred and ninety-four miles without a stop, and a minute ahead of scheduled time in spite of that signal against us at Taunton and the slowing down for the PW operations.'

'What's "PW"?' I asked.

'Permanent way, you ignoramus. Stop a minute. I want to speak to the driver.'

He was back in a few minutes.

'Our train leaves for Okehampton at three twenty-five,' he said. 'Now, we'll just have a chat with one of the officials here to begin with.'

We found our way to one of the officials, and Godfrey Page presented the letter of introduction.

'Ah, I've heard of you, Mr Page,' he said. 'You unearthed that strange affair at Warchester, didn't you? Well, I see you've come down to have a look at this Okehampton mystery. Can I do anything for you?'

'Not at present,' said my brother-in-law, 'except to tell me if the train in which the murder took place wasn't a bit late in starting from St David's.'

'Aha,' laughed the other, 'we Great Western men always like to get a rise out of the South-Western, you know. Yes, she *was* three or four minutes late.'

'That's all I want to know. It confirms me in a little theory, though. If I find out anything further at Okehampton I shall trouble you again.'

'Certainly. Anything we can do for you, please ask me. But it seems to me that it is a South-Western job, Mr Page.'

'Ah! I'm not so sure that your line isn't mixed up in it!'

Arrived at Okehampton we quickly found our way to the hotel. Godfrey Page made himself known to the detective-inspector on the premises and we were ushered by him into the room where the body of the murdered man had been taken. He lay in the bed, quiet and serene, with quite a smile upon his face.

He was a man of some five and thirty years of age, with very dark moustache and beard and a bronzed countenance which even death had not been able to stamp with pallor.

'Are there no marks about him?' asked Godfrey Page of the inspector.

'Only this,' and he turned down the sheet and showed the man's right arm, on which a small dragon was tattooed in black and red.

'Hm!' said my brother-in-law, 'looks as if he'd been in the Far East. Only a Chinese or Japanese artist could have done that.'

'Yes,' said the inspector, 'there was a silver dollar along with his money, too, which corroborates that.'

'Were there no marks on his clothes?'

'No.'

'May I look at them?'

'Here they are.'

The inspector narrowly watched Godfrey Page as he turned over garment after garment till he arrived at the shirt. It was an ordinary white one, but with a nasty red stain upon it that told its own tale.

'It's no use,' said the inspector, 'there's no name upon it.'

'By George, though, there's something else. Look, have you noticed this?'

And he pointed to a faint pencilling inside the starched linen cuff.

'What is it?' asked the inspector. 'Looks like a pencilled note. Strange we never noticed it.'

'You gentlemen don't always look everywhere. But I'll just jot that down, please. It's interesting.'

And he entered the following in his notebook, a copy of what had been scrawled on the dead man's shirt cuff: 242, E3 Great Marlow.

'I'll wire to Great Marlow at once,' said the inspector; 'it looks like a clue. It may be he's known there. It might even be the number of a street he knows, or something of that kind.'

'It might be,' returned Godfrey Page dryly. 'I'll only detain you one moment. Was anything else found on him besides money?'

'Only this knife.'

It was an ordinary, rather large, clasp knife. My brother-in-law opened it.

'The big blade's broken,' he said, 'and freshly done, too. Ah, and see how loose it is.'

'Now, sir,' said the inspector impatiently, 'if you've quite finished we'll go. I hope you won't mention what you've seen.'

'Not I. And you're really going to investigate at Great Marlow?'

'Certainly!'

'Ah! Perhaps the bit of blade broken off that knife lies somewhere by Great Marlow.'

The inspector stared at him with astonishment.

'I've heard of you as a sort of private detective where railways are concerned,' he said, 'but, if you'll excuse my saying so, you don't seem to know much about this kind of thing.'

'And perhaps you are as strangely ignorant of railways,' retorted Godfrey Page, 'but I don't bear you any malice. If I'm ever in a position to help you, I will.'

'Now,' he said to me, as we regained the street, 'there's just time for us to make a little purchase, and then we'll catch the five-twelve train back to Exeter.'

And, taking me into an ironmonger's shop, he bought a small screwdriver and put it into his pocket.

Arrived at Exeter we sought out the friendly GW official, and my brother-in-law at once began:

'I'm going to ask you for some rather curious information. We shall stay the night at Exeter, and if you can get it by tomorrow I shall be much obliged.'

'What is it, Mr Page?'

'Find out on what train the third-class coach numbered 242 was running the night before last, and where it is to be found tomorrow.'

The official promised to do so.

Godfrey Page refused to say another word on the subject that night. The next morning we went to St David's and sought out our friend.

'Well?' asked the 'railwayac'.

'I've got you the information, but I don't see how it will help you. Number 242 third coach is one that at present is kept at Plymouth as a spare carriage in case there is an abnormal number of passengers for the Paddington express. The night to which you refer it ran—'

'On the eight-twenty p.m. from North Road, Plymouth, arriving here at 10.03.'

'How on earth did you know that, for it's quite true?'

'It was only my little theory,' said Page, with a smile, 'but go on.'

'It was put on to the up-corridor express at Plymouth because some passengers, arriving by a P&O steamer, increased the demand for room on that train. You know, perhaps, that if we have over twenty-four P&O passengers we run a "boat special", but not if we take them by ordinary express. On this occasion only sixteen travelled to London.'

'And where is number 242 now?' asked Page impatiently.

'Here.'

'Here?'

'Yes. It was running back to Plymouth last night and I took the liberty of detaining it here because you seemed interested in it.'

Godfrey Page was jubilant.

'Let's go and see it at once,' he said, drawing the screwdriver out of his pocket.

'What do you want that for?' asked the official.

'You'll see,' was the only reply he would make.

We very soon reached the siding where the third-class carriage was standing. Page counted down the fifth compartment and climbed in. We followed.

'Now,' said he to me, 'what do you see? Notice that!' And he pointed above the door. There I read as follows: 242, E. 'All the compartments are lettered, you see,' went on Page, 'and E, of course, is the fifth compartment from the end, commencing with A. Now look at those photographs!'

As is customary in Great Western carriages there were

photographs of places of interest along the line over the seats.

'Great Scott!' I exclaimed.

'Great Marlow! you mean,' said my brother-in-law triumphantly, for there, before me, was a photograph of that picturesque Thames town.

'Now,' said Godfrey Page, 'I'll give you my theory, and then we'll see if it's correct.

'A man, travelling in a train the destination of which he is seemingly ignorant of, is found murdered. Not a single scrap of paper of any kind remains upon him to prove his identity. His money being left proves that robbery of *that* was not an object. The two men whom we assume committed the crime were following him, and he was flying from them. He was evidently acquainted with China or Japan, and his bronzed face suggested a recent return from abroad.

'Let us assume that he landed at Plymouth from the P&O boat and took the eight-twenty express to Paddington, travelling alone in this compartment. Let us further assume that he discovered that his enemies were on board the same train, having watched for his arrival at Plymouth, and further that he had in his possession some very important paper or letter that it was their object to obtain.

'He knows he is watched and is in danger. First, then, he hides the paper and scribbles the key to finding it again on his wristband. Then, as the train draws up at 10.03 on the left-hand side of the island platform, here he sees another train, the Okehampton one, which ought to have been starting at that very moment, standing on the other side of the platform. Thinking to escape, he rushes across and takes a seat in it. But he is observed by his followers, and they do the same. Then the murder takes place, and they search in vain for the hidden paper.'

'But where did he hide it?'

'Behind this picture of Great Marlow,' said Godfrey

Page, commencing to unscrew the panel of it. 'He broke the blade of his knife in doing what I'm doing now.'

Breathlessly we waited while the four screws were withdrawn. Then the panel was removed, and out dropped a large sheet of thin tracing paper, many times folded. We undid it carefully.

'A map,' exclaimed the railway official.

'Yes, but what a map! Look, Tom!'

'A plan of a fortress apparently,' I said.

'A plan of Port Arthur!' cried Godfrey Page.

There, sure enough, was the map of a fortress, with guns and other points marked out with care, and brief explanations in French.

'I'll tell you what,' said Godfrey Page, as he commenced screwing up the panel, 'it's my opinion that we three had better keep this little discovery to ourselves. For, depend upon it, even if we handed this over to the police, the murderers would never be discovered.'

'Why not?'

'Because in all probability they are police themselves.'

'Russians?'

'Exactly so. He met with a spy's fate.'

'But who was this map intended for?'

'My dear fellow, our government would have paid well for it, eh?'

On further consultation we agreed to say nothing to the police. Just before we took the train back to Paddington, Godfrey Page said to our friend the official: 'By the way, they take tickets at Reading from the passengers in the eight-twenty p.m. from Plymouth? You might try and find out if three fewer tickets than were issued at Plymouth were collected that night?'

'All right, Mr Page, I'll drop you a line.'

On our way home my brother-in-law was much puzzled how to act. He had retained the map in his possession, and he was talking of destroying it when suddenly an idea occurred to him.

'Tom,' he said, 'do you ever come across Colonel Sylvester now?'

'Occasionally I meet him at the club.'

'Ah! Isn't he something to do with the Secret Service?'

'Yes.'

'Good. Let's sound him. Ask me to meet him at your place to dinner and leave the rest to me.'

A few days later the dinner came off. We three men were lazily smoking our cigars afterwards when Godfrey Page exlaimed: 'Mysterious affair that at Okehampton the other night.'

'Very,' said the Colonel, with a quick look at him.

'I was down there a day or two afterwards.'

'Indeed!'

'I made an interesting discovery.'

'What?'

'I found a curious thing in a railway carriage.'

'May I ask what?'

'This map,' replied Godfrey Page, taking it out of his pocket.

The Colonel seized it eagerly.

'Good heavens!' he said. 'Have you told anyone of this?'

'Only two beside ourselves know it.'

'For goodness' sake say nothing, Mr Page. If the Russian police knew you had that map, they'd – they'd—'

'Murder me as they did the man who brought it to England, eh?'

The Colonel was pale and trembling as he laid a hand on Godfrey Page's arm.

'Tell me,' he said, 'the police know nothing of this?'

'Nothing.'

'What do you propose to do with it?'

'I thought *you* might find it more useful than I should,' he said significantly.

The Colonel put it in his breast-pocket with a sigh of satisfaction.

'You are a wise man, Mr Page,' he said. 'I am extremely obliged to you.'

'I wonder,' remarked my brother-in-law a day or two later, 'how the inspector got on at Great Marlow? By the way, I've had a letter from Exeter. There *were* three tickets from Plymouth to London missing at the collection at Reading!'

www.ingramcontent.com/pod-product-compliance
Lightning Source LLC
Chambersburg PA
CBHW030357030726
47497CB00002B/374